THE GIRL NEXT DOOR

BESTSELLING AUTHOR OF *THE REBOUND*

J. R. ROGUE

THE GIRL NEXT DOOR

OZARK OMENS
BOOK 1

J. R. ROGUE

Copyright © 2022 by J. R. Rogue
All rights reserved.

All rights reserved. No part of this publication may be reproduced, distributed or transmitted in any form or by any means, including photocopying, recording, or other electronic or mechanical methods, without the prior written permission of the publisher, except in the case of brief quotations embodied in critical reviews and certain other noncommercial uses permitted by copyright law.

This is a work of fiction. Names, characters, places, and incidents are a product of the author's imagination. Locales and public names are sometimes used for atmospheric purposes. Any resemblance to actual people, living or dead, or to businesses, companies, events, institutions, or locales
is completely coincidental.

J.R. Rogue
PO Box 984
Lebanon, MO 65536
www.jrrogue.com
contact@jrrogue.com

CONTENTS

Author's Note	xi
My name is…	1
Prologue	3
Chapter 1	9
Chapter 2	19
Chapter 3	30
Chapter 4	36
Chapter 5	53
Chapter 6	63
Chapter 7	67
Chapter 8	84
Chapter 9	89
Chapter 10	94
Chapter 11	103
Chapter 12	112
Chapter 13	117
Chapter 14	132
Chapter 15	148
Chapter 16	161
Chapter 17	176
Chapter 18	189
Chapter 19	198
Chapter 20	204
Chapter 21	213
Chapter 22	221
Chapter 23	230
Chapter 24	241
Chapter 25	253
Chapter 26	267
Chapter 27	271
Chapter 28	294
Chapter 29	297
Chapter 30	311
Chapter 31	318
Chapter 32	329
Chapter 33	343

Chapter 34	359
Epilogue	372
Acknowledgments	375
About the Author	377
Also by J. R. Rogue	379

For Sita, the last vampire...

*She revels in a region of sighs:
She has seen that the tears are not dry on
These cheeks...*

                                          EDGAR ALLAN POE

AUTHOR'S NOTE

In the summer of 1992, I moved to the Ozarks from Orlando, Florida. The shock of moving from the city to rolling hills was immediate and strange. In my earliest years in Missouri, I fell into reading about vampires and writing heartsick poetry.

The small towns of Grovespring and Hartville, Missouri, shaped me, and the winding gravel roads and small-town bubble I lived in stayed with me—making this story what it is.

It has taken me six years to finish The Girl Next Door, the first book in the Ozark Omens series. And though a part of me wants to share details of this story's many versions—on the page and in my mind—I want the version I am giving you now to be the one that takes hold of your heart.

Many hours of research into Romanian, Ukrainian, and Russian vampire folklore shaped this story, as well as research into Roman, Greek, and Nordic mythology. In addition, I was inspired by songs, novels, tv shows, and movies as I created the universe you're about to enter. The mythology of the Ozark Omens series is intricate and dark, resulting from sleepless nights delving into research and my imagination.

Blurring the lines between poetry and prose, The Girl Next Door is a fever dream of a story. But this is only the beginning.

Welcome to Hart Hollow, Missouri.

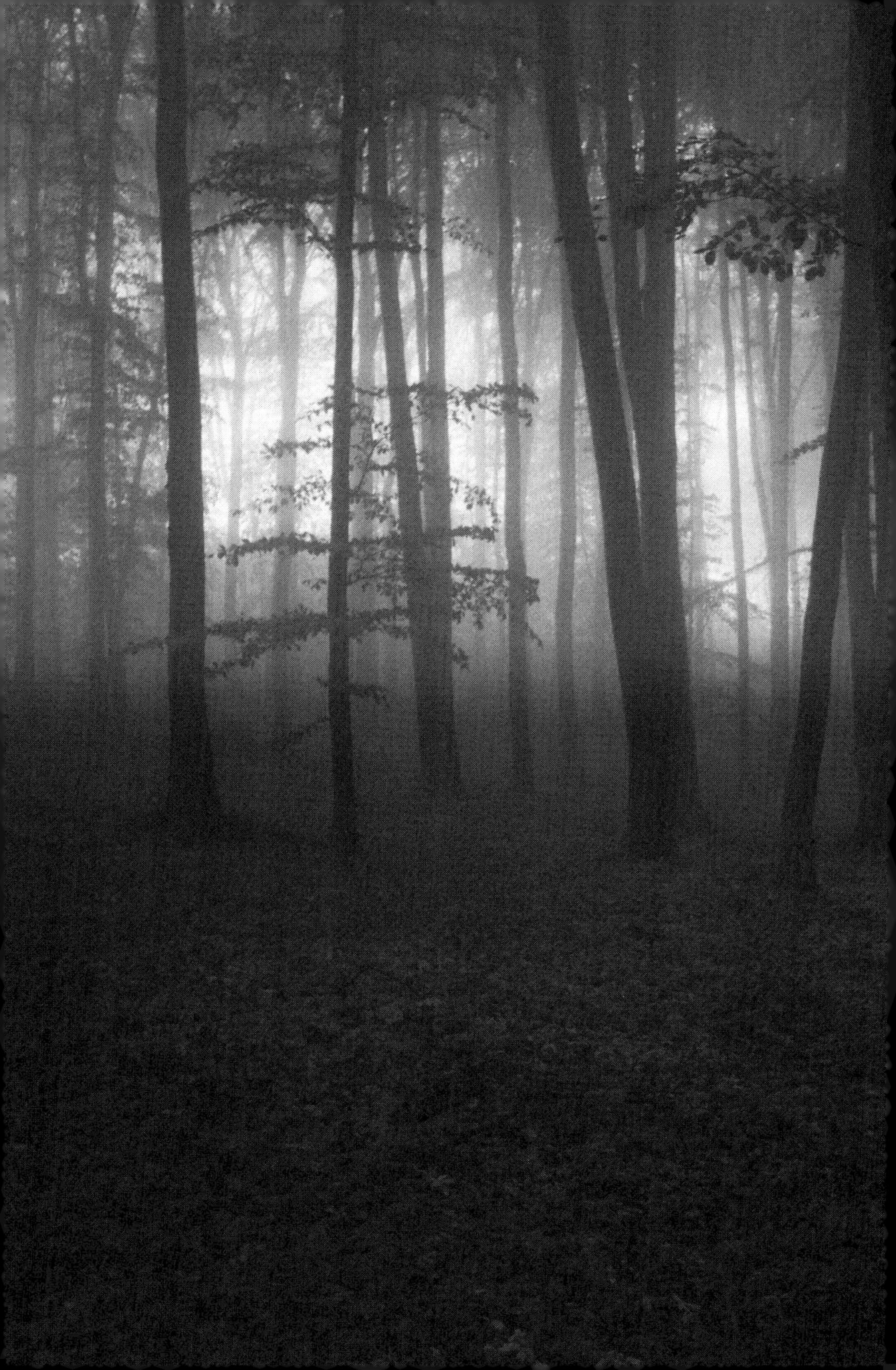

Bless me, Father, for I have sinned.

I cannot promise to be less a poem, more a boy.
For I am neither.
Not beast, not man.
Something more.
Never a father, forever a dream.
I am what you unleashed.
I am what she made me,
and I am frightening, frightened.

My name is Nicholas Hemming,
and this is my confession.

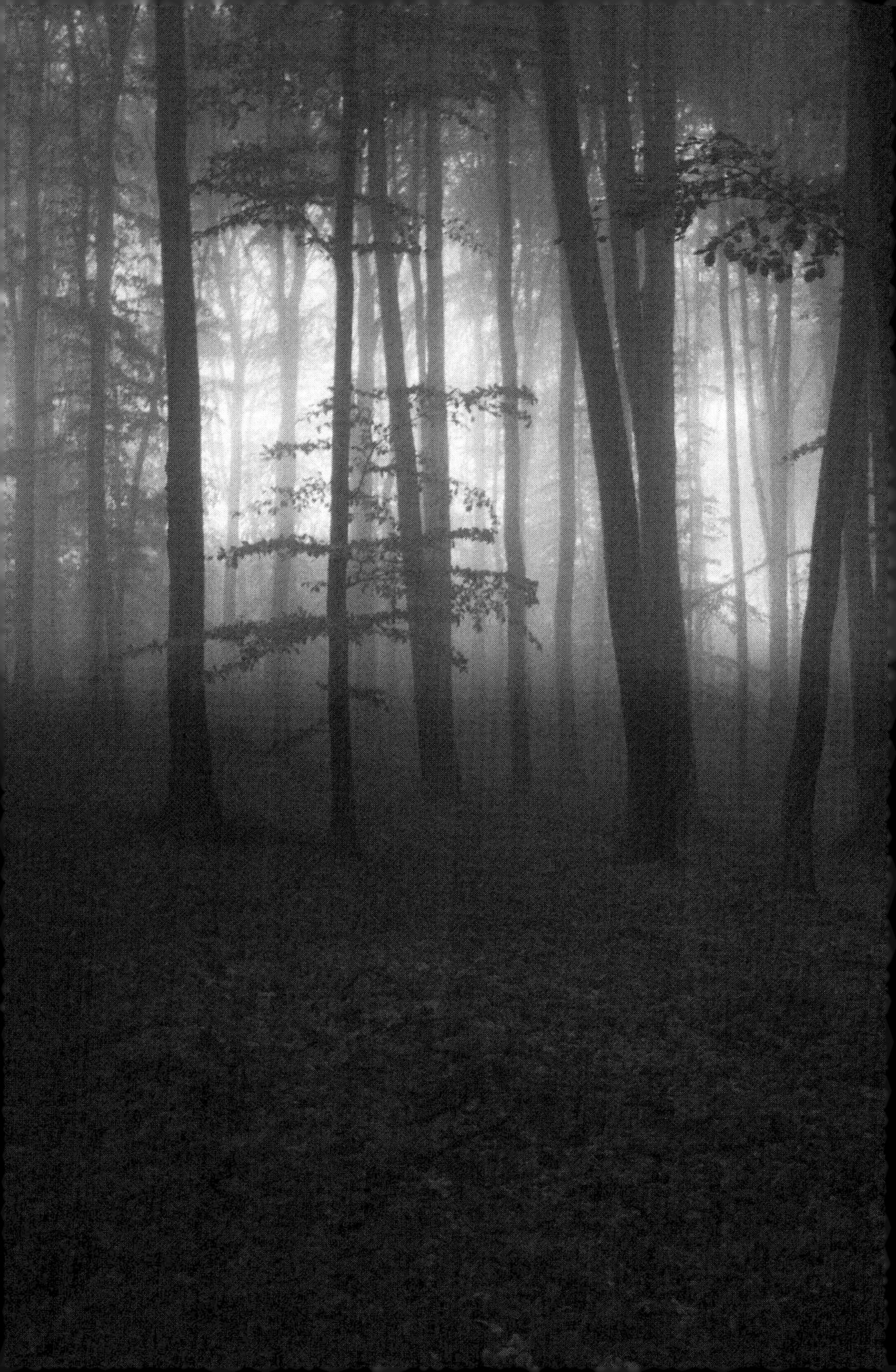

PROLOGUE

She didn't see him watching. The girls never did. And though the late summer heat was oppressively hot in the Ozark woods she roamed, Amber liked the feeling of peace that washed over her every time she escaped to the wooded area beyond her father's church.

Junior year was starting soon, and she was dreading the first day. A ticking clock ticked and tocked and rocked her as she slept, reminding her that each sleep brought her closer to the first tardy bell, the first slam of a locker door, echoing. Specifically, the locker she shared next to her boyfriend, Eric.

Breakups were never easy, and Amber had suffered the weight of her inevitable decision to end her relationship with Eric Childress —basketball player, baseball player, and a member of the National Honor Society—the perfect boyfriend on paper.

It kept her up late all summer, the nights she slept, anyway.

Her dreams had become more akin to nightmares. They were filled with slow, dramatic darkness and comical violence

She wasn't sure what had brought on the sudden night terrors, but to give into them was to be asleep, and that beat the alternative—awake, eyes trained on her doorknob, willing it to remain still.

In the safety of daylight, Eric wanted more and more from her body with each passing month of their relationship, and she couldn't give herself to him, not without angering another's possessive eyes and hurting the one she enjoyed touching her.

She'd prayed about the impending breakup moments earlier in the church, but it didn't feel real to her unless she prayed under the shade of green trees, where she felt utterly alone and blissfully shielded.

So she escaped when she could—changing in the church bathroom before walking out the back door into the heat, her favorite spot in mind.

A hundred yards into the woods was a felled tree, and Amber had spent hours there throughout her childhood. Though she no longer played with her siblings on the dead wood, she felt comfort when it came into view that evening. She jogged to it, hoisted herself up, and felt the rough bark on her bare legs, her denim cutoff shorts riding up.

Her father, Pastor Hughes, chastised her for showing so much skin every time she changed into her favorite shorts, but her mother reminded him they lived in a furnace and admonished him for the critique. Interactions such as these made Amber feel bolder and more capable of standing up to Eric when she ended their relationship. More capable of living the way she longed to, in the arms of the one person she wanted to dream of.

Amber was practicing her speech—playing with the necklace circling her neck—when he found her in the woods. She didn't hear him coming, but when the Deacon walked out of the brush,

PROLOGUE

Amber clutched her chest and gasped a little. The scent of her fear was potent, though the feeling was fleeting.

"Deacon Rex," she said, pulling her hands behind her back.

Hart Hollow's Deacon wasn't an imposing man, wasn't a cause for fear, and her tension fell away—just slightly.

She was still alone in the woods with a man. A godly man, but still a man. The hairs on her arms stood straight for a moment before she relaxed.

Deacon Rex was blind, handsome, soft-spoken, and a staple in the community. And though some might say the young Deacon was a rival of her father's, Amber didn't see it that way. *We are all children of Christ*, she reminded herself.

Deacon Edward Rex lived on the hill at the Steele Heart Catholic Church and Rectory, the only Catholic church in town. Attendance was slim compared to the many Baptist churches in the county, but the attendees were devout, often driving from the more remote areas of the county to listen to the Deacon speak. Steele Heart Catholic Church had been without a Priest since Father Dodson had passed away the previous winter.

Amber had often fantasized about attending another church in the community, if only to escape her father's gaze and expectations.

And sometimes, his hands.

Pastor Hughes doled out punishment unflinching, painting it as love.

Amber twisted the useless purity ring on her finger as the Deacon stepped closer, his dark glasses glinting in the light that peaked through the trees. "My apologies. I believe I caught you in a faraway moment," he said, his voice calming. "What are you hiding from, Amber?"

The question caught her off guard, and the tightness in her shoulders lifted just slightly. She'd been hiding from many things that summer, longing for the alone the woods offered. And she felt closer to God there in the trees—could hear him clearly. His voice was muffled when her father was around.

"Nothing," she smiled, twisting her hands together into a knot. "What are you doing here?"

The Deacon smiled, stepping closer. He had his cane in his hands, and he seemed so fragile, so incredibly human. He reached the felled tree she sat on, placing a hand on the bark, twisting around. When he sat down, he let out a long breath, then smiled again as he stared forward. "I enjoy being in nature and often walk on Sunday evenings."

"All the way down the hill and out of town?" Amber asked, turning toward the Deacon. The Deacon lived in the rectory on the hill. Steele Mansion had been bought by the church over a hundred years ago. It was tradition for the Priest and Deacon to live in the house connected to the small church, and she wondered how lonely it was for Deacon Rex now that Father Dodson had passed.

"Sometimes," he said, staring ahead. He looked strange to her in his attire, and she took him in as if he had just appeared to her on the tree, as if from thin air. He wore a crisp white shirt, grey pants, and shiny black shoes. His attire was not suited for evening walks in the woods, but she didn't point that out.

"I enjoy being in nature too," she admitted. "God is out here, isn't He?" she asked, feeling warm from the heat.

The Deacon turned to her, wide grin, incisors a little sharp. The briefest of thrills ran through her as her eyes tried to make sense of the unnatural, a strange cocktail of horror and want. And when he lowered his glasses, showing her his white eyes, she fell deep into the pool. He could smell it, her warring fear and desire.

Every want felt like a defiance of her father. And the Deacon's eyes were a mirror, showing her all she could not grasp under her father's roof, under his rule.

"God is out here," the Deacon replied, reaching out with his left hand, gripping Amber's neck, pressing the chain of her necklace into her flesh. "What would you like to confess?"

ONE

"Here it is, Nicholas. Hart Hollow Missouri," Valerie called quietly from the front seat of her Ford Fiesta, waking me from my shallow dream state.

With a yawn, I sat up, stretched my arms to the ceiling, and grazed my knuckles on the worn fabric. I'd spent the previous two hours of the trip from Denver to Missouri in and out of sleep, the warm summer air making it impossible to drift off properly.

Though I was old enough to drive, my *Aunt* Valerie was reluctant to allow me the privilege unless she was woefully tired. Plus, her passenger seat driving took all the fun out of the act. As a result, our trip had taken twice the time it needed to.

I leaned forward between the seats, running a hand over my face as Valerie stopped at a flashing light in what appeared to be the town square. I attempted to climb over the center console, but Valerie swatted me. "Stop doing that. We're almost there. Just stay back there."

I huffed out a breath, a remark on my tongue that was better left there. Our arrival in the small, forgotten town was a fresh start, and I'd promised to be less of a dick to Valerie. She was all I had when I arrived in Hart Hollow.

Valerie put the car into gear and turned as I moved to the rear passenger window. I saw a man with a cane and glasses walking along the sidewalk.

The buildings we passed were brick, worn down—gone from my vision in a flash. As soon as we arrived in the downtown area, we were passing neighborhoods. Some homes were beautiful, some derelict.

The houses suddenly stopped, and we were approaching a road leading up to the Hart Hollow school district, the yellow buses announcing its presence. My new school sat on the hill to my right, but Valerie turned left as I pressed my nose to the glass, trying to see up the incline.

I shifted in my seat, moving to the center console again as we paused at a stop sign before turning left. The town was quiet, and we saw no cars as we pulled up to the Steele Heart Trailer Park entrance. A remark was there, a joke ready to fall from my mouth, but I bit my tongue instead. I'd vowed to be better to Valerie. The prior two years had been rough for us both—since the fire and the deaths at the ranch.

If our hearts had been made of steel, would we be unscathed right now? I pushed the poetry aside, playing the part of a normal teenager when I asked, "Which one is ours?" before glancing at Valerie.

She swept her red hair off her face, leaning her head into the headrest of her seat. Then, casting a fleeting glance at me, she pointed to the trailer in the back of the park, by a dark circle of trees. "That one."

I leaned forward slightly.

The trailer was a little less dilapidated than the rest, and as far as I was concerned, it was the mother fucking Hilton compared to the crammed car we'd been in for hours and the motels we'd been living in for the past two years. "Nice. I like it," I remarked, offering Valerie a reassuring smile.

She nodded before inching forward.

Everything we owned was on the floorboard, in the trunk, and scattered across the front seat. Items hastily shoved into bags and boxes the night we left, very few things added in the years since we crossed the state line out of California when I was fifteen. Our nomadic lifestyle meant spending little, blending in. Our budget went to food for the two of us and clothing for me. I'd gained several inches since we left.

Valerie pulled the car into the grass next to the trailer, put it into park, and cut the engine. I stretched, raising my arms again, finding resistance once more.

"The landlord said the key would be under the mat. Go look for it, and I'll start getting things out of the trunk," Valerie said after a moment.

I nodded as I reached for the door, dying to stretch my legs. When I stepped out of the car, my back popped and I cursed low, turning away from Valerie as she rounded the vehicle. She hated when I used "foul language."

The August heat was suffocating in Missouri, and I pushed my shaggy hair from my forehead as I walked toward the front porch. It wasn't quite in line with the trailer, but you could reach the door. The mat in front of the entrance was faded and off-center. I squatted down, lifting the corner. A silver key was there, just as she'd said. I snatched it, let the mat fall, and then turned to Valerie. "Got it."

She rounded the trunk with a box of clothes in her arms. "Okay, open it up. I'm sure it's stuffy. He said the last tenant moved out six months ago. Let's open the windows."

I opened the screen door, reaching for the doorknob. I stepped back a little when it opened. "It wasn't locked," I said as Valerie reached me, opening the screen door more with her shoulder. We stood side by side at the entrance, and I looked down at her. "I'll go in first," I said, dropping my voice.

I wasn't scared. Walking into an empty trailer in broad daylight was nothing. Every morning when I woke from one of my fitful and brief sleeps, I reminded myself that the dead could not find me here. The horrors I'd seen in darkened rooms in the past haunted me, but in dreams, those images remained.

I pressed my hand to the front door, pushing it wide. Valerie clutched the box to her chest next to me, craning her neck to see inside.

"Flip the light. There should be electricity," she whispered.

I reached for the light, flicked it on, and watched it illuminate our new home.

It was dusty, hot, and smelled like the color of the walls—bland. There was a brown couch on the far wall, one end table, and a glass coffee table. Light shone in the kitchen from the sliding door that led to the back.

As Valerie stood in the doorway, I walked through the kitchen to the bedroom on the right side of the trailer. When I turned the light on, I saw a full-sized bed and one nightstand. Satisfied that the room was empty, I flicked the light off, and closed the door.

Valerie had stepped into the trailer, still cradling the box of clothes. "It has two bedrooms. Yours should be down the hall."

I passed her, then flicked the light on in the bathroom, giving it a quick once over. Satisfied, I left the door open and walked to the back room, finding my new bedroom.

CHAPTER ONE

Before me was a worn desk against the wall, a dresser with stickers covering it, and a twin bed. Glancing out the window, I saw a line of trees visible through the dirty glass. I squinted, wondering if my eyes were playing tricks on me or if there was a headstone in the woods. Blinking, I walked away, convincing myself it wasn't an omen.

I placed my hands on my hips as I looked around the small room, trying to place the feeling bubbling to the surface. *It was mine.* All mine. I didn't have to share a room with Valerie. I didn't have to sleep in the car's backseat. I didn't have to worry I would wake anyone when the night terrors came.

When I walked back out to the living room to Valerie, I couldn't help myself. My lips turned up of their own accord, and my eyes watered with the first smile I'd genuinely felt in years.

Dusk was giving way to nightfall when I got away for the first time that day to explore the woods. Valerie was cleaning the trailer, making it a home. And I was in her way, so she told me to get some fresh air, explore my surroundings, *and play outside.*

As if I'd ever played, as if I remembered how to play. She wanted to forget where we came from, but the wound was fresh, still raw. Even two years later.

I walked into the small circle in the woods and, like an open mouth, it enveloped me.

It was a cemetery, just as I'd thought, though small, worn down. Forgotten.

When I looked back in the direction I came, to our trailer, my heart rate sped up, then galloped when I saw the fresh grave to my right.

I'd had dreams about that place before we arrived, but they never made sense. Not until that moment. They'd started six months before we'd left California. Dreams red and dark, with a sky full of stars. I would lie in the cemetery at night on a fresh grave, eyes wide open, staring at the moon.

Always a full moon. Two snakes writhed on my chest. The hands always came from beneath me, reaching for the serpents, finding my cool flesh.

When I would break free, I would always see the hands pulling the snakes beneath the surface, eyes white. Blind snakes. One albino, one dark as night.

Every night my dream form would stumble back in horror, watching the arms become shoulders, become a body, become a woman. Naked and covered in dirt, red hair fell over her shoulders. One snake in her mouth, half-eaten, the other in her outstretched hand. An offering.

When she reached me, I would grab her wrist and open my mouth to eat the second snake as my other hand cupped her dirty breast.

I would wake up only after devouring the snake's head entirely. The dark snake. Every time.

I'd never seen the fresh grave in my waking hours until that moment. I couldn't tell if it looked like the one in my dream or if I was just on edge, making horror real to feel justified in my sleeplessness.

I rubbed my eyes and blinked twice, looking around the graveyard. The dry summer grass crunched beneath my Converse tennis shoes, worn and faded.

The day's events caught up to me, and sleep was calling—I always resisted it because of the dreams, often staying up too late. I often feigned sleep and slowed my breathing, so I wouldn't worry Valerie. But now I had my own room, and I could stay awake as long as I pleased. I knew I was still under the microscope Valerie held to me, but I was convinced her watchful presence would ease. Valerie was worried about my mental state and the after-effects of where we lived. It was as though she was always waiting for me to explode, unleash something, hurt her. I believed it was because of the men—the father, his sons. I didn't take it personal. And she didn't take it personally that I never wanted to be touched.

My mother and father died in California. Valerie almost died. Or so I thought. I would learn that truth and fiction blurred for her, and her visions were not confined to dreams.

I walked to a worn headstone and hoisted myself upon it. I pulled a book from the back pocket of my jeans, then the flashlight from my front pocket, clicking it on.

Valerie agreed to stop at a bookstore on the drive here, and I'd grabbed a copy of *Salem's Lot* from a rummage bin, and a collection of short stories by Edgar Allan Poe. I should have grabbed Poe for my night reading since the mascot for my new school was a Raven.

I had little experience with proper schools; changing towns and districts since we'd left the ranch hadn't helped me catch up with the real world. But I loved to read, and I would devour any story put in my hand. At the ranch, I wrote poetry that I often burned at our nightly bonfires. Nothing was sacred or private there. They pressed the family upon us. Everything was shared. Even our bodies, enthusiasm faked or ignored.

I pushed away the thoughts, the memories of probing hands, and focused on the story in my own hands. Before long, the lights in our trailer went out, and Valerie opened the back door, hollering for me to come in soon.

I yelled back that I would, though I wouldn't, and I knew she wouldn't notice. Valerie had an early morning interview at a café in Hart Hollow. She'd been on food duty at the ranch. It was her passion to feed people. She was beautiful enough to be a server, but she told me she was applying for a kitchen job. I enjoyed her food, though it never satisfied me, and I always left the table hungry, my slim frame begging for something more.

As the hours passed, the night fell over me like a warm blanket. The heat was still stifling, but I preferred it to the alternative.

The dark didn't scare me—not out in the open. It was the darkness of my room that frightened me. The promise of no exit, of one door and no way out.

I glanced at the trailer, my room, and the window. There was an old picnic table by the trailer, and I was already planning to push it below my window so I could sneak out easily. My mind was constantly looking for escape routes and exit plans. Ways out.

The women weren't here; they couldn't get me. They were dead.

But the mind was a perilous labyrinth, and I often found myself trapped in it.

The nights we slept in the car on the road were my favorite. Though cramped and subject to my complaints, I preferred it to the lumpy motel beds. The car was full of windows, and I could see out, could see danger before it caught me. The nights spent in motels were filled with fitful tossing under the sheets or stories told in my head as I pretended to be gone from the world.

And on some nights, I thought of my parents.

I was ashamed of the fact that I didn't miss them. It was because of them we lived on the ranch. Because of them, morbid dreams and darker memories haunted me. *If our hearts had been made of steel, would we be unscathed right now? Would this body be a weapon, no longer a plague? I am what you unleashed.*

CHAPTER ONE

I closed my book and hopped off the headstone, closing my eyes tightly, pushing the violent and dark poetry away. I didn't have my notebook; I didn't have anywhere to go with the words.

I'd made a promise on the way here, scribbling in that notebook as Valerie drove. I wouldn't let them get me here. I wouldn't let their memories haunt me.

I wouldn't be the little boy they abused.

Shoving the novel in my back pocket, I started walking toward the trailer, out of the cemetery.

I saw her then, for the first time, in flesh and red. She was sitting on a headstone just as I had been. How I hadn't seen her before, I'd later know and understand. But that night, I thought she was a ghost, some waking nightmare.

The headstone she was perched upon wasn't worn like the one I'd just left.

It was grand, beautiful; some would say it was an omen to touch something so lovely. It didn't belong in the small clearing of those woods, tucked farther into the trees, but close enough to still be a part of it. One word was scrawled in the stone. *Salina.*

The girl before me believed in omens; she would tell me this later. But on that night, she told me nothing.

Her legs were crossed, her hands gripping the stone. She was wearing a sheer, black robe, untied. I was too far away to see what it barely hid, but she was naked beneath it. Her long red hair was swept behind her shoulder on one side, and on the other, the long strands covered her breast.

It was the woman from my dreams. The snake charmer.

The Devil.

I waved my hand in greeting. I don't know why. It was absurd. As if my body was being moved by a puppeteer high in the night sky.

She didn't wave back; she didn't move. Not for a moment. I dropped my hand, but I didn't leave the woods. We just stared at each other, and when I went to step toward her, I stopped short as she hopped off the headstone. I could see her body then, every pale inch. She took a couple steps forward before turning toward the treeline. Her robe billowed behind her, and her red hair blew in the hot summer breeze. I stood there like a frozen stone as she walked into the woods.

Wordless.

Soundless.

Through the trees, I could see a house, and it seemed to be her destination.

She hadn't made a single sound. And all I could hear was my beating heart as she slipped from my view.

Sleep did not come for me that night.

TWO

The week leading up to my first day at Hart Hollow High flew by. Valerie dipped into our savings to buy me school supplies. She wanted me to get a haircut, but I refused, clinging to my defiance. I'd never been allowed to grow my hair out on the ranch. I couldn't look like *a girl*. Long hair was for women. I disagreed, but they didn't welcome my opinions and voice on the ranch. I was cattle.

Since the trailer park was across the road from the school, I walked to class that first day. And as I crested the hill, the yellow bricks of Hart Hollow coming into view, I smiled, thinking I could be whoever I wanted to be when I stepped into that building.

I was wrong, but my naivety was powerful, and I rode that high as I found my locker, as I walked to class, though I felt like every eye was on me.

I wasn't paranoid. New kids were a delicacy at Hart Hollow High. And at the beginning of my first class—world history—a dozen sets of eyes ate me alive when my teacher, Mr. Pitts, asked me to go to the front of the class.

"Class, this is Nicholas, our new student from all the way on the West Coast in California. Everyone say hi to Nicholas." The teacher said California, like Ca-li-for-nia. Like the word made no sense—as if it had never been said before.

The class repeated after the teacher, lackluster and bored. *Hi, Nicholas's* echoed in the small classroom. I gave a wave and a hello, attempting to walk to my seat.

Unfortunately, the teacher wasn't done with me.

"Nicholas, or Nick?" he asked, adopting a tone that told me he wanted to be my *friend*. He was that kind of teacher. Though my experience in the classroom was woefully limited, I'd picked up a lot about the real world in the two years Valerie and I had traveled.

"Nicholas," I said.

"Okay, I like it. You shouldn't shorten such a nice name. Nicholas, why don't you tell the class something about yourself?"

Jesus Christ. I reached up, rubbing the back of my neck. My shirt felt itchy, and heat crept up along my spine. There was nothing I could tell that classroom about my life that wasn't straight out of a horror story for most of them. *Let's see, I grew up on a ranch with a crazy-ass blind leader who made us drink blood because God told him it would show us the way.*

Maybe it wouldn't have been horrifying to everyone if I had told the truth. Maybe some would act horrified and wonder where the ranch was so they could go there. The zealots would find me, eventually.

I went with the stomach-able version. The one my *Aunt* Valerie was peddling.

"Well, uh. California isn't all big city lights and all that. There are farms and ranches. That's where I grew up. A cattle ranch. But, my aunt and I moved out here for a change."

The teacher cleared his throat. "And this is the first time you're in a real classroom, is that right?"

Thank you, Captain Asshole, for telling the entire class I may or may not be stupid. It didn't matter that I wasn't—or that I was likely smarter than half the students in there. He'd put a target on my back. Did he know nothing about teenagers?

I gave a tight-lipped smile. "I've been going to public school for the past two years. And yeah. Ranch life was more ... life learning, I guess."

"That's okay, Nick. We'll make sure you're up to speed in no time."

Nick. *Nick* ... I saw a few students in the back corner snickering, and a guy leaned over to whisper in a girl's ear. "Who let the Crypt Keeper in?"

The girl watching me had wide green eyes and long legs. I watched back, waiting for her to smile at the idiot's joke. She didn't, and instead, she slowly opened her knees. My first day and some girl was trying to give me a peep show. The Midwest was awfully welcoming.

Mr. Pitts waved a hand for me to take a seat, and I grabbed my backpack from the floor, walking from the front of the room. I could hear whispers and cursed my hearing.

Sometimes I wished I were deaf.

The empty seat left for me was next to a girl in a pretty dress. She watched me the entire time I walked down the aisle, then casually looked away when I sat down.

I could hear the teacher talking about what to expect from the school year and informing us of his office hours. I listened as I got out my new school supplies, and the girl next to me in the pretty dress leaned over, offering a hand. "Hi. I'm Kyrie."

I reached for her hand, finding it warm. I didn't want to touch her, but I didn't want to draw attention to my touch aversion just yet. "Nich—"

"—olas." She laughed softly. "Yeah, I know. We all know. You're the fresh meat."

"What's that mean?" I asked, leaning toward her. Past her, the girl who'd spread her legs for me glared at Kyrie.

Kyrie smiled, and her eyes told me she was blushing, but her skin was too dark for me to tell. "People don't move to Hart Hollow. They leave. They leave without a word. So, anyone who comes here is fresh meat." She pointed to the guy in front of her. "I've known him since preschool." Then, she said of the girl behind her. "Known her since 1st grade."

I smiled widely at her. "Ah, I see. So what do I get for being fresh meat?"

Kyrie smiled, the corner of her mouth turning up. "You'll find out. You go to church?"

I shook my head. *Don't invite me to one.* "No. We didn't have a church on the ranch." Lie. The ranch *was* a church. The kind you can't escape.

"Well, my daddy is Pastor Davis, and he preaches out at First Baptist on South Street. You and your aunt should come this Sunday. We're always looking for fellow worshippers."

"I'll run it by her," I lied. I had no intention of continuing my relationship with *The Lord*. It had brought me a life of pain and mornings spent begging for forgiveness for sins I never asked to take part in. I could still feel their hands on me when I slept. Which is why I rarely slept. I hoped that would change in Hart Hollow, but the memory of the red-haired girl had kept me up the week leading up to my first day.

"Good," Kyrie said, smiling like she'd won a prize. It almost made me want to visit her father's church. But there was nothing I could offer this pretty girl that she needed.

I offered my hand again, pretending to be normal, and Kyrie took it. "Friends?"

Her eyes dimmed a little, and behind her, I could see the guy who had been whispering in the peep show girl's ear, eyeing us. "Friends," Kyrie agreed.

The class went by slowly, and I focused the rest of my attention on the teacher and our first lesson. I'd taken history classes in the other schools, so I felt confident I could pass the class.

Ten minutes before class let out, a man came to the door, knocking on the frame.

"Principal Garrison, what can I do for you?" Mr. Pitts asked.

The tall man stepped in, smiling widely. He was balding, with a spare tire middle and muscular arms. His smile was like a politician's. "Mr. Pitts, happy first day! I apologize, I meant to be here at the start of class, but some paperwork came up, you know how it is." The two men laughed the way boring adults do. "We have another new student that will join your brilliant world history class. A foreign exchange student, to be exact." He raised his eyebrows at the word foreign.

Mr. Pitts lit up, clapping his hands together like an asshole. "Oh well, this is a wonderful surprise." He peered around the principal to the person in the hallway, and Principal Garrison stepped further into the classroom, ushering in someone, a girl with long hair.

All I could see was red hair, full lips, and pale skin.

Those piercing blue eyes of hers locked on mine the moment she looked into the classroom. Her smile was faint, but I could see it.

"Students of Hart Hollow High, this is Sorina Oleksander. She'll be staying in our beautiful little town for the school year."

"Sorina, Sorina! Where are you from?" Mr. Pitts asked.

The red-haired girl looked at the teacher, and for a moment, it seemed as if she were appraising an insect, something beneath her.

Her voice was deep when she spoke, different than I expected. "Romania."

Mr. Pitts said nothing, mouth half open as if he expected her to elaborate.

She didn't, and the silence fell over us like a fog. When I cleared my throat, Sorina looked at me.

"Great, great. You'll have to tell us a little about yourself tomorrow. For now, I know there isn't much time left, but why don't you take that seat right behind Nicholas? Wave Nicholas," Mr. Pitts requested.

It was so fucking stupid, but I waved like a jackass as a question manifested in my mind, like smoke, like a dark river—*what are you?*

"He's our other new student. Maybe you guys can be friends," Mr. Pitts said, and I thought I was going to punch that man in the face before the end of the year.

Around us, the students talked, gathering their things as if their bodies were in sync with the length of the class, anticipating the bell.

CHAPTER TWO

My eyes caught on Kyrie. She had her lips pursed and her arms crossed. I guess she didn't like someone sitting by the *fresh meat*. And maybe didn't like Sorina.

Kyrie looked pretty in her floral dress with a cardigan over it. Her dark hair was styled in wavy curls, butterfly clips holding it back from her face.

Sorina didn't look like she belonged here. Didn't look like she belonged in this decade.

She reminded me of an antique.

I could feel every hair on my arms stand up when she sat behind me. I glanced back at her and saw only her red hair, a curtain between us, as she fiddled with her backpack. It looked like a prop, a foreign object to her.

Before I could speak, and I'm not sure I would have had the balls to say anything, the bell rang. A rush of bodies moved around me, and I felt Kyrie brush against me. On purpose, likely.

I didn't like that.

I didn't like being touched.

But I would soon learn the town of Hart Hollow cared little for what I wanted.

◯◯

At lunch that first day, I took a seat alone. The room of students before me was a mass of people who knew each other, and I could hear them catching up on their summers. There was laughter and whispers, and some watched me as I moved about the room with my tray of pizza and applesauce.

At the end of a row of tables, I set my tray down, then my backpack. I felt like I was in a dream. I'd never had the naked at school dream, school being the least of my worries in life and a welcome challenge after we left. But walking into that room felt like something of a nightmare, though mild compared to my own demons.

I kept my eyes on the mushy pizza as I settled into my seat. When I glanced around the room, I saw Kyrie watching me. She was sandwiched between two guys, and when they saw her looking, they followed her gaze. One narrowed his eyes, and the other leaned into her hair, saying something.

She rolled her eyes and grabbed her tray, getting up.

Maybe she meant it as a mercy, but it felt like she was drawing an arrow, letting it loose.

I looked up at her as she approached. "Hi, friend," I said, ensuring she knew where our new relationship stood.

"I couldn't let you eat alone. Don't worry. Everyone will warm up to you," she assured, setting her tray down next to mine. "Plus, everyone is just a little on edge."

"First day stuff?" I asked, pinching off a piece of pizza and turning my body toward her.

"No." She moved closer to me, leaning in. "About a week ago, Pastor Hugh's daughter, Amber, went missing."

I felt a chill but pushed it away. I didn't know that girl. It didn't matter. "Runaway?"

Kyrie shook her head. "I don't know. It wouldn't be the first. It's like I said, people don't come here. They leave. It's just ... weird, and it has my daddy watching me like a hawk. Like if someone took her, they must be after Pastor's daughters or something." Her laugh was shaky.

"I'm sure it's just a dad thing," I offered, like I knew any fucking thing about the way dads were *supposed* to act with daughters in the real world.

"You're sure, or you know?" Kyrie's brown eyes could draw you in. I would remember that later when she was gone. And that day, she looked at me like I was a shiny new toy, a pet she wanted to adopt.

"Yeah," I said.

"Which one?" She smiled.

"If you're looking for something wrong with me, yeah, my parents are dead."

Her brown eyes softened. "Well, you told the class you moved here with your aunt, so …"

"So you were fishing?" I would have bumped her shoulder or touched her if I were a normal person. I would have flirted with her, eased her. But I wasn't a normal person. And how Kyrie couldn't see that like a blinding neon light, I would never know. Or maybe it as that she could see something was off about me, and that's what drew her in.

"Maybe," she said, reaching for a piece of her pizza. "Why did you move here?"

"I don't know." I sighed. "Not really my decision. I just go wherever my aunt wants to go. She said she wanted to move to the middle of the US, the middle of nowhere. So, here we are. The middle of nowhere."

"Have you lived in many places?" Kyrie asked.

"We tried out a few places before landing here," I said.

"Think you'll stay?"

"Maybe." I shrugged. "My aunt got a job at the café down the road."

"No way! My family and I eat there every Tuesday night and on Saturday morning. Is she a waitress? I haven't seen anyone new there."

"No, she's a cook. She loves cooking, so maybe we'll stay. She likes it. Things are slow here."

"Is that a bad thing?"

"No," I said, meaning it. After two years on the road with no proper home, I was happy to settle down. I liked that Hart Hollow was in the middle of nowhere. It felt like I could hide away. I was wrong, but that feeling of being slightly off-balance that first day of school was everything I needed for a moment. "So, are you one of those people who'll leave this place behind?"

Kyrie smiled around a bite of pizza. "Yes. I don't want to marry someone I've known since we played on the merry-go-round and have babies here in Hart Hollow. I want to leave as soon as I graduate."

I don't know what came over me then, but I put my finger in my apple sauce and smeared a bit on her nose.

"Oh my God, why did you do that?" Kyrie shrieked and pushed my hand away.

Why *did* I do that? I felt warm all over and ... buzzing. I didn't touch people. I didn't *want* to touch people. It was a rule. And there I was, touching this girl. Just her nose, sure, but something wasn't right. The off-balance feeling from earlier was more pronounced, more vivid in its wrongness.

Kyrie pretended to be disgusted by the applesauce on her face as I looked around the crowded lunchroom, the buzzing in my ears growing louder.

CHAPTER TWO

My eyes stopped wandering when I saw blue eyes and red hair. Sorina was leaning against the wall on the opposite side of the room, arms crossed, jaw up. She was watching us, and I felt her everywhere. I felt her in my head, in my chest, down to my dick. I shook my head a little, seeing the ghost of a smile on her lips. She blinked, and I did too. Then, when she pushed off the wall and took her eyes off me, I felt like a cold bucket of water had been dumped over my shoulders.

The warm feeling I had moments before was gone. My desire to lean toward Kyrie was gone, and I found her high-pitched laugh grating.

She could tell something was wrong and looked around, following my gaze. A trail of red hair was all she caught as Sorina left the lunchroom.

When Kyrie turned back, her eyes had changed. I could see the jealousy there. Or *something* there. "You're not the only fresh meat."

"You gonna tell me what happens to fresh meat or leave me wondering again?" I asked, handing her a napkin.

"Leave you wondering," Kyrie replied, reaching for the tray.

THREE

Valerie's new job at the Family Café in Hart Hollow wasn't hard work. Not to her, anyway. It was busy, familiar, and held a sense of home. She was used to feeding people. It was her assigned position at the ranch. And though she longed to leave that life behind and the horror experienced in their last hours there, she found comfort in the routine of making meals for people, in keeping her hands busy.

Idle hands were …

It'd been one week since she started at the Family Café.

She went to bed early and rose early to feed the morning crowd, which consisted of farmers and locals. No one passed through Hart Hollow. It was a forgotten town, buried in winding roads and the hills of the Ozarks. She liked it there. She enjoyed the people. God-fearing people. It was familiar. The people they left behind at the ranch were pretenders. It's what she told herself when she heard their screams. And she often did in the night, and she wondered if Nicholas did, too. He had trouble sleeping, but he hadn't left the trailer yet. Not far from it, anyway. She suspected he sat on the bench behind the trailer. There was a

CHAPTER THREE

small cemetery behind their new home in the woods, and she knew he harbored a fascination for them. She'd found sketches in his backpack once, dark poetry, and after nearly being caught snooping, she never looked again.

Though she acted as Nicholas's guardian, she often felt they were more like siblings because of the nine-year age difference, and she often still felt like a kid at twenty-six.

The patrons of the café called her young lady when they saw her leave the kitchen, complimenting her on her cooking. It was a run of luck that the previous cook was ready to retire when she visited looking for a job. She studied under the woman for a week before she was on her own with the part-time workers that came in a few times a week.

She'd lied on her application, saying she was the head cook on a cattle ranch in California. Then, she lied again, saying the ranch owners had moved.

They hadn't moved, not the leaders of the *ranch* they'd lived on.

They were dead.

It was a late morning in Hart Hollow as she reminisced about the past. The early rush had come and gone, and the café was empty as she headed behind the building to take a break where the lone server was smoking. The front door had a bell that chimed out back, so they could take these moments.

Charla smiled at her when she stepped out into the scorching morning air. She puffed out a cloud of smoke and grinned around the grey. "Hey. Smoke?" she asked as she pulled a pack from her front pocket.

Valerie shook her head. "No." She didn't have vices such as that. And this was a new leaf. Left behind were envy, greed, and the spite she often felt when she looked at familiar faces. *Tabula Rasa.*

"Smart. I'm trying to quit," Charla said, shoving the pack back into her pocket.

Valerie nodded, unsure what to say. It's why she could never do Charla's job. The thirty-something woman was friendly and outgoing. She charmed the customers and made great tips. Well, as great as you could get from farmers in forgotten towns. But you didn't need much to live in Hart Hollow. The line between the well-to-do and the less fortunate was thin. Easily crossed.

Before Valerie could suffer another moment of wondering what to say or do with her hands, the bell chimed above the two women.

"Shit," Charla said, moving to throw her cigarette in the dirt.

"I'll seat them. Finish your smoke," Valerie said, her voice a whisper.

Charla smiled, bringing the cigarette to her lips. "Thanks. I'll be in in a second."

Valerie nodded, walking into the building.

Waiting at the door was a tall man in dark slacks, a white button up shirt, and black glasses. He held a cane in his hand, and his eyes were trained on the wall.

She could tell he heard her approaching, but his lack of sight was apparent in how he moved his head back and forth. "Good morning, you're new, aren't you?" the man said, smiling.

Valerie furrowed her brow as she approached. "Yes. Hi. Charla is just out back. She'll be inside in a second. I can get you seated, though."

The man was handsome, dark-haired, and broad-shouldered. "And who is seating me, may I ask?" His voice betrayed his appearance. He seemed older than the skin on his face suggested. Yet, he had no wrinkles and a smile that was all teeth.

"I'm Valerie. I work in the kitchen. I started a couple of weeks ago."

The man offered his hand, and Valerie stepped forward to take it, finding his palm was cool to the touch.

"I'm Deacon Ed Rex. Nice to meet you."

Valerie felt a chill as she pulled her hand away. "Is there a Catholic church here in Hart Hollow? I hadn't seen one when we moved in."

The man's smile grew wider. "Yes. It's smaller than the Baptist congregations here." He hitched a thumb over his shoulder. "Steele Heart is on the hill overlooking the town. On Steele Bluff Road. Are you Catholic?"

Valerie shook her head, then blushed, grateful he couldn't see her. "No, but I'm looking for a fresh start here. A new church." She finally spoke the words she'd refused to say out loud, especially not to Nicholas. She knew he would reject the idea. Their ideas for Tabula Rasa were quite different.

Deacon Rex nodded his head. "You should join us on Wednesday nights, then. Father Dodson sadly left us recently, so I've been practicing my public speaking since he's been gone." He chuckled. "It's not that scary when you're speaking the Lord's word to a dozen people."

Valerie smiled. She liked the sound of that. No crowds. No pressure. No swaying believers like back on the ranch.

"That sounds nice. Maybe we'll come."

The Deacon nodded. "We would love it if you and your husband came."

Valerie shook her head. "No, no, I'm not married. I meant my nephew and me. We just moved here."

"How noble. Raising a child is no small feat for a young woman like yourself."

Valerie cocked her head. "How do you know I'm young?"

"Do I not have eyes?"

"Yes, but—"

The Deacon smiled. "I'm jesting. Yes, I'm blind, but I can read a voice like a face. So forgive me. I just sense the freshness of youth in you."

"I'm twenty-six," Valerie said, wondering why she was still conversing with this man. He made her feel warm.

"And how old is your nephew?"

"Seventeen."

"Ah, the throes of youth and adolescence. Teenage hormones and defiance. Am I right?"

"Mm, somewhat." Valerie didn't know. Not really. Nicholas was practically a stranger to her. They'd spent little time together on the ranch before they left. Family units meant nothing when you were all one big *family*. And in the two years they'd traveled before landing in Hart Hollow, they'd been busy. Valerie with work, gathering money for their new life. And Nicholas with new schools and studying, trying to catch up with a world that didn't belong to either of them. They slept in motels and forged addresses on paperwork for jobs and school districts. Lying was an exhausting endeavor.

"Well, we would love to have you," the Deacon said, just as Charla emerged from the back.

"Deacon Rex. Here for your usual?" the waitress asked.

The Deacon looked beyond Valerie, and she wondered if he moved in such a way to appear normal. To make other people feel more comfortable with his blindness.

"Yes, Charla, I am." He patted his stomach and smiled widely. He was very handsome, Valerie thought, as Charla led him to his table.

She retreated to the back, patiently awaiting his order. She loved cooking for people. And would love to cook for this man, especially.

FOUR

My first two weeks of school at Hart Hollow High felt like quicksand, a slow descent into a world I was not familiar with.

At the schools I'd jumped through during the two years Valerie and I traveled, I took little seriously except my schoolwork. I was engrossed in catching up and playing pretend in the world of the living. I didn't make friendships; instead, I actively avoided them to bypass questions I didn't want to answer.

Where are you from? Where do you live?

In Hart Hollow I fell into many of the same habits, but this time I memorized the faces of the surrounding students, sketching their likeness into permanence in my notebooks. Creating poetry out of the mundane. I'd been burning the candle at both ends, but it was comforting, in a way. Because being consumed with school meant I wasn't consumed with my dreams, with wondering about the red haired girl from the cemetery. I hadn't walked around the town at night, but I would soon.

Kyrie and I became fast friends, and when she told me she liked to befriend the rare new kid at Hart Hollow, I didn't question her

—or reject the friendship bracelet she gave me. I didn't wonder why she wanted to shield the new kid from the politics and intricate web of high school. She was a kind soul. I was a damaged one.

She also liked to talk, and that worked with my taciturn nature. I could escape to the places in my mind safe from my dreams, where I created poetry. And Kyrie didn't notice. Or pretended not to as she caught me up on the lives of each of my fellow students.

I wondered from time to time who Kyrie's friends were before I arrived, though. I didn't seem to take anyone's spot.

After dodging her request for days, I finally agreed to have dinner at Kyrie's house. Though the silence of my trailer was comforting —Valerie was often going to bed early, worn out from her early shifts at the café—I knew I couldn't deny my new friend forever. The home cooked meal at Kyrie's home was amazing, but I was glad when the night was over. Pastor Davis had been eyeing me all night as though I were there to take his beloved daughter's virginity.

I tried to show him I wanted nothing to do with Kyrie in that way by calling her *buddy* and *friend*, but it didn't seem to do me much good. It was clear from the way he continued to look at me. The most genuine smile I received from him was right after I announced I was leaving.

Did I think Kyrie wanted to fuck me? No. But she was fascinated with me for some reason. I chalked it up to being new, but the mystery of who I was would wear off eventually, and I mused that maybe soon she would try to befriend the new girl.

I shook away the image of Sorina on the headstone as Kyrie joined me on her front porch. "Can I walk you home?" she asked.

I glanced back at the open door. Kyrie's father nodded at me, then retreated around the corner to where I knew his office was thanks to the tour Kyrie led me on of her home.

I reached up, rubbing my neck. "You don't have to. It's just down—"

"I know where the trailer park is. There's only one here."

Last week in science I heard a kid call me "poor-rich." I didn't know what he meant, so I asked Kyrie. She said it was because I lived in the nicest trailer in the park, and my clothes were name brand. I didn't see what good that did for me. Some tall basketball player still mumbled the words "trailer trash" as he walked by me after that class. It didn't matter that I had nice things. I was still beneath them. The difference between me and the other kids who lived in the trailer park was that I didn't give a shit what anyone thought of me.

I let out a sigh and feigned a smile for Kyrie. "Then you know it isn't far."

"Nothing is far here," she said as she reached for my hand. "But I want to leave this house for a minute and speak earnestly."

"Earnestly?" I gave her a half smile, my eyebrow-raised as I pulled my hand from hers. Kyrie often drifted into an elegant way of speaking, and I found it strange and oddly comforting.

"Yeah." She shut her front door, clasping her hands behind her back, bouncing a little on her feet. "Without my mother and father hovering. Or everyone at school hovering. We can talk about tutoring."

"Ah, yes. Better get my dumb ass on track." I knew I wasn't stupid, but I was still catching up.

CHAPTER FOUR

Kyrie brushed past me down her front walk. Flowers grew at the edges, a barrier between the concrete and the perfectly manicured yard. "You're not dumb, Nicholas."

I followed, hands in my pockets. "I'll remember you said that when I have my first pop quiz." I was trying my new reality out, wearing it like a story.

Kyrie stepped into the road. There were no sidewalks on her street, but the road was quiet. "I'll have you ready for that. Don't worry. I'm top of my class."

I caught up to her quickly, long strides matching hers. Kyrie was tall. Five foot ten to my six foot. She had an older brother who graduated ten years ago. He was the star basketball player, and just as smart as Kyrie. I'd learned a lot about her in a short period. "Maybe I'll take that spot from you."

She grinned, pushing her hair behind her ear. "You can try."

"Your parents are nice," I remarked, changing the subject. Nice and normal. Warm and doting.

"Yeah, they're wonderful. I wish your aunt could have come. They'd love to meet her," Kyrie said as she played with the hem of her dress.

"Would they like to meet her to see if she exists and make sure you didn't bring a vagrant into their home?" I asked.

"No, silly. They just know all of my friends' parents. That's the way it is here. Everyone knows everyone."

"Tell them to stop in at the café," I offered, watching the trees as we walked along the road. The trees in Hart Hollow seemed old and watchful, as if something lived in them. Trees held secrets. Told them. Maybe that's why the ranch had been so barren—like a desert.

"I told them she works there. It won't be long before they decide to compliment the chef and welcome her to town," Kyrie said.

"And ask her if she wants to join Sunday service?" I asked, raising an eyebrow. I had no intention of ever stepping foot in a church. That part of my life was buried. Only resurrected when I wanted to bury it again in my notebook.

Kyrie smiled sheepishly. "Yeah. They'll do that. I'm sure. I won't tell them you're an atheist, though." Her tone was light, but I knew her heart was heavy with her new knowledge that I didn't believe in God. If she knew where I came from, maybe she would understand. Or maybe not. I'd learned how Jesus lovers could be.

I hadn't shed my ruined skin, hadn't brushed off the way the hands of God-fearing women could feel on your flesh.

Or God-fearing men.

"That would have been a great dinner conversation." I laughed.

The walk to my trailer wasn't long, and I noticed Kyrie's steps slowed as if she wanted to stretch out our time together.

I didn't mind. I'd been itching for a long walk, and the heat had kept me from it. The evenings were cooling, however slightly, and wandering Hart Hollow was a routine I would welcome. When you were walking, you weren't sleeping. You weren't dreaming. My dreams were hands, open mouths, tongues lapping at my skin.

I shuddered at the thought.

Kyrie noticed. "Are you cold?" she asked, reaching for my arm.

I raised my arm before she could touch my skin, running a hand through my shaggy hair. "No. Just a chill. I don't know," I said.

We paused at a stop sign, words hanging awkwardly between us. Kyrie looked right. "Do you want to go up to the school?"

I glanced back the way we came, then toward the trailer park entrance. "Won't your dad wonder where you are?"

"We won't be long," she assured me, walking toward the school, waving a hand for me to follow.

I jogged after her. "We spend every day up there, isn't that enough, bookworm?" I asked, trying on a nickname for her. We were both bookworms. She just preferred schoolbooks, where I preferred fiction. And in books, friends had nicknames for each other.

Kyrie smiled when she glanced back at me. "Yeah. But it's more fun when it's deserted."

We walked along the road leading to the highway, then crossed. There were no cars around, and no light reached us as we walked up the hill to the entrance of Hart Hollow. Once there, Kyrie turned left, toward the playground.

To the playground's right were the softball and baseball fields. Hart Hollow had two sports. Basketball was the other.

Ahead of me, Kyrie ran toward the swings, leaving her sandals on the pavement before tiptoeing into the gravel.

She grabbed the chain of one of the swings just as I stepped next to her forgotten shoes. I stared at them, sketching their likeness in my head.

"Push me?" Kyrie asked, moving backward. She smiled widely when she let go, gravity propelling her toward me. Her dark braids waved with the wind, and her teeth were bright white against her complexion.

I nodded and walked around the swing set, admiring the way her dress looked in the fading summer light.

She swung back to me, and I grabbed the chain, ensuring I didn't touch her hands. Her long legs kicked back and forth as she moved with gentle ease.

I was jealous of her. Jealous of the way this small town had shaped her. I wondered who I would have become if Hart Hollow had been where I'd grown up. Maybe I'd have tried to kiss her, had charmed her father at dinner, and maybe I would have helped her mother with the dishes. Maybe I would have happily said Valerie and I would love to join them for the Sunday service. Maybe I would believe in God.

I didn't believe in anything except the dark, the wretched things that happened in it.

The sound of my name pulled me from my dark wonderings.

"What?" I asked, certain Kyrie had said it a couple times.

She glanced back at me as she swung. "I asked if you were ready to go home?"

"Sure," I said, grabbing the swing's chains, slowing her sway. My eyes wandered to the back of the school, the dark shadow that led around the gravel drive. I knew there were school busses back there—and the woods.

Trees were everywhere, surrounding the town like sentinels, and I wondered about their secrets.

Kyrie stood up, walking around the swing to me. "I've always loved coming up here in the evenings. But I don't anymore. Not since Amber went missing. The only reason my parents let me walk you home is because you live close. So I just wanted to do this for a second. I hope you didn't mind." Kyrie's voice reminded me of a piano, haunting and pretty when she spoke like this. I'd only known her briefly, but I felt drawn to her. Not in the way she was drawn to me, perhaps. But the concept of friendship ... it was foreign, mystifying, and beautiful.

I smiled for her benefit, reaching for my back pocket involuntarily. My notebook was there, waiting. "I like it here. I know my aunt wants to stay, so this feels different from the other schools. Like, maybe I can put down roots. Maybe I'll come up here sometime."

"At night?" Kyrie asked.

I nodded. "I've always enjoyed walking at night. I like to clear my head. I haven't had time to explore the town yet on foot."

Kyrie smiled widely. "Come get me when you do."

"I like to walk *late* at night."

"Come to my window," she said, looking behind her, as if she worried her parents could hear her from their house. I knew the clichés and what they said about preachers' kids. *Naughty, troublemakers.* Kyrie wasn't that. She was pure and intelligent. She wanted to explore and test the boundaries set in place by her parents. She loved them but didn't believe their word was almighty. I wondered if she felt like bending the rules and words of her almighty God.

"Maybe," I said, grinning.

My smile faded away when I looked past Kyrie to the school's roof.

Sorina stood there, black dress waving in the warm breeze, eyes black in the night.

I felt the color drain from me, felt the way I shivered. I didn't warm, or feel dizzy, as I had that day in the cafeteria. I'd avoided her gaze since that day in school, but I always felt her watching, waiting for something from me. She hadn't been to school that day, though.

"Nicholas?" Kyrie asked, a tremor of worry in her voice. I couldn't stop her from placing her palms on my arms and giving me a small shake. I didn't even think to brush her off. I blinked hard, looking down into her eyes.

When Kyrie turned to see where I had been staring, Sorina was gone.

◎

After Kyrie and I left the school, I walked her home. We laughed about it—hers genuine, mine forced. *You don't have to walk me home, that's what I was doing,* she'd said.

But I insisted. I was worried for her after seeing Sorina on the roof, half tempted to convince myself I dreamed it, that my dreams and waking hours were blending together.

When the rain came, I opened my back window. My favorite thing to smell was rain on leaves. I felt like I belonged somewhere when I pretended it was nostalgia—pretended my life was different. I often wrote stories of other lives, dreamed dreams that felt like memories. When I didn't have the nightmares, I dreamed of a cold rain, sharp grey and black angles.

A place I had never been to.

I knew it wasn't real—that the dream wasn't a memory—but I liked to pretend it was.

I looked out my window, closing my eyes, sniffing the air. I smelled mud, wet gravel, and the air was not cool, but humid. It wasn't like my dreams, but it was real and new.

The slanted front porch in front of the trailer was small, no place to spend time, but we had a sliding glass door in the kitchen and a small back deck with a roof. Itching to be anywhere but my room, I tiptoed through the house as Valerie slept, opening the sliding door before pulling one of our new dining room chairs out

CHAPTER FOUR

onto the deck. My view was the woods, not wet pavement and passing cars, but it would do.

I let my eyes turn the greens trees vivid, more alive than they appeared in the dark. I let my eyes take me from my reality, but before I could begin telling myself stories in my head, I saw a light on at the house beyond the woods, through the creeping fog.

The house beyond the trees looked like it was from the 1800s. It was beautiful and dark, imposing, shrouded in the shade of the trees even in broad daylight. I often stared at it when I spent time in the cemetery. I came there to be alone, but maybe to wait. To look up and see Sorina's slight frame on a headstone. But she hadn't come back.

I looked up into the sky and wondered if Sorina was there, watching me from her own roof, soaked in the rain. It's all I could see above the trees that separated our homes, and it was vacant. A black knife in the blacker night.

With Valerie fast asleep, I ran to the house. I wanted to ask her what she was doing on the roof of the school, why she'd been absent from school that day.

I wanted to ask her *what* she was, the question always felt like a shadow in my mind, hovering.

It never disappeared.

I couldn't shake that first day of school, the way I felt warm all over, reaching for Kyrie as if I were someone else. I didn't want someone fucking with me, making me do things I didn't want to. I'd left that life behind.

Her looming Tudor-style house was one of the biggest in town. I couldn't see it now, the green of the trees was too grown this time of year, but I moved to it, pulled to where I knew it sat, looming. I ran through the rain, soaking my Converse like a kid.

The house had no driveway; instead a paved road ran through the property. I exited the trees onto the short road. Each end had a gate. No one had a gate here, and Kyrie had told me the gates were new one day when she was chatting on about the town. She seemed to know everything about everyone, and her interest in Sorina was pointed.

The sky was open above the road, and my hair soaked as I stared up at her window. Was it her window? I assumed, but I didn't know. Not yet.

I sprinted to the porch and took the steps two at a time. There were two wicker chairs to the right of the front door. I sat in one, weighing my options, grateful for a place to dry off.

Eventually, I pulled a notebook from my back pocket and grabbed the pen that I shoved between the pages. I wrote there, kept company by the cemetery, in her chair. The rain and the slow fog seduced me.

I was halfway through a poem when I heard something in the woods. I had the strange thought that she'd meant for me to hear her, and if she'd wanted to sneak up on me, I never would have known she was there.

"What are you doing here?" Her voice was deep and strange as she stepped from the woods, her luminous skin glowed in the dim lighting. So much of her flesh was visible in her tiny black clothing. Something stirred in me, an ache in my chest.

I closed my notebook and pulled it up, waving it back and forth a bit, in answer.

"What are you writing?" Her voice softened slightly as she drew nearer, her bare feet squishing in the grass. Her hair was drenched.

"A poem about a dream I have sometimes," I said as I pulled my foot up into the seat, wrapping my hands around my ankle.

The porch didn't creak when Sorina reached the landing, not as it had when I stepped onto it earlier. I wasn't surprised. When I wrote about her, which I always did after the dreams, I wrote her as a tiny deep red bird, soaring through a pitch back night sky. She was always being chased by some*thing*, but I couldn't finish the poems.

"Let me read it." She held out her hand, and I hesitated for a moment, fearing the steel of her eyes. Eventually, I relented and handed the notebook over. Sorina looked at the open page for only a fraction of a second before flipping through the other pages. Her eyes took everything in, like she was reading every word. Which was impossible.

I didn't have to wait long for her critique.

"This reads like … what is the word for it?" I noticed then why I thought her voice sounded strange earlier. Her accent was gone. When the principal had brought her to class my first day, parading her like a trophy, I'd shivered at her voice, her thick accent. It was gone now. She continued, "This reads like *porn*. Yes, that's the word they use for it."

I jerked my eyes to hers. There's no fucking way she could have read everything in my notebook in that quick flip through the pages. "What? It does not."

"Do you know anything about men and women?"

"I know a lot about men and women," I seethed. The poems in those pages, the ones I wrote as I touched myself, had nothing to do with what I knew about men and women. What happened at the ranch was not the same as the stories I poured into my notebooks. What happened there was a violence against my flesh. What I wrote about was an exorcism. The girl from my dreams, blood dripping, ecstasy on her tongue—that was healing.

"You need a muse," she offered, handing the notebook back to me.

I took it, purposefully touching her fingers. She locked eyes with me as I slipped it back in my pocket. "I have one," I said.

The air felt sultry between us. And when she asked me if I wanted to come inside, I nodded.

I saw little of the house that first day. After she shut the door behind me, she started walking up the staircase in front of her, leading me down a dark hall and into a bedroom.

What I assumed was *her* bedroom.

We did not speak as she opened the shades, letting the moonlight in.

When she motioned for me to sit on the bed, I did. She didn't join me, instead she walked to a black ornate vanity. She took a seat, looking at me through the mirror in front of her before she spoke again in her timeless and placeless voice. "How was school today?" she asked, reaching for a brush.

I relaxed into her headboard before I spoke. Being near Sorina felt strange and familiar. Though I'd spent mere moments with her since we'd met—I'd spent hours with her in my dreams.

I felt like I knew her, but that was merely a want.

"School was okay," I said

"That seems like a lie," Sorina said, pulling the brush through her wet strands.

I smiled. "Today in English we went over poetry, which is my favorite," I said, thinking of her assertion of my poetry. *Porn.*

"I'm hardly surprised." Her lips curled up, and in the mirror I could see how sheer her clothing was.

"What does that mean?" I asked.

"I wasn't surprised by what I read in that notebook. Poetry … it fits you."

I softened. "Yeah, that's what they said."

"Who?" she asked, moving the brush to the other side of her head.

"Mrs. Vaughn didn't make us read anything out loud or anything. We were all quiet for twenty minutes, writing. Mike Walters and Bobby Morrison were behind me, laughing the whole time, and when I turned mine in, Mrs. Vaughn started reading it immediately. She didn't do that with the others."

"Something on the page pulled her to it." Sorina sounded faraway as she brushed her hair.

"Yeah, I guess. She told me it was 'lovely.' I wish she hadn't said anything." I laughed.

"Why? Did the boys harass you?"

I noted her language, the forceful sound of certain words. *Harass. The boys.* As if she wasn't as student herself. "Yeah. Bobby shoved me in the hall and called me a faggot."

Sorina's voice was dry when she said, "How original of him. Boys like that will be bullies their whole lives. The strongest thing a man can hold inside of himself is compassion, empathy. The most beautiful men are the quiet ones. At least, that's what I believe." Her blue eyes pinned me to her headboard. It's the most I'd ever heard her say. And I wanted to tell her I wasn't scared of Mike or Bobby. It wasn't about that. Some part of me felt like I could rip them to shreds. The way I felt inside rarely matched my slim frame. I felt caged.

I looked at Sorina then and didn't tell her about my fears. Didn't tell her about the rage bubbling beneath the surface. I asked her a question. "Do you have a boyfriend back home?"

Sorina's brushing stopped, and she looked at me in the mirror. "I've never had a ... boyfriend." The word sounded foreign on her lips, just as the other words had. *Harass. The Boys.*

"Bullshit."

"I've kissed boys and I've had ... sex with boys. But never one to keep."

"How old are you?" I asked, wondering why I was drowning like a river near her. I didn't grasp, just yet, why I was asking such a thing.

But that time I didn't think about it, and I asked a version of the question haunting me.

"I'm not ready to answer that question, Nicholas Hemming."

"Fine," I said, my tone stating plainly between us it wasn't.

"Would you let me read what you wrote for the class?"

"I don't have another copy of it. I turned it in."

She turned in her seat, holding out her hand. "Let me see your notebook again."

"Okay," I answered, sliding off the bed. I walked to her, and once again, when I handed her the notebook, I let my fingers touch hers. "Would you like to come over to the lamp?" I asked. The lamp was closer to the bed, to where I was.

"No, I can see fine."

I walked across the room, climbing onto her bed again. After a few minutes of her silent page turning, I asked her questions. She never told me to be quiet. She answered as she poured over my poetry a second time, more slowly. More *human*.

"Where were you born?" I asked.

"*By the sea.*"

"Do you miss the ocean?" I asked.

"*Every day.*"

"Do you believe in God?" I begged for a no.

"*Yes.*"

"Are you done yet?" I teased.

"*No.*"

"What are you most scared of?" My heart beat fast.

"*I'm not scared of anything.*"

Her answer felt like a lie, but as I watched her read, eyes roving slowly, almost performative, I let it stay between us. Finally, I spoke again, unable to help myself with her. "There's a school dance in a few weeks. I'm thinking about going. Are you going to go? I've never been to a dance."

Sorina stopped reading. "You should. It would be good for you."

I didn't like the way she said it, like I was a pet. Or a child. "If it's lame we can just walk home." I looked away, embarrassed that I'd used the word *we*, and my eyes caught on a quill on her nightstand with a glass jar of ink next to it. Next to the lamp sat a large notebook, black leather. A red string stuck out at the end.

Sorina closed my notebook, pulling my eyes to her as she stood. She didn't move for a moment, and if I blinked, I would have thought she disappeared, that I was in a dream state. She shook her head, then walked to the other side of the bed, crawling onto it. She didn't lean on the headboard like I had so brazenly done, instead she leaned against one of the posts at the end. After a long sigh, she stretched her legs out, resting them on my lap. I didn't move.

Sorina's voice was dreamy when she asked, "Are you going to take Kyrie?"

I reached out, placing my palm on her calf. Touching her was nothing like touching anyone else. It calmed me. The slight buzzing in my ears, the swelling anxiety, it fell away when I touched her flesh. "Do you have a better idea?" I asked, having one of my own, needed her to say it.

She shook her head. "No. Take your pretty friend. Have fun," she said.

We said little else that night, and I thought of nothing else but Sorina as I walked home—her blue eyes, her flesh, the pink of her nipples visible through her wet clothing.

I smelled of her. Of her home—earthy, like pennies in a well. And when I fell to bed, the nightmares did not reach me.

But I dreamed—writhed, touched myself in the dark.

And that was a nightmare in itself.

FIVE

If you had asked Valerie, she would have told you plainly that she'd never been the good daughter. The most loved daughter.

She'd been the daughter of pity. The daughter of social status. The daughter of *this is a good deed*.

Valerie Hawkridge's mother and father adopted her from a Seattle foster home when she was five years old. Her mother said her ruddy hair drew her to her. She stood out. She reminded her of autumn, Libby Hawkridge's favorite season. She reminded her of falling leaves and apple cider.

Of course, Valerie was a child, not a season, but it got her out of the foster home, so she didn't complain.

She went from the foster home to a three-story house in the suburbs. She went from sleeping on a cot to wearing a uniform on her first day at a cute little private school. One more piece of her new parents' perfect, cookie-cutter life.

She went from being an orphan to a daughter. A *sister*.

Her new brother was five years older than her. And her new sister was only ten months older. It didn't take long for them to be attached at the hip or behave more like twins than two little girls that were only related by law.

Serendipity loved to remind Valerie that she was ten months older than her when she did wrong, when she wanted to tattle, and when she tried to confess all the cruel things her new sister did.

Valerie was the perfect daughter; she'd styled herself that way.

Serendipity *appeared* to be the perfect daughter.

Behind her laughter and embrace was resentment.

Why did they need to bring Valerie home? Why did they need a new daughter when they had her?

Serendipity never spoke those words out loud, but Valerie felt them when her eyes landed on her some days. They were thick as thieves, but the older sister was the only thief. The younger was the lookout. Valerie was the cover-up.

It had started small.

Serendipity killed their brother's fish. Valerie covered. Said it was her.

Serendipity stole twenty bucks from their father's wallet. Valerie covered. Said it was her.

Serendipity convinced her new sister it was okay for her to take the blame. She had no real parents, so she could be forgiven easily.

Serendipity said Valerie was *dirty,* and if she helped her, she would be clean one day.

She couldn't see what she was then. A child's eyes were so pure. She wanted to belong, and with Serendipity, she did. Even if it was just as a scapegoat of sorts.

When they hit high school, Serendipity was the most beautiful girl in their class. She was five foot ten, legs for days. Her hair was jet black, and her ivory skin always drew men in. Her classmates, the teachers, everyone.

Valerie was popular by association. She shouldn't have been—not with her frizzy, red hair, braces, and awkward way of speaking. Not according to the laws of high school.

There is a price to pay for being an imposter.

Everything you think is yours is not. It was borrowed. It could be taken from your wanting palms.

In their sophomore year, Valerie fell in love for the first time. His name was Gregory, and he was all things beautiful. He liked to smile at Valerie in the English class they shared, and before long, he was leaving notes in her locker, walking with her between classes. Every day brought a new thrill.

Until Serendipity found out.

She told Valerie she was too good for him. He was dirty, but she was finally almost clean. She had covered for her many times, so close to atonement.

The game, so clear to Valerie now, had held her hostage. Serendipity hovered, ensured Valerie wasn't lingering in the halls with the boy she liked.

Serendipity had been in Valerie's bones.

Two weeks later, Serendipity let Gregory finger her in the back of the school bus.

They sat together at lunch. He walked Serendipity to her classes.

And Valerie was a shadow. A mistake.

Valerie never said a word about her loss. She was dirty. And she believed it justified the screams, the revenge she took. And it felt true when the man with the scar took her away from her life, away from those who would punish her for what she did to Gregory and Serendipity.

These were thoughts Valerie wouldn't allow herself to indulge in very often. The memories became hazier and hazier with each passing year.

But sometimes the images gripped her. The sounds woke her. And on those mornings she woke covered in sweat, her back aching, she wished she wouldn't have woken up at all.

After pulling herself into the shower and washing away every dirty feeling in the dark as tears streamed down cheeks, Valerie shook her head and closed her eyes, firmly shutting the door to the past.

When she stepped out of the shower, reaching for a clean town, she smiled into the mirror after her hand wiped the steam away. She was reset. New. *Serendipity meant a beautiful fate. She never deserved the name.*

The Steele Heart Trailer Park felt clean before the sun rose. Valerie liked to drink a hot mug of coffee on the tiny front porch each morning before heading to the café. She sat on the steps as the world woke up, the sounds of birds singing and distant cars on the highway her soundtrack.

She was working a later shift that day, so she slept in ever so slightly. And when she opened her front door after dressing, she squinted into the early morning light.

She preferred the dark.

She preferred the illusion that the world was fast asleep.

Before her, the lime green trailer across from their driveway was quiet—as every trailer in the park was on weekend mornings. There was a large dumpster in the front yard, and a haphazard couch hung off the porch.

As Valerie sat down with her mug, she remembered the park owner had hired a few men to clear it out. While bringing in groceries the previous evening, Valerie had heard them saying they were tired of cleaning out the *trash* and complained about the needles they found under the bed.

She'd smelled what they cleared from the trailer. Animal feces. Rotten food.

The trailer park was a mixture of townsfolk. Right next door to the now vacant *trash* trailer was a sweet little doublewide.

Valerie had heard that living in the only trailer park in town meant she lived on the *bad* side of town. But she mused that Hart Hollow was too small to offer much of a definitive line between the good side of town and the bad. Everything blended together.

There was a large house behind their trailer that sat just through the trees. It overlooked the trailer park and the cemetery and was only separated from the supposed trash by the elderly trunks and branches whispering toward the sky.

She would've loved to rent a house like the one so close. But she'd wanted to blend in, so they'd rented a trailer instead. It was a temporary fix—she'd dreamed of living outside of town, away from people. Though she did still keep a knife on her at all times, the convenience and warm safety of living in town snuck up on her.

Nicholas could walk to school, and she could avoid school drop-offs.

She could avoid buying him a car, and the nagging feeling that if he had one, he would leave her and the town behind.

She knew he wanted the freedman a car promised. And Valerie wanted him to be ready to start his own life when he turned eighteen, but she wasn't prepared to let him go.

Playing *mother* had not been part of her plan.

Leaving the ranch with Nicholas had not been part of the plan.

But when the screaming started that last night and she saw his eyes—blood red—she'd taken him with her. Maybe it had been atonement, a deep dwelling plea to God for forgiveness for what she had done to her sister—and Gregory.

No, no. Leave it there.

Setting her coffee down, Valerie slipped her feet into the sandals she kept on the front porch. She walked down the steps, pulling her flannel shirt tighter around herself. The air held a chill in the morning, and fall was approaching.

She walked down the gravel road that circled the trailer park until she arrived at the entrance, where the mailboxes stood in a row. She was hoping the movement would make her manic mind stop spinning back to the past like a broken game of spin the bottle. The world and her mind quieted as she flipped through their mail. Coupons, PTA meeting paperwork, and an advertisement from a local church were all she found.

And in the quiet, with nothing more than the gentle rustling of paperwork, Valerie felt a strange warmth wash over her …

And then came a chill …

The hair on her arms stood tall.

She straightened her back and turned slowly, quick enough to see a flash of red in the woods behind the trailers, but not quick enough to see anything more.

CHAPTER FIVE

Though he'd been groggy—and protested—when she woke him up, Valerie convinced Nicholas to join her at the café for breakfast. She was working a quick shift with the other cook that Saturday morning, and the flash she'd seen in the woods while checking the mail left her reluctant to leave him behind.

He closed his eyes when he got into her car, leaning into the headrest, sleeping in the front seat, though the drive to the café lasted only a few minutes.

She spoke low when she pulled behind the café to park. "Do you think you want to get a part-time job?" she asked.

Nicholas opened his eyes, looking around. He looked disoriented for a moment, then recovered, remembering where he was. "Why? Do I need to? I thought this was—"

"It is. It is," she'd said. The words unspoken between them.

This is different.

This is a new start.

Tabula Rasa.

He'd held odd jobs while they traveled. Hanging out in a car or a motel after school wasn't exactly exciting. Nicholas often waited tables while Valerie worked in the kitchen. They never said they were related. And that was the truth. But they also never said they were masquerading as aunt and nephew.

Nicholas unbuckled his seat belt, stretching. "I want to focus on school. I'm thinking about joining a club, or … I dunno … a sport or something."

Valerie turned to him. "Really?" Nicholas didn't have an athletic build. He was tall and slender, had an artist's hands.

"Yeah. Maybe Art Club, or … they have a writing club at the school too."

That fit him. The sport comment had thrown her, but maybe he just threw it out to see her reaction.

"You should. We want to—"

"Appear normal," Nicholas finished her sentence, his voice dipping low. He opened his mouth slightly, as if to say something, but then closed it. When he spoke again, his voice was different. "I'm going to call my friend and see if she wants to come up and eat with me."

"What's her name?" Valerie asked. She was glad he had a friend. They hadn't been able to talk much about how school was going. She was always so tired after work, often napping when Nicholas came home, waking only long enough to cook dinner, which he ate less and less.

"Kyrie."

"Are you—"

"No," Nicholas said, reaching for the door. He stepped out of the car, shutting it in Valerie's face. She closed her eyes for a moment, almost said a prayer, but thought better of it. A face flashed in her mind, and it was the Deacon's. She'd been thinking of him lately at work and warming when he came in to eat. And she hated to admit it, but she thought of him as she drifted off to sleep, too.

He was even in her dreams.

Maybe, she thought, if Nicholas had a friend, she could have one too.

The Deacon was shaped differently from the men she usually desired. The opposite, in every way, of her first love, Gregory, and of the man with the scarred face.

CHAPTER FIVE

The Deacon could fill a door frame. His hands were large, his thick fingers wrapped around his drink when he sipped his water in the late mornings. He always came in close to when she was ending her shift. He took a seat by the window—as far away from the kitchen as one could get—and he looked out that window. She wondered what he was watching, what he could see with his blind eyes. What he *heard*.

And some days, she wondered what his hands would feel like around her neck. She thought she'd like it.

Valerie had been drawn, in the past, to tender looking men. Dark eyes and lips more pink than most. Slender fingers and soft voices, though the words they often enticed her with were lies.

The Deacon's voice was old, deep, and she felt it everywhere.

It commanded.

How did a beautiful girl like Valerie end up a virgin at twenty-six? In high school she was the redheaded, brace-faced younger sister of the most popular girl in school. She only wanted one boy, and he was taken from her.

In the earliest days of her life on the ranch, Valerie thought she had fallen in love for real. She'd let the scar-faced man map her body, let him play her like an instrument. She made sounds. She hummed. She wanted to give in all the way. But the voice in her head wouldn't allow it. The dirty reminder. The planted seed. Partly because of Serendipity's words. Mostly because of her deformity.

The scar-faced man had found it, but he had not cast her out, and he didn't make her leave the ranch. He'd kept her, but he never touched her again.

Valerie was good at bottling. Stewing until the anger inside spread to her bones, her fingertips, her toes. Until she became rage …

Saving it up.

Exploding on contact.

She used to steal Serendipity's toys, her things. She would break them, burn them, or throw them in the trash. She never caught Valerie, but that wasn't the point. She wanted her sister to wonder. To search in vain. She wanted some sort of power over her.

Serendipity liked to steal for show. To show you what she had taken. To make your changed face a pleasure party for her eyes. Instant gratification. Not Valerie. She liked to watch the insanity grow slowly. She liked to watch the search grow and swell. The warmth that simple pleasure gave her sat well in the pit of her belly. She never let her desires show.

As she sat alone in the front seat, Valerie outlined the Deacon's figure in her mind; her tongue traced her incisors, and she blinked twice, wondering if a man who could not see could love a woman like her. He couldn't see her marred parts.

Couldn't see her ugly.

She jumped when Nicholas knocked on the passenger window, pulling her from the sighs that echoed in her head.

"I'm coming," she said, briefly wondering what those words would sound like in a dark room, alone with the Deacon.

SIX

They're coming.

It was ritualistic—a loop. And the time had come to feed, to find rebirth in the town. Deacon Rex crept down the stairs in Steele Mansion and made his way to the elevator. When his bare feet stepped in, he was fully dressed. Grey. White. Heavy. Stifling as he traveled down to the deep parts no one knew about.

The house on the hill was old but the caves were older.

The water rushed by, calming as it entered the lake. The cave opening that fed to the water was obscured, and no one dared float by.

The locals called the cave haunted; a feeling of illness came over them when they considered fishing the waters. They knew better, as their fathers before they did.

Don't go far upstream in Casador Lake.

The mouth of hell sits there.

They weren't wrong.

When The Deacon exited the elevator, he stripped his coat, his white button up, and his pants. Clothes were for the mortals ...

For the animals he walked among and pretended to fit in with.

Here he did not need to hide, though he had nothing to fear from the townspeople. Or any people, for that matter.

Amber laid on the bed, eyes on the ceiling, when he walked into the cell. Iron and rock and earth—soundless. No one could hear her scream.

She hadn't stopped trying. But now she was tired.

She pinched the skin of her wrist, reached up to her throat, missing the necklace she lost that day.

Her tie to home.

Her connection to God.

Connection to the girl the gift came from.

She didn't flinch when he came to her, naked, made of marble. White eyes open, seeing nothing.

She knew he wasn't going to rape her. He hadn't tried. He had no use for her in that way. Instead, he fed on her sorrow, her cries, and her family's anguish as they mourned the young girl who *ran away for a better life*. The girl who got away from that small town.

He didn't need to feed often, could go years without the drink...

Without a bite.

But it was time, and the strength it took to swat the fly that was Sorina was nothing he could spare. He had more important things to worry about.

A more important daughter to transform.

CHAPTER SIX

Valerie wouldn't be like the rest. He wouldn't let her mind sour, wouldn't let her turn against him.

But he would have to separate her from the boy. He wasn't part of the plan; not *that* plan, anyway. And the crumbs the Deacon had left as he followed them across the land hadn't been enough to convince Nicholas to run away. He wasn't ready for him yet, but the free will he'd granted the boy was often unpredictable.

Dreams were potent, and he could plant them with his touch. And Deacon Rex had been many people on their journey. A stranger in a gas station. A hotel clerk. A sales associate at Kmart. Light touches, almost accidentally. *Infections*. And when Nicholas and Valerie looked at him then, he was many people, fading away as soon as their eyes left him. He shape-shifted, poking tiny holes into the fabric of their minds. Led her here to be devoured. Led him here to blot out the sun.

He needed the boy on task. He knew what Nicholas Hemming was. He'd set him loose with one purpose in mind. The boy's fate —his destiny.

The Deacon closed his white eyes and turned his face to Amber. She nodded, although she didn't know why. She knew his eyes were useless, but also knew he saw everything.

She rolled over, opened her legs, and exposed the flesh of her thigh.

He knelt to her, kissed her knee, then moved higher, biting. She closed her eyes, and only after a sharp cry, gave into the warmth. It spread from her thigh to her sex, to her nipples, to her throat. A warm hand around it.

The guilt would come later. She was the dirty thing her father preached about.

Vile girl, broken thing.

Deacon Rex didn't care what she did as he fed. It didn't arouse him when she touched herself or moaned when she came. She was cattle; she was meat. And when she was happy, even when his teeth made her feel like she was on a glittering drug, it didn't feed him.

Later, his belly would be full of her as she sobbed in her cell, dirty with her desire. That's when he grew hungry for something else, something primal. But he didn't want her.

Not for that.

That was for the daughters. The scattered and fractured bloodlines he had created. *Pure.* A single line needed to remain pristine. One single line for the day his kind had to make a choice. Stay in the darkness, or feast on the herd in the daylight.

The time for the dead to hide would soon be over.

And he would be ready.

SEVEN

It was an awakening that night. A brutal assault on my senses. I waxed and felt like the crescent moon. So desperate for her. So desperate to please the girl with the red hair—a huntress, what a marvel she was in my dreams. The need to taste her was ingrained in me—a memory, a destiny of sorts.

I didn't believe in that sort of thing then, not yet.

But I would. The memories of another life, my birth, were buried far too deep to pull to the surface; the universe was not yet ready to rip the bandage off, to expose the cruelty of fate to the light.

I would touch myself at night, furious and fading images of her behind my eyes, starkly contrasted to what was there when my lids closed.

To pull yourself from a whispering grave is to exhume the long buried.

I didn't know it yet. The cave in the grave hadn't spoken to me yet.

It was long before those dreams. Before the shivering and the fainting in class.

I would have liked to have been a mythical creature, especially after I read or wrote in my notebook.

Maybe a werewolf, shape-shifting my way through the centuries, through the world around me.

I imagined it manly, to be a beast. To rip the flesh from those who harmed me. It was a lofty dream many boys fantasized about, aiming their rage at bullies or abusive parents.

Instead, I aimed it at dead women, at the hands that touched me.

Mary was the worst because she seemed to be the kindest. She was closer to my age, mute, blind in one eye. Half of what *he* was.

I didn't know what rules and punishments Markus doled out to the women on the ranch. But I knew something happened in the dark.

In my dream that night I was on Sorina's roof, watching the stars.

"Do you think the stars talk to us?" I asked. I could feel her eyes on my face as I memorized the constellations. She propped up on one elbow, no shame in her attention.

"Everything talks to us. You just have to listen."

"I imagine, up there, there is no good and evil. Not like there is here. There is no hate, no disease, no suffering." My voice was deeper in my dream, but my words brought forth the image of a child. A child I could never be.

"I won't let you suffer." She reached over and ran her hand through my hair.

I said, *"I used to suffer every day."*

And dream Sorina said, *"I can take her away, you know that, right?"*

"Yes." I barely got the word out, vowing not to ask. I couldn't sentence someone to death, could I?

CHAPTER SEVEN

"Do you want me to?"

"Some days, yes. Most days, no. I shouldn't love her, but I do." Dream me pictured Mary, but the image was distorted, flickering. Valerie's face was in the static.

"Sometimes we have to hurt the ones we love."

I said, *"I think religion is killing her."* I didn't know who dream me meant anymore.

"Revenge is a religion, too, you know. It's mine."

"I don't want to be that way." I closed my eyes, throat hot.

"You don't have to be that way. I can carry that for you."

And then I woke, drenched in sweat, though there was a chill the night I met Diana. I was grateful the reoccurring nightmare of hot, needy, greedy hands that left me with a film all over my skin had left me alone for one brief night, but the dream I'd been given made me feel unsteady.

I looked at my bedroom window, the cause of my chill. It was open, and though it was an unanswered plea, I desired the tapping of fingernails on windows. Hers, red and sharp. But she never came, except in dreams.

The moon was full that night. And my disappointment at the surrounding silence faded after a moment.

I was going to walk that night.

I was going to resume the ritualist loop I'd begun making through town a few nights earlier.

I felt restless and determined as I threw the covers off and ran a hand over my face. When I closed my eyes, I steadied my breathing. The house was still, Valerie likely asleep. She always seemed to sleep heavily, and that was a solace.

I'd been exploring the town in small increments as I tried to clear my mind and shake off the dreams.

Plus. I was looking for Sorina.

Though I never saw her, I felt her watching me, and it made me feel less alone.

Taking care to be quiet, I slipped on a pair of jeans and a T-shirt. After grabbing a flannel and my Converse, I'd slipped out my window to the bench below it to put them on.

The air was often hot and sticky, a heat unlike what we experienced in California. A heat that clung to every part of you, suffocated you. But at night, it faded away, crisp air flowing through open windows as cicadas sang, trying to tell me every secret of the town and it's inhabitants. I still didn't feel like a resident.

Hart Hollow was in the shape of a cross. We map what we are moved to believe. What is mended into our bones. Past the bridge leading out of town sat a bar and gas station, though we never got gas there.

Early after our arrival, Valerie scoffed at the idea when I suggested we stop in one Saturday as we left town to stock up on my school clothes.

"Let's stay away from the bars, Nicholas. New leaf, fresh start." *Tabula Rasa.* She didn't say the words, and I didn't argue as I turned to the window and pretended she didn't sometimes sound like my mother—or others on the ranch.

After leaving the trailer park, I crept down the road, past Kyrie's house, onto South Main. There I turned right, past the town's main cemetery, and over the bridge, out of town.

Once I arrived at the Lazy Lee's gas station, I stared at the small bar. It couldn't be bigger than the trailer we lived in and looked

CHAPTER SEVEN

like an old garage. The bay doors were open, exposing the patrons to the night.

To me.

There weren't many there that Thursday night, and I knew I couldn't get in, but I was drawn to the dirty place. The people inside were night owls like me. That was a want, perhaps, but I didn't know how unlike me they were. Not yet.

I walked toward one of the open bay doors, planning to sit on the pavement outside, when a voice called me.

I turned to the right, finding a tall woman with shaggy, black hair smoking a cigarette, piercing blue eyes boring into me.

She'd said my name.

I walked toward her. "How do you know my name?" I asked.

She threw her cigarette on the ground, using her boot to extinguish the cherry. "Small town. Everyone knows who the new people in the trailer park are." She shrugged before hitching her thumb toward the bar. "You can't go in there. You're what, sixteen?"

I raised my chin. "Small towns don't know my grade? My social security number? They aren't curious about the birthmark on my thigh?" I mocked.

The woman laughed, mumbling something that sounded like *some are*.

"I'm seventeen," I said. "And I wasn't going in. I was just going to sit outside."

"This isn't exactly a fancy diner with nice outdoor seating. Don't get me shut down, kid," she said, her voice raspy.

I wondered if it was from the cigarettes, and I didn't like being called a kid. I didn't feel like one, and I wasn't sure I'd ever been one, either.

"Nicholas," I replied, crossing my arms. "Not, *kid*."

"Okay," she said. "*He who mocks.* Nicholas, don't go near my bar, okay?"

"No promises—"

"Diana," she answered, extending her hand.

I shook it and eyed the entrance to her bar. Above the old wood was a sign, the name hand-painted. *Moonies.*

I pointed to it, then asked, "Diana Moonie?"

She shook her head, coming closer. "No. I didn't name it."

"Good, because the name sucks."

Diana laughed again, walking past me to the back of a truck. She opened the tailgate, hoisting herself up. I joined her. "What are you doing out past midnight on a school night, *Nicholas?*"

I rubbed my palms on my jeans, staring across the gas station to the road past the park. "I'm a night owl."

"Yeah, well, teenagers go missing around here. Maybe you should stay home. Small town people don't take kindly to teenage boys stalking around in the dark. Especially ones who just moved to town."

I smiled wide, looking her in the eye. "How would they know? Everyone's asleep."

"Not everyone," Diana replied, looking past the gas station to the bridge.

I followed her gaze, red hair drawing me in.

CHAPTER SEVEN

We sat in silence as Sorina approached. When she was close enough, I took in her clothes, the pale of her skin. She wore a long black skirt—slits on each side; her legs flashed with every step—fishnet tights and black combat boots. I heard nothing as she walked up, no boots on gravel, no sway of her hand. She was always quiet.

She didn't halt her step, but she eyed Diana and me before she walked into the bar.

I followed her every move, and she watched me in return.

Beside me, Diana spoke. "Don't go getting a schoolboy crush on that one," she said.

I turned to her. "Why is she allowed in the bar?"

Diana shrugged. "Drinking age is slightly different where she's from, maybe?" She said it like a question, but it didn't halt my interrogation.

"In Romania?"

"Maybe, I don't know. I've never been there." Diana swung her legs.

"Bending the rules for her. Nice." I shook my head. But I thought I would have bent every rule for her.

"You don't want to hang in that dingy bar with the locals on weeknights. Trust me."

"Why does she?"

Diana laughed. "She doesn't."

"You know her, then?"

"Yeah. She's waiting for me. And she's probably pissed I'm talking to you." She shrugged. "I have a tendency to say shit I shouldn't."

I narrowed my eyes. "Has she talked about me?"

Diana grinned as she rolled her eyes. "God, *teenagers*. You're so hopped up on hormones and shit. You're just a young pup when it comes down to it, huh?" It was another nonquestion for me, and I had no time to mock or retort before Diana hopped off the tailgate and turned to me. "Go home, Nicholas. Maybe I'll let you in another night. But, for now, let the big girls talk."

I watched her walk away into the bar. Diana closed one bay door, then the next. But not before I saw Sorina leaning against the wall, watching me until she couldn't.

The darkness was my shroud, my mystery. And her eyes brought me out.

Rejected, I walked back toward town. But before I reached the bridge, the dirt road leading to the right caught my eye. I knew what was atop that hill. The Catholic church Valerie had mentioned.

I had no desire to go there, but the city park was within view, so I turned toward it instead of heading back into town. The gravel crunched beneath my feet, and the town was eerily quiet. The sounds of the bar faded.

Once I reached the park, I left the road, strolling across the grass to Casador Lake. There was a body of land jutting out, and when I got close enough, I noticed it was a small island in the lake. A wooden bridge connected the park and the small piece of land. I walked toward it and imagined laying on my back as I sketched the night, but I stopped short when I noticed a man standing in the center, staring at the trees.

He was completely naked—dark brush strokes along his arms.

The sight of his white skin in the moonlight struck me, and I crouched down, my heart beating fast.

CHAPTER SEVEN

I didn't know what to do. In all my brief wanderings of Hart Hollow, I'd yet to see another person, save for the town Sheriff when he patrolled.

I was a ghost in the night, never fearful.

Until now.

If the naked man heard me walk up, he would hear me leaving. I closed my eyes and listened, hearing nothing but the wind in the trees and the soft music of Moonie's.

I crouched there for an unknown amount of time, waiting for something. Seconds? Minutes? I couldn't be sure. But when my legs started to ache, I knew I needed to leave, retreat somehow.

When I opened my eyes, a hand slid around my throat, and another clamped over my mouth.

Cool lips pressed to my ear. I felt fear in her voice. "Don't move. He knows you're here."

My heart thundered in my chest, and my body tensed.

Sorina's voice was deep. Hypnotic. "You're going to leave back the way you came. Don't come back here, Nicholas. That will be your blood on him if you do."

I squinted in the moonlight, trying to see what she meant. I saw what the dark strokes had been. There was blood on him. She was right. My eyesight had always been keen, and I didn't know why. Not yet. And when I sniffed the night air, I smelled it then. *Copper.* Like pennies in my mouth. I shivered, a deep ache in my belly, traveling to my chest. I wanted something, but I wasn't sure what it was. When I exhaled, Sorina leaned into me. Maybe she didn't mean to because she pulled away a fraction just as quickly as she pressed to me.

We stood together, her hand leaving my throat, then my mouth. I turned toward her, looking down at her slight frame. She had to be five feet to my six. As slender as me, as pale. Eyes just as blue.

"What the fuck are you, anyway?" I asked in a whisper. The question always rising when she was in view. She was ... off ... unnatural.

She was on me again, hand gripping my neck, hand over my mouth. "Not here. He might want to play."

She took my hand then, leading me away from the island. I felt another shiver. I didn't know it, but the man on the island had turned, white eyes watching us. Lips turned up in amusement.

He wanted to play.

Just not yet.

Sorina didn't speak until we crossed the city limit sign over the bridge.

She cast furtive glances over her shoulder as we walked, her eyes trained on the park, the lake, and the island.

I broke the silence when we passed the Casey's gas station; nerves shot. "What the fuck was that back there?"

"Don't go back there, Nicholas. I know you want to wander the town at night, but don't go back there."

I sped up, passing her. "Last I checked, we aren't friends. We barely know each other, save the orders for someone else." I was defiant then, and eager to shed the past. I was told how to live at the ranch.

How to breathe.

CHAPTER SEVEN

How to eat.

Every moment of every day was meticulously planned out for me.

I didn't want that life anymore, and I was exercising my independence more and more each day. It helped that Valerie was busy with her own new start. Her eyes were often vacant, and she was so busy with work and creating a new life for us that she rarely paid attention to me. It served me well.

Sorina said my name, voice deeper. It felt like an undead ghost was speaking through her. I didn't understand it then, and when I would learn the truth, I would believe my dark past had caught up with me.

I turned around, looking at her. Her fists were balled at her side, and her chin was up. Her eyes looked almost black in the night, and I blinked a few times, then shook my head.

Finally, she shook her head, and I smiled.

"What? What was that?"

Sorina strode forward, glancing down the road past Kyrie's house and on to the trailer park. Her voice was softer when she spoke again. "Control is hard to give up, especially when it's newly claimed after years of having none."

"Okay."

She turned to me, blue eyes clear in the night. "Don't go down there again. It's not safe."

"And to the bar?"

She smirked. "Diana won't let you in. Not unless I say it's okay."

I crossed my arms. "And why does she have to wait for your permission? She said she runs the bar."

"We're close."

"Didn't you just move here?" I asked.

Sorina turned down the road.

I wasn't eager to get home, but I followed.

"You're close with that girl, and you just moved here." She pointed ahead, to where I knew Kyrie's house would come into view in a block. "Did you ask her to the dance like I suggested?"

"We're friends," I repeated.

Sorina glanced at me. "And that's all she wants to be."

"Is that a question or a declaration?"

"It's the truth. So don't let your little ego convince you otherwise."

"What, because she's religious?"

"No, that's not why she doesn't want to fuck you, Nicholas."

I kicked a rock, jarred by her words. I was both fascinated and annoyed by the way she spoke.

"Well, that works out great because I don't want to fuck her either," I declared. I didn't want anyone touching me, wanting me. Greedy hands and mouths made for nights like these. When I couldn't sleep.

But when I dreamt of something different? Something that didn't hurt? It was a girl with red hair and long black nails. Black eyes and fangs. A blood-hungry thing. A demon. A ghost.

And in those dreams, I welcomed the hands, the mouth, her flesh. My eyes were red, black hair long and coarse. I wasn't human, and it felt like I dreamed her into existence.

"You should leave this town, Nicholas," Sorina said, glancing idly at Kyrie's house as we passed.

It was dark, but I saw a lace curtain move slightly.

"I'm pretty sure I'm not in charge of where we live. My aunt likes it here. She's finally feeling settled."

Sorina glanced at me, eyes roving over my bare arm. I was thinner then, lean, six feet tall, and gangly. I had turned to gluttony after we left the ranch, famished when we stopped at roadside diners and gas stations. But my teenage metabolism cannibalized everything I ate.

I would grow bigger and stronger.

Soon.

Sorina reached out and brushed fingertips over my arm.

It didn't hurt when her flesh touched mine. "You should eat more," she said, and I wondered if she could read my mind.

She couldn't. But she felt me.

I couldn't feel her yet.

Not the way I wanted to.

"I can't afford double lunches," I said.

"Make your own meals from now on at home, Nicholas."

We were at the entrance of the trailer park when I turned to Sorina, annoyance swelling. "This has been fun. Thanks for saving me from the weird naked man and the ominous commands, but I think I'll call it a night."

Sorina was unfazed by my anger, my mocking. Instead, she walked past me toward my trailer. When I caught up to her, she looked up at me. "I have something for you. It'll fix your problem."

Before I could think better of it, we walked into the trees to the small cemetery between my trailer and her house. Sorina crawled onto a headstone again, quiet, like a cat.

I shook my head, and she cocked an eyebrow. "You think I disrespect the dead?" she asked.

I crossed my arms and walked to a fallen tree, using it as a seat. It wasn't where she sat that piqued my interest; it was the way she moved. "On the ranch, we had a cemetery," I said. "A place where we knew the face of everyone on the headstones. Well, the older people, anyway. I was young. The dead weren't old, really. Many died young. I can see now it was … what was happening there with the … *family*."

"On this … cattle ranch? This is where you grew up?"

I nodded my head. I had told no one where I was truly from or what it was like. But though she couldn't hypnotize or control me now, something about Sorina's eyes made me want to peel my skin off and confess my sins—whatever they were. Though I had this gnawing feeling that what I considered a sin, she would not.

"I didn't know the word for it. Not while I was there. I just know I … hated it."

"It was a cult," she stated, pulling something from the inside of her shirt.

I continued. "The leader … his name was Markus. We called him *Father*. There were mostly women there; very few men could stay. Often they would grow up, age out, and they were pushed out of the community."

"So Markus could fuck all the women, right?" Sorina asked, sitting completely still.

I nodded my head. "For … for the most part. My mother and father were there. He and his brother brought my aunt in. I don't

CHAPTER SEVEN

know if they would have let me stay in the end. I guess it doesn't matter. I didn't want to, but I didn't want to leave the family." I wanted to leave, to burn the place down. And when I thought about leaving, the family I didn't want to leave was Valerie, for some reason.

We weren't close. We weren't blood related. We weren't really family, not in the traditional sense.

But I felt like she was a prisoner, just as I was. I didn't know what they did to her, if they doled out the same punishments disguised as pleasures to her. But I knew my uncle, the man who fished her from the sea of people who didn't live on the ranch, the outsiders, didn't want her. And I thought maybe that was a solace for her.

"And your parents are dead?" Sorina asked.

I swallowed. "Yes."

"I'm sorry. You're better off away from there, though."

I stared down at my Converse, a lump in my throat. "I know. I know I had parents, but ... we were all *his* children. The men who were there ... they were molded after Markus, trained. And the women were—"

"Like cattle? Bred? Is this why you lied and said you were on a ranch with cattle?"

Tears threatened my eyes, and I closed them tight. "Yes."

"What do you dream about, Nicholas? What keeps you from your bed, wandering this town at night? You should run away. Leave your aunt behind. She won't want to leave. She can't leave this town. He already has her marked."

I glared at her. "Who has her marked? What are you talking about?"

"The man out there? Where you came from? Markus … he was a false God, and he's been punished?"

"He's dead."

"She took you from a terrible place, but here? It's worse. He's seen her coming. He's drawn her here. He's known every move you've made. That man we saw earlier? He'll devour this whole town to get to her."

I stood then, dizzy from her words. They made no sense, not yet. But I would learn Sorina often talked in riddles and broken songs. "What the fuck are you talking about?"

She hopped off the grave then, bringing the item she had pulled out of her top to me. It was an offering; her pale hand was a cup, and I would drink from it.

When she was close enough, I saw the joint. I'd seen someone with one once, outside of a diner. The musky odor drew me in, and I'd walked toward the man before he gave me a dirty look and walked to his car.

I knew what it was, but I was hesitant. It'd been ingrained in us at the ranch to keep our minds and bodies pure. What a fucking joke.

But the spear was not a weapon, not in his mind.

"What's that?" I asked, though I knew.

"It'll help you sleep. No more dreams, no more nightmares."

"You know, we had a D.A.R.E. meeting at school last week. You weren't there. I don't think you should give drugs to a fellow student."

"I'm not a student there," Sorina said, procuring a lighter from her pocket. She lit the joint, then pulled a slow drag. Her eyes turned black for a second, and I almost didn't see it. After that, I convinced myself it was a trick of the light.

When she was done, she offered the joint to me, and I took it, pulling it to my lips.

I imagined I could taste her as I inhaled, eyes closed, registering a hand around my wrist, an urge to keep it there. I held my breath until Sorina motioned for me to release it.

She smiled then; it was the first time I saw her teeth. Her incisors were slightly longer than the rest. I imagined them on my neck, my chest, and the skin of my thigh.

The euphoria that overtook me was instant. The small places she'd touched me pulsed, and when I looked at her, her teeth seemed to elongate, her eyes turned full black, and her hair glowed red.

"Fuck, is this … is this what it's always like?"

Sorina took the joint, bringing it to her lips. When she was done, she puffed the air into my face. "No. You won't find anything like this anywhere else."

I remember little else after that. I know Sorina took my arm and led me out of the woods to the bench by my window, and somehow she carried me in through the open window and laid me in my bed.

She said I wouldn't dream, but what else could the memories be? I felt her crawl under the covers, strip her clothes off slowly, and help me with mine. She didn't touch me; she laid there, watching me, watching my eyes fight fatigue, pushing the hair from my brow, whispering something in my ear. Though I didn't know what.

EIGHT

On the hardest nights, Valerie remembered their coupling, the forms of their body, so unlike anything she imagined she and Gregory would have done. He'd treated her like folded glass. So *delicate*. Did he not know the old wives' tales? That redheads could endure pain to a greater degree than any others?

She wanted him to do such things to her.

Through the cracked door, she'd seen Gregory's white knuckles, Serendipity's black hair wound tight. Her sister glistened, sweat on her brow, and her face was pure ecstasy. Valerie felt like an intruder—watching them like that. The loud voice she wanted to wield stayed small inside of her, and she watched Gregory's narrow waist move back and forth behind Serendipity. The thud of their skin slapping together over and over muffled her heartbeat, and there was a ringing in her ears.

Valerie's vision had blurred as she gripped the wall and stepped back away from the sight.

It was heartbreaking to walk away from the deceit, to walk away from the crime of sister on sister. To keep it quiet

CHAPTER EIGHT

And she could not.

Instead, Valerie walked to the bathroom down the hall, far from their slapping skin. Her own was hot and flushed. She wanted to run water and splash some on her face, but she didn't want them to know she was there. She couldn't look herself in the eye as she left the room, slinking down the stairs. When she reached the front door, she opened it wide, the winter air slapping her in the face. She closed her eyes and stepped back.

In another life she would have slammed the door loud enough for them to hear. She would have forgotten the way the betrayal felt like a knife every time she was near them. She would have made sure her sister didn't get caught by her parents after they returned from their movie.

But in that life, she didn't. She closed her eyes, wiped her tears, and slowly shut the door. She walked into the kitchen and grabbed the knife from the block. Cold German steel, forged and heavy.

On the hardest nights, Valerie remembered *that* night, and she had nowhere to go with her aching chest.

But now she had somewhere to go.

She left the trailer before dusk, earlier than she needed to leave to prep the kitchen. She wanted to see the church, see where the Deacon worshiped, see if forgiveness could find her in the dark. The townsfolk said you could see the entire town from the lookout point across the gravel road, and Valerie parked there to get a look at the home attached to the small Catholic church.

With the radio down, she pulled her car right onto Steele Bluff Road, driving up the hill past a couple of houses until she saw the grand estate on her left. A short rock wall stretched along the edge of the drive, and it opened to a well-kept driveway that led through an opening. No gate, no *No Trespassing* sign—though the trees promised watching.

On the other side, she saw the lookout point and a patch of gravel to the right. She rolled down her windows as she pulled in, cutting the engine.

There was a lone light on in the large house, and she squinted her eyes, but could see nothing, no one, not even when she exited the car.

He saw her, though.

Valerie walked along the gravel, finding a small staircase encased in wildflowers leading to the lookout. After casting another fleeting glance at the home, she turned away and walked down the steps.

There was a white building with a small green door on the side that she noticed as she descended. It had a lock on it. When she passed it, her eyes caught on the American flag on the front of the building. She peered behind it to the hollow space inside.

It made her shiver. There was nothing but darkness there, though she knew it would be less fearsome when the sun came up.

Ahead of her was a wide rock ledge. She walked to it, opting to sit down and cross her legs.

In the distance, the sun's warm glow could barely be detected. The heat of the lost summer wrapped around her. *Muggy.* According to the calendar, it was fall, but it still felt hot most days, and she was ready for the cold. She'd missed it, and memories of her life before the ranch always brought shivers, a longing for the cold of a long night.

She and Nicholas had traveled the coast of California to the heat of Arizona, never far north, zigzagging across the west, aimless but drawn somewhere. Their time in Colorado had been in spring

CHAPTER EIGHT

and summer months, dry air that seemed to rip your breath from you. And all the while, the center of the continent pulled her to him, drew her in.

She didn't know why, and when the truth would look at her, she would fall into its eyes; though it would not be the angel she imagined, and she would shiver at the horror, warm at the need.

She felt eyes on her then, but pushed the feeling away. Where they came from, there was always an eye on you. Watching, preying, waiting for you in the dark. How could one man create such pain?

She'd fantasized about killing Markus in his sleep many times while living on the ranch.

Before he could rape another one of the girls when they came of age.

Before he could plan more brutality for Nicholas.

She'd imagined stabbing him in his dead eyes, the ones he claimed were taken from him.

And she had. She'd killed him, killed more. Just as she had killed her darling sister and her beautiful Gregory.

She needed to repent, to atone for her sins.

She wanted to speak to the Deacon. Prayed he would be her confessional, her awakening.

She hugged her knees, laid her cheek on them, and closed her eyes as she thought of the moment. The town was eerily quiet, warm, ready to float into the day.

There was no confessional on the ranch—not the traditional kind, anyway—and she craved it. Needed it. *Deserved* it for what she had endured.

Gregory's cries, the screams of her sister, and the cries of the children as the slaughter endured throughout the night—she could hear them.

And some of those screams made her smile.

NINE

The first time I saw Amber Hughes was at the grocery store with Valerie as she finished up the last of our weekly shopping.

Having grown bored looking at magazine and comics, I'd meandered to the front of the store to browse the board by the exit that had help wanted requests, yard sale advertisements, and other various community news tacked to it.

When my eyes caught on the grainy photo pinned to the board—Amber Hughes in black and white, forever immortalized—I knelt to my knees, studying her face. She had a wide smile and dark eyes. Her hair was long and curly. Above her face sat one word in all caps: *MISSING*. Below it was a plea for information regarding the whereabouts of their daughter, a prayer, and the names of Pastor and Mrs. Hughes.

As I stared at her face, a shadow passed over the board, and I turned around to see Eric Childress standing outside, staring inside the grocery store. His eyes seemed to look through me, as if he'd have been staring at the poster whether or not I was there. After a moment, he blinked, stepped back, and looked me in the eye. He hadn't been in the grocery store while Valerie and I shopped, and he never came in. I watched him drive away in his truck as I pushed the cart out for Valerie.

Eric and I had never talked in school. He was a senior, a basketball player, baseball player, and a member of the National Honor Society. Mr. Childress was the Sheriff of Hart Hollow, and his mother was the Elementary School Principal. They lived in a neighborhood close to the trailer park, just up a hill in a nice home.

The first time I heard Amber's name from his mouth was a week later, in early October, in the locker room. I'd just finished my last period of the day, which was gym. Embarrassingly, I'd been falling asleep in class occasionally. My late night walks, my nightmares, and the hours I spent trying to catch up on studies caught up to me from time to time. Though I should have been, I was rarely tired—save for the nights I didn't sleep at all.

I'd only been caught sleeping in one class, surprisingly.

Classes with Sorina were the easiest to feel that calming warmth you feel when you're sleeping somewhere safe. And I was never caught in those classes, as if she had settled a grey fog over me, a shield.

I didn't take my clothes off in the locker room with the rest of the guys. They seemed comfortable in their bodies, unafraid to walk around nude after their showers. I always changed in one of the bathroom stalls in the locker room. It set me apart and made me stand out—but not in a good way.

I heard the names I was called when I slipped from sight. The idiots I went to school with assumed I couldn't handle their naked bodies and that I lusted after them. I just couldn't handle anyone seeing *me* naked.

CHAPTER NINE

I was sitting on the stool that day, my head against the stall door. I'd been waiting for my classmates to leave and had fallen asleep sitting there in my jeans with my shirt clutched in my hands.

The voices woke me.

Jarring.

Raised.

One noticeably upset, the other trying to calm the agitated voice in some way.

It was Eric and one of his teammates.

I jolted awake at the sound of a locker slamming before I heard the voices.

"I keep having this fucking dream. Last night I fucking had it again."

"Eric, man, you gotta stop this. Stop."

There was a loud noise, a fist to a locker, an inaudible curse. "You think I fucking want to? You think I want to dream about my missing girlfriend being pregnant? And that fucking look in her eyes ... so fucking scared ..."

"No, no man I know. And I know you said—"

"We never fucked. Her daddy was all in her head about it," Eric said, the sound of his feet moving, his voice moving closer.

I pulled my feet up, wrapping my arms around my knees. The space was cramped, and I made a vow then to get more sleep so I wouldn't nod off at school again.

"Never? Not even once?" the other guy asked. "Listen, I know how those preachers daughters can be sometimes. I fingered Lane freshman year in the back of the bus when we went to that game in Waynesville."

"Amber is nothing like that slut Lane, Justin," Eric said, his shadow passing by the crack in the door.

Justin said nothing, and the locker room was silent for a long while. The only sounds were Eric and Justin changing into their basketball uniforms.

I saw Amber's face then. The grainy photo clear in my mind. Eric's haunted look outside the grocery store.

Finally, Eric spoke again. "Everyone is just carrying on like she isn't gone. Like she left on purpose. She would never do that. She isn't some runaway. Some *loser*. We had plans. We were going to go to college in Springfield after we graduated. Far enough to have our own lives, close enough to come back home to see our parents. She wants to be a nurse, did you know that? Her dad wanted her to go to SBU, but she was going to do what she wanted. But, I don't know. We'd barely talked all summer. I called while I was in New Mexico with my mom at my uncle's, but she was always somewhere else."

Eric's voice was close, and I could see his shoes as he leaned on the stall door. I held my breath. There would be no excuse for me hiding in here while they had this conversation, and I didn't want to fight at school.

"And your dad?" Justin asked.

Eric let out a laugh, and it held no warmth. "Oh, *Sheriff* Childress has many a theory. All revolving around me driving her away."

"Your dad gonna arrest you?" Justin said, going for a joking tone.

"He isn't going to arrest anyone. This is fucking Hart Hollow, Misery. What do you expect?"

"So what are you trying to say with the dreams, man? You don't really think she was pregnant? Do you?"

CHAPTER NINE

Eric's voice was low, laced with frustration. "I don't know. Maybe it's ... I don't know. Maybe she was keeping something from me. But ... she looked beautiful."

"When?" Justin asked. "When she was pregnant?"

Eric's voice was faraway, but clear. "Yeah."

They moved around in silence after that, clothes shuffling, shoes squeaking on the floor.

And as I hid, I thought of a dream that haunted me. I had no idea what else happened in Eric's dream, but I'd been pulled to the dark some nights, images of a pregnant Sorina in the dirt, belly bulging, hands inside her pushing. And blood. Always blood.

The look in her eyes matched the one Eric described of Amber.

Beautiful but scared. So fucking scared.

TEN

I reluctantly took Sorina's advice and asked Kyrie to the fall festival dance.

My first school dance. I made it clear I was asking her as a friend, Sorina's voice in my head—*she doesn't want to fuck you.* Though I still felt love from Kyrie when she looked at me. I didn't know how to accept love that didn't come with strings, and the delicate dance of friendship with the opposite sex was more complicated than anything we would do on the floor that night.

The first time I saw the three Clement siblings together was the day before the dance while Kyrie and I had dinner at the Raven's Nest.

The brother walked in with all the swagger of a guy fresh out of high school and the contempt of a guy forced to tote his younger sisters around. We locked eyes as he walked past our table, and I was struck with the forethought that he was someone I would know. Eventually.

Though not obvious, I tracked the siblings' movement into the next room where the pool tables sat, listening to them as I picked our order up from the counter, unsure what I was listening for.

CHAPTER TEN

I'd kept Eric's dream confession to myself, as I had my own dream, the mirror of his. Sorina in a white dress, a nightgown, swollen belly, hands tied behind her back, breasts large, filled with milk for her unborn child.

"Tell me what you are." My dream voice was manly, rough. It came out wrong.

"Why do you waste time asking questions you already know the answers to?" Her voice was a song as she writhed.

"I don't know. I need you to tell me."

"Let your aunt lie her way through life. Let them all. But you, you stop wearing that skin."

"I'm so tired of you and the way you talk. It's all riddles. You flip things. It's for show." I waved my arm to the side, revealing the stage in our school, the dream morphing.

"I'm not trying to impress you, Nicholas. This is just my sound."

"Whatever," I spat. "Keep fucking with my head. It's been years of this bullshit. This back and forth. Why are you obsessed with Valerie?" The Valerie of my dreams was suddenly in the room, tied to a stake on the stage. I could smell smoke but see no flame.

"What would you like for me to be obsessed with? You? That skin you wear? The bits under your clothes? Your blood? Your lips? I am. That's why I moved next door. One day you will be too busy to bar your door."

I woke in a sweat, aroused, confused. Rested.

And angry.

At what, I wasn't sure.

When I returned with our food, finding Kyrie staring out the window, I snapped my finger in her face, pulling her attention to me. "Where'd you go?" I asked as I sat.

Kyrie yawned. "Nowhere. Just tired. I studied all night for my chemistry test tomorrow. We shouldn't have tests on days we have dances. It's not fair," she said, reaching for her food when her fries and burger were placed perfectly in front of her, a neurotic habit of hers I found endearing. When she looked up at me I saw the bags under her eyes.

"Did you get the sour cream fries?" I asked, looking into her basket. I hadn't paid attention when I grabbed our tray, lost in my own thoughts.

"Yes. And you can't have any. You got onion rings, live with your choice." She laughed, looking past me to the other room where the pool table sat. Where the Clement kids laughed and joked with each other.

I stuck my straw in my Pepsi, throwing the wrapper at Kyrie. "So, I've been meaning to tell you. I uh, fell asleep in the locker room last week and—"

"You fell asleep … in the locker room?"

I waved my hand. "Yeah, uh. Anyway. I heard Eric Childress in there talking to Justin Miller."

Kyrie leaned back, her eyes wide. I remembered the first day then, the whispers in class. Not from Eric, but from Justin. *Who let the Crypt Keeper in?*

"And what was he saying?" she asked. "He's … I heard he isn't taking it well. That the coach is on him about his game. He's … off. Not handling it well. He had a job at the feed store behind the Cafe, but he just stopped showing up. He's not like that."

I took a long drink of my Pepsi, then grabbed a fry from Kyrie's basket. "He's been having dreams that Amber was pregnant."

Kyrie blinked, then shook her head. "No way."

"No way?"

CHAPTER TEN

"No way. She would ... she never would have cheated on Eric. They'd been together since ... since they were kids. Kinda. I mean, they were boyfriend and girlfriend in kindergarten. Then they got together in high school. They had plans. Everyone knew they were going to go to college in the same town."

"Sometimes people change their plans," I offered. "Right? What if she changed her mind?"

"And got pregnant? By Eric?" Kyrie asked.

I cleared my throat, then said, "Or someone else. He said ... he said they never did it."

Kyrie pushed her food away. "So he's spreading some rumor that she got knocked up by someone other than him. That she not only broke a vow to God, but cheated on him? Nice of him to spread rumors like that about his missing girlfriend."

"I don't think he's spreading that around. It seemed like when he was telling Justin, it was like ... a confession. Like he'd never told anyone about the dreams before."

Kyrie's hand moved, resting on her belly. I tried not to look at it.

"Maybe she was pregnant. Let's pretend that's true for a moment."

"Okay," I said.

"Maybe that's why she's gone."

"Ran away with the other guy?"

Kyrie shook her head, leaning close, her voice dropping. "Maybe whoever the dad was took care of it."

When I heard people in Hart Hollow talk about the missing Amber Hughes, they mourned her potential. Mourned all she was supposed to be. Pristine. By her parents' side. Not a runaway.

But I knew what it meant to run away. To leave your life behind. There's a reason people did it.

Kyrie spoke of Amber like she was dead, like she knew her fate. It was unsettling. "She should have been the fall festival nominee for the senior class. It would have been her. I know it," Kyrie said, eyes dark.

I wanted to reach for her hand across the table, comfort her in some way. But I didn't. I sat there, listening.

It was the only comfort I could offer. The room in the back erupted in laughter, and Kyrie's eyes flitted briefly past me.

I pulled her attention back to our table. "Is it a pastor's daughter thing?" I asked. Kyrie was the junior class nominee. She'd asked me to be her escort, but I declined. I didn't want to walk across the gym floor in front of the entire school. Or suffer through the awkward expectation that I kiss Kyrie if she won. So she asked her lab partner from science instead. He agreed.

"What thing?" Kyrie asked.

"Who are the underclassmen nominees?" I asked. I didn't pay attention to the announcements. The only name I heard as the announcement was made in the gym during a pep rally was Kyrie's. The other names drowned out as I daydreamed. I probably wouldn't have been able to place faces to names, anyway. Though the school was small, I was still playing catch up.

When Kyrie looked at me, her eyes looked darker than usual, frightened in some way that she pushed back. "They're all pastors' daughters," she said.

CHAPTER TEN

When I returned home from the Raven's Nest that day, Valerie was cleaning the kitchen and stocking groceries from the grocery store.

Wordlessly, I helped unload and grabbed a broom to clean. Certain tasks were just ingrained in us.

Finally, she spoke. "Did you know there's a Catholic church on the hill overlooking the town?"

I grabbed the dustpan, sweeping the dirt from the floor into it. "Yeah. Kyrie told me."

"The one who ate at the café with us?" Valerie asked. The question seemed for my benefit, as if she had met any other *friends* from school.

She hadn't.

And when Kyrie joined us for breakfast that Saturday, Valerie had barely spoken before pretending she needed to start her shift early, instructing me to walk home. She could pretend to be pulled away that day but couldn't pretend to be normal in front of my friend.

"Her dad's a preacher. She gave me a brief history of the churches in town," I said.

Valerie nodded, reaching for a dish towel. "The Deacon who lives on the hill came into the café not long after we moved here. He's a nice man. He invited us to see his service sometime."

I felt it then. A cold anger washed over me. It wasn't the first time I'd felt the strange sensation, and it wouldn't be the last. It would only get worse.

I dumped the dust in the waste bin, turning to Valerie. "Why would you want to do that? After what we left?"

Valerie crossed her arms and cleared her throat. "We mustn't let what happened in California color our view of God. Markus was an evil man, but he's dead now."

"And we would have been dead if he got his way. Because *Vampire Jesus* told him so." I used air quotes and glared at her, my teenage petulance making me feel normal in a way. I never fought with my parents. I was too frightened of them.

"There are no such thing as vampires."

"There's no such thing as *God*," I seethed. "What benevolent being would allow someone to use his name and do what Markus did to them? To my mom?" I swallowed, and it hurt. "To me?"

I felt something like love for Valerie. It wasn't family or friendship. Just the bond two people felt when they experienced immense trauma together. I didn't understand it then; I would, as things got worse between us, as one fell and the other healed.

"I know, Nicholas. But if we're going to start over, this is part of it."

"I don't want to go to church. You can't fucking make me," I said, voice deep. Beneath my ribcages, something rattled, and I felt a vibration around us. A warm line ignited from the base of my spine and sped up my back and into my throat.

What the fuck?

Valerie looked around, and I realized she felt it too. "What was that?" she asked.

"I …" My neck felt hot, and my body felt cold; I swayed a little with the exertion.

It was the first time my anger would move out of my body and be felt by others. But it wouldn't be the last time.

CHAPTER TEN

Moving to Hart Hollow woke something inside of me—a beast, a dark shadow slithering between my bones. I was close to my other half, to my partner. I just didn't know it.

I shoved my anger aside and leaned against the counter. I tried to make my voice even when I spoke again. "I'm ... I'm not going to church."

Valerie was rattled; I could see a quiver in her movement. She eyed me with suspicion, something like fear. "Okay. What about dinner?"

"Dinner?"

"The Deacon invited me to dinner, and I told him I had a nephew, and he said he would love to have you as well."

"Is this a date?"

Valerie shook her head, but I saw the blush. Her lies sounded almost believable. "Deacons can't date. It's a Catholic church, Nicholas."

In our travels, Valerie had turned to study, trying to understand religion and how it worked. I thought it was to know why Markus hurt others. To understand why whatever happened to us happened.

Markus had sex with all the women on the ranch.

All but Valerie. Lips weren't as tight as you would think on the ranch. Put three people in a room, and two will whisper. One will devour secrets.

The whispers said she had a deformity. She was unclean, not fit to breed. And besides, she was an outsider.

It was likely Adrian who told others. Markus's son brought Valerie in as his partner, but quickly discarded her. She bonded with my mother and never left. Stuck in the kitchen, never paying the highest price.

There were other whispers, too. That I wasn't my father's son. That my mother slept with another man while out fishing. While out bringing in fresh blood for manual labor to develop the homestead on the ranch.

Outsiders could not fornicate with the women.

That was saved for Markus and his sons.

I didn't look like my father. He had sandy hair and dark brown eyes. I had black hair and blue eyes. My mother looked like my father. The truth of that knowledge was like a kick in the gut when I finally broke free.

I shook my head, pushing away the horrors of our past.

"Dinner when?"

"Tomorrow night," Valerie said, a warm smile spreading over her face. I enjoyed seeing her smile. After everything we'd seen, I didn't want her to be sad.

And who was I to say anything? She was becoming friends with the town Deacon. I was friends with a preacher's daughter. Maybe we couldn't escape our religious chains, no matter how hard we tried.

"The fall festival dance is tomorrow night," I reminded Valerie.

She smiled, wiping her hands. "It'll be an early dinner. You can go to the dance after. How does that sound?"

I gave her a smile, forced, hoping it would land.

It did.

"Sounds great."

ELEVEN

Shortly after we moved to Hart Hollow, Valerie and I had walked along the town square, learning the architecture, learning our new home. While in a thrift shop, a pop up tent had caught my eye. When I asked Valerie if we could buy it, her eyes had misted, and she'd said yes. I ignored the emotion. I never got a childhood, and though she never talked about her time before the ranch, I suspected she never had one herself.

Until that night, I hadn't set up the tent. But after Valerie went to sleep, I snuck out the back door and set the tent up next to the picnic table. It sat just to the right of my bedroom window. The opening of the tent faced the cemetery, and by flashlight, I read my newest book, a large and worn copy of Stephen King's *It*.

I worried that she wouldn't come. I had seen little of Sorina since she gave me the joint, since the night I slept soundly and hard, with no dreams. When I saw her at school, which was rare, she smiled a knowing smile at me. It was infuriating, and I clung to that annoyance as I glanced beyond the trees, searching for anything bright. It was two in the morning when I gave up. I clicked off my flashlight and pulled my sleeping bag tight as I cursed myself.

I heard her singing when I closed my eyes, and I was smiling for a few seconds before I stopped myself. Too lost in the dream of her voice. Thinking I wanted to see her so badly that the tenor and tone came from the recesses of my mind. But it was real. I heard the rustle of her dress in the cool October air as I sat upright.

When I saw her silhouette, I shivered. "Hey stranger," I whispered as I threw back the portion of my sleeping bag that was keeping me warm. "I haven't seen you walking lately," I added. I held back the part about my walks that made me feel like a child. I hadn't walked past the bridge since that night. Since I saw the man with blood on his flesh. It was too close to my dreams, too close to a waking nightmare.

"What are you doing in this?" Sorina said, ignoring my observation about her absence. She eyed the tent like it was something childish, or something she didn't understand. "Why are you sleeping in the backyard?"

I had no answer for her other than I wanted to see her. And wandering the town and sitting at the picnic table hadn't brought her to me. I hadn't knocked on her door. I was playing a game. I wanted her to chase even though everything inside of me told me I was born to chase her.

If I had been in my room, would she have knocked on my window? I didn't know, worried she wouldn't.

So I made myself available to her.

I didn't know how to play the games the guys and girls at school did to get each other's attention. So I was trying to figure it out on my own.

And it had worked.

"I don't know." I laughed, low, the lie having no chance at fooling her.

"Let's go for a walk," Sorina said, crawling out without another word.

I followed.

We walked in relative silence down the road, past Kyrie's house, and back toward the school, one road over from one of the two main streets. The cop patrolling never saw us, though when I thought he might, Sorina pulled me into her and down an alley to avoid the headlights. It felt like a game. Like a *dream*. And I wanted to smell her, smell another joint from her fingertips, smell her in private places.

I imagined her letting me lead her if I tried to take her hand, but I never reached for her.

Eventually we made it to the school, and when we walked to the playground, I wondered if she would want me to push her the way Kyrie did when we snuck up there. Instead, Sorina walked into the baseball field and over the fence. Again, I followed, eyes seeing everything in the dark.

The pond wasn't too far into the woods, and the grass grew higher the closer we got. Despite the October chill, Sorina was wearing a skirt and fishnet stockings. The weeds caught in the delicate fabric, ripping, but she didn't seem to care.

She stripped when she reached the pond, and I felt a thrill, a deep need to chase her into water.

Instead, I stared at the pile of clothes, though we both knew I wanted to look at her.

I heard the water moving as she entered, and it pulled my gaze to her despite my thinly veiled restraint.

When I looked at her, I saw her bones and moonlight reflecting off her skin. She was a magnet, but her eyes couldn't hold me for long.

As if hypnotized, I looked beyond the water, into the woods, a slow pull making me blink. When I saw nothing there but the dark and a flash of red light behind my eyelids, I shook my head.

"Is it cold?" I asked when I looked back at Sorina.

"Not to me," she answered, and I thought I knew what she was saying.

After a moment, I kicked my shoes off and walked to the edge of the pond, stepping into the water. It was chilly, and I shivered at the life there, going no farther. It wasn't stagnant or calm. "What the fuck?"

"A creek feeds this pond," Sorina said, looking down into the dark. "The water comes from the earth. From somewhere darker."

"Do you want me to come in?" I asked, shivering at the meaning.

"If you want to," she stretched out the last letter, singing again.

I was self-conscious of my skin in front of everyone, still hiding in the locker room despite nearly being caught by Eric and Justin before. It was worth the risk, worth letting no one see me exposed.

I pulled my shirt over my head, then my jeans. My boxers stayed on.

For a moment, Sorina spun in the water, then looked at me. The white of her eyes reflected in the night. "Take them off, Nicholas." The hair on the back of my neck stood when she spoke. Her voice was older than mine at times. Older than everyone's.

I said, "I don't like to be naked in front of people."

And Sorina said, "I am not people."

"I know." I heard the double meaning, the wondering I had felt. "How old are you?"

"How many times must we do this?"

"The questions will stop when you actually answer." I shrugged and reached for the elastic of my boxers, turning when I pulled them off. When I turned back to the water, my dick was in my hands, cupped and covered. Sorina's eyes were on my eyes. I wanted her to look me over. But she sometimes gave me what I needed in my dreams, not what I wanted. It was jarring to see the gift in the flesh.

She held my stare as I entered the water, never wavering. When submerged to the waist, I took my hands away from my dick and moved them along the water's surface.

She looked me in the eye and smiled, blue eyes bright. "So demure."

"I'm not."

"So scared of everything. Just like her."

"Who?" I asked.

"Your *aunt*."

I didn't want to talk about Valerie. Not after agreeing to the dinner with the Deacon. I was angry at her, and a small part of me felt betrayed. I pushed the thought away, moving in the water toward Sorina.

"Tell me about your parents." I said it like a command, not like a question, hoping to inch the power play in my direction.

Sorina moved closer in the water, looking up into the sky when she answered. "Why?"

"I'm curious. Are they together? Are they waiting for you back home in Romania?"

Sorina smirked, and I didn't mention the accent, the way it disappeared when we were alone together, and appeared again the rare times I heard her speak in school. "I haven't seen my mother in a long time."

"Why haven't you seen her? Did you have a fight?"

"Yes, and no. I haven't seen her since I was sixteen."

"That wasn't that long ago."

"But it was," she said, and her voice was so faint, and so different for a moment. She sounded like the young girl she appeared to be. When she looked at me again, so close I could almost touch her, her voice changed. "Something bad happened. I had to leave. I've been taking care of myself since then."

"What about your father?" I asked, kicking in the water, feeling a droplet hit my head. I didn't notice Sorina was silent as I looked up into the sky. The moon was bright, a crescent blade in the night, and when I closed my eyes, more droplets hit me, splashing in the surrounding water. The pond had been cool, and my body felt tight, but the temperature dropped even more when the rain came down in earnest.

When I looked at Sorina, she dipped down below the surface, rising after a breath, pushing her red hair from her face. She looked up into the sky like something threatening was there, more than the rain. She swam to the shore, and I followed. She didn't dress when her feet squished into the dirt surrounding the pond. She held her clothes to herself, casting glances at the sky and beyond, to where our homes were. When she started walking, I hurriedly pulled my clothes on, my skin resisting, covered in dirty water. She was nearly to the fence dividing the mangled field we'd walked through from the well-manicured baseball field.

She didn't speak as we walked home in the rain, but the silence felt different from the silence we'd enjoyed as we walked the town. It didn't feel like she had a coy secret she wanted to share with me. It felt like she was keeping a dark secret from the world.

I didn't know if I wanted to know what it was.

···

Sorina's bathroom had a clawfoot tub that sat beneath a large window overlooking the cemetery. I followed her in, curious and wanting, as she reached for the drawers beneath her sink and began searching for something. I was always astounded at how silent she could be. "What are we doing here?" I asked, running my hand on the edge of the tub.

"I'm going to give you a bath." She said it slowly, letting me take in every uncomfortable word. When she turned, she had a lengthy silk scarf. She used it to tie her long red hair up. There was so much of it, and touching it was something I thought about in the mornings, as my dreams faded.

Again I hesitated, just as I had on the shore of the pond. It was one thing to swim in the dirty dark water with her, another to let her touch me this way.

"Do you want me to turn around?" she asked, and I knew she didn't want to. Nakedness, and skin, it didn't matter to her.

"Yes. I do." I gave in to her request because I wanted her to take something from me. It's all I knew.

Sorina turned around and looked into the hall, and I stared at her hair, her bony shoulders. When she heard me begin to undress she did the same, and I faltered for a moment, but picked up the pace, wanting to beat her. I stopped when I was in nothing but my boxers because the bathtub was empty. I didn't want to stand around awkwardly with my dick in my hand again while she filled it. "The tub," I started. "Should I fill the tub?"

She was naked when she turned to me. "Yes. Fill it. I'll be back." She left me and I wondered if she was even looking for anything.

After I turned the faucets, making sure the temperature was just right, scalding, I noticed there was a cart with glass bottles near the tub. I pulled the stopper from one and sniffed it. It smelled like lavender, and I poured some of the liquid into the hot water. The steam filled the room, and the mirrors offered no reflection.

When Sorina returned, I was naked, submerged in the water and bubbles. I looked away when I saw her small pink nipples. She had a small glass vial in her hands, and she set it on the cart before climbing into the tub behind me. Her tiny legs wrapped around me, and I had an urge to grab her knees, pull her forward. I wanted to feel her against me, every part that, from other women, felt like a weapon.

Sorina's palms made contact with my back, and I let out a groan. Her thumbs pressed into the muscles at the base of my back, and there was a new scent in the air. Pungent and familiar.

"Do you want to leave here one day?"

"Yes." I groaned, her hands hurt, but I needed it.

"Me too."

"Why did you move here?" I asked as I closed my eyes.

"I came looking for something that's mine. I can't leave until I can get it back."

"What is it?"

"Do you know the best way to kill a bird?"

"No."

"I do. You can't rush it. You can't let yourself be seen as a threat. Become a part of the surroundings. Become familiar." Her hands moved to my hair, and when I closed my eyes I saw red, the white of the moon, and the cemetery. The headstone she sat upon that first day.

I wanted to ask her what she was talking about, but I was suddenly tired, her strong hands easing away every fear and memory I had. They felt like a cure for everything, when touch often felt like a knife. I sighed deep, and Sorina's mouth was near my ear. "Are you tired?" she asked, and I nodded, my eyelids fluttering.

When she reached for the vial she had brought in, opening it in front of me, I only half opened my eyes. And when she brought the dropper to my mouth, I obeyed as she told me to lift my tongue. She dropped something there, and it smelled like the joint she'd let me take a drag from. The relief was nearly immediate, and after she set the vial on the cart, she looped her arms underneath mine, keeping me from sinking into the water.

We sat like that for a long time, skin to skin, my breathing becoming deep. I don't remember going home, but I made it there somehow.

TWELVE

I woke the next morning groggy, a thick fog clinging to me like a blanket. There were memories on the fringes of my mind, and I couldn't make them clear—make them permanent. I was naked and my head fuzzy, but the insistent pounding my ears registered was coming from my front door.

I threw my covers off and left my room after yanking on a pair of boxers, walking down the small hallway leading to the front door of our trailer.

I opened it without hesitation, and when Kyrie saw me in my boxers, sleep in my eyes, a look of annoyance on my face, the anger she must have been feeling to make her pound on the door like that washed off and was quickly replaced with annoyance.

"Why aren't you dressed?"

"For what?" I asked, walking away from the door.

Kyrie stepped in and surveyed her surroundings. We had little, but the place was clean. Valerie was obsessive about cleanliness, perhaps because of the filth we often lived in on the ranch. I

CHAPTER TWELVE

walked to the kitchen and grabbed a glass from the cupboard, filling it with water as Kyrie looked around.

"Where's your furniture?" she asked, dark eyes watching me as I guzzled my water.

I needed to get rid of the fog surrounding me, the haze of the night before. I smelled like Sorina. "We just don't have much yet," I said, unfazed. I had a bed. I had a desk. It was more than I'd ever had, and that was enough for me.

Kyrie smiled as she walked into the kitchen. "There are a lot of yard sales in town on Saturdays. We could go. You need a bookshelf, maybe a lamp."

"How would I get the furniture home? I don't have a vehicle of my own," I said as I walked past her to the hallway. My tone was light, though my words felt somewhat forced. Kyrie had a habit of wanting to fix things—test scores, awkward situations ... *me*.

She followed me to my room. "I'm sure my dad would let me use his truck to get you whatever you needed."

I grabbed a shirt from a hanger in my closet, then turned to my friend. "Okay, second issue. How would I pay for it? I don't have any money. I don't have a job or anything."

"Maybe your aunt could give you some? I'm sure she wants furniture and hasn't had time to get any?"

After pulling my shirt over my head, I sat on my bed, rubbing my eyes. Something about her energy was off. "Kyrie, what are you doing here?" I asked before getting up from my bed and walking to my dresser.

"I thought I could drive you to school."

"I don't live far. It's across the street," I replied.

"I saw you last night. With her. With the foreign exchange student. I forgot she existed." She laughed. "I guess I hoped you had too."

I ignored the last part of her reply. "I thought you might have. We walked by your house."

"What were you doing out so late with her?"

"What were you doing up so late?"

"I had a bad dream."

I turned to her. "About?"

Kyrie walked to my bed, shaking her head. "I don't know. Something in the sky, like a bird or something. And some place in the woods, with this glowing circle. And I woke up because I heard something on the roof. Or maybe it was just the dream, I don't know. So I went to the window, and I heard voices. I saw you guys walking. But later, I heard the sound on the roof again."

"Maybe it was a squirrel?" I was grasping, and my mind was reeling. The circle intrigued me.

Kyrie sighed, watching me as I grabbed my discarded jeans from the floor. I sniffed them, then put them on.

"Do you have a washer and dryer?" Kyrie asked.

"No."

"You can come to my house and do laundry if you want."

"My aunt does it at the place behind the Mill on Spring street."

"I know where everything is here, Nicholas." Kyrie sighed. "You don't have to tell me where the laundry mat is."

"My bad," I said, holding my hands up.

"I'm just saying we could study, and I could tutor you while you do your laundry."

"Maybe," I replied, searching for my Converse.

On my bed, Kyrie wrung her hands, glancing at the door.

"Are you okay?" I asked. Sorina said Kyrie didn't want me, but I wasn't sure if that was true. It wasn't arrogance, but there was something in her voice when she said Sorina's name. Maybe it wasn't jealousy; perhaps it was fear. I couldn't be sure.

Kyrie's voice was low when she spoke again. "I heard my parents talking about Amber the other morning. They always drink their coffee together and talk. Anyway, they said the cross on top of Amber's father's church was vandalized, broken off the top, in the parking lot. It happened the night she went missing. We have a cross in our front yard. Did you see it when you came over? In the rose bushes?"

"I think, I don't know." Everything in Kyrie's home and the area surrounding it was pristine. Beautiful. Maybe that's why nothing stood out to me. I was drawn to the dark—the ugly.

"This morning when I left, it wasn't sitting up straight. So I ran back in and told my dad and mom so they could fix it. They looked … I don't know. Worried. Scared. I'm surprised they let me leave."

"I'm sure it was just—"

"A storm?" she suggested, eyebrow raised. "There was no storm last night, just rain."

"Maybe—"

"Vandals? We don't have that here. I'm not looking for comfort or coddling. I get enough of that from my parents. Do you think I should be worried?" Her voice told me she was worried already. And comfort or coddling was not something I knew how to offer.

The warning was unnecessary. Before I spoke, I thought of the woods beyond the pond, and the way I felt a slight pull to it the night before. Then I thought of the dinner Valerie and I were to have at the Deacon's before the dance.

I cleared my throat. "That depends. Do you think she ran away? Or do you think there's something to everything Eric said?" I asked.

"I wish I knew."

THIRTEEN

The house was grand. *Old.* The exterior of the first floor was red brick, the second story covered in grey, and ornate designs flanked the windows. At the top of the mansion I could see open windows, and a grand chandelier in a single room above all else. Ivy crawled above the front door, and to the right hung a sign that read *Steele Mansion*.

I stood on the gravel, hanging back for a moment, taking it all in before the Deacon greeted us at the door, swinging it wide and grinning. "My guests," he said, hissing on the S's.

He wore black glasses and held a cane. He was younger than I imagined, closer to Valerie's age. But that's not what stood out about him.

I stared at his cane, his black glasses, and then I looked at Valerie, hard, sniffing the air. She did not turn her face, but I knew she felt my acid eyes on her.

She had a pie cradled in her hands, and her smile was only for the man before her. I cleared my throat as I stepped up to the door, willing her to look at me. She didn't. Something flashed across his face. However fleeting it was, I saw it.

And it felt like he saw me.

He didn't want me there.

I was spare parts, an unfortunate circumstance.

He wanted Valerie alone.

As she spoke to him, I couldn't help the anger that swelled over me. *How stupid. How fucking stupid,* I thought. Maybe she wanted to be close to this man because she thought it would spare her the horrors men subjected a woman to. But I could feel it.

The man of the cloth wanted her. I stepped closer, invading their space as they spoke. I felt like a jealous dog warding off a stranger.

I shook the Deacon's hand when he offered it, finding it slightly cold. I ran hot.

"Come in, come in. I was just getting started in the kitchen," he said politely, his voice reminding me of something, though I wasn't sure what.

"You cook?" I asked, my voice deeper than I registered as normal.

"Yes," the Deacon replied warmly. "I may not have sight, but smell and taste are the most important part of cooking. And I have no one to cook for, not since Father Dodson passed. So this will be nice."

Though stately and beautiful on the exterior, the mansion held little magic for me once I entered. Maybe Sorina's home had spoiled me, but the mansion didn't appear to belong to anyone. The Deacon's scent was everywhere, but faint, as if he only existed in the home in passing. I sniffed the air again, rubbing my nose, feigning allergies.

I could smell his scent, more potent, somewhere deeper inside.

CHAPTER THIRTEEN

"Where's your restroom?" I asked as Valerie and the Deacon walked down a hallway.

The Deacon turned to me. "Down that hall, to the right."

I walked down the hall, their voices growing smaller as I moved past the bathroom. When I entered the dimly lit room with high ceilings, the scent of the Deacon grew stronger. The room was round, and at the end was a pew. It was a tiny church with stained glass windows surrounding the circling wall.

I cleared my throat and marveled at the echo of it.

It was beautiful and dark, frightening when you had a past like mine. *This* was his home. This place. A framed photo of Jesus stared back at me, and I chilled. I'd seen pictures and crosses depicting the likeness of the son of God very little since leaving the ranch. I averted my gaze when he came into view, shoving my past to the dark like a dirty secret. Markus had his own image of his savior. Long hair, similar to the commercially sold figure. But his eyes were always weeping red and gouged out.

Dark.

The Jesus on the wall staring at me in that small, round church looked like Markus's Jesus. The eyes were closed, but the dark shadow on the cheeks resembled blood. It looked like the Deacon as well. I didn't feel well surround by the walls that circled me, and I felt someone watching me. I closed my eyes, certain it was the memory of Markus. But when I turned around, I jumped out of my skin at the sight of the Deacon. His scent was so strong in the space I hadn't felt him behind me.

"It's beautiful, isn't it?" he asked, crossing his arms.

"Uh, yeah. Sorry, I know you told me where the restroom was, but I saw the light. I couldn't help myself." The lie fell out. No light pulled me, just his scent.

"Don't apologize for being drawn to this place. I am drawn to it often."

I rolled my eyes, grateful he couldn't see it.

He cocked his head in response, as if he had. "I'm going to get back to cooking. Stay in here as long as you'd like, Nicholas."

I didn't want to stay in the church, but I did, waiting for him to be out of sight. The sound of my name from his mouth sounded false, like he was telling me a lie. When he was gone, I turned back to the circle room, shoving my hands in my pockets. Kyrie said the Deacon's flock was a small congregation, the townspeople preferring the Baptist services to the old building on the hill.

It was all the same to me. Baptist, Christian, Catholic. No matter what type of believer, they all worshipped the same imaginary man in the sky. They all used him to justify their cruelty, their rape, their murder, their incestuous pairings.

When I closed my eyes, I could see her, the woman with the wild blonde hair, the pale man at her side. The liberators, the ones with the match. They burned the ranch to the ground, and Valerie and I had been the only ones to escape.

The girl had looked like a witch. It was the only word that came to mind when I remembered her.

But witches didn't exist. Neither did the vampires that Markus called God.

I didn't believe it there. Didn't buy into the horror sold. But here, here in Hart Hollow, I felt something. Some ominous cloud hovering around me. The woods beyond the pond where Sorina and I swam flashed in my mind, and I shook it away.

I knew who the monsters were in this world.

Men.

Us.

The women who touched me.

I left the Deacon's small church, closing the door behind me. Closing his scent off, and something sweeter.

After using the restroom, I walked into the kitchen to see that Valerie had taken over, as she often did in the kitchen. The Deacon walked around an oval table, setting our plates and adjusting our silverware.

"Deacon Rex, what will we be drinking?" Valerie asked, looking over her shoulder.

I watched them, wondering what his first name was, and why Valerie was using his title like a caress.

Hands together in prayer, the Deacon answered, "I have water, juice, wine."

"Nicholas, grab the juice and put it in the center of the table," Valerie instructed. Her voice sounded maternal, and I didn't like that.

"No wine for me?" I joked, glancing at the Deacon.

He smiled in my direction.

"No underage drinking on the hill, Nicholas. Unless you want to come by Sunday night and drink the blood of Christ."

Valerie laughed. I did not. It wasn't good if that was supposed to be a joke.

"I'm sure you'll run into enough temptation at the dance tonight, though," the Deacon continued. "Stay away from the punch bowl."

I huffed out a breath. I didn't really want a drink. I saw the way everyone at the ranch acted when they got drunk.

Worse.

Mean.

Horny.

I needed a smoke, though. Or whatever the hell Sorina had put under my tongue last night.

"How long until we eat?" I asked.

"Twenty minutes?" Valerie estimated, taking the lid off a pot.

"Do you care if I walk outside? The house is beautiful, Deacon …" I said, trying on my most flattering voice.

The Deacon nodded. "Ed Rex, you can call me Rex. Just go out that door right there. It leads to the backyard.

I thanked them both and slipped out, pulling a joint out of my pocket as I skipped out of the house. *Rex, Rex. Red Rex. The reign of Red Rex.* I rolled the Deacon's name around in my head, making poetry of the word and the color that haunted me, as I tried to figure out why Ed Rex sounded familiar.

The lawn was immaculate, and my Converse made little sound as I walked away from the mansion. I'd tucked a lighter in my jeans. After grabbing it, I turned back to the house, nearly choking on the joint hanging out of my mouth when I saw her. It dropped to the ground, and I clenched my jaw.

Sorina was on the roof, black dress moving in the wind, her blue eyes staring at me.

She looked angry.

When she crawled down the roof, she looked inhuman and made no sound. She landed on the grass, jogging across the grass to me. I reached down, grabbing the joint just as she took my hand, pulling me to the edge of the yard. There was a small gap in the

CHAPTER THIRTEEN

brick fence. She pulled me through, taking the lighter from me when she turned. I liked her hand on mine.

She flicked it to life and motioned for me to pull the joint up. After she lit it, she took it from me, taking a long pull before placing the joint between my lips.

It was almost intimate, and I could feel her delicate fingers on my wrist. Then she let go.

"What were you doing on the roof?" I hissed.

"You shouldn't be here."

"I was invited. Pretty sure you weren't."

"Invitations mean nothing. You shouldn't be here; it isn't safe."

I rolled my eyes, staring back at the house. I could see in the windows. Valerie's shape moved in the kitchen, but the Deacon wasn't visible.

"Trust me, I don't want to be here. But Valerie is, uh … friends with the Deacon and wants to go to church up here. I said no to Sunday service but compromised on this dinner thing."

"She shouldn't be here either," Sorina said.

"What harm can he do?" I asked, not wanting to know the answer. The red, weeping Jesus from the small church stayed with me.

"I think you should know better than to assume he's harmless."

She was right. I knew better, but diving deeper into our past with Sorina wasn't something I was ready to do. Not yet.

Why open your fears for someone new when you could hide them, play at being normal, be an unscarred human instead of this mangled mess of a person I seemed to be then. I cleared my throat, the scent of the Deacon still strong. "Maybe that's why I'm here. To watch after her."

Sorina leaned against a tree, her black dress hanging off her loosely. I could see the points of her nipples, the faint outline of her hipbones. The fabric wasn't sheer, but it was thin. I didn't think she wore anything under it, almost as if it were a formality to wear anything at all. The air was chilly. She should have been cold.

I'd never wanted someone before. Not the way a normal person should. The urgent flood of desire normal teenage boys felt—that was lost on me, taken from me.

But when I looked at Sorina, I wanted to bury myself in her, taste her, bite her. Not out of obligation, not out of order, but out of want.

And the hardest part to grasp, to stomach, was that I wanted her to do everything back to me. I wanted her to touch me, too. I wanted more than the feel of her hands on me as she washed me in her tub. I wanted something darker.

Shoving away my want, I snuffed out the joint, returning it to my pocket.

Sorina shook her head and reached for me, so I handed over the joint, and her fingertips grazed my palm.

"Why are you here? The real reason. No ominous fucking riddles. You're like a walking omen." It was a lie, but I wanted to jar her. She was like a poem, a dark and haunting one. English was my favorite class, along with mythology. I enjoyed being lost in the stories, the other worlds. Even in their horror, they were safe because they couldn't get to me. Not the way a bitter memory could.

"To watch you. I'm here to watch after you."

CHAPTER THIRTEEN

"I never asked you to." *I'm here to chase you.* The thought was red in my head, circled by light.

"And I never asked to want to, but I do."

"And I never asked to fucking dream about you, but here we are. Two new kids in a town that no one gives a shit about, hiding in the woods."

"What happens in the dreams about me, Nicholas?" she asked, her eyes on me, but also one the house, as if every bit of her was tuned into it, waiting for someone to come out. To pierce our meeting with an arrow.

I didn't want to be crude or scare her away. But the words I wanted to use would frighten someone like Kyrie off, not Sorina. I wanted to say they were wet dreams because I woke up soaking in sweat—soaking in tears. And there were other dreams, too. Dreams of her mouth on me, a slow release. My arousal mixed with the horror. She was a winged demon, with fangs, talons, a screeching cry that could kill you. A tail ripped off, red spilling all over the ground.

She was horrifying and beautiful in her wrongness. And though we existed together more often in night, in the dreams she was bathed in sunlight at times. "I—"

Valerie called for me then, and Sorina ducked down, hiding her red hair and pale skin from view.

I turned away, a faded goodbye falling from my mouth as I walked through the gate and back to the lawn.

○○

I imagined his eyes white and unseeing behind his glasses. Not unlike Markus.

Not unlike the winged thing in my nightmares.

Vampire.

That's the word I'd used for it, though it was more grand and horrifying than the romantic image peddled in movies and books at that time.

That wretched being was at the forefront of my mind on the ranch. The all-seeing being.

The son of God is a vampire, Markus had said.

If the thing from my nightmares were human, it would look similar to the man before me, serving salad onto a plate, smiling at Valerie as if he could see her.

"Nicholas," I heard Valerie say. It wasn't the first time she'd said my name.

"What? Sorry," I said, glancing at the Deacon.

"I asked if you minded if the Deacon said grace. I told him … I told him that where we came from, our relationship with God was … soured."

"Soured?" I raised an eyebrow, glancing at Deacon Rex again. He was smiling. Some corner of the mouth thing. I would recognize it later. More teeth, then.

Valerie said, "Yeah." Then looked down at her hands.

"Are you asking me if it's okay that he says grace?"

"Yes." She looked me in the eye, a pleading look. She was checking in with me and the kindness was foreign and considerate. We had danced around each other for years, roaming the country. And now she was playing at the good *aunt*. I hadn't had a mother figure, and I didn't want her playing at one now.

CHAPTER THIRTEEN

But later, I would miss this moment when the consideration turned to resentment, demands, and commands.

"It's fine," I said, looking at Deacon Rex. "It's fine."

He placed his hands on the table, bracing himself. He drifted like water. I could see he was firm beneath his white shirt, wired muscles straining. Did the church have a gym? It was weird. But the body is holy or whatever.

Deacon Rex brought his hands together, interlaced them, lining up his index fingers, pressing them to his mouth as if he had a secret. "Bless us, O God. Bless our food and our drink. Since you redeemed us so dearly and delivered us from evil, as you gave us a share in this food, so may you give us a share in eternal life."

When he was done, he turned to Valerie, and I did too, but not before shivering at his last words. *Eternal life.*

She had tears in her eyes, and I hated it. They were the words used to hurt us, to justify monstrosities placed upon our skin, all in the pursuit of the unattainable. Eternal *fucking* life.

Maybe she didn't understand because she had been left alone, like the Virgin Mary or some shit.

I grabbed my fork, ready to stomach through the meal. Everything Valerie made tasted amazing and left me with a stale aftertaste. Sorina said to stop eating what Valerie made me.

How much of this was from her hands? How much from the Deacon's? It didn't matter. I'd eat a snack after the dance if I was hungry.

"How are you liking the town, Nicholas?" Deacon Rex asked, watching me with his eyeglass-covered eyes. I wanted to rip them from his face.

"It's not bad. Small. But … that's fine."

"It's a small town full of fine people. Made many friends?"

"A couple."

Liar.

I'd made one. Or two, if you counted Sorina.

"A couple of good ones is all you need. What are their names? I know everyone in Hart Hollow. It's part of the job."

"Uh, the other new student, she lives next door. And Kyrie Davis."

I watched his face as I answered, saw the twitch when I mentioned Sorina, even though I'd kept her name out of my mouth. His look of otherness turned to a smile when I said, Kyrie. "Ah, Pastor Davis's daughter."

"Yes."

"How's she doing?"

I stared at him when I spoke, somehow antagonized. "Worried. I guess before we moved here, another preacher's daughter went missing. Amber Hughes. She's worried that whatever happened to Amber will happen to her." I closed my eyes, wondering why the fuck I had let that out. An image of a man patting his dog on the head came to mind, and it made me sniff the air, searching for an unknown predator, a master.

I hated being in that house.

"Ah, it's sad what Amber Hughes is putting her parents through. It's hit them hard. But you cut and run when you don't want this life, this small town family. Amber wasn't the first runaway to leave Hart Hollow, and she won't be the last. The best we can do is pray for her soul. Pray she finds her way back home, or to her own version of home."

CHAPTER THIRTEEN

"I guess you're in the right business to not have to worry about that kind of thing, huh?" I said, setting my fork down. I was done with the dinner, ready to get to the dance.

"And what kind of thing is that?" Deacon Rex asked, turning his head to one side. Now he looked like the dog.

I grinned when I spoke, and Valerie glared at me, as if she knew what I would say next. "Well, you're celibate. No children. So you never have to worry about them."

Deacon Rex grinned, and I could see the malice there. "My parish is my children. God's children are my children. And I love them all, so very much."

Before I could speak—a red remark on my tongue—a distant cry from outside made us all turn toward the front window. The scream was inhuman, a shrill sound coming from the direction of the road. We all stood, and after, I would remember their faces. Valerie looked concerned. Deacon Rex looked like an actor in one of the school plays I'd sat in on in the gym during my free period.

"It's likely a coyote," Deacon said, sniffing the air as I had, an almost imperceptible movement. I watched Valerie leave the table, rushing toward the hallway that led to the front door, drawn to the sound.

The shriek sounded again, and she walked faster. I followed, down the hallway, crowding Valerie as she opened the front door of the grand home and took a few steps onto the front porch. I brushed past her, shielding her.

When Deacon Rex and I reached the front steps, I saw something on the road beyond the front gate. I could see better in the dark than most. It's why I didn't fear walking the town at night. The shape moved slowly—almost *twitchy*—and behind me I felt Valerie sway backward slightly. After steadying her, I shoved the Deacon aside as I rushed down the steps, skidding to a halt when

I saw dark hair and long legs. It wasn't a dog, but something else. Something bigger. "Don't go down there," I said, and I turned to see Valerie next to me, her face white.

I glanced back to the house and saw the Deacon standing at the door, one hand on his cane, the other brushing his long hair from his face. His brow was pinched, as if his eyes were narrowed at me.

The night swelled with the autumn chill, with fear, with a gnawing feeling that we were being watched by the thing struggling in the road. I hummed with a desire to help whatever it was.

Deacon Rex called down to us. "Don't go down to the road. I'll call the game warden or the Sheriff."

"What will they do?" Valerie asked. We were still like children in some ways regarding the workings of society and the roles others played.

"They'll put it down. Put it out of its misery," Deacon Rex said, walking down the steps to the well-manicured lawn, one slow step at a time. I felt like I was still watching an actor in a play, that he didn't belong there in such a beautiful place.

Everything about the home was in sharp contrast to another piece. The windows were eyes watching, the round church quarters beautiful and haunting with the stained glass windows. The front step was grand, and the interior pristine in some places and derelict in others.

Vines crawled to the east side, searching for the sun.

When Deacon Rex reached us, he placed a hand on Valerie's other shoulder. I took my hand from her, and it almost looked like he smiled.

CHAPTER THIRTEEN

The shriek came again, but this time it sounded far away. We all looked to the road, and the dark mass was gone.

"Oh my. Oh, where did it go?" Valerie asked.

"I don't know, but we better get inside in case it comes back. They're tricky animals. They try to lure their prey out. But, we're smarter than that." Deacon Rex's voice was far away.

Everything about him gnawed at my senses and made me feel irrational anger. He reminded me of Markus, though Markus looked like a dulled version of the Deacon.

I wanted to sketch him, immortalize the small ticks I saw, the moments when his facade dropped.

I would draw his true face one day, which would be what my nightmares had foretold.

The omens I carried in my blood.

I stood still on the lawn, staring at his broad back as he walked across his lawn, unseeing eyes trained on the town over the hill. I knew he felt me.

I spoke with a firm voice, looking at Valerie. "I need to get to the dance," I said, pointing to my watch.

The Deacon turned, a smile on his face when he glanced at Valerie. "I'll grab your coat, Valerie. I won't keep you," he said.

Not this time.

The words echoed in my head, unsaid, but heard by some part of me I hadn't woken.

He hadn't woken.

FOURTEEN

Valerie and I rode home from the Deacon's place in silence. I stared out the window as we descended the hill, breathing out when the scent of Deacon Rex seemed to finally be gone. I was looking for something. Maybe the animal from the road. Or a flash of red—Sorina's hair. I saw nothing but trees, dark and reaching.

When we returned to the trailer, Valerie went to her room after a monotone goodnight and a plea to get to the dance safely.

Kyrie was picking me up, and I was glad to avoid the awkwardness of her father's protective gaze.

I sat on the front porch waiting, looking for Sorina again, but she never came. Eventually, I saw the headlights of Kyrie's car. She rolled down the window and waved as she pulled into my driveway, and I jogged over, getting into the passenger seat.

The fall festival dance wasn't formal. No fancy dresses expected as they would be for the winter formal, Homecoming, and Prom, or so I'd been told, but Kyrie loved dresses, and she couldn't help herself. She had on a long floral number with a cardigan over it.

CHAPTER FOURTEEN

She wore Doc Martens with thick socks. Her black hair was in a casual updo thing girls did, and she wore deep red lipstick.

I told her she looked beautiful not just because I knew it would make her happy, but because it was true. She smiled as we drove up the hill to the school. After we parked, she reached for the door handle, but my words stopped her.

"Something weird happened at the Deacon's house tonight."

Kyrie pulled the door closed, turning to me. "What happened?"

I turned in the seat, leaning my head on the window. "Deacons ... Priests ... all that. They're celibate, right? Like, that's what they're supposed to be, right?" I knew the way religion could sour a mind and make a person do awful things. But I hadn't the slightest idea of the innerworkings of each religion, and I had no genuine desire to know. Not until that night.

"A Deacon that has the goal of becoming a Priest, yes. They're celibate. Why?"

"I think he wants to fuck my aunt." The thought that had been swirling in my head on the hill tumbled out. I'd smelled it, his want.

Kyrie flinched, then pulled her cardigan over herself. "Nicholas ..."

"I don't like him. Something is off about him. I mean, dinner—"

"It wasn't a date, Nicholas. Friends have dinner. Look at us. And the Deacon doesn't have many people who come up there. He's all alone now without Father Dodson. And if your aunt is interested in joining the church, dinner doesn't seem weird, right? He's courting her, but not in that way."

"Are you willfully naïve?" I asked, and the look on Kyrie's face wounded me. Because I'd put it there by being a fucking asshole.

She didn't speak. She didn't retort, and I'd known she wouldn't. I was a coward as well. Instead, my friend pulled the keys from the ignition, opening the door. "I'll see you inside," she said, slamming the door.

I sat in Kyrie's car for quite some time, hating myself. I didn't want to go to the dance anymore, but I didn't want to go home. And after what I'd seen on the hill, I didn't want to wander the town. So I was fucked. I needed to go inside, but I lingered in my misery, in dreams. I hoped I wouldn't dream that night because of the smoke, not as I had the night before. I heard Sorina's words from another dream. *I can take her away, you know that, right?* And with those words, unbidden, the image of Sorina devouring the snake emerged in my mind, like smoke. I stiffened in my seat in ways only she could release.

Before I could close my eyes, slipping back into the dream that felt like a memory, a car drove up the hill, tires squealing. I recognized it from the trailer park. Two girls from my school lived there in the park. Twins. One twin being the girl who'd spread her legs for me the first day of school. Jessica Clement.

The car flew around the parking lot in a circle and finally parked next to Kyrie's car.

The windows were down, and music blared from the speakers. A puff of smoke slithered out of the driver's window. Jessica was smoking, and her twin sister, Nicole, sat beside her, glaring ahead.

The two girls opened their car doors at the same time—mirrors—then slammed them in sync as well. Nicole walked ahead, yelling something at Jessica who threw her cigarette onto the ground, yelling back.

I remembered my first day of school then. The way her brazen teasing had elicited a feeling of embarrassment in me.

CHAPTER FOURTEEN

And, admittedly, arousal.

Fuck. This. Night.

I closed my eyes, wondering if Kyrie would care if I just sat in her car the entire night. She had Nathan Dolan to escort her for the crowning. The dinner with Deacon Rex had me off, itching to tear something apart or be patted on the head. I shook away the fog of her scent just as the hairs on my arms stood up. I opened my eyes to see someone walking across the parking lot to the car.

Sorina's eyes were on me, and my own roved every inch of her. She wore a short skirt, too flimsy for the cool night air, and her legs were covered in her fishnet stockings again, feet in her black combat boots. She wore some sort of lace bra and an oversized flannel over it. It was definitely breaking the dress code, but no one ever reprimanded her. Gone was the thin black dress from before. I missed it and then quickly forgot it as she walked to the hood of Kyrie's car, placing her palms on it, climbing slowly until she stared at me through the windshield. I watched back, a small smile taking over my face.

"What the fuck are you doing now?" I asked, reaching for the door.

When I shut the car door, she turned on the hood, sitting. I stood between her legs, far enough away that she couldn't wrap them around me as she had in her tub.

"Why aren't you inside?" she asked.

"You changed," I said, ignoring her question.

"How was the rest of your dinner?" she replied, ignoring me in kind.

"I don't know. How was it?" I asked, wondering if she lingered nearby and had been listening. If she had seen the black thing in the road.

"I'm asking you," Sorina said, sliding off the hood.

She was so close to me I had to back up a little, but she slipped her finger into my jeans, pulling me back.

I reached down, wrapping my hand around her wrist, pulling her finger from my jeans, a wash of anger flittering over me, dropping me into my past, where grabbing and pulling, and softly violent taking left me scarred. She dropped her hand.

"It was fine. Ended early."

"Why are you out here and not inside with your date?" she asked.

"I was mean to her. She went inside."

Sorina smiled, genuine, her teeth glinting in the light. "Walk me in?" she asked, reaching out her hand.

I offered my arm and her own slipped into the space I left for her as we turned toward the school. I leaned down to Sorina, speaking in a hushed voice. "The Deacon said Amber Hughes was a runaway. Said we should pray for her."

"The power of prayer? You don't believe in it?" she asked.

"No," I said, stepping onto the school's front steps. Two teachers sat at the door, Mrs. Vaughn and Coach Richards, watching as each student came in. They checked our names off on a list, and I noticed when Mrs. Vaughn checked Sorina's name, she blinked rapidly before shaking her head and ushering us in. I glanced back at her as we walked down the hallway toward the gym.

Sorina was small and dainty on my arm. Other students in the hall watched us as we walked by, and just as we were about to step into the gym, I felt a warning ripple through me. But not before Sorina flinched, turning back.

At the entrance, Deacon Rex smiled at the teachers.

CHAPTER FOURTEEN

"Deacon Rex, how nice of you to come," Mrs. Vaughn said. "I thought you were chaperoning the winter formal?"

The Deacon smiled his broad smile, his eyes likely crinkling behind his glasses. "Yes, but I thought I would get some practice in. Unfortunately, we don't have many young people on the hill. I'm afraid I'm out of practice with our young, hopeful next world leaders."

Mrs. Vaughn smiled, and I rolled my eyes. As if anyone from Hart Hollow High would change the world.

Well, maybe Kyrie would.

Sorina pulled my arm, dragging me into the gym.

When I turned to her, I saw a faint red color around her eyes. Before I could ask her if she was alright, she said she needed to use the restroom and left me alone.

⌬

I was genuine with my apology, and Kyrie quickly forgave me. I didn't think she was ignorant or naïve. I wanted her heart sometimes. Wanted her *love*. But I'd lost it long ago. If I ever had it to begin with.

We sat on the bleachers as our classmates mingled, dancing. I didn't dance, or have any desire to, and when Nathan asked her for a dance to prep in case she won the title of queen, she left me alone on the bleachers. I breathed out when she walked away, content to observe my classmates, as I often did.

That was the first time I spoke to Jessica Clement. I smelled the cigarette smoke before I saw her; she smelled of tobacco and warm vanilla sugar, a perfume I would grow to associate with her.

She sat next to me with a dramatic sigh, her twin across the room with a group of people, watching us.

"Hi, loner boy. Where's your date?" Jessica asked, crossing her legs.

"Kyrie?" I asked, pointing to her in the crowd as if she didn't know exactly where she was.

"Why aren't *you* dancing with her?" Jessica asked, turning her body toward me. It wasn't the first time I'd been on the receiving end of Jessica's flirtations, and it wouldn't be the last. "I don't know how to dance," I said, hoping for a nail in coffin situation, but she took it as a challenge, a flirtation.

She held out her hand as she stood, eyebrow raised. Resigned, I stood, but I didn't take her hand as I walked out to the dance floor. I pulled my hands into my sleeves, and when I placed my hands on Jessica's hips, mimicking those around me, no part of my flesh touched her. Not purposefully. Jessica put her arms around my neck, and I turned away from her, unsure of why I agreed to this. We moved slowly, circling. If this was dancing, it was lame.

"How come you never talk to anyone?" Jessica asked, looking up at me. I towered over her.

"I do," I said as I looked around for Sorina.

"Not really. You talk to Kyrie. You talk to that scary girl from Romania. You don't talk to any of the kids in the trailer park. Too good for them?"

I looked down at her, a feeling of dread washing over me. Then, before I could answer, I saw Deacon Rex by the punch bowl. His dark glasses turned my way, a small smile on his face as Mrs. Turner spoke to him.

CHAPTER FOURTEEN

I felt him everywhere, half expected him to whistle for me like a dog. I looked down at Jessica again, blinking my eyes. "I'm just ... I don't know."

"Shy?" she supplied.

"I guess." I knew the word, and how it painted me, but it wasn't accurate. I just didn't want to talk to people. I didn't want a lot of friends. I didn't even know how to *be* a friend. So I was starting small. And it wasn't going well for the most part. Being a dick to Kyrie earlier proved I had a lot to learn about just *being* with people, existing with them in a space that wasn't tangled in religion, abuse, and horror.

Jessica groaned, then smiled. "God, you have no idea what that does to us girls."

"What do you mean?"

"You're like this new kid all the way from California. Fucking tall, and you have those blue eyes and that voice. And you're like, shy and shit. Everyone wants to know about you. See what's under this." She squeezed my shoulders and slid her hands forward as if to slip them under my flannel. I moved quickly, grabbing her wrists.

She grinned, raising an eyebrow. "Are you a virgin, Nick?"

"Nicholas," I said, grinding my teeth, avoiding her question. I didn't have an answer. I'd never fucked anyone. I'd never made love—whatever that meant—to anyone. I'd been used. My body was not my own, and it felt foreign to me.

Felt *frightening*.

Each day away from the ranch was a reclaiming, a way to get back to myself. I wasn't there yet. I still felt like I belonged to the hands, to the mouths, to the dark.

I dropped Jessica's hands as the song faded out. I didn't want her hands on me; I didn't want her asking me intimate questions when she barely knew me.

Questions I was sure the Deacon could hear, somehow.

Jessica smiled again, leaning up on her toes. She brought her lips to my ear, and I could tell she was still smiling. "It's okay, one of us will find out eventually." When she pulled away, she winked at me, and I stared, jaw flexing.

I walked back to the bleachers just as Kyrie returned. Her brows were pinched, and she reached her hand to me. I pulled it away, running my fingers through my hair. "When does the ceremony or whatever start?" I asked, taking a seat.

Kyrie stared across the gym, watching Jessica join her friends.

"Soon. Nathan and I were talking about what to do if I win." Kyrie sat on the bleachers, adjusting her hair and her cardigan. She always looked perfectly put together, but something was off about her as she stared across the gym.

"What do you mean?" I asked.

Kyrie turned to me, answering as if I knew what the hell she was talking about. "He's going to hug me and give me a kiss on the cheek. I wanted to make sure we were on the same page."

"Oh." I said, as I saw a flash of red across the gym. "Hey, I'll be right back."

The dance was in the older of the two gyms in the school. The newer gym was strictly for sport events, but the old gym was attached to the stage where school plays took place. The curtains were drawn on the stage, but I knew it wasn't vacant when the curtain moved slightly.

I smiled as I walked across the gym floor.

CHAPTER FOURTEEN

No one stopped me or seemed to notice me as I snuck up on the stage. My fellow students moved around, laughed, and danced as the crowning drew nearer. And before I duck behind the curtain, I saw Kyrie take Nathan's hand and lead him to the hallway where the nominees and their escorts would line up.

The lights in the gym, dim before, warmed as I slid away.

Sorina was sitting on the stage when I stepped behind the curtain, close to it, peering through a slit where the two curtains met.

I walked to her, taking a seat next to her. She'd shed her flannel and was using it as a seat. I tried not to stare, but with so much skin exposed, I felt that familiar want. That slow drag of desire. I wanted to smell her, run my nose along her neck, inhale her. I wanted to wrap her red hair in my fist, expose her jaw.

Something primal was moving within me every time she was in view, intensifying since we swam in the dirty pond near the school. But I acted out none of my fantasies, instead I sat on the stage with her, trying to see what she was looking at.

"Where did you go?" I asked, stretching my legs out in front of me.

"The bathroom. I told you that," she said, staring straight ahead. Her voice was hushed and monotone. Bored.

"For an hour?" I asked, looking at her profile.

I couldn't help myself then. My hand felt like a puppeteer had it on a string. Or maybe it was my true want, what I did next. I reached out, brushing her long red hair from her face.

She closed her eyes then, turning away from the light in the curtain. Her long fingers wrapped around my wrist, and she didn't push me away. Instead, she pulled me closer. I threaded my fingers in her hair, leaning into her.

"You should be down there, Nicholas. With a girl. Any girl. Someone ... normal. Even if just for a little while." Sorina said this as I pushed her jaw up, exposing her neck. I leaned in, inhaling her scent, feeling brazen, unlike myself. Jessica's flirtation with me didn't make me want her, want any of my classmates. It just reminded me of my dreams, who I really craved.

"I want to be here," I said. I wanted to be in the shadows with her, hiding away, far from the eyes of the Deacon, the teachers, Jessica, Kyrie, everyone.

"You don't know what you want, Nicholas," Sorina said, pushing me away. She stood, but she didn't leave. She walked in front of me, obscuring the light. She sat down between my legs, then spun around, facing the gap in the curtains again. She pushed herself back until her back pressed against my chest, then wrapped her arms around my thighs. I gripped her shoulders, pulling her closer, pressing my face into her hair. She smelled like dirt, amber, and pennies.

She pushed back, and I wrapped one arm around her torso, sighing. "What are you doing to me? I need to stop dreaming about you," I whispered, my body hard and wanting.

Sorina tilted her head. Just slightly. "Let's play a game, Nicholas."

I liked the words from her, and only her.

A game.

"What's the game?" I asked, pressing my forehead to the back of her head.

CHAPTER FOURTEEN

"This is a game of sounds and mirrors. You win when I make one. You mirror me. You make no moves of your own. You can make as many sounds of your own as you want. You do to me what I do to you, nothing else."

She turned around, crawling into my lap. I kept my hands still. My breathing sounded loud, maybe just in my ears, maybe to her. I couldn't tell. But it didn't matter. No one could hear us above the chatter, the music, the announcer when they began calling out names, starting with the freshman fall festival candidate.

I closed my eyes as I felt Sorina run her hands over my chest. "Put your hands behind your back, and keep them there until I tell you."

I opened my eyes, then obeyed.

She reached for the end of my T-shirt, ran her hands underneath. I let out a moan when she found my nipple and squeezed. "No mirror yet. Just listen to the sounds you're making. The sounds I'm making you make."

It was the first time someone had touched me that way without making me want to throw up, to cry, to end my life. It was the first time I didn't want to crawl out of my skin. It was unlike the way she touched me in the bathtub. That was slow and soft, gentle and clean. It wasn't sexual, not really. Though my mind went there.

Sorina pushed my shirt up, exposing my chest, then bent her head, taking my nipple in her mouth, swirling her tongue around it. I thought of a mirror, what she was saying I could do to her. It scared me. I'd never touched a woman willingly. I'd never wanted to make someone wet and wanting of me. I'd just closed my eyes every time it happened. Waiting for it to be over, to be used and discarded.

Sorina leaned up, running her hand over my face, her thumb touching my brow. I was tense there, lost for a second in the past. "I won't hurt you," she said, pressing down into my erection.

"What if I want you to?" I asked, surprising myself.

"There is a pleasure in pain sometimes. I can show you," she whispered, pushing my shirt back up, taking my other nipple in her mouth, biting down a little. I moaned, nearly falling back, nearly touching her. But I listened, I knew how to obey.

She pulled my shirt off then, dropping it on the stage. I heard the sophomore candidate being called as I fell backward, closing my eyes. When I opened them, Sorina stuck her finger in her mouth, wetting it, then continued her touching. One finger swirled my nipple, and the want was in the knowing. Knowing everything she did I was going to do to her. I flexed my hands at my sides, wanting to reach out, to touch her, but I didn't. She noticed, and it was then I saw the faint redness around her eyes again. As if she had been crying.

She reached for the hem of her little lace top then, pulling it over her head, exposing her breasts.

I'd seen her rosy nipples before, felt her naked skin against by back, but now she was exposed, staring down at me, red hair darkened by the shadows.

I leaned up, and she nodded. Tentatively, I reached out, cupping one breast, leaning in. I rubbed my nose along her nipple before I wet it with my tongue, and the taste of her made me want to howl. Rip something apart. When I sucked her nipple into my mouth, she did not make a sound, and it spurred me on. I sucked, pulled, bit at her, my hands kneading the plump flesh. When I pulled away, a string of spit lingered between my mouth and her nipple. Without looking at her, I moved to the next, my desire like fire, my determination to pull some sound from her possessive. I sucked at her, pulled her closer to my erection, swirling my tongue around the small bud. I felt her move, her hands graze my hair, but no sound. Nothing that my sensitive ears could find. It made me angry, made me feel feral. I let her tit fall out of my mouth, a wet sound making her eyes open. A smirk on her mouth.

"What's the point of this game?" I asked, my voice gravely.

"To show you what it can be like when ... when you want it."

I pushed her off of me, angry, and her small breasts bounced, and her face darkened.

"By making no sound? Shouldn't both of us be making sounds if we both want it? Because if not, then it's too much like—"

Sorina's face turned white, and she stood. "I'm sorry. I didn't think—"

"You have no idea where I've been. What, just because I told you a couple of things, you think you know? And you think because they ... they—"

"Raped you," she offered.

"Fuck you," I said, unable to wear that word. I reached for my shirt, ready to leave. Before I could get it over my head, Sorina grabbed my arm. I glared at her. "If you think I need ... lessons ... you're a little late. You think I don't know what to do? They fucked in the open, you know? Or no, they *loved*. That's what it was. *Love*. The love of each other, the breaking of flesh. You know they fucking drank each other's blood? Markus and his vampire Jesus bullshit. There's no such thing as God, no such thing as fucking vampires, but you walk around all gothic and ominous. I should stay the fuck away from you."

"But you can't," Sorina said, and I wasn't sure if there was happiness or sorrow in her voice.

But I knew she was too close. "I know what to fucking do," I said, voice low.

Sorina nodded, stepping back a little. "Then show me. No more games."

I smiled, dropping my shirt to her feet. "No, let's continue the game. Where did we leave off?" I asked.

I reached for her then, fisting her long red hair in my hand. I lowered her to her knees, and when she looked up at me, the smile was back. Warning and deadly. Something like desire.

"Put your hands behind your back. No touching," I ordered.

Sorina complied, and I reached for my zipper. Her eyes followed, widening a little, then she looked back up at me. She didn't look away as I slid my jeans down, stepping out of them. I pushed my boxers down just enough to pull myself free. I was hard, desperate for some part of her. I brushed my thumb over my tip, and it was wet with pre-cum already, our fighting and the way she touched me earlier arousing. But not as arousing as my anger.

Her smirk.

I brought my tip to her nipple, mimicking the way she'd touched my own with her finger.

I heard Kyrie's name announced as I wet Sorina's nipple, then the next. She was looking down, watching everything, until finally she looked up, a look of sleepiness and warmth all over her pale face. I'd never seen her cheeks red, but they were now. Still, she was silent. I knelt down, one hand securing her arms behind her back, the other grabbing one of her breasts. I leaned down, tasting myself on her, my earlier pleasure nothing compared to this. I devour her nipple, flicking it with my tongue, sucking it hard. When I let go of Sorina's hands, she grabbed me. One hand in my hair, the other reaching for me, small fingers wrapping around my length. When her own fingers brushed over the head of my dick, I pulled away, ready to be her mirror. I flipped her onto her back, desperately grasping her skirt, pushing it up. I pushed her panties to the side, and with no preamble, pressed one finger inside of her, feeling how wet she was, pulling it out, pressing it over her clit. I heard it then, the sound from her mouth. A whisper of something, a desperate *yes*, falling out. I swirled my finger over her clit a couple more times, my mouth hovering close, blowing on her. I barely remembered the things I'd seen in my past, that wasn't where I'd learned to do what I was doing.

It was books, dark telling of desire such as this. Detailed scenes describing all the ways a man could make a woman come. I knew how to do it. I knew how to make it come to life. But that's not what I wanted right then.

I needed more.

When I looked up, Sorina was biting her lip, trying to be silent. So I pulled my finger away, giving her just a second before I flicked her clit with my tongue, then sucked it.

Her thighs pressed against my ears, but not quick enough. I heard her cry out my name, and it was all I needed.

I pulled away, wiping my mouth and Sorina looked up, eyes wide, as I smiled.

I reached for my discarded clothes on the floor, and stood, winking. "Looks like the game is over," I said, before walking away.

FIFTEEN

I didn't stay for the crowning of the queen.

Instead, I ran out of the school, frightening the teachers at the entrance, shoving a student as I exited. The Ozark air hit me like a cold slap to the face, and when I made it to the end of the parking lot, the reality of the night took over.

I ran down the gravel drive that led to the highway, running across, through the trees, until I made it to the trailer park. My lungs were empty and my chest ached. I wanted to howl into the night like an animal.

I didn't know who I was on that stage, who I became. Shame and anger flooded me, my neck hot and aching.

I'd wanted to press Sorina against the far wall of the stage, rip her panties away, bury myself in her. I'd wanted to hurt her and beg her to hurt me. I'd wanted to feel everything and nothing all at once. But feeling nothing with her was never an option. She looked like a release, burned like a cure.

I didn't want to be cured. Not yet.

CHAPTER FIFTEEN 149

When I looked at our trailer, I saw a light on in the living room. The last thing I wanted to do was face Valerie, so I walked past my back window, to the woods. I closed my eyes, listening, not sure who I wanted to hear.

Sorina leaving the school? *Keep dreaming.*

The cicadas sang on, and then I heard a voice that was not from my dreams.

"What are you doing, sniffing me out?" a voice said from behind a tree to my right.

I turned, seeing a guy around my age in a white T-shirt, jeans, and scuffed-up boots. It was the guy I'd seen with Jessica and Nicole at the Raven's Nest. I'd seen him around the trailer park but never at school. He took a long drag, and I smelled the inviting pungent odor of a joint in the air.

"What's your name, new kid?" he asked.

I walked to a headstone, glancing at Sorina's house through the trees.

"Nicholas."

"Nice to meet you, Nicky. I'm William the Third." He bowed, a cocky grin on his face. "Lord of Steele Heart trailer park since … I've been here since I was nine so"—he squinted his eyes, maybe doing math in his head—"since 1982."

When he smiled at me I saluted him. *Fucking awkward.* "Nice to meet you, *Billy.*"

He laughed at my reply, then stepped forward. "You know it isn't safe to follow strangers into the woods around these parts, right Nicky? Or was it all rainbows and glitter where you came from?"

I raised an eyebrow, pulling my leg onto the headstone. Billy looked like Jessica and Nicole. Acted like Jessica. "Hardly. But I'm not a teenage girl, and that seems to be who's in danger around here, right?"

I thought of the thing in the road at the Deacon's house earlier in the night. The screams sounded like a woman—a siren. Not a beast laying in the road, writhing. Something inhuman but also not of this earth, more like the monsters and animals I'd read about in Stephen King books. But what did I know? At that point, I was playing catch up in real-time, the real world confusing and blinding but far brighter than the nightmare world I had lived in.

Billy laughed. "Yeah, and godly girls. I'm neither, so I think I'm safe." His voice was joking, but something melancholy lived there. I liked him already.

"So, what's the deal with this town, anyway? How often does this ... runaway thing happen?" I was eager to hear someone else talk about it. Kyrie was my sole source of information on Hart Hollow, and I needed a fresh perspective. And I didn't want some bullshit answer like the one I got from Deacon Rex. *We should pray for her.* Fuck off.

Billy took a long drag. "Would you wanna stick around this hellhole? God's hand is mighty, blessed be," he mocked. "Look at us heathens, walking over graves," he teased and gasped. "We must bathe in the blood of a virgin next. You a virgin?"

I shook my head. What the fuck was with that question being thrown at me tonight? "No." *Yes, if it was my choice. Does it count when it's taken from you? Taken in the name of God?*

Billy smiled wide, running a hand over his stubble. "I saw you with the Davis girl. Don't go down that road, buddy."

I eyed him. "Why not, buddy?" I didn't know why I was mocking him, maybe I was still being a mirror. Something told me he wouldn't mind though, and I could be myself with him.

He pointed at me. "I, William Clement, once loved a godly girl, a lamb of the lord. And lo and behold, she ran away from his town. Which makes no sense, since living out her life here was all she ever wanted and preached to me."

"When was that?" I was relieved his reasoning for staying away from Kyrie wasn't something that would force me to punch him in the face.

"Oh, about four years ago. We were fifteen, in love, a *secret* love, mind you. Couldn't let daddy Payne know about her fucking the trailer trash who snored through Sunday service when he showed up. Which, I only showed up to so I could see her in her pretty dresses, but that should count for something, right?"

I shivered. "Which church was that?"

"It's about ten miles out, the Little Creek Baptist Church on Highway F. They're gone, though. Her parents left. Couldn't handle lying, I guess." Billy took another drag, and I wanted to grab it from his hand, take it for myself. I stamped down the urge, my adrenaline from earlier waning.

"Lying?" I asked.

"Yeah. Smiling, lying, pretending life was fine and dandy when their precious daughter had ditched the town and their *blessed be* home."

"Oh."

"I mean, if you believe she ran away, anyway."

At this, I hopped off the grave. A flash of red caught my eye, and when I turned, I saw nothing. But I knew that didn't mean Sorina wasn't there, listening. "What do you mean?"

Billy walked to me, offering me a drag of his joint. *Finally.* I took it, inhaling slowly, trying not to seem too eager and green. It felt good but not as good as what Sorina had given me.

Another flash of red.

Billy continued. "Well, the vampire took her. Duh."

I choked on a breath as I handed his joint back. "The ... what?" *Please, not this fucking shit again.*

"You didn't know? Hart Hollow is the forgotten town where dreams die, God rules, and the Vampire King resides high on the hill."

My vision darkened like someone had draped a heavy blanket over the night, over the trees. "I think you took too many hits of that, man." I wondered if saying the word had awoken something. I never should have uttered the word vampire on that stage with Sorina. Never should have snuck into that church on the hill. The likeness of God's son haunted me.

Billy laughed. "Ah don't believe in the bogeyman, then?"

I laughed a bitter laugh as I drifted back into my past. "Nah. I once knew someone who did, and he hurt a lot of people because he believed Jesus Christ was a vampire."

Billy's eyes widened. "Who did?"

I cleared my throat. "Someone I used to know back where I used to live."

"Where did you live?"

I offered my partial truth to him. "On a ranch in California."

He seemed disappointed in my answer. "Ah. How'd that work out for him? Because we don't talk about the truth around here."

I ran a hand through my shaggy hair, turning around in a circle. "Well, he's dead."

Billy nodded, pulling out a lighter. I recognized it as a Zippo. He held the glinting silver up to the light, his thumb on the bottom, his index, middle, and ring fingers all on the top. He squeezed the lighter, and it popped open, shifting in his hand. It was a neat trick.

"I probably shouldn't be running my mouth to new kids in the woods about all this shit, anyway. I'll end up dead like your friend."

My throat tightened. "He wasn't my friend. And I doubt you'll end up six feet under for telling me that."

Another flash of red caught my eye in the trees, and I knew Sorina was up there. *Watching.*

"Oh, I never said six feet under. That's not where you go when he gets ya."

"I feel like there has to be another explanation for people leaving," I tried.

"Like what, MoMo?"

"What's MoMo?"

Billy grinned widely, waving his hand in the air. "Oh, the Missouri Monster," I thought Billy was pulling my leg at first, but as he continued on, I could tell he wasn't. "Great beast of a thing, watches in the dark and stalks the woods. Eats up little kids at night. *Don't go far, kiddies; MoMo will gobble you up if you stay out past curfew. Stay under the streetlights, and peddle fast little kiddies. You can tell he's here by his stench.*"

I thought of the animal in the road again, the screams. "And what does MoMo look like?"

"Big black beast. Spotted up by St. Louis in the 60s. Might say it's Missouri's own Bigfoot."

"So, we have Bigfoot and vampires? What about werewolves? Do we have those, too?"

Billy put his hand on his hips. "Nah, that's fairytale shit, man. Don't be dumb," he joked.

I laughed, and Billy came closer.

"In all seriousness, I know you probably think I'm high or whatever, but be careful in this fucking town, man. You either never leave or get taken."

"I'm sorry for your loss," I said, practicing the words. I'd learned this was something you said to someone who lost someone they loved. We never said it on the ranch because every death served a higher purpose, according to Markus. So we weren't allowed to mourn, cry, or feel loss when someone was ... sacrificed. Feelings meant death. Insubordination meant death.

Or worse.

Billy shrugged. "Ah, it was just a kid thing. We were young." His words were casual, but I could see the pain in his dark eyes.

He walked toward the opening in the trees, toward the trailer park. "Don't stay out long, Nicky." His eyes glittered up to the trees, as if he knew she was there, too. "And don't do anything I wouldn't do, little non-virgin."

Then he was gone.

And she was with me.

When I was sure Billy was out of earshot, I shot a look in the direction I'd last heard noise. "Hear all that?" I asked, walking to the edge of the woods that separated the cemetery from her lawn. Sorina followed out of the dark, a black dress dragging the dirt behind her. She'd changed out of the clothes I'd taken off her earlier. She was how she was in my dreams. The sheer black, the lace, the red. She was how she'd been on the hill, before the screams and the Deacon's scent. I could smell it again now.

Sorina's voice was measured when she answered, "Momo, vampires, werewolves, and your Jesus king."

"What was that up on the hill?" I asked, walking out of the woods.

Sorina was suddenly in front of me, hands on her hips. "Where are you going, Nicky?" she tried on Billy's nickname, and I turned to her.

"You don't call me that."

"You let him call you that."

"Maybe I need some more friends besides Kyrie and … whatever we are."

"You could do worse than Billy Clement."

"Glad you approve." I walked past her.

"Where are you going, Nicholas?" My name sounded like a caress when she said it, and I could feel it everywhere.

"Your house. That alright?"

"But I didn't invite you," she said, beating me to the front door. I noticed then that the windows reminded me of the church on the hill. *Vampire King resides high on the hill.*

"Stop me," I dared. Something about the night was frightening and arousing. The figure that lived in the dreams, that had haunted me for years before she existed in my reality was influential and old. The version of her that walked in the night looked like her now, in the flesh, but different, darker, a humming around the form when I was lost in the nightmare world. I remembered the blood dripping from her mouth, the way it made me want to wake—to reject my want for her.

I reminded myself that the only vampires that existed were in stories, fairytales, and horror novels.

In Markus's mind.

And why would a vampire want to dominate a small town like this one? With all that power, wouldn't you want to devour the world?

Sorina reached for her doorknob, turned it, swinging the grand door wide.

The house didn't look like it belonged here; it was old and beautiful, not old and worn down like many homes here. Time was clear in the style but not the condition, and when I stepped in I determined the house looked like her—ivory, red, black, ornate gold fixtures. Down the hallway, I could see a glittering chandelier. I walked toward it, hearing the front door shut. The last time I'd been in her home, I was nervous, missing the intricate details of her space as I took the stairs. I wanted to take my time. I felt bigger than my body, stretched at the seams. I was in the beast's den, the haunting nightmare of my dreams. Of my fantasies. But I felt like the beast.

"Nicholas Hemming, don't get caught up in the regret of a lovesick teenager who lost his little girlfriend."

I stepped into the kitchen, black cabinets stretching to the ceiling, a small window above the sink. A mahogany kitchen table was in the center of the room, with four chairs surrounding it.

Everything looked … unused. Like the house was ready to be sold or photographed. *Staged.*

I ignored her, walking out of the room into what looked like a sitting area. I could sense Sorina following me but couldn't hear her. Eventually, I found the staircase I knew led up to her room. I took each step slowly, the wood creaking beneath my footsteps. Again, Sorina followed, but the floor made no sound beneath her.

CHAPTER FIFTEEN

She probably weighed around a hundred pounds, if I had to guess. The outline of her ribs could be seen beneath her dress when she moved the right way.

I walked to her bedroom door and opened it wide. Lace curtains, red accents, and the small vanity in the corner where she'd brushed her wet hair. I stared at the large four-post bed, the covers perfectly in place. When I laid there the other night, it felt unused. She'd joined me, but how often did she sleep in the bed? My mind was racing, making up stories and stringing together poetry.

"Would you say this your room?" I asked, staring her in the eye.

"You could say that."

I crossed my arms. "But would *you* say that?"

She raised her chin, the blue of her eyes fading away, the black getting larger.

I felt nothing as I stared back, defiant.

Sorina shook her head as if she were shrugging off a nightmare, a wilted try at something. "No. I would not say this is my room. Your wording, your intention, it will never get by me, Nicholas. You say I'm a riddle—an omen—and I say you are a poem. But I am not in the mood anymore. And I think you should leave."

"Why?"

"I'm hungry."

"So? I can talk while you eat."

She smiled then, and I again noticed her teeth, her long incisors. "Yeah, you can. But that may spoil the meal."

I waited for the warning I felt when something terrible was about to happen. The ache in my chest. But nothing happened. My mind told me to fear her, but I never felt that feeling. Not the way

I had when I met the Deacon. I felt ready to spring, ready to chase.

"Why were you hiding on the hill in the woods tonight?"

"It's not safe up there."

"The vampire king on the hill, like Billy said?"

"Don't listen to him."

"Why not? I think he may be the only one in this town telling me what I need to hear. Not you, not Diana, not even Kyrie, but she just doesn't know what's going on. Maybe I should introduce her and Billy."

"Bold of you to assume everyone in this town doesn't know each other and hasn't broken bread together at some point in that little café your *aunt* is hiding out at. The roots of this town run deep. They follow the same cycle as their fathers, their mothers, and so on."

"Except the ones that leave," I said, thinking of Amber's missing persons poster.

"No one leaves. They just go somewhere no one can find them."

I reached out, grabbing the post of the bed. "Stop talking in riddles." My vision blurred, and I recognized the change in my voice, the deepening. It'd only happened a few times in my life, and every time it did, people around me looked scared of me. I remembered the night on the ranch, the last night. The way Valerie trembled, then grabbed my hand, taking me away.

She could barely look at me for weeks after we left, but never left me. I kept waiting for it. For her to leave me behind.

She didn't. Though, at times, I wished she would.

CHAPTER FIFTEEN

Sorina wasn't scared of me. Instead, she stepped closer, invading my space. She reached up, placed her hand over mine, and pulled it from the bedpost.

The wood was fractured, and a crack edged down from the place I'd grabbed it.

"I'm sorry, I don't know ..."

It happened then. My body came alive, crackling. And it didn't hurt, not the way it had on the stage. Sorina let go of my hand, gripped my neck, and brought her mouth to mine.

I'd been used before, stripped bare.

But I'd never kissed someone. I wasn't worth that; I didn't want it from the women on the ranch. Grown, using a child. They were vile, walking demons in my mind.

Sorina's mouth was soft, pleading. I exhaled, and her tongue slipped in, lapping with mine. It was all it took to make me hungry.

Desperate for her.

Her hand threaded in my hair, and I wanted her to touch me. I wanted her to feel me everywhere. I grabbed her back, pulled her body to mine, and mimicked what I knew a body could do and what women wanted to feel. I'd watched it before. Seen the way humans turn into animals in a wide room. The room was small, warm to her coolness. I gripped her dress in my hands and pressed against her as her mouth turned hungry, too.

I was hard, and I pressed against her small body. Then, just as a moan escaped my mouth, she pushed me away, hard. My back was against the wall, and I'd flown three feet.

Sorina's hair was wild, her erect nipples straining against her dress, the vein at her throat visible.

And her eyes were all black.

Inhuman.

When she spoke, she sounded older.

Ancient.

As if a demon had slipped inside her skin.

"Get out of my house. Now—" She ended her command with a name, but it was not my own. Her tone warped it, and the *S* was violent and angry. *Skull.*

I didn't waste a second, didn't ask her what she'd called me. I left. Frightened and aroused and hungry.

Wondering who won the game this time.

SIXTEEN

The weeks following the fall festival dance moved at a sluggish pace.

At home, Valerie kept her distance and never brought up another dinner at the Deacon's house. I wondered if the experience with the animal frightened her, or if she felt the same way I had on the hill.

Afraid.

I endured half a day of silence from Kyrie for ditching her and missing out on her crowning, but she quickly forgave me, as she did with everyone.

She'd stopped talking about Amber, her fears, and I hoped my life was curving back to an easier course, but I knew it was just wishful thinking. Though Kyrie wasn't voicing her fears out loud, she seemed to be in her own world all the time. I hadn't been over for dinner again, and I hadn't asked her to eat with me at the café. I was playing at normal and had stopped walking the streets at night, hoping to see Sorina at school. Maybe a part of me was hoping if I wasn't wandering at night she would meet me in the middle, show up in the day. But my hopes were dashed. She stopped showing up. And her name was never called for attendance. It was as if she didn't exist.

In her place, others found me.

The blonde woman from the ranch came to me as I slept. I saw the blood, her red anger. I saw the dark-haired man next to her, his raised finger as he pointed at me, whispered to her. I heard her say words she hadn't that night, but her deep otherworldly voice was the same. *From their blood, a prophecy will be woken, no cycle broken, twin Princes of black beast. Treachery, the wolf who chases the bright bride of the sky.* I would wake every time she said his name, the wolf.

I smoked in the cemetery with Billy to escape my insomnia. We talked about our lives, the town, and our plans for the future. He told me again I should get out of Hart Hollow and showed me his uncle's truck on the grass by his trailer, telling me it was for sale.

He talked about his sisters, Jessica and Nicole, and he asked me to promise to look out for the two girls at school. I told him I'd barely spoken to his sisters, but he insisted I watch after them. He invited me for dinner at his house on more than one occasion, but I declined. I'd never had a male friendship, and I wanted to keep my friendship with him simple. Adding his sisters to the mix didn't appeal to me. But what I wanted and what was in the cards rarely aligned. Our worlds were about to be shaken.

On a Wednesday after lunch, during our free period, Kyrie pulled me behind a curtain to the back of the stage in the old gym. The drama club was practicing on the old wooden boards that hour, but they didn't mind us. They were all on stage or on the court, watching or running lines. Plus, everyone loved Kyrie and would deny her nothing.

Kyrie frowned when she looked at me, and I remembered how tired she had looked that morning at our lockers. "You'd never like, climb my roof, would you?"

My chest tightened. "What?"

"I heard someone on my roof again last night. Really late, after three a.m. Something woke me up. I don't know if I heard something in my sleep or what but I was suddenly wide awake, and I heard something up there. It walked around a little, and then nothing. But I heard ... like ... this weird gust of air. As if it flew off." She winced, knowing how her words sounded.

I nodded, deciding I needed to sit on the floor for this conversation. Kyrie joined me, stretching her legs out in front of her.

Her voice was low when she said, "I think I'm losing it. And I feel like everyone is watching me now, waiting for me to do something weird, something out of character. Like I'm a runaway waiting to happen. My parents won't leave me alone in the house. I'm not going to climb out my window. I'd break my neck. And now I'm hearing these noises." She sighed, rubbing her hands over her eyes. "Nicholas, I ... I wanted you to love this town when you moved here, just the way I always have. But, after what you heard Eric say, I don't know. My head keeps spinning. What if she *was* taken by someone? It's not the first time this has happened ..."

I crossed my arms, leaning back against the wall. "You're not the first person to say that to me."

"Who else did?"

"Billy Clement. He lives in the trailer park. We smoked together the other night."

Kyrie frowned. "You smoke?"

I let out a laugh, running a hand through my hair. "That's what you got a from that? Not that someone else is sure girls are going missing, not running away. You landed on me smoking?"

Kyrie rolled her eyes, glancing back at our classmates. "You shouldn't hang out with William Clement."

"Why? Because he smokes weed?" I asked, smirking.

She whispered-yelled, "He's a drug dealer!"

"Aren't you supposed to be all nonjudgmental and nice and shit?" I asked, raising an eyebrow.

Kyrie scooted closer to me. "I'm being nice and watching out for you. My friend."

Though I'd kept Billy at arm's length, I liked him and our nightly chats about nothing. Every conversation in my life seemed to be fraught with riddles and resentment. Sorina and Valerie brought out varying shades of dark in me. And spending time with Billy was something I enjoyed. "Well, he seems nice. Smoking doesn't make him a degenerate. If you think that, then why are you friends with me? I smoke, so what? I smoked with Sorina, but maybe you don't need another reason to dislike her."

Kyrie moved closer again. "I'm not trying to be judgmental."

I leaned away. "You don't like how people look at you and the assumptions they make because you're a pastor's daughter. Well, you shouldn't make the ones you make. What are people who live in trailer parks, bad people? I'm sorry, as you know, I grew up on a ranch. I don't know all this cool society class shit. Is he a bad person because he does drugs? Well, I do too." I was getting angry and defensive over a strange girl who kissed me and threw me out of her house weeks ago and some guy I met in the trailer park and had a few smokes with. Kyrie had been a good friend to me since the day I stepped foot in the school. I needed to give her some space to … be normal. But I was also protective of the other people in my life. However few.

Kyrie eyed me, shaking her head before she dropped her eyes. "No, I didn't mean … I don't know. I'm sorry. I'm not perfect.

And that's another thing people assume, and you're using it on me, too. Sometimes I ... I don't know."

I almost reached out, placing my hand on hers, but I didn't. "No, it's okay. I ... I don't know. Maybe we should talk to Billy and see what he knows if you think something is happening. See if it's just a gut feeling, or maybe he's seen something. Maybe he's heard something from family. Has his family been here long?"

Kyrie nodded. "Ages. Like mine."

"Well, maybe his family is a little more apt to speak frankly than yours."

Kyrie glared at me, but then smiled. She knew her parents.

"Where could we meet after school? The Raven's Nest?" I asked.

Kyrie smiled. "Yeah. But we might look suspicious."

"Why?"

"Why would two high schoolers be hanging out with Billy Clement?" Her glare told me she knew why people would assume we were hanging out.

Drugs.

"He's only nineteen," I reasoned. "And he lives in the trailer park with me."

"It's going to look weird."

"Well, if you stop dressing like Mary Poppins, it may not," I joked.

Kyrie looked down at her dress and smoothed out a crease. "Fuck off."

My eyes grew wide, practically bugging out of my head. "I'm sorry, what?"

She looked me in the eye, half a smile, half a frown. "You heard me."

I laughed loudly, and a few theatre students looked back at us. I mouthed a "Sorry" and watched Kyrie blush. She was pretty, smart, a good friend—everything some high school kid should want. But I felt nothing, not in that way, and it made me hurt. Liking Kyrie would feel normal, right?

Nothing about me felt normal or right.

I wanted the girl next door, and she didn't want me anymore.

If she ever did.

Two days later, we all walked into the Raven's Nest looking like a bunch of suspicious assholes. We didn't fit together. Not even in the slightest, but we found a booth in the back, ignoring stares from the staff when we ordered, and the customers as we passed them.

Billy brought Jessica and Nicole in his Camaro, and the sisters sat across from me and Kyrie.

I could feel the tension between them. They weren't friends, and I didn't know the history there. Small towns are their history, relationships, intersecting, and crossing names off lists.

Two guys played pool by the front windows, but otherwise, we were alone on that side of the Nest. I cleared my throat, hoping to get started before our food was brought out. "So, I know we look a little ... weird here. None of us have hung out. Well, not since I moved here; I don't know what your history is—"

"Everyone in this town has a history with everyone. Moving on," Kyrie interrupted.

CHAPTER SIXTEEN

Jessica rolled her eyes and zeroed in on me. "You wanna talk about the missing girls? That's old news. And not like I care. I definitely don't fit the profile of the runaways." She eyed Kyrie briefly.

Billy turned toward his sister. "Jess, quit. You know as well as I do that no preacher's daughter hitches it out of this town."

Jessica glared at her brother. "Rumors, Billy. Just fucking rumors."

"Yeah, well, maybe they're not. I don't think Sam ran away, and you know that," he said.

"Just because you think she was gonna settle for trailer trash skanks like us because you kissed when you were fifteen doesn't mean anything, brother. Know your damn place, and you won't get your heart broken."

"Sam? Samantha Payne?" Kyrie asked, interrupting the sibling squabble.

Jessica rolled her eyes. "Yeah. Her dad was the preacher out of town on Highway F. Little Creek Baptist Church. You remember them? They had a big farm. She was Billy's secret girlfriend."

Billy crossed his arms, shaking his head. "It wasn't a secret. We were fucking fifteen—"

Jessica sneered. "*You* were fifteen. She was eighteen. She had a car. She just didn't want her jock boyfriend knowing she was finding dates in the kiddie pool."

"Wait ... she was older than you?" I asked Billy.

Billy sat straight. "I've always looked older than my age. For a while, we went to church out there with my aunt Rita before she moved to Montana."

Jessica asked, "Gonna say the bogeyman kidnapped her, too?"

And Billy glared at his sister. "You know how this fucking town is. They take this shit seriously. Every pastor is selling something, And they sure don't enjoy competition."

"What's that mean?" Kyrie asked, eyes alight with anger.

"Everyone is selling something, and a pretty little preacher's daughter brings all the high school boys in, don't you? They need to be saved. Better go fish."

Kyrie stood up in the booth, hands braced on the table. "What? And I'm the bait?"

Billy eyed Kyrie's pretty dress, and I saw her blush under his gaze. I could almost smell her sweat. He held up his hands in surrender. "Have a cow, Davis, damn."

High school hierarchy and mating rituals made no fucking sense to me, but I didn't need this kind of thing right then. I stood, raising my hands. "Could you guys stop it? If all we're going to do is fight, we might as well leave."

"I don't even know why we're here, Hemming," Billy growled.

I could feel Kyrie's emotions grate at the sound of his voice.

"Because if something is happening to the pastors' daughters around here, then Kyrie is in danger. And she's my friend. And if you want to know what happened to Sam, then we need to stop whatever is going to happen next. So what do you know? What do you remember about the time before she went missing?"

"She went into the Archer house the night before she went missing, Billy," Nicole said, half whispering as she placed her elbows on the table. It was the first time the other sister had spoken.

Billy shot her a look. "Shut up."

"What house?" I asked, just as Kyrie spoke up.

"The haunted house on Archer. It's right in town."

CHAPTER SIXTEEN

I'd walked by all the houses in town, and to be honest, I knew a few of them could be what one would describe as haunted if they let their imagination get the best of them. But they just looked like empty, sad houses. They were scary if you hated bugs and spiders and rats. But I hadn't grown up watching scary movies and hearing scary stories. My life was a horror tale before coming here.

Now, the madness *was* here.

"It's just an abandoned house people sometimes drink and smoke in. Nothing more," Billy said.

"I heard you guys fighting about her going there without you," Nicole whispered.

Billy didn't hear her, and Kyrie gave them a dirty look. Probably because Billy said they smoked.

"That house freaks me out. I won't go in it. It gives me nightmares," Jessica said.

"Watching those fucking movies gives you nightmares," Billy mocked. "I should tell dad."

"Like he gives a fuck," Jessica replied, and I could hear the hurt in her voice. She wished he gave a fuck.

"So, does anyone own the house?" I asked, glancing at Nicole, who had gone silent again.

"Someone has to. I don't know; it's never been for sale. It's been a shithole since I was a kid," Billy said.

"Should we find out who owns it?" Kyrie asked, leaning back into her chair. Then, after a second, she snapped her finger. "Mrs. Sampson works for the city. She attends Sunday service every week. And Wednesday nights, too."

"What are you gonna do? Kindly ask her for personal details on a gross house in town?" Jessica asked.

"I don't think that's a bad idea," I said, looking at Kyrie.

"I'll just say I've always wondered who owns the creepy house on Archer and see if she says anything. It's worth a shot, right?" Kyrie asked, hopeful.

Billy leaned forward. "Or, while you're playing pretty pastor's daughter and asking her your little question, I can steal a key to the courthouse."

"Shut the fuck up," Jessica groaned.

"No, I'm serious. I can do it. Just get her out of her pew for a few minutes, and if she leaves her purse behind, bam. I got it. I'll pretend I dropped something."

Kyrie sighed. "You're forgetting about the absolutely absurd part of that plan—you being at my dad's service."

"That's why we gotta work up to it. Find a reason for me to be there. Which is where you come in," he said, pointing to his sisters.

"Jesus Christ, what?" Jessica asked.

Billy raised his other hand, pointing at Kyrie. "You three gotta be friends." Jessica and Kyrie cried out in protest as Nicole stayed silent. Billy ignored them. "Yes, you three become friends. But, Jess, you gotta stop acting like a carbon copy of me and start acting like you want the lord to save your soul. Nicole, you're fine. Keep ... doing you."

Nicole reached for her drink, smiling.

"No one is going to buy that shit," Jessica replied.

CHAPTER SIXTEEN

"Yeah, they will. You just gotta sell it. And pretty boy here is already chummy with God girl, so it'll be fine. We're already laying the groundwork by being seen here now."

"I like it," I said, earning a high five from Billy.

The girls grumbled in their seats but didn't say no.

Before Billy could regale us with more of the plan formulating in his head, I stopped him. "Before we do anything, I want to see this house."

Billy and his sisters pulled out of the Nest, followed by Kyrie and me. I could understand my friend's hesitation, her annoyance. But there was something else. She had some sort of beef with Jessica, but I didn't have time to question her about it on the short ride through the town's lone stoplight before we turned left toward the school.

When we pulled up to the house, I looked out the window. The house could certainly be described as creepy in the right light. I'd missed the house because I rarely went down the main road, or any of the side streets on this end of the school. I always cut across the highway to my house and took the street by Kyrie's house to get to the Nest and on to the bar.

Billy, Jessica, and Nicole got out of the Camaro on the road just ahead of us. Jessica crossed her arms, eyeing the house as Billy waved his arms wide like he was showing off some art he made, like he'd made the damn place creepy. Nicole stayed in the car, looking out the window.

Kyrie heaved out a dramatic breath, then we exited the vehicle, and when I walked up to Billy, he slapped me on the back. "See, just a creepy house. Creepy to some, an opportunity for us degenerates," he replied, turning his dark eyes on Kyrie. She stood close to me, so close I could feel her bare arm against mine.

I stepped away, a strange hum in my ears and an unmistakable dread crawling up my spine. I blinked and everything was dark, a red in the house seeping out.

I blinked again, and it was light.

I shook my head as I stepped closer. An obscured stone walkway led to a porch with no steps on the right side of the house. In the center of the home, five windows arched out, likely what was once a beautiful seating area in a front room. Second-story doors opened to nothing, where balconies must have been, now gone. The windows were black, mirroring the nothingness within. The house must have been white before—when it was still beautiful. The paint was washed away, showing the grey of the wood beneath, weather lashed and old. The main entrance was to the left of the clustered windows, flanked by stone columns and planters, where nothing grew.

I walked toward the house. "You're right. That's a creepy house," I said, keeping my voice even.

"It's not half bad on a summer night when you wanna forget the world," Billy said, his voice faking bravado, laced with something darker.

I tried to imagine him getting wasted there, sinning. Doing all the things Kyrie's dad said would damn you to hell.

In this town, in this world, there were sides. Lines drawn. The druggies and the pure. The trailer trash and the good ole townsfolk. But where I came from, it all blurred. The drugs, the sex, the promised ones. I couldn't understand their cliques and their rivalries. I didn't care about them. All I knew was my friend was scared, having bad dreams, and hearing things. And I wanted to

CHAPTER SIXTEEN

make sense of something for her. If that meant blending what the town deemed as my world and hers, then that's what I would do.

"So, what do you think? Are we gonna steal some keys? Fake some friendships? Figure this shit out, Davis?" Billy asked.

Kyrie glared at Billy. "Call me *Kyrie*. I'm not one of your buddies."

I shot Kyrie a look, and she looked chastised.

When I focused my attention on the Archer house again, I imagined how it would appear at night and closed my eyes briefly, allowing my imagination to take me there. I saw a crack of lightning and two black dogs on either side of the house. A ring of red light, not unlike what I'd imagine in the woods by the pond, glowing behind it. There was something strange about the house; it didn't seem quiet and uninhabited. Billy said kids came here to drink and smoke, but a heavier presence lingered. I thought I smelled the Deacon, and I opened my eyes, looking around to ensure he wasn't standing on the sidewalk watching us. But there was no one there: just the occasional car passing by or someone walking on the sidewalk. No one yelled for us to get off the lawn or told us it was private property. It was a forgotten house, a part of the scenery that likely held no importance to the inhabitants of Hart Hollow. If someone were passing through, they might want to take a photo of the old home, but it looked otherwise lost. I wanted to know who owned it. The desire for knowledge surged in me as my friends bickered around me.

I reached down and fingered the bracelet at my wrist, the one Kyrie had made me. I felt that strange animal humming in my chest, and I couldn't help myself. I looked around to ensure no one had heard it, to ensure it was all in my head. But they were still carrying on, though Kyrie stood still, staring at the structure like a statue. She was lost somewhere, eyes on the roof. And I remembered what she told me, that she had heard something on her roof. The thing from my nightmares came to mind. The winged beast.

Before I could ask her if she was okay, a car came down the hill from the direction of the school.

It was sleek, purring, and Billy grinned widely when he saw it. "Look at that. Just fucking look at that," he said.

Jessica brushed past me and stared at her brother, her hand on her hip. "Look at what?"

Billy looked at me, then at his sister, before pointing to the car as it parked. "Look at what? At *what*? That's a *lady*, Jess. That's a Pontiac Firebird and ..." He squinted his eyes. "Please tell me it has a red velvet interior. Please. Hemming, go ask your girlfriend if she'll take me for a ride."

Ignoring Billy, I stepped closer to the road as the window rolled down.

I hadn't seen Sorina outside of school in weeks. She was never in the cemetery. The lights were never on in her house. She'd vanished since we touched on the stage, since she kissed me in her home. Since she told me to leave.

Since she scared the fucking shit out of me.

And then there she was, parking across from us, opening her car door.

Despite the chill, she has dressed in ripped denim cut-off shorts, her fishnet stockings underneath, and her black combat boots. She had a ripped T-shirt with the words *Fleetwood Mac* on it. Her red hair was pulled into a high ponytail. She looked beautiful and clean, unlike the dark thing she often was at night. The kind of being who swam in dirty ponds, crawled from dark rooftops.

With a slam, she shut her car door and leaned on it, staring at the house as if we weren't there.

CHAPTER SIXTEEN

I turned to my ragtag group of new ... friends. I didn't know what we were. "I'm gonna go talk to her. Kyrie, you can leave me here. She'll either drive me home, or I'll walk."

My friend looked annoyed. "Are you sure?"

"Yeah."

Billy winked at me, and Jessica glanced between Sorina's figure and my face. "That witch is scary. Whatever." She walked away, heading toward Billy's car.

I couldn't disagree. Waving bye to reality, I crossed the street. When I reached her, Sorina pulled out a joint, twisting it in her fingers. "Peace offering?"

I jogged the rest of the way. "Someone could see you, Jesus—" I didn't finish. There was no such thing. I didn't believe in fairytale men who absolved your sins.

But I did believe I needed an explanation from the girl standing before me.

And maybe I owed her my own.

SEVENTEEN

Sorina took us out of town, down Highway 38 in her Pontiac. I hadn't been that way yet, and it made me realize I desperately wanted wheels of my own.

I knew we had money, but I wasn't sure Valerie would part with it to buy me one. She'd purchased two small safes after we arrived in Hart Hollow. One sat in the bottom of my bedroom closet and was filled with the wages I'd earned while we lived our nomadic lifestyle doing odd jobs and waiting tables.

I'd seen a help wanted sign at the Nest earlier, but when Valerie had suggested I get a job, I'd protested the idea. Maybe I needed to rethink it. I wanted my own spending money and a way out of situations I didn't like, like the dinner with the Deacon. If I'd had my own truck, I could have faked being sick and gotten the hell outta there when I got that terrible feeling. Which would have been as soon as I showed up on his doorstep. As soon as I smelled him.

Beside me, Sorina was quiet, the windows down, fall air whipping her ponytail around.

CHAPTER SEVENTEEN

After driving about ten miles, she turned down a drive to what looked like a summer camp. Cabin buildings lined the woods, and a pool with a chained fence was in the center.

Sorina cut the engine, then exited her car. She never lingered.

I followed.

When she got to the fence, Sorina pulled on the chain link, exposing an area that had been cut.

I didn't go through, opting to grab the fence instead, motioning for her to go ahead—like a gentleman.

She slipped through the fence with no sound, not a part of her snagging. When she reached the other side, she placed her hand where mine was, and I let go, following her in.

I walked past her, heading to the other side of the pool, staring into the sky, half expecting the thing from my nightmares to arrive. Bad shit always happened when I was around her. Waking or dreaming.

Sorina pulled out the joint again, then a lighter. I walked back to her when I smelled it, heard the clink of the metal in her hand. She took a long drag, then held it up to me, an offering.

I shook my head.

"So, what were you doing at the Archer house?" she asked, blowing smoke from her nostrils.

I crossed my arms, walking around the pool. "I don't know. Might hang out there with my new friends. We're trying to find out who owns it."

Sorina grinned, incisors catching my eye. "A few of us know who owns the house."

"Who?" I asked.

"Me. Diana. We have deep roots."

I tested her. "Yet you're both *new* to town, just like me," I said, turning my head to the side, a smirk there.

"What's new is old, sometimes."

My smirk fell away, and I bit my tongue, drawing blood. "Ah yes, the lovely fucking riddles and poems. Missed those. Where have you been?" I asked. I could hear the breaking, and I knew then that Sorina heard it too. Felt it. The nightmares had been worse since she'd been absent. I hadn't been sleeping well. What haunted me was that first night after she kicked me out. I felt like she was in my bed with me, holding me close. I felt her bare skin against mine, and it didn't hurt. It didn't make me sick; I wanted to rip my skin from my bones and light it on fire.

It made me feel safe. I'd never felt safe in my life with someone else. Sometimes when I was alone, I felt safe, but never with someone. Not even with Valerie.

"Why are you hanging around those kids, acting like you're Scooby Doo's gang or something?"

"What the fuck is Scooby Doo? That brown dog?" I never had a childhood, and when I was free of the cage of the ranch, I immersed myself in literature that was beyond my age.

"Sorry," Sorina said, taking another long drag. "Sometimes I forget you're not like the rest of them. That you don't get those … references. And I should just speak how I am."

I was tired of the riddles, the way she danced around everything. "Then just talk to me however the fuck you are."

Sorina walked around the pool toward me but I walked away. Something resembling hurt flickered across her face.

She tried again. "Why are you making friends?"

CHAPTER SEVENTEEN

"Isn't that what normal teenagers are supposed to do?"

"You're not a normal teenager. I think you know that," she said.

"Thanks for the reminder," I replied.

"I ..." Sorina opened her mouth, then shut it, her lips a hard line. Something passed over her face. A decision of some sort. "I thought I said to leave town."

"Instead of being a runaway, I think I'd rather figure out what happened to the others."

"It's not safe. And they can't help you understand what's going on. They can't stop it. *You* can't stop it. Not without putting a target on your back."

"So I'll just leave the target on Kyrie?"

"Take Kyrie with you, then. Just leave."

I arched a brow. "I thought you said she didn't like me like that?"

"She doesn't. I didn't say run away together and get married. I just said take her with you."

"And what happens to the next girl?"

"The rituals of small towns, that's not your problem. It's mine."

I stopped my escape and let Sorina make it to me. I felt like my body was on fire whenever she was near me. I could still feel her lips, her small body wrapping around me, what I thought was a dream, but maybe it was real. I was tired of wondering.

"That night you gave me a smoke for the first time. Did you sleep in my bed?"

"Yes."

"Did you touch me?" My throat hurt, and I closed my eyes, willing the past to stay there.

"Not like that. I just …" she looked away into the trees. The dark of her eyes growing. "I held you. Slept. I left when I heard Valerie waking up."

"She could have seen you."

"She's blind to anything to do with you now, now that you're here. She has a weak mind and a sour soul. But, she'll take to it."

"To what?"

"His … congregation."

"The Deacon?"

"Yes."

I shook my head, denial thick. "She hasn't talked about the Deacon since that night we had dinner with him. I told her I didn't want to go to church, but she thinks … we can start over with God or something. I don't know."

"God has nothing to do with what's he's selling her."

I remembered my fear, my words to Kyrie that night. *I think he wants to fuck my aunt.* "Should I be worried about her?"

Sorina smiled, and there was nothing but sadness in it. I didn't understand it then and would be blind to it for a while. Then, I would feel it too.

"You should fear her." Her voice was a whisper, and I laughed at her comment. Scared of Valerie? No. She wasn't a shell anymore; she wasn't cowering. She'd gotten us out of that hellhole, that awful place. We weren't close, never felt like family, but she took me away from it all. I owed her my life.

Sorina walked away to the edge of the pool, then dropped, going for the laces of her boots.

I asked, "What are you doing?"

CHAPTER SEVENTEEN

And she looked up at the sky. The sun was fading away. It was getting dark earlier, fall enveloping us in her cool embrace.

"Going for a swim," Sorina said, looking me in the eye. "And you're going to join me."

I walked to the edge of the pool, crouching down. My eyes roved over Sorina as she took her boots off and shimmied down her shorts. I watched her unapologetically because I thought maybe she wanted that. To distract me. But I was already distracted. The pool was much cleaner than the dirty pond, and I was curious to know if I would feel that strange pull again when we entered the water. When I blinked, I saw the glowing red circle in the woods by the school.

I removed my shoes, then my jeans, before ripping my shirt over my head. I stood in my boxers, eyeing the water, then staring off into the distance, to the trees.

When I looked up at Sorina, she had her own shirt off, and she hadn't been wearing a bra. I saw a glimpse of her nipples before she dove into the water, red hair moving like blood.

I joined her, diving in, remembering hot days on the ranch, the derelict pool on the back half.

When I surfaced, Sorina was on the opposite side of the pool, at the shallow end, walking around in slow circles. Her breasts were just above the surface, the light from the building beside us shining on her pale skin as the sun left us.

"I'm going to Moonies tonight. I want to talk to Diana about the house. Maybe I'll get more out of her than you," I said, swimming to the end of the pool, grabbing the ledge. Sorina walked closer, eventually reaching a spot her feet couldn't touch, swimming out.

"A Priest, Father Scott, built it after the Civil War, in 1880. Ten years before Steele Mansion was built. Did you see the building that looked like a church across the street?" she asked.

"Yes." There were churches everywhere.

"It's not a church. Not anymore. It's now a ... they call them a Veteran's Hall. But it used to be the lone Catholic church in town. Then ten years later Captain O.R. Steele, a Civil War soldier for the Union, moved to Hart Hollow and built Steele Mansion on the hill. The Captain attended the Catholic church across the street from the Archer house and grew close to Father Scott. It didn't take long for the Captain to decide—after everything he'd seen in the war—that he wanted to become a Deacon."

My heart stopped at her words, but she continued.

"The new Deacon studied under Father Scott, grew closer to the Lord, grew closer with the community. And when Father Scott died, and Deacon Steele took his place, he moved the small Catholic congregation to a new church adjoining his home. The old church within city limits was sold. The house across the street, without Father Scott to attend to it, fell into disarray. It was willed to an unknown man, a man who never visited Hart Hollow, Missouri. It was planned that way. It was built on a crack, a fault line."

"Are there earthquakes here? I thought that was just in California."

"They happen here, few and far between. Most people don't feel them. But certain kinds of people do. If there was one right now, I'd feel it. So would you."

I closed my eyes, trying to digest the information she had given me. I gave up, coming back to her comment. "Because I'm ... not a normal teenager," I said, making air quotes.

"Yes."

CHAPTER SEVENTEEN

"How do you know so much about a town you just moved to?"

"My family has always come here ... for the exchange." Her words sounded fake, lies she barely concealed.

"Your mother, from Romania, she came here too?"

"Yes," Sorina said, swimming closer. I felt like prey, like a lamb, and she was the wolf.

"Why did you kiss me?" I asked, reaching for her in the water, grazing her leg. "Why are we—*what* are we doing?"

She ducked under the water, and I felt her close. Hand on my hips, mouth at the hem of my boxers. She kissed me, then swam away, breaking the surface behind me.

I was hard. Angry. Confused.

I turned in the water, splashing some on her face. She looked incredibly young when she smiled, wiping the water away. It was her mouth, the sharp canines, the slant of her jaw. But when I looked into her eyes, she didn't look young. The black was taking over, pushing away her blue. "Do it again. And this time, don't make me leave," I said, almost begging.

"I will if you leave that house alone. If you leave all of it alone," she said, swimming closer.

I grinned, and it felt wicked. She invaded my space; her legs going around my waist as her hands gripped shoulders. I grabbed her hip with one hand under the surface, the other arm keeping us afloat. She was so small, dainty, almost gaunt. She looked like a ghost, and I wanted her to touch me; I tried to touch her, but I didn't know how to do it without feeling the way I felt on the stage, full of heat and rage. I never agreed to her terms, couldn't allow myself to.

Sorina pushed her wet hair from her face, eyes close to me, breath on me. It was cool. "I want you to pretend I'm someone else," she said, hand gripping my neck.

I furrowed my brow.

"Jessica," she said. "If you will not leave, live a normal life here. Pretend you don't hear the whispers; pretend you can't feel the dread. Date and fuck, go to prom, and play on the basketball team, Nicholas. Do all the stuff that was robbed from you before. You have a chance to start over here. Don't get caught up in the omens."

I wanted to do what she said. To live a normal life. The kind of shit I read about in books or watched on the TV shows I caught after school sometimes. I wanted to sink into a blissfully ordinary life, but the wolf was at the doorstep. *My* doorstep. All of my ominous wonderings and nightmares led to him—the winged beast of my dreams, the savior Markus had described on the ranch. The savior he said would take us all away to the promised land if we did what he said. Jesus Christ, the Vampire King.

What a fucking joke. What a fucking lunatic.

I swam backward, bringing the two of us to the pool's edge. When my back hit the side, Sorina's arms gripped the ledge, bringing her closer to me. I could feel her nipples on my chest, her breath at my ear. "I can teach you how to be normal. I've gotten good at pretending."

I laughed, shaking my head. "You're fucking awful at it. Everyone thinks you're a freak."

Sorina pulled away, but I felt her nip at my earlobe before she did. Her black eyes peered at me, and I let mine see everything. Her lips, her jaw, her neck. When my eyes landed on her small breasts, I thought I could hear her heart beating. I remembered the way they felt between my teeth, under my tongue.

CHAPTER SEVENTEEN

"Do you want to be a freak, too? I can teach you that as well. Though, I think you'd be a quick study," she teased.

She ground into me, and I think I growled. Something animalistic came from my throat, and the blue of her eyes glinted in the light. I saw recognition there. She knew what it was; I didn't though. Not yet. I thought I saw fear, arousal, and a sad acceptance. None of it made sense.

"I'm sorry about what happened to you, Nicholas," Sorina said, low, almost apologetic. "My hands can hurt, but they won't hurt you," she whispered, trailing her fingers down my neck, to my chest, thumb grazing my nipple, then she gripped my ribs.

"Do you want to play a game with me again?"

I closed my eyes and saw a fleeting shadow on her face, an upside-down cross, an omen.

When I opened my eyes, I nodded. "Yeah," I groaned. Let's play."

She dove beneath the surface, gripping me, taking me in her mouth with no preamble, no warning as I closed my eyes and prayed my mind would stay there in the present—stay on her.

A strangled moan escaped my lips, unabashed, and I felt safe in the open, where no one could hear me, watch, hold me captive. I didn't expect it to last long with Sorina under the surface, but she stayed submerged. Her hands gripped my base, her throat taking me in. I clutched the side of the pool, head falling back, hips surging forward, but in a flash, my mind broke—taking me back to when everything was taken from me. I opened my eyes, the present flashing to me as I reached below, grabbing Sorina's ponytail, pulling her to the surface.

She wiped her eyes, streaks of black across her cheeks, and my name, *Nicholas*, fell from her mouth in a question, as I pulled her close and kissed her hard.

It was still a lesson, and I felt unsure, but my mouth moved knowingly. My tongue swirled with hers, and when I pulled her flush against me, she pressed her center to my hard lines. Her hands gripped my hips, the dips and bone, the muscles that seemed to become more defined every day. When I pulled away, I pressed my forehead to hers. "I want to ... I want nothing done to me." I didn't wonder if she would understand my words. She understood everything—my silences, my pauses, my body language.

She reached up and wrapped her hand around the back of my neck. "There is *to* you, and *for* you. One day you will feel the difference, feel the heart behind the hands. With the right person."

I didn't argue that she *was* that person. That she was what I needed. I simply wanted to bring sounds from her mouth, fall into the game again in some way, so I pulled her from the water, small frame, pale skin under the light. I spun around and placed her on the edge, and her hands on my shoulders fell away as she fell back, knowing what I wanted to taste, to touch.

The air was chilly, and our bodies mirrored the night, but I wanted the cold. I felt warm all over, like I could scorch the water, make it steam as I pressed against Sorina's thighs, spreading her legs. I stared at the sliver of black silk covering her, saw that she was swollen around it, flushed red. I thought I could hear her heart beating, but I wasn't sure what was real anymore.

I locked my hands around her thighs, pulling her closer, hearing the rough sound of her flesh dragging along the concrete, though she didn't let out a cry, didn't protest. All she did was reach up, cup her breast. I hoped it was all real, not for show after my anger on the stage when she was silent, making me feel like I was one of them—one who takes.

Pushing the past away, I focused on what her mouth and done to me, the swirl of her tongue, the graze of her teeth. It should have frightened me, with remnants of my dreams on the edges of my memories, but it didn't. My chest ached and dreams and wants blurred. I imagined Sorina running into the woods, her sheer black dress, me in pursuit.

It made me hungry; it made me alive. I pulled the small fabric to the side, exposing her to the chilly night. She arched off the ledge, and I moved closer, inhaling her, moaning. I felt like an animal ready to feast. I closed my eyes, inhaled, and breathed out a hot breath.

I thought I heard my name again.

I couldn't be sure, and the only thing I *was* sure of was that I wanted to do something *for* her, as she'd said. I wanted to practice on her what I wanted her to do in return. So I lost myself in her body, licking, sucking, pressing my fingers to her slick wetness, listening when her hand on my wrist told me what to do. She clenched around my fingers as I worked her, clutched herself as I stared on in amazement. When did a teenage boy have the dark goddess from his dreams before him?

Never.

Now.

Forever.

I crawled out of the pool, my wet body covering hers. And though I wanted to bury myself in her, I was afraid of her—afraid of myself. Afraid I would break open and she would see me for the boy they hurt, not the man I was becoming.

Sorina looked into my eyes, her own almost black, and I saw a red circle in her eyes, two reflections. I blinked, and it was gone as she pushed my shoulder down, climbing on top of me.

She tugged at my boxers, and that's when everything stopped. The night blinked, and the stars were ink for a moment, and I let out a breath that was more a cry than a plea.

Sorina stopped just as I grabbed her wrists. I push the blinking memories from my mind and kissed her with every broken piece of me to quiet my cry.

Her wet hair tickled my neck and jaw when she pulled away. "I'm sorry," she said, her hand on my face. "I'm sorry."

When I opened my eyes, I felt tears fall, and I hoped she couldn't see them, though I knew better. "Just let me touch you. I want to touch you," I said.

Everything was still fresh, my wounds and my scars. She carried her own, but I would learn how hard hers were, scarred over and over again, deeper than mine. She was hard, and I was soft in so many ways.

That night it was my hands.

She rolled over, and when her beautiful mouth opened in sighs, I wanted to kiss her teeth and red tongue. I wanted to know everything I did for her was bliss.

I wanted to know that the dark part of me that wanted to tie her up so she couldn't touch me was quiet.

As I nipped her nipples, bit her rib cage, and sucked at her wet heat, the voice quieted. All I could hear was her; and all I could see was what the moon showed me.

EIGHTEEN

My frame of reference for what a normal household would look like back then was the television shows I'd been watching after school since we moved to Hart Hollow, and Kyrie's house. So when I walked into Billy's trailer, I knew their home did not fit the mold.

There was a couch in the living area with a bed pulled out. No coffee table. No end tables. Instead, there was a dresser and some metal structure where identical work shirts were hung.

Kyrie walked in behind me, an unsure look on her face as she reached for my hand. I gave it a squeeze, quickly letting go.

From the kitchen area, Billy grinned at me. "It's a real house of horrors, isn't it?"

I walked into the kitchen, Kyrie close behind. "The one on Archer, yeah."

"No, I meant—"

"I know what you meant." I recognized it then, though I didn't quite understand it. Billy's shame couldn't get him if he made a joke first, if he owned who he was.

He didn't have to make excuses for me; what did I know about class and everyday life? Nothing.

But maybe the show was for Kyrie.

Billy motioned to the living room. "My dad made the living room his bedroom so my sisters could each have their own room. He works at the Barrel Mill in Lenore. Night shift."

It explained the bed, the dresser, and the quilts adhered to the wall with what I would later learn was a staple gun. The staples were embedded haphazardly in the wood-paneled walls.

Billy's sisters came down the opposite hall. Jessica had a bag of Cheetos in one hand, and Nicole had her arms crossed. I didn't know her well yet; she'd barely spoken at the Nest, and they didn't look like twins, not identical. Nicole looked shrunken in herself. Like she wanted to hide from the room.

Jessica walked into the kitchen, offering the snack to Kyrie. She shook her head.

"Okay, Princess," Jessica said, hopping onto the kitchen counter. "Where do we do this? Not the living room. Dad hates it when you even look at his stuff."

"Well, he'd be here more to watch his stuff if he wasn't stuffing that widow behind the Mill after work every day," Billy said.

"God, Billy, don't go there. We have guests," Jessica said.

It would always be like that; Billy would say something disparaging about their trailer, their life, and their father. And Jessica would fight back while Nicole watched on.

I would grow to feel at home in this family's presence.

"If you would move out and get a real life, dad could have his bedroom back," Jessica snapped.

CHAPTER EIGHTEEN

Billy walked over to this sister, putting her in a headlock. "And if you two freaks would get a life out of this damn trailer, maybe sharing a room wouldn't seem so bad, and then dad could have his room back. But you two losers have no friends and spend every waking hour in those rooms watching *America's Funniest Home Videos*. So spoiled, I say." He laughed, letting go of Jessica. "I never had a TV when I was in high school."

"Maybe you should have stolen one like dad did then," Nicole said.

"I would have gladly taken a stolen TV, Nicole," Billy replied. "But I was too busy watching your bratty asses when I was in high school, so when would I have had the time to lounge around and watch *Ren and Stimpy* or read *Sweet Valley High?*"

Jessica threw a cheese snack at Billy, and he swooped down, catching it in his mouth. He chomped on the bright orange puff, then opened his arms wide. "Let's take this meeting to my bedroom, shall we?"

We followed him past the tiny pantry area to the master bedroom. Nothing was masterful about it, but it was the largest room in the trailer.

Billy flicked on a small lamp as we walked in, heading to his bed. Jessica walked to the front of it, taking a seat out of the floor. I pulled out a chair from a small desk, offered it to Kyrie, and took a seat on the floor in front of her. It was … cramped, stuffy in the room. A small breeze rushed through the window, and streamers taped to the glass extended as the cool fall air passed through.

Billy leaned against the wall, eyeing me. "So what's the plan, fearless leader? What'd the red-haired witch have to talk to you about?"

The blush was immediate, and I was transported back to the pool for a moment, to the things Sorina and I did.

She taught me things with her touch, let me taste her, then left me on my doorstep, bewildered.

Billy's face morphed into a salacious grin. "You dog ..."

I heard Kyrie shift behind me. "What?"

"You hooked up, didn't you?" he asked.

Jessica leaned forward. "With the Romanian chick? Dalton is gonna be pissed."

"Dalton Wakefield?" Nicole asked.

Jessica nodded her head. "Yeah, she's all he talks about in math, because he has English with her, and he will not shut up about her."

I'd never talked to Dalton Wakefield, but from what I'd gathered, he was one of the most popular guys in school. A junior like me, he was the captain of the basketball team and the baseball team's pitcher. That's about all I knew.

Behind me, Kyrie placed her palm on my shoulder. "Did you?"

I didn't brush her hand away, and I didn't answer her question. Instead, I stood up, running a hand through my hair. "I don't think we're here to talk about my ... life. We're here to talk about our *plan*." I felt territorial about Sorina, protective of our moments. I finally had something private, something my own.

"Okay, what is it then?" Jessica asked.

I glanced at her, my eyes quickly moving to Nicole. There was something in the way she looked at me. Like she'd been watching me for a while. I would later learn she had been since the first day of school.

Though I'd told Sorina I would leave the house on Archer alone, I couldn't. My friends wanted this, and Kyrie was scared. The information Sorina had given me on the Archer house hadn't quelled my curiosity. It only worked to fuel it. I wanted to know why Sam went into the house, and if it had anything to do with her disappearance. I cleared my throat. "We go to the house at night. Different nights. We have to see if anyone is going in."

"All of us? Like every night?" Jessica asked.

"No, we'll take turns teams of—"

"Two," Nicole said.

"That doesn't work," Jessica countered.

"She shouldn't go," Nicole said, pointing at Kyrie. Her voice had that same haunted sound it did at the Nest when she mentioned the house, causing us to go down this path.

"Why?" Kyrie asked, and though I knew she had no desire to enter the house, she sounded curious now that she was being told she shouldn't.

"Do you want to go in?" Jessica asked, leaning forward.

Before she answered, Nicole, continued, "Isn't she why we're here? You're afraid you're next, right?"

Kyrie nodded.

"And I want to find out if something happened to Sam," Billy said from the bed, his voice a little deeper.

"Okay, let's make a schedule," Jessica said, standing from the floor and tossing the bag of Cheetos to her twin.

And so began our dumbass plan.

○○

I walked Kyrie home, the silence deafening, surrounding us like a thick fog in the night.

Before we left the trailer park, I'd grabbed a flannel from my trailer and offered it to Kyrie. She took it, pulling the fabric close around her. I knew she was stewing on her thoughts, her convictions, and conflicting emotions. Maybe regretting our new, strange group of friends.

Finally, when her house was in view, she spoke. "I've lived here my whole life, Nicholas. Hart Hollow is all I know. And, it's not always enough. Sometimes I want to run away just like the other girls. Where I can be myself, without my parents telling me who I should be."

I glanced at her and asked, "Who do they tell you should be?"

Kyrie sighed. "My mom wants me to be just like her. I think maybe so she'll feel better about her life. She wants me to settle down with a nice man, maybe with a farm, and he'll decide to preach the word of the Lord like my father. I'll come over to my parents' house on Sundays, and we'll make pies together after morning sermons."

"Do you think your father wants you to be like your mother?" I asked.

"Yes. Because then I'll be manageable. He can understand me if he can control me. But I'm not like her. I don't like the things she does. Not all of them ..."

"Do you think the other girls felt the way you do? And they really ran away?" I asked, eyeing the perfect flowers in Kyrie's yard in the distance, the pristine lawn. Everything about her life seemed perfect to me in comparison to the checkered history of my own, and all the things I could never tell my friend.

"I thought that was a possibility," she said. "Because I could understand it. It was always there, just under the surface, that

CHAPTER EIGHTEEN

same feeling I thought they must have felt. And I thought, *good for them*, when my father lamented their wildness." She laughed, sad and lost somewhere.

"And now?" I asked.

"I-I don't know. The dreams, the nightmares. I just. I wonder if they felt it too."

"Well, maybe we can find that out. Is it only the daughters of pastors? Or is it—"

"Is it just them who get noticed? Who get missed?" Kyrie interrupted, finishing my question.

"Yeah," I said.

She shrugged her shoulders. "I guess we can find out. Let's add it to the investigation list." She sounded almost amused by our mission, like perhaps deep down she was enjoying it.

"You can handle being around them? The trailer park kids?" I asked, smirking.

Kyrie smiled in return and said, "It's not that … it's not … I don't know. Maybe I should be nicer."

"Isn't that what you're supposed to be?" I joked. Unfortunately, the joke didn't land, and Kyrie whirled on me.

"Yeah, it is what I'm *supposed* to be. No personality. Nothing beyond the good little church girl. I changed that with you." She waved a hand at me.

I jerked my head back. "With me?"

"Didn't you know? Girls and boys can't be friends. Not *teenage* boys and *teenage* girls. My dad hates it. Hates me hanging out with you. Can't understand what I'm saying when I say we're *friends*. He can't fathom it. Because he and mom met when they were our age."

"So, he thinks we're secretly dating?" I asked.

"He thinks you're going to deflower me."

We both laughed at the absurdity of it all. Kyrie liked to touch me, and I always pulled away. But I saw it now as nothing more than her affection, the way she showed the people she cared about that she cared about them. The touch of a hand, the kiss of a cheek, a hug when she thought you looked far away. I didn't know it then, but I loved her. I wasn't *in* love with her, but I loved her like a friend, and I'd never had a friend before. I'd had family, broken leaders, and those who took from me.

Kyrie didn't want to take from me, she wanted to be close to me, and I'd been keeping her at an arm's length because I thought she wanted me the way the women had. It wasn't ego; it was instinct. Trauma manifested into a shield.

"I promise, I'll never want to deflower you. I'll save that for your future husband."

Kyrie flinched at the word, and I didn't understand it, not yet. So in the light of Kyrie's front porch, I did the only thing I could think to do; I spoke her language. I pulled Kyrie to me and hugged her swiftly and tightly, letting her go just as her arms reached my back.

My face was an apology when I pulled away, hers was one of acceptance.

I thought I saw a curtain move behind Kyrie, and I stepped back. "Well, I'll see you in school tomorrow. Let's talk at lunch. We can get the twins to sit with us. Go over the plan," I said. "The study plan," I amended, louder.

"It's pizza day tomorrow." Kyrie smiled, walking backward toward her door.

CHAPTER EIGHTEEN

I grinned wide. She had no idea how delicious it was to me, after all the bad things I'd tasted in my life, but she knew it was my favorite. That's what friendship was—knowing people, caring for them, loving them.

NINETEEN

Valerie could not help the smile that stretched her face that day when the waitress returned, saying a customer wanted to compliment the chef. She knew who it was, knew his order, knew this schedule. She'd been feeding him, watching him come and go with no word, for weeks. Ever since that night on the hill, the Deacon had been a shadow in her daylight hours, a menace in her dreams.

It wasn't wise to have a schoolgirl crush on the Deacon, but if he didn't *want* to be looked at in such a way, why was he so beautiful?

Pretty flower, full of thorns.

The words came back to her. It was how the man with the scar once described her, and now it was how she thought of the Deacon.

She walked out into the café, hands clasped, and the Deacon stood from his table, reaching for his cane. He was tall, with broad shoulders she wanted to reach for. She chastised herself for these thoughts, the lustful desires, but was never successful in banishing them.

CHAPTER NINETEEN

She reminded herself that he wanted to share the lord with her in the right way. Not the way Markus had.

She smiled when she reached him, hoping he could sense it. "Good morning, Deacon Rex, how are you today?" she asked, hoping her voice sounded just right, just perfect enough to make him stay in her life.

"I'm well, Valerie. And you?" he asked, almost shy. She watched him move, shifting his weight on his feet, tilting his head. "I hope ... I hope the night we had dinner didn't scare you off. I hadn't heard from you in a while, and ... Being up on the hill, away from town, animals, they ..."

Valerie's heart stammered at his words as he trailed off. *He hadn't heard from me? From me?* She'd been so embarrassed by her fear, her goodbye that night laced with shock and something else. The scream of the animal had taken her back to the last night in California. She saw the strangers who'd entered the property, the fire, her own hands dripping in blood. She'd heard a cry like that animal's that night, in the distance. She'd fled with Nicholas, hoping to never see what could make such a sound. And then it was there, on the hill, so close. And she'd felt like her past had followed her like a black dog.

An omen.

She cleared her throat and smiled at the Deacon. "I can hardly hold you responsible for the beings of the night," she whispered. She did not know the ways he would bend her. But she had been frightened, worried. An all too familiar unfamiliar dread had settled over her, so she did what she always did after she left his property.

Put her head down, did her work, isolated.

The Deacon's voice was warm. "For that, I thank you. How's Nicholas?"

Valerie stepped forward, moving to the seat opposite the one the Deacon had vacated. There were no other patrons in the café at the moment, and the lone waitress was behind the counter, working on her crossword puzzle. She was likely listening, but Valerie tried to ignore that. The Deacon always came after the rush when the café was quiet. Maybe he liked the quiet as much as her, she wondered.

"He's fine. He forgot all about the thing in the road as soon as we left. I'm sure he has bigger concerns. He's a normal teenage boy, I guess." She knew it was a lie. She didn't view Nicholas as normal and didn't know anyone she would call such a word.

"So he's rebellious. Raging with hormones. Petulant. A little lost?" The Deacon smiled, retaking his seat. He leaned his cane on the table, and it slid away, along the table, toward Valerie. She reached for it, halting the fall, and so did the Deacon, their hands touching briefly.

She felt a charge at his cool touch, a burst of energy straight to her center. His touch did what he desired, what he wanted. She didn't understand it, couldn't know the manipulation. The traps being laid. It was familial, and she buoyed the desire.

The Deacon pulled the cane toward him. "I'd hoped, as some time has gone by since, that maybe you talked to him about coming to Mass on Sunday? Or to confession tonight? I know he was vehemently opposed to the idea before, but ..."

It was Wednesday, and she'd been counting the days. She always counted the days between Sunday Mass and Wednesdays, when he said he liked to be present in the small, round church for confession. She's hoped the Deacon would reach out again after the disastrous dinner. She wanted to be chased. It didn't matter if Nicholas wanted to go; she would go. She'd bought a new dress. Well, new to her, at the thrift store just past the four-way stop.

CHAPTER NINETEEN

She'd bought a Cosmopolitan at the Town and Country Supermarket and decided how she would do her hair.

She felt foolish when she tried a few styles, staring at her reflection in her bathroom mirror at the trailer, cursing herself. *What the fuck am I doing?* She'd wondered.

But she knew what she was doing now with him sitting in front of her in the café. She was searching for a friend, maybe more.

Something she'd never had before.

She'd always wondered if something was wrong with her, something dark in the pit of her writhing, that came from her biological parents. It manifested into her belly, her heart. Her deformity. That which kept her pure on the ranch, untouched—*Virgin Valerie*. Delegated to the kitchen, to the shadows. She liked it where she could observe, could watch as the sins mounted, the tower high.

She never liked Markus, *the* Father. But God? God, she loved. She loved his word, his life, the meaning she desperately craved. They'd twisted it on the ranch, but she never left. Couldn't leave. She had nowhere to go after what she'd done to her sister and Gregory. And she had a purpose there on the ranch. Feed them. Nourish them. Her creations were beautiful, and she found art in food, in the bounty. But it never nourished the men she fed. A curse. But she was oblivious to it. And besides, most of the inhabitants of the ranch were women. Daughters of Markus.

For years, she was unaware, just as they were. Or pretended to be.

And when the truth came to light, the ranch burned.

It burned, and she fled. Taking Nicholas with her. Penance for living in the house of a pretender. Penance, perhaps, for the things she'd done.

She'd never stepped foot inside a church. Not a proper church, though while on the road, she could have tried. There was the church on the ranch, but she didn't consider that real. She thought of Charla's words one afternoon when the Deacon had left, not speaking to Valerie, not drawing her out. She'd said God had never been her thing, she never believed in an all-knowing man who lived in clouds. *Everything happens for a reason? Bullshit.*

Wanting to orbit the Deacon was laughable. She wasn't sure why she was doing it. It was simple on the surface, if she left her wonderings there. It was his calm voice, the smile he wore.

Valerie was attracted to him. And she was rarely attracted to anyone.

The God and the Monster. We'd make a pretty pair.

She wondered if he could exorcise the demons writhing in her blood, wash away the sin from her hands. If anyone could, it was him.

The Deacon cleared his throat, and Valerie came back to the present with a jolt. "I'm sorry, I didn't mean to startle you, Valerie."

"You—you didn't startle me," she whispered, wondering sometimes if he could see her.

"You just seemed a bit faraway for a moment there. Where did you go?"

Valerie smiled, placing her hands on the table, looking at the chipped polish. Her pretty hands had been waiting for him to show up, but the show was just for her. He could not see her feeble attempts to look beautiful. "Nowhere," Valerie said, shaking her head.

"Well, I won't keep you then, Valerie. I know you have to get back to work." He smiled, and she was softened by it. The Deacon was handsome in all his sharp edges. "I just wanted to let you know the church doors are always open. My doors are always open. And my phone is ready." He reached into his pocket and grabbed a piece of paper and a pen. He scribbled his phone number and slid it over to Valerie, brushing his fingers against hers.

She blushed and couldn't recall the last time she had touched someone willingly.

"Have a good day, Valerie. And a good Thanksgiving coming soon." He saluted and smiled again. She watched him stand, taking his cane, taking sure steps out of the door. She watched him through the glass as he walked away along the sidewalk. Charla was likely watching her, but she didn't care.

The Deacon was not a pretender. And she wanted to follow him.

She would follow him to Hell in search of Heaven.

TWENTY

I respected closed books, those that begged to be opened slowly, revealed page by page. That's who Nicole Clement was. And though I wasn't the one she wanted flipping through the pages of her mind, I was the first to slip in that day in late November before Thanksgiving break.

"I'd like you to pair up. Find a partner," our teacher said, earning a collective groan from my classmates as I stared out the window, watching leaves fall off the ever-watching trees. I glanced back at my classmates, watching their faces scrunch up in annoyance. It was a popularity test, a bullseye on those with few friends. I was one of those people, but it didn't hit me the same way. I was happy to have the few friends I had. Even if our sole purpose for hanging out was to solve the town mystery.

I looked around the room, locking eyes with Nicole, and she gave me a small wave. It was the first time we had communicated directly, away from the others. She was the quiet twin, and she faded away in the room when Jessica was bulls-eyeing the attention. I nodded, and she picked up her books and came over to my table, sitting at the empty seat.

CHAPTER TWENTY

Her smile was less bright when I saw it up close. "Hey," she said, sitting down.

"Tell me you're not going to drop me as a partner if I fuck this up," I joked, trying to ease her. Kyrie and I had been studying together since my first day, and though it was sometimes apparent that I had little high school history, I read all the time and penned every thought in my head, helping to make up for the experience I lacked.

"Does it look like I'm rolling in options for a partner? I think you're safe," Nicole said, opening her book before absently running a hand through her hair.

"Okay, but don't say I didn't warn you," I replied, opening my own.

We followed along with the teacher for the first half of class, then huddled together when he assigned the chapter to study. I was eager to discuss our subject, and when Nicole looked at me, I could tell she felt the same way.

"Mythology fascinates and scares me. Do you think it was real?" Nicole asked, staring at a sketch of Odin.

"I don't know. I'm not sure I believe in anything," I admitted. "Though I do enjoy the stories, and the way writers use the stories to create modern interpretations."

Nicole stared at me, dumfounded, then blinked. "You're not like the boys here."

I smiled, not knowing how to take that. "Okay."

She shook her head. "And you don't believe in anything at all? Not even God?"

"No," I replied, firm.

"Sometimes I don't either," Nicole said, brushing her hair away from her face. She was pretty in a way you had to study. Unearth. Her hair was often in her face, her clothes baggy. She smelled like soap and a flowery perfume.

"Is that so bad?" I asked.

"Here in Hart Hollow it can be," she said, staring at the words on the pages. "And I wish I still did."

"Believe in God?" I flipped through pages of the book, pausing briefly at each sketch.

"Yeah, I guess I don't anymore. Not really," she said. "It's hard, after what happened."

"Did you know Amber?" I asked.

"Yeah, she was my lab partner in biology last year."

And there it was, hidden away. The strongest tie to the most recent runaway girl. My body hummed with the knowledge, something Nicole had failed to mention during our meeting of ragtag sleuths.

I leaned in close. "How come you didn't say that at your house the other night?"

"I don't know," she said, and I saw the lie on her lips, heard it in her tone. I didn't know it yet, but I could sniff out a lie and smell it in the air.

"Nicole ..." I said, leaning closer, ready to pry, but she didn't let me continue.

"We were friends," Nicole said, her voice low. "We shouldn't have been, she was ... she was who she is, and I'm ... well, you know."

I shook my head. "I don't know, though everyone keeps telling me I should know. I didn't grow up knowing all these rules and things you guys have. Living where we live makes us bad, and being who she is, someone like Kyrie, makes her good? Aren't we all a little bit good and bad? Like Athena," I mused, referencing the chapter we had read recently. I couldn't get over Medusa's fate.

"Yes. But her boyfriend—"

"Eric Childress?" The captain of the basketball team, his name meant something in that small town. His father was the Sheriff, and his mother was the vice principal of the elementary school, which could be found on the other side of the cafeteria. The entire school shared the same cafeteria; that's how small it was. But I knew nothing different. It was vast, crowded, a labyrinth I was happy to traverse. It beat the alternative.

Nicole leaned closer, hiding behind her hair. "If we were talking about an assignment or anything in the hall, and Eric walked up, she would turn her back to me, act like we hadn't just been talking to each other. I was nothing when he was near, and she acted like …" She stopped there, a blush taking over her face. I didn't press further, but I would later.

"I'm sorry."

"For what?" she asked.

"That she treated you that way. And that you miss her."

Nicole's green eyes held a glimmer, looking at me like she had been seen for the first time in a long time. I didn't know what it was like to have a sibling, let alone a twin who was more enigmatic than you, overshadowing you every time she was in the room. But I knew what it felt like to be invisible or think that you were. Strangely, moving to Hart Hollow, starting school there, and making friends had been the first time I'd felt anything remotely like a family—like I mattered.

"I miss her," Nicole whispered. "And, I could never tell anyone because they'd never believe that we were friends or anything," she admitted. "She was a prep, I'm—"

"I believe you," I said, meaning it. Nicole didn't strike me as someone who would lie. She had secrets, that much was certain. But she kept them to protect herself, to protect someone else.

She laughed then, almost in a way that sounded like relief, then wiped her eyes. "What was your old school like?" she asked.

"Ah, it was okay," I replied, wanting to avoid lying to her. Maybe I needed to tell my new friends about my past, where I came from. Valerie had warned me to stick to the script, never divulge our pasts. I didn't know where I came from yet, but I'd adopted the last name whispered in the dark the night the fire came. Hemming. The woman with the wild hair and the blood called me Hemming before Valerie and I fled.

So when Valerie asked me what name I wanted to go by, I chose my middle name and the name she'd uttered. *Nicholas Hemming.* My first name never felt like my own, and I smiled at the words when we obtained the falsified birth certificates. Nicholas Hemming. No middle name. A fresh start. Valerie had kept her first name and had given herself a generic last name.

A fresh start for us both.

A clean slate to be wiped with blood.

After school, Nicole came over to study. I figured getting her alone was the only way to get more information out of her. I knew there was something she was hiding, and I needed to know what it was.

CHAPTER TWENTY

We sat at the picnic table in my backyard, bundled up in our hoodies, below my bedroom window. Nicole remarked on the placement. "So, how often do you sneak out?" she asked.

I laughed, glancing at the tree line where the cemetery was. "From time to time."

"To meet up with Sorina?" Nicole asked, curiosity thinly veiled, but less sharp than the rest of our group.

I smiled in response, though I didn't feel it. "No, I mean, I see her around town when I'm walking."

Nicole opened her book, adjusting her backpack on the bench. "Why do you walk around town?"

"To clear my head. I don't sleep well." *I am the dream, and the dream is me. Your existence is her undoing.* I reached for the notebook in my pocket but stopped myself. I didn't want to write poetry in front of Nicole, and I hoped the words wouldn't slip away from me.

"Must be nice," she remarked.

"Not sleeping well?" I asked.

"No," she corrected. "Not being afraid of who will find you in the dark."

The dark didn't scare me. Maybe it was because I could see clearly when I walked the town, when my feet made soft sounds on the road. "What do you mean?" I asked.

"I wish you would tell us where you're really from," Nicole said, startling me. "I've been watching you since the first day, and you're ... different."

"What do you mean?" Again, I repeated myself, this time with a different question.

"It's like ... like you're Amish or something. You know there's an Amish community not far from here? You remind me of them—

or how I imagine they are. You don't know things a normal teenage boy should know. What was the ranch like where you grew up? No TV? No, like ... real people?" It was the most I'd heard Nicole say, away from everyone else, away from school. She was opening up in front of me, and I liked her.

"I guess you could say that," I said.

"So you're like the Amish people?" she goaded.

"I guess. What did you mean when you said it must be nice?" I asked, circling back.

Nicole rolled her eyes, and in that moment, she looked like her twin. "You're a boy. You can walk around town at night without a care in the world, right? When new people move here, it's mostly to escape something. Escape the city, crime, and all the scary things in the world. Dads move their families here because it's safe. But what they don't see is ... nowhere is safe when you're a girl. Are we investigating a string of missing boys? No. You don't have to worry about anything."

I bristled at her words. I knew she was right in a lot of ways. And maybe that's why saying what happened to me and my past was so hard to get out. I was ashamed. Ashamed I didn't fight.

"If you want to walk around the town at night, you can come with me," I said, not sure if I meant it. I was always baiting Sorina out into the open. But I hoped I didn't have to do that anymore.

Nicole smiled, shaking her head, knowing where my thoughts lingered. "Sorina might not like that."

"We're not ... I don't know." I pulled my leg onto the bench, turning my body to the cemetery.

Nicole brushed her hair from her face and narrowed her eyes at me. "Jessica might get jealous."

CHAPTER TWENTY

I turned toward her sharply. "What?"

"She told me you would be an easy lay back on the first day of school. That she'd break you."

I flamed red, my stomach rolling. *Break you.* "I'd rather she didn't talk about me like that," I said, sounding like a puritan or however the fuck Amish people must have sounded.

"I told her she shouldn't say stuff like that, but she never listens to me."

"Aren't twins supposed to be in tune and connected and all that? You two seem so—"

"Opposite? Yeah. Everyone can see it, but they don't know how awful it is to feel it. I wish we were close. How wonderful to have someone born with you, growing up with you, and next to you throughout this life? Right? That's supposed to be this nice thing. And it's not. We've always fought, always been at odds. I don't know, we don't have many pictures from when we were little, but when I see one where we're smiling together, it feels like I'm looking at some other babies. Not little versions of us. You know, she always wanted to pump me for information about Eric, too. Since she knew I was partners with Amber."

The hairs on the back of my neck stood up. "Why?"

"She likes Eric. Always has. As far back as when we were in kindergarten and he was in first grade. They used to be boyfriend and girlfriend when we were seven, before everyone broke apart into their groups. Until we all realized that Eric's family had money, and ours didn't. It was simpler then, before we knew words like prep and skank, and ..." She looked away.

"Do you think Eric would have ever been into her?"

"Not in public. Just like Amber and me couldn't be friends in public. Who knows? She sneaks out too, you know. The evil twin. She enjoys being that."

"And you're the good twin?" I asked, wondering what it would be like to be so closely tied to someone in such a way. Not knowing I would soon resent the connection.

"Only if you believe in that stuff."

"And I don't," I said.

"I know you don't." Nicole smiled. "We're good and bad, like Athena, right?"

I believed that for everyone but the being in my dreams, the demon who haunted the sky at night.

And sometimes, I didn't believe it of myself, either.

Some part of me felt dark, feral, and ready to snap. Like my waking hours were make believe, and my dreams were more real than anything else.

TWENTY-ONE

Valerie loved old televisions shows. And on the nights they'd been able to stay at motels while living on the road, she'd soaked up many, caught up on all they offered.

Hart Hollow was a relic. A throwback to simple times. To the 50s or 60s. It suited her, this new life she was carving out. However lonely it was.

She drove to the Town & Country Supermarket that night, avoiding the missing persons poster for the Hughes girl.

Everything inside was familiar.

Everyone was familiar.

She'd learned the names of the teenagers who worked there, the manager, the patrons. The same ones she saw going in and out of the café. She knew she was now one of them, a citizen of Hart Hollow, but she still felt different. *Separate.*

A young new girl named Janessa worked that night. She smiled and waved when Valerie came in and she nodded, ducking into an aisle. Valerie did not feel up to talking after her long day at the café. She'd went home after her shift for a nap but needed milk for the dinner she planned to make. After she grabbed the milk, she rushed to the magazine rack by the checkout as she heard someone walk in.

"Hello Deacon Rex, how are you?" Janessa asked in her singsong voice.

Valerie cringed and grabbed a magazine as the only two normal people in the building talked.

Valerie's milk felt warmer in her hand, but she didn't want to interact with the Deacon in front of the young girl. It made her face feel hot, and she worried her thoughts would be plain on her face. She couldn't have that.

She rounded the corner and ducked down an aisle, grabbing a cereal box, using it as a shield. She listened to the Deacon and the young girl converse, their conversation naturally turning to God.

"I never got to ask you how long your family plans to stay in Hart Hollow. Are they enjoying the community?" the Deacon asked.

Janessa sighed, a breathy thing, and Valerie rolled her eyes. "I think so. My father was a pastor in Orlando, but he said the city was getting too big. He didn't like the crime."

"Well, you'll be free of that here in our one stoplight town," the Deacon assured.

Valerie peered around the corner, and she saw the Deacon's jaw tense, almost as if he could see her.

"That's what he thinks too. So I imagine we'll be staying. He's thinking of finding a church to lead here, too."

Valerie walked farther down the aisle, away from their conversation, but close enough to know when they were done talking so she could check out in peace.

CHAPTER TWENTY-ONE

She felt like a fool—like a teenage girl all over again—wanting what she couldn't have.

Wanting what Serendipity would take.

And every girl, every woman, had her face. She avoided looking at Janessa as she checked out, afraid she might slap her, confuse her with her dead sister. But she didn't, and a few minutes later she was safe in her car in the parking lot, nerves shot.

The knock on her window was deafening. She pissed her pants a little. And when Valerie looked up to the owner of the knuckles to blame, she was glad she didn't say the Lord's name in vain.

Valerie rolled down her window and smiled at the Deacon as she squeezed her thighs together so he couldn't smell her. She was feeling like an animal around him.

She blinked at him, her reflection in his glasses small. "I'm sorry, hi," she said as she brushed her fingers along her hairline. "Were you just inside? I didn't see you," She said a silent curse, dropping her hand away as she reminded herself that the tried-and-true tricks wouldn't work on a man such as this. A man with eyes that did not see, and a heart that belonged to God.

"Yes, I was," the Deacon said, raising a bag. "Dinner for one."

Valerie smiled, rustling the bag in her passenger seat for good measure. "Dinner for two, here. Though I doubt Nicholas will eat it. I got him a box of cereal, just in case. It's all he wants lately," she admitted.

The Deacon smiled warmly, leaning down. Valerie moved back, intoxicated by his nearness. "I believe I caught you in one of your faraway moments again," he said, pursing his lips.

"Perhaps," Valerie admitted.

"If young Nicholas wants cereal tonight, I would be happy to host you for dinner. As I said before, my door is always open. And you have my number."

Valerie nodded, the Deacon's scent in her car, so near. Valerie promised to let him know. To use the number he gave her. To ask Nicholas if he would like to join her.

To want was to be weak. And Valerie didn't want to be weak, but there she was.

Wanting.

Again.

After she made it home from her brief encounter with the Deacon, she cleaned all afternoon. And when Nicholas returned home from school, they started their game, playing house, pretending to be normal.

She asked him about his day, his homework. He asked her how work had been. And when all was said and done, all the niceties performed, they went to separate parts of the trailer.

Later, Nicholas feigned disappointment when she told him she was leaving for the night, heading to dinner with a friend. He barely tried with his lie, but they both acted the part.

Grateful for their fake family, Valerie ran to the gas station, picked up pizza, and brought it back to him. She knew he would likely eat the cereal as dessert, and the solitude was a peace offering, for show, for his fake sadness.

He retreated to his room, and she knew later he would go to the cemetery. Maybe smoke with his friend. She could smell it in the air but said nothing.

CHAPTER TWENTY-ONE

It's why she didn't feel guilty for leaving the boy behind in favor of her own heart.

The Deacon was grilling when she walked into his backyard. He smiled at her approach. And it felt good to be smiled at. His teeth were straight, perfect.

"How was the rest of your day?" His voice was warm, like honey and second chances. A trick of the light, perhaps. Perhaps they reflected her desires.

"Tiring. And ... Nicholas said he wanted pizza, so I gave in. That's why I'm here," she lied, wondering if he could tell. She was slowly thawing around the Deacon. She could hear weakness in her throat, crawling to get out, but she choked it down. She wondered again what it would be like to confess to him.

He didn't ask about Nicholas when she'd called, saying she would join him. He didn't ask why she'd changed her mind. He's simply said he was grateful to not dine alone. And she'd smiled into the phone.

As the Deacon prepared their meat, Valerie eyed the house and the round structure of the area that was the church. She was scared to go in, but knew she wanted to. Perhaps it was another reason for the dinner. She wanted to see it alone, without the townsfolk and their voices echoing in her mind. She wanted nothing but the Deacon, and God, if she could hear him.

She turned to the Deacon, clearing her throat before speaking. Smiling when he turned her way. "I know I haven't told you much about ... our church in California. But it's not just Nicholas who has his reservations. I thought it would be nice to see the church tonight. In the quiet. But what if I don't go in tonight? What if I can't? What if I never can? What if this backyard is my church, for now?"

"You'll make it to church when you're ready. I've known you were meant to be there ever since the first time I met you in the café."

"Are …?" She stared over the lawn, past the road, to the overlook. You could see the whole town from there. "Are … Deacons ever allowed to date?"

She heard the clink of a plate to her left, as the Deacon shut the grill. She kept her eyes away, heard the rustle of his clothing as he stepped closer to her. She closed her eyes.

"I enjoy this friendship we have, Valerie, and I want more, yes. I think we both know that." He paused, the *but* on his lips. She waited for it. "I have thought for many years that I wanted to be a Priest. And to do so … you and I could never be together. But if my decision is to be a permanent Deacon, I would not be bound to celibacy. I have been ordained to nurture and increase the people of God in this community in the absence of a Priest. It is my duty to lead the prayers, to proclaim the gospel, to preach the homily, and to give Holy Communion."

Valerie nodded, tears in her eyes. When the Deacon spoke, everything inside of her quieted. Everything she loved about the Deacon was everything that told her he could break her heart. She'd foolishly entertained the idea of living on the hill with him, serving the community, being two godly people that inspired others. And when reality hit, she always remembered who she was. Murderer. Cruel hearted sister killer. Deformed.

Before she could be once again caught in one of her faraway moments, Valerie excused herself, confessing she was worried the potatoes might burn. Another lie, stacking up like building blocks. But she didn't know what she was building.

After a moment the Deacon knocked on the door, likely with his shoe.

CHAPTER TWENTY-ONE

She opened the door, and the Deacon stepped inside with the large platter holding the thick steaks. The air had been crisp out there, but he hadn't worn a coat. Valerie walked to the Deacon, inhaling his scent as he passed, and shutting the door to the cold behind him. "Do you need any help with that?" she asked, making her tone even and warm. She marveled at the way he moved. His cane was hanging over his forearm, and the plate was neatly balanced.

"No, I got it," he said, setting the steaks down with a loud clink. He turned around, inhaling the savory odors in the room.

They stood there for a moment in the quiet, before Valerie snapped and asked, "Would you like me to get the plates down? Set the table?" She felt suffocated and exposed after their conversation in the yard. There was a clock on the kitchen wall just above the fridge. The minutes ticked loudly, as if they were in her skull. She began to ask another question, but the Deacon stopped her, stepping close. "I wasn't always a believer, Valerie. I want you to know that."

She nodded, eyes wide.

He continued, "And I want you to know, any decision I make about whether I want to be a Priest or remain a Deacon, will have everything to do with you, and what you want."

Valerie's voice was small. "You-You didn't know this was what you wanted for your life, always?"

"No. My love for the Lord wasn't always inside this heart." He made a fist, tapped it to his chest. "I won't lie. I would be delighted if you came to Mass some Sunday. And I would understand if whatever fear you have because of your past kept you out of that church. I would care for you either way. But we won't have a future if God will never be an integral part of your life. I didn't want to have a serious conversation like this on the first date. I just wanted to get to know you. I asked you here for dinner because I like you. Because I sense good in you. I can read people easily, it's always been a gift of mine."

"So ... this is a date?" Valerie laughed, wiping at her eyes.

"Yes." The Deacon crossed his arms, chuckling. "Honestly, Valerie, I just wanted to have a nice evening with a pretty girl. I didn't want to discuss ultimatums before we even sat down to dinner. We don't even know each other that well."

"No, we don't. And yet, you said ..." *I want more ...*

"Valerie, let's start over. Let's approach this as friends. Maybe that won't be so scary."

Her heart deflated at his words, but a strange sense of calm came over her. It was familiar—men wanting, then retreating.

Like Gregory.

Like the man with the scar—Adrian.

Her heart deflated and rebuilt itself from the rubble. Every part of her that wanted also warned. She almost reached back, almost grazed her fingers over her deformity. *If we are friends, he will never know I am wrong.* "Okay. Friends. Let's eat dinner as friends." She walked to the stove, opening the lid to the potatoes. She stirred as the Deacon walked to her, his voice at her back.

"Deal. Friends. Friends until we cannot," he whispered.

And then he left the room to set the table in the dining room.

He did not see her face when she turned around, a confession on her lips. But he would hear it in the dark of his church.

TWENTY-TWO

There were few cars parked along the road at the top of the hill that night. Valerie walked up the driveway after parking in the road. She didn't want to appear as though she thought she was special because she'd dined with the Deacon in private.

Once at the house, she walked up to the door before she could stop herself. She opened his front door and maneuvered herself through the house like she belonged there, until she reached the side door that led into the church. She hesitated for only a moment before entering.

She didn't go inside the church after their dinner and had turned the moment over in her head as she tried to sleep every night since she'd last been there. She knew she could not linger. Could not allow herself to question if she would go in. So when she saw the door, she reached for the handle, reminding herself who would be on the other side.

The townsfolk had come in a side entrance that led straight to the church. She felt like an insider for a moment, coming in through the house. Like she was special. But she quickly chided herself and walked in, avoiding eyes and smiles.

The confessional was in the corner, the door closed. No sound came from inside, secrets kept and held by the Deacon's kind and steady ear. Valerie sat in the back, her hands clasped in her lap, counting seconds and minutes as they passed. The only sound was a cough from someone nearby or the opening and closing of the confessional door. As each person came in and out, Valerie felt excited and nervous. She didn't know what she would confess or say to the Deacon when she was inside the small space, so close to him that no one could hear her. Maybe she would tell him about her sister and Gregory. Run him off for good, get what she deserved.

She shook her head, a silent *no* in her mind like a ghost. No, she wouldn't do that. But maybe the last night in California? She'd killed and hurt those who hurt, but she'd taken Nicholas. Saved him from the fate of the others. That counted for something. Right? She closed her eyes as the last man left the confessional.

She smiled meekly at the man as he left the church and stood, wiping her sweaty hands on her pants. She walked slowly to the door, placing her pale hand on the ornate knob and opening it. When she was safely inside, she let out a breath and looked over, through the partition, to the Deacon. His glasses were off, and she felt an odd thrill. She wanted to see his eyes, but they were closed; his head leaned back, chin up, firm jaw in full view.

"Valerie, Valerie," he said, and she hoped it was off script, something just for her.

She smiled, head down. "Deacon, how are you this evening?"

"So very well, now," he said, turning his face to hers slightly.

The silence enveloped her as she waited for more. But nothing else was said, leaving Valerie shrouded in her fear, in anguish.

Unable to sit in it any longer, she began. "Bless me Deacon, for I have sinned. It has been ..." she faltered. "This is my first confession. These are my sins." She crossed her legs and closed her eyes. "I have taken a life."

"Whose life did you take?" the Deacon asked, no change to his voice. He sounded as he always did.

"The church in California. I ... the reason I said it might be hard to come in here ... I—" she was failing, fumbling for words in the dark. She'd practiced it all, but reciting the words in the bathroom, staring at her own reflection, it was nothing like being in that small space with him. "I fell in with bad people, and I should have left. But I couldn't. I had nowhere to go. I'd burned every bridge in my life. I had no family left. So people were looking for me, for, for something else."

"What were they looking for you for?"

She laughed sadly. "I'll save that for another day. But, anyway, on the ranch, bad things happened to people. But never to me. They left me alone. But I wanted to leave. So much. And one night, strangers came to the property. And, I thought, maybe I can help right this. Maybe I can help save people from this in the future."

The Deacon was silent, and she went on. "I killed some of the women. Women who had hurt Nicholas. I should have done something sooner, helped sooner. Taken him from there. But I didn't. I don't know that I could have helped him, or if he would have come with me. He was such an angry boy, mocking and mean at times. But they made him that way. And ... I don't know. I wasn't myself that night. The fire and the screams, I couldn't help myself." She lied. She could help herself and helped herself to the taking of lives. And when she'd tasted a spatter of blood on her lips, she'd liked it. And nothing terrified her more than that. The long, dormant thrill she'd felt when she killed her sister and Gregory ... it came to life again. It spoke to her. So she'd fled, new beginnings in every town. New ways to outrun what was inside of her. *I couldn't help myself.* She turned the phrase over in the dark, and the Deacon sat silent.

She didn't want to be like Markus. To worship at the altar of the make-believe. But she'd believed it somehow, saw the winged God in her dreams on the ranch. The dreams had left her only to return the night she ate dinner with the Deacon, after he'd told her he *wanted more.* She saw God, his son, wandering. She saw the Deacon's face and woke in a sweat, aroused, and she once again craved that copper sweetness.

She pushed the thought away, struck by the silence of the Deacon.

After closing her eyes, she spoke again. "I am truly sorry for all my sins."

The Deacon opened his eyes then, and she turned to him. His head was down when he spoke. "I can tell you're shaking, Valerie. You don't have to be afraid. I am bound to hold our confession."

"It's not that," she started.

"Then what is it?"

"I don't want you to think … think—"

"You have expressed contrition. I can hear it in your voice, Valerie. You were protecting Nicholas. Can you say it for me? Speak clearly the Act of Contrition?"

Valerie shifted in her seat, turning away from the Deacon's profile. "My God, I am sorry for my sins with all my heart. In choosing to do wrong and failing to do good, I have sinned against you whom I should love above all things. I firmly intend, with your help, to do penance, to sin no more, and to avoid whatever leads me to sin. Our Savior, Jesus Christ, suffered and died for us. In his name, my God, have mercy." Valerie closed her eyes, steepled her fingers, and brought them to her forehead.

The Deacon looked at Valerie with his white eyes, but she did not see, did not look up as he spoke. "May our Lord and God, Jesus Christ, through the grace and mercies of his love for humankind, forgive you of all your transgressions. And I, an unworthy Deacon, by his power given me, forgive and absolve you from all your sins, in the name of the Father and of the Son and of the Holy Spirit. Amen."

Valerie's lips moved, saying Amen with the Deacon.

"Give thanks to the Lord for He is good." He looked away, smiling as he reached for his glasses.

Valerie said, "His mercy endures forever."

And the Deacon said, "Your sins are forgiven. Go in peace."

When Valerie looked through the partition, her words faded as she said, "Thanks be to God."

The Deacon was not there, and the shutting of the door as he stepped into the church, leaving her alone in the confessional, echoed in her heart.

After she gathered herself, she opened the confessional door. The Deacon was kneeling, his back to her. He mumbled something before standing and walking to the first pew. He sat town, turning to her, his glasses on his face.

The sight of him in his grey shirt struck her, and she warmed. She'd only seen him in his lay attire when he looked like the people whom he served. Now he looked important, as important on the outside as he made her feel on the inside.

She walked to him, taking in the empty pews, before turning her gaze upward to the second level. The pews there were empty too, the windows showing the dark of the night.

The Deacon patted the pew, and she sat next to him.

"What else is there, Valerie? Speak to me as your friend. Not someone seeking absolution."

She wanted to curl into him. To feel his arm around her as she spoke. But she knew that wouldn't happen. Not yet. *Friends until we cannot.*

"I have these dark thoughts," she said. "And I don't know what to do with them. I have dreams and desires. I try to control them. And I do, for the most part. But I was born wrong. I have this thing ... I don't show people. I've never been intimate with a man. And that's not normal, right? I'm twenty-six."

"You're unmarried. I don't think there's anything abnormal about that, Valerie. I, too, have urges."

"Like what?" she asked, looking up at him.

"I have never faltered. But the day I saw you, I questioned my faith. My purpose. I thought *I want her.*"

"Saw me?"

The Deacon smiled. "I can see, though I do not have eyes. I see you now, in all your peculiarity. All of your turmoil. I have given myself over to this life, this restraint. And when I look at you, I don't want to restrain myself."

"I would never want to tempt you. I enjoy being near you because it keeps everything in my head quiet, and still," she said, lies and truth mixing.

"And you make everything noisy. But, in the best way, Valerie. I know you have felt alone for a long time in his life, but you don't have to be if you join me here."

"For church? For confession? For—" She searched for the word, what she wanted him to take from her, to make her feel again. She'd almost felt forgiven in the confessional.

"I have been unable to think of anything else since you had dinner here alone with me. I have been unable to think of anything else but my decision. A future Priest, or a permanent Deacon. I love the people here. I want to lead them. I selfishly don't want to follow another. I want to hold the mantel. But, I've been waiting a long time for you Valerie. I want to lie with you. I want you to be my wife. That first day, when I said we would love to have you up here, I misspoke. What I want to say is I would love to have you forever."

Valerie's heart exploded, and she turned in her seat toward the Deacon. He stayed still, staring ahead. She took his hand. "Nicholas would never live up here," she started.

The Deacon finally moved, turning toward her. "Are you not his guardian? There is plenty of room."

"I'm not ... no. I'm not his guardian. Not legally. He'll be eighteen in less than a year. I worry that when that happens, he'll want to leave. I don't know. He's enjoying school so much. He has friends for the first time in his life."

"Friends?" The Deacon asked, and something strange flickered over his face. "That's wonderful for him. But it won't fill the gaping hole in his chest. He needs guidance. Someone to be a positive male role model in his life. I can be that for him."

"I don't know," Valerie said, and she pulled the Deacon's hand up to her face, kissing his knuckles.

The Deacon leaned close, and she tilted her head, but he pulled away. "I think what you seek, you can find in the dark. You have a deep-seated hunger within you. You worry you are wrong. *Altered*. But you are not a red woman like that."

At his words, Valerie pressed his hand to her lips, where she gripped it limply. "I dream of blood, Deacon. And my hair is red. I think you're wrong. I think maybe you don't know me the way you think. Or, I am not who you hope I am. I let people down. I always have. I've never lived up to the expectations set for me. My mother didn't want me."

"Your mother was a fool playing games. She wanted to hide you away, but you're found now."

Valerie looked at him hard, trying to read his face. She wanted to take his glasses off, see every part of him. She looked away and whispered her next words. "I don't know my mother. No one does. I was left at the front door of a fire station."

"Valerie, look at me," the Deacon said, and she shook her head, looking everywhere but at him. The moon's light could be seen outside, filtering through the tall windows. She knew it was cold outside, with December so close, and she felt incredibly at home then in the Steele Heart Church. What she'd wanted, he'd confessed. He was not like Gregory or Adrian. He wanted to lay with her. He wanted to marry her. The Deacon leaned down, pressing his forehead to hers, and she wondered what it would be like to kiss him. To kiss *God*.

His voice was deep and old when he spoke. "When I first felt your presence, I felt family. I haven't felt family in a long time. I would never admit this to those who come here looking for guidance. But I want you to be my family here. I want you and Nicholas and I to be together."

"If I move up here, the town will talk. They'll want me gone. Your congregation—"

The Deacon gripped her throat, and Valerie finally looked at him. "Will understand, or not. I do not care. We are a small and loyal group. They will grow to love you as I do. They will have no choice," he said.

To Valerie, it almost sounded like a threat. And the image of the winged beast from her nightmares flashed in her mind.

Instead of leaning forward to press her lips to the Deacon's, to confess to him that when she first saw him she felt the same, she pulled away. "My God, I am sorry for my sins with all my heart," she repeated, pulling away.

"Valerie, look at me," the Deacon repeated, but again, she did not listen. Some voice inside of her told her not to.

"Thank you for insisting I face my fears. I am so very glad I stepped foot in this small church," she said, standing. "I have a lot to think about. I feared you would look at me differently after my confession, but you have given me your own confession, and it is the one my heart longed for." She spoke hurriedly, staring at her shoes. She could see the Deacon stand in her periphery, but she did not look at him. "I have much to think about. I must say goodnight now," she said, hurrying for the door. She thought she saw a shadow on the wall, wings and dark things, but she did not stop. She walked through the Deacon's home, to his front door, out into the snow.

TWENTY-THREE

One cold night, it snowed. I saw fat shadows fall by my window as the moon shone brightly. I grabbed my jeans from the floor, swiped my notebook from the nightstand, and went to grab my coat from my closet.

I was imagining what words would hit the page as I sat in the cemetery writing, as winter spoke to me. But my brief joy over the white flakes in the dark sky was short-lived, and before long, it rained.

Defeated, I hid under my covers, mocked by the minutes and hours on the clock across the room as they ticked by.

The trailer was quiet. Valerie was asleep after an evening out again with her friend ...

A friend who I strongly assumed was the Deacon, though she spoke in vague language each evening as she stepped out. *They've asked me over for dinner. They just called. They're a good friend.* I knew it was Deacon Rex but wasn't sure what to do about it. She was an

CHAPTER TWENTY-THREE

adult. She would be safe. The girls who had been stolen from Hart Hollow were exactly that ... girls.

Resigned to stay in, I grabbed the Walkman Billy had loaned me from beneath my bed. I pressed play, the sound of the band creeping into my ears.

A few songs in, I glanced at my window, my instincts speaking to me when all else failed.

I'd vowed no one would ever sneak into my room.

I would never let that happen again. And perhaps that was the strongest reason for my insomnia.

Sorina's pale face stared back at me, and her red hair looked almost black when I stepped in front of her. She didn't ask me to open the window, but the question was there. *Will you let me in?*

She'd only been in my room once before, when I was high and sedated, but I couldn't forget how she felt curled under my blanket with me. I thought it had been a dream, and she'd told me it was real. That night was not where I went when I drifted off, though. I went to the stage, the pool, the uncovering of myself under her hands.

I slid the window open, and a strange thing happened when I heard the rain. She didn't crawl in like some inhuman thing, make me marvel at her unnaturalness as she had on the hill, slinking down the Deacon's roof like a snake. Instead, she reached out to me to help her through, and I did not hesitate to touch her. She was so light, like a bird, and when I pulled her through the window, she clung to me as her feet hit the ground, wet soles on the carpet. I didn't close the window, mesmerized by her glow. She appeared almost translucent when she looked up at me, wet lashes, red lips wet from the rain. She didn't shiver, but I did.

"Close the window," she said, voice dripping with something I couldn't name, not yet. Later, I would recognize it.

Hunger.

I let go, walking around her to the window. When I turned back, I looked at what she was wearing. Black panties, no bra, a sheer black thing skirting the edges of the floor. I couldn't tell if it was a robe or a shawl. I didn't understand women's clothing or half of the things she wore, but I could see her small breasts, ribcage, and the sharpness of her clavicle.

She was flesh, bone, and soft in small places my hands wanted to touch again.

She looked too human to be wearing so little out in the cold. Too fragile.

I pressed a finger to my lips, then stepped closer. "We have to be quiet. Valerie's asleep. I was about to leave, but then—"

"The rain."

"Yeah."

Sorina walked to my bed. "Can I have a shirt?" she asked, pulling the sheer fabric from her wet skin. I moved to my closet, finding a grey shirt showcasing a band I didn't recognize. I walked to her, and she turned around, bare, making me hum.

I averted my eyes after only a moment, and the smile on Sorina's lips told me she didn't mind. I'd seen every bit of her, every white moment, and she'd seen me.

She pulled the shirt over her head, then walked to my hamper, reaching for my dirty towel. She brought it to her wet hair, wrapping it around the strands, sopping up the water.

I walked to my bed and sat down, leaning against the wall.

"I saw you with Nicole the other night," Sorina admitted once her hair was dry enough.

"We were studying," I said, voice suddenly gruff.

"And talking about missing girls?" Sorina asked, walking to my door. She pressed her ear to the cheap wood, closing her eyes for a moment.

"Yes. We talked about Amber. Nicole was close to her," I replied.

Sorina turned back to me, fingers of one hand still grazing the door. "Nicholas, I think you and your friends should leave this alone."

I laughed, squaring my jaw. "Yeah, you said that before."

"Will you not listen to me?"

I crossed my arms, rocking my head. "I spent my entire life on the ranch taking orders. I'll never do that again. Take blind orders. Because that's what you keep giving. Cryptic orders with ominous warnings. And the other night, what was that, a bribe?"

Sorina turned to me like I'd wounded her. Her big blue eyes seemed to flash darker. Outside, the rain fell herder. "A bribe? How do you mean?" Her voice sounded strange and familiar all at once. Gone again was her Romanian accent, the voice she used when others were around. She had no accent. None. I doubted anyone could study her voice and know where she came from. I was starting to think she came from my dreams, that I'd manifested her.

"You ... what we did. Was it so I would listen to you? You said you'd kiss me if I agreed to leave the house alone."

"No. And you never gave in, did you, Nicholas?"

I smirked. "Then what was it? What we did?" I was begging for meaning, needed it like air.

"It was what I wanted."

"And what about what I want?"

Sorina walked to the bed, her legs between mine. "Was it not what you wanted?" She crawled onto the bed, her thighs around mine. I didn't uncross my arms, but felt myself respond to her.

I wanted to touch her again, explore her skin, and practice how she told me to move. I'd never touched the women who took from me. I was there for a purpose, and to get them off wasn't it. The purpose was to get me off, to break me, to make me more beast than the man I'd been masquerading as.

Instead of showing Sorina what I wanted, I reached up, grabbing her by her ribs, moving her off me. I was turned off—my mind working against me, reminding me that I was, what they'd done to me.

We were mirrors, glowing brightly with our scars, all internal.

Raped, the word like a slap in the face, a wound to the chest.

"Stop fucking around and tell me why you don't want us trying to find the missing girls. What if it was you? Would you want someone to come find you?" I asked.

"I've always wanted that. It hasn't happened yet. No one looks for me." Her voice was small, and I leaned closer.

After a moment of silence, I shook my head of the sorrow. "What? Wait, what?" I stammered.

Sorina lay on my bed, rolling to her side. She pulled her small legs up, wrapping her arms around herself.

"Did-did someone take you from somewhere?" I asked.

"It was a long time ago. Forget it, Nicholas," Sorina said.

CHAPTER TWENTY-THREE

My voice rose. "Ah, great, more cryptic bullshit. You both should have stayed in my dreams."

At that, she sat up. "What?"

"Nothing, it was a long time ago," I mocked.

Sorina narrowed her eyes. "Who else is in your dreams?"

"No one. Just you. Every night I dream of you," I said. The rest of the sentence died on my tongue. *In the dark, with you, I am unafraid.*

Every night dreams of her, every night nightmares. First her, then the winged beast, the sharp teeth. And on the worst nights, the women—bastard daughters of a maniac.

Sorina looked away, and I saw the thin black rope around her neck.

I moved closer. "What's that?"

She looked at me and grabbed my wrist. "You can't wait to play. I can feel it."

"Is that what you brought that for?" I asked, warming all over. I had a fire in my chest, the desire to burn alive when anyone else moved to me. But she played this game with me in a way that made me feel safe.

"Yes," she said.

I didn't know it was a symbol, a restraint in name, not in reality. The rope couldn't hold her. But I didn't realize it then.

I knew it made me feel safe, even though her hands … I wanted them all over me.

I reached for her shirt roughly, pulling it over her head. And that time I didn't hide my eyes, I looked at her hungrily, and when our eyes met again, I moved closer. "Okay, let's play."

There was a certain beauty in the pace of our touching. Every move was slow, deliberate, and hushed—so we wouldn't wake Valerie.

I grabbed Sorina by her hips, hoisting her up, and she clutched my forearms, blue eyes wide as I pressed her against me.

The relief was immediate. She squeezed her thighs around me, and I pulled her wet hair to the side. My mouth was hot against her cold skin, and she leaned her head back, almost sighing, out of control ever slightly, making my desire to push her over the edge aflame inside of me.

In my dreams, in the stories I told, I saw us—flesh to flesh—as we moved.

On that night, in the waking hours of dark hearts, I mimicked the dream me, the fictional me.

She grabbed my head, moving me to her breast as if I needed guidance. I took her nipple in my mouth and gripped her back, raking my hands down. She winced and when we locked eyes, hers were black, and I blinked as she closed them.

I let her nipple slip from my mouth and grabbed her face, making her look at me, but when she opened her eyes, they were blue. And the smirk on her face was telling. Just as in dreams, in fantasy—she was playing a game, teasing me, taking me to the edge.

I flipped us over. Ripped my shirt over my head and grabbed her thighs as I looked down at her. Again a thin strip of dark fabric was all that kept me from what I wanted to taste.

Sorina went to speak, and I reached for her jaw and pressed my thumb to her lips. "If I want instruction, I'll ask," I said.

With a smile, her hands went up and gripped the headboard, and I raked my eyes over every bit of her exposed flesh. Her pink

CHAPTER TWENTY-THREE

nipples, her sharp hipbones, the blue veins beneath her pale skin. I grabbed the rope, securing her wrists to the cheap metal rails of the headboard, then knelt down, hands hooked under her knees as I breathed on her panties—wet and cold from the rain and snow, but warm, too. Warm for me.

When I let go of her right thigh, I gripped the fabric covering her and pulled it to the side. I saw pink, her little bud, the way she throbbed, and I thought I could hear her heart beating in her chest but I tried to convince myself I was going mad. I wasn't, and that heartbeat would be a beacon one day when she was away from me.

I leaned forward, running my tongue through her folds, across her clit, before swirling around. Sorina made a slight sound, and I smiled as I licked more, my right hand wrapping around her thigh, locking her in place. Sorina's grip on the headboard was forgotten, and her hands grasped for me, but she couldn't reach. When I glanced up at her she was smiling with with her eyes closed as I tasted and pulled from her.

I pressed two fingers to her opening, slipping them in, curling them, and she pushed up against my mouth. That was different; that was new. The way she responded.

And I was fucking hard, pressing into my mattress, aching to feel her around me. She made me feel safe and alive, exhilarated and worthy of hands to my flesh. She was taking from me and giving to me. It was both of us.

We both wanted each other.

I'd never felt that in my life, and my eyes were greedy with every new sight. I'd always closed my eyes when they took from me, but in the dark of my room, I watched every move, insatiable, licking and touching.

Unable to handle the ache any longer I pulled away from her sex and ripped the rope from her wrists and the headboard. I flipped her onto the bed face first, pulling her to the edge, bending her over. I kicked her legs apart and dropped to my knees, hands raking up the inside of her thighs, she tried to lean up, and I pushed her face into the covers.

"Shhh," I hushed, biting her flesh, pushing her thighs apart. I fisted her long red hair when I licked her from behind, then yanked when I stuck my tongue inside her pink hole. She hissed out a breath, and with my other hand, I spread her lips, finding that little spot that made her legs tremble. She pressed back, pushing her slick heat into my face. I was ravenous, lapping at her, hoping the game was one she would lose. I didn't care if I woke up Valerie, not really.

She was not my mother, not my keeper.

And I was tired of not knowing what it would feel like to be inside Sorina.

Her legs trembled as she gripped the sheets. I tugged at her hair, slipping my hand around her neck as she moaned. The sound was cut off, but I felt her cry, and it only made me eat her more earnestly. My length pressed into the side of the mattress, and the friction made me moan into Sorina. She released my name on a sigh, and I stopped, my tongue slipping out of her.

Then I let go of her hair and pushed my boxers down, bringing my tip to her wet slit. I could have slid in easily, and my chest burned with need. Instead, I rubbed my tip over her, then down to her folds, over the swollen nub. She pressed back, my name slipping from between her lips again, and I placed my palm on the small of her back. My other hand gripped her hip as I pushed her into the mattress and lifted her until she was at the perfect angle.

CHAPTER TWENTY-THREE

Then I slid in slowly, achingly gentle. My hands left her as I pressed forward, and I grabbed my hair, pulling, before biting down on my fist. I wanted to curse, to shake the house again. I wanted to stay inside her forever, feel the heat, her warmth, her perfect angles, and her softness.

I had no idea what home was, but inside that trailer in a forgotten town, I was warm and safe, feral and deadly. I felt like my destiny was with her, and every nightmare of my life had led me to that moment.

I fell forward, pressing my chest to Sorina's back, my mouth close to her heart. "Fuck, you feel so good." I moaned.

She turned, kissing me as I gripped her small breast, my other hand coming to her throat. I lifted her, held her tight as I stood, never slipping out of her as I walked us to the wall. She placed her hands on the cheap paneling, and I laced my own with hers, only letting go to hold her as I slipped in and out.

She was weightless.

I was insatiable, and she whimpered as I slipped out only long enough to turn her around.

As natural as it had felt to take her from behind, I wanted to look into her eyes.

I wanted to see if they were black or if I was losing it.

She wrapped her legs around me as I pressed her into the wall. And when I came, I buried my face in her neck, inhaling her red hair as I cried out.

I didn't care who heard us because I didn't care anymore. I was hers; she was mine. Even if I was a fool to think so, I felt it that moment. My dark room was clear, her scent was all around me, and the world was dead. I was tired of purity and perversion clutching my hand in my life.

I vowed to have no master, no keeper—no one to silence me when I swore, tell me what to eat, keep me bound to anything. No one but her.

Exorcising the past was all that mattered.

I kissed Sorina's jaw, clutched her throat, and spilled myself inside her like a heathen. She made me feral, alive; I felt immortal, and looking back, there is nothing like the cocksure defiance of a teenage boy.

Especially one inside of a girl he is addicted to, a girl he never thought would walk out of his mind and into a reality that made sense, that felt like home.

TWENTY-FOUR

Every moment Valerie spent with the Deacon she learned something. She had still never touched a Bible—she felt too dirty for that—but she enjoyed being in the small round church every moment they weren't eating dinner or talking in the living room. She let the Deacon read to her. Let him teach her, scrub her clean.

And she let him touch her.

Small moments.

She placed them on her tongue when she slept at night. She would push her fingers into her flesh, where his hands had been—his fingers grazed her shoulder, his arms wrapped around her when he hugged her goodnight, the light kiss he placed on her temple. She touched all of those places, licked her fingers clean. If he knew where her fingers lingered later, he would want to pray for her.

More than he already had.

The wicked do not wed the holy.

She told herself this truth every night after she left him. Fed herself the bitterness. Convinced herself he would tire of her, eventually. That's why the nights were the hardest. During the day, she remembered his words, his promises and his confessions. She remembered his wicked smile when she would arrive for dinner, and every gift of his scent told her he wanted her.

She'd spent Thanksgiving with the Deacon, and though that made her heart warm, Nicholas did not join. She'd kept her visits with the Deacon secret at first, but after his confession that he wanted her, and wanted her to live on the hill with him, she told Nicholas she was spending time with him. It went as she had suspected. Nicholas rewarded her lies with that mocking face he often wore and his cold indifference.

Their make-believe family was paper thin, and she was ripping it to shreds with each deceit and defiance of her promise of new beginnings. She knew he thought she was circling around to the dark, but she did not believe so.

The Deacon was not Markus.

The Sunday night she saw his true face had been slow and calming. She'd attended Mass. Spent the evening eating dinner with the Deacon before going home to check on Nicholas. She found him in the cemetery with his friends. Instead of telling him where she was going, she left a note in the kitchen. A lie. She said she was going to confession. But every moment with the Deacon felt like confession. And she'd considered telling him about her sister that night, but he had other plans and steered her away from the confessional.

The Deacon said he wanted to show her something, and she marveled at the thought, dipping into dark places. She knew where his bedroom was but had never been there.

"Did you know the first elevator in the Ozark's is in this house?" the Deacon asked, his hand resting on his stomach. He was

CHAPTER TWENTY-FOUR

sitting at the kitchen, fresh from a shower. Valerie studied his knuckles, the firmness of his arms in his button up shirt. He looked casual, so different after how he'd seemed in the church in this grey and white. She was in his home, a part of his private life. It felt wrong and alive. She didn't know what to do with her hands and then reminded herself he could not see her.

"No. Where is it?" she asked, leaning against the door frame as she watched him.

The Deacon stood, not reaching for his cane. She wondered why he only used it when he left the house. Perhaps his home and church were familiar; he was like an ordinary man in that holy place.

He was hardly ordinary. He seemed special to her—glowing with an otherworldly presence that spoke God into her ear.

"I can show you."

Valerie cleared her throat as she pushed off the wall. "Why did you not let me confess earlier?"

The Deacon smiled wide. "You're so very different than everyone here, Valerie. I have been listening to the people of Hart Hollow for so long, and their voices are so familiar to me, so comforting. But yours, it's special. I didn't want you to confess again until we were alone."

"Can we go now?" She wanted to confess, because the last time she had, he'd confessed his own feelings. She needed more. Needed more to combat her warring thoughts, her nighttime voice.

"How about we go after I show you the elevator," the Deacon said.

"Where does it go? Is there a basement?" she asked.

"Yes. But it doesn't go there. Missouri is known for the beautiful caves beneath us. Labyrinths. The entire world is below. I find creatures of the night to be fascinating. I have since I was young."

"Things that see in the dark scare me," she lied. She didn't want him to know about the dreams—the snakes, the dark things that walked the woods, the one that looked like the thing she'd seen on the hill. She regretted the time she'd spent away from the house on the hill, full of fear over the thing in the road. She knew now that the Deacon would never let anything harm her. Knew that even the darkness inside of her, and all she'd done that night at the ranch, wouldn't make him look at her differently. She'd been forgiven for her sins, but for years she had been someone else, never herself.

Never who she was the night she hurt them. And the night she took her sister's life.

The confession was lodged in her throat. Alive and waiting. So she steeled herself to go down into the dark, knowing that when the resurfaced she could confess her darkest night to him.

"I'll be with you," the Deacon said. "Nothing will happen. I want to show you the way the lake looks from beneath. It's beautiful and serene. I can hear God there. And I think you need to listen to him too."

Valerie nodded and let the Deacon lead her out of the room. They walked down a hallway to a staircase with a beautiful door.

"This is the basement. It's in there," he said.

Her heart thundered in her chest, and she wondered if she was incredibly foolish. Following a man into the dark. She gripped the knife at her side. She never left the house without it. Always felt the sheath biting into her skin. A souvenir from the last night on the ranch. She'd seen the wild-haired woman drop it. And she'd snatched it up for herself.

CHAPTER TWENTY-FOUR

It always hummed in her hand, felt alive.

She touched it as she walked down the steps, then turned back, watching the Deacon. He was calm, moving down behind her step by step, so cautious. So silent. She wondered if he was ever worried he would misstep, fall down into the dark.

When she reached the basement floor, she stepped to the side, allowing the Deacon to pass her and lead her to the elevator door. It was covered with an iron gate. He pressed the button to the right, and she heard movement. The doors opened slowly, showing her a dated box.

"Is it safe?" she asked, wishing instead that she was walking into the confessional.

"Yes. I have it serviced regularly. It's perfectly safe. I go down there quite often. Since Father Dodson passed. It's quite lonely here," he said. "For now."

Valerie stepped inside and the Deacon followed, moving close. His scent was of the earth, copper, clean and warm. She wanted to touch him, tell him she was still thinking about his words, still trying to figure out how to broach the subject with Nicholas.

She shook a little as the elevator went down. She wasn't sure if it was because she didn't trust the machinery, the Deacon's closeness, or if the dreams she often had were frightening her. She saw rushing water in her dreams. Sometimes she saw the thing in the road. Sometimes she saw her sister. And sometimes it was a winged being with a crown covered in blood beckoning her to a seat beside him.

It was why she wanted to confess.

She was no artist, not a writer like Nicholas. She could not sketch her dreams into reality as he did. She had no talent to let the dark out. She had only this—her want for absolution; her wish for this man. She wanted a family.

When the elevator stopped, she jolted a little, reaching for the iron gate and for the Deacon's arm.

He stepped forward, one arm reaching for the door, the other taking her hand. It felt cool to the touch, and she pressed close to him; she could hear the water and smell the lake. When they stepped out, she looked down at the rock surface. It glistened with moisture. She looked around, her mouth hanging open. It was a cave, stunning and dark and magnificent. There were torches lit, illuminating the shadows. She wondered if he'd been down earlier to light them, hoping she would be brave enough to join him.

Ahead of her, the mouth of the cave opened to trees and, beyond that, a sliver of water. She stepped closer, eyesight adjusting, nose inhaling the fresh scent of the earth. She was about to smile, but movement to the right stopped her.

When she looked at the thing moving in the corner, her eyes strung, her mind stuttered, and she tried desperately to make sense of what she was seeing.

It was a mattress on the cave floor. A chain hammered into the wall. And at the end of that chain, a girl. She had curly blonde hair, dirty clothes, and a blanket half thrown over her lap.

Her mouth was gagged, and her eyes bulged at the sight of Valerie.

Before Valerie could think, she whirled toward the Deacon, fear gripping her throat until it was his hand there, wrapped around her like a vice, like a caress.

She grabbed his arm, yanking it, but it did not budge. He felt like rock, the steel of a chain. Like her past. Every step leading to that moment flashed in her mind, and that voice inside told her what she always knew.

You're stupid, Valerie. You cannot tell pure from poison.

CHAPTER TWENTY-FOUR

The Deacon smiled, and for the first time, the smile made her want to scream. She tried to then, and before the sound could come out, the Deacon kissed her. Forceful, aggressive. She couldn't keep his tongue out of her mouth, and it was long and hard, the muscle flicked, tasting every bit of her. She tried to bite down, and the Deacon laughed; she could feel it when he pulled his tongue out, blood around his mouth.

She went to scream again, but this time the Deacon reached up with his free hand and removed his glasses.

He repeated his words from the night in the church when she confessed. "Valerie, look at me." And this time, she had no choice. His eyes were white, and around the edges, there was scarring. She could not scream. She could not move. She was limp in his hand, arms dropping to her side.

She was a tiny doll, and he was the puppeteer.

His wicked smile made her blood turn cold, and she shivered in his clutch.

And then he let her go. She did not run. She did not move. She stood still, staring into his eyes, transfixed. She felt warm all over.

"You're so beautiful, Valerie," the Deacon said, an almost parental tone falling out. He sounded proud. "So obedient. I love when they're new like this."

Valerie stared, the girl in the cave moving in her periphery. She could not look at her. Could not move.

"Look at her. Look at her again, and tell me what you see."

Valerie took a breath and felt like a heavy bucket of water had been poured over her. She jerked to the side, and the blonde-haired girl was not there. Not anymore.

Chained to the wall, in her place, was a girl with dark hair and a wicked grin around the gag.

Staring back at her with malice and triumph was Serendipity. In reality, the girl there looked nothing like her dead foster sister, but the illusions planted in minds were often potent. And being near the Deacon, so close to his heart, she had no chance of breaking free from what he wanted her to see. She brought her hand to her mouth and stifled a gasp.

"She didn't deserve you. She was not your sister. A sister would not take as she did. I can bring you to them, the sisters you seek, the flesh and blood you know is out there. And your mother? I can show you her, too," the Deacon said.

Valerie turned to him, away from the grinning girl, tears in her eyes. "My mother? Serendipity always said she was dead. That she died after she left me."

"How would she know? Tell me you do not linger in those falsehoods. She aimed to hurt, to cut. And you let her."

"I ... just wish I knew her name. I wish I knew why I'm like this ..." She wanted to know. Desperately. It's all she could think about. Her whole life. A mother to love her, to come back for her. To tell her why she left her there. If it was the fleshy deformity. If she had to. If she missed her at all. She'd missed her mother dearly, making up her reality and form. She saw red. Red hair that gave her a copper mane. But the mother in her dreams had red hair like blood, red hair like the glowing red circle she saw in the woods in her dreams—the one she wanted to walk through.

"Why don't you ask Serendipity? She kept so much from you. Make her tell you," the Deacon said, teeth sharp.

Valerie blinked at him, unsure what she was seeing. So like a horror movie. And the most horrifying thing was that she wanted to touch his incisors. Feel them on her flesh. She looked at the girl chained to the wall. Dirty and sad, alone in the dark. Sister. Taker. Killer. So like Valerie, in some ways. Sisters in kind. She stepped toward her, and the girl thrashed. Something like *help me* sounded in her muffled cry. She knew it wasn't true. Her sister would never ask for help. Didn't ask for help when Valerie had taken her life. So sure she would always come out on top, even as the life left her. So wrong, so deserving. She thought she had stayed for that last gasping breath, that stupid smirk sliding away. But had she? The memories blurred with the dreams, with the years past.

"How is she here? I killed her. I wanted to confess tonight. I needed to."

"Did it satisfy you? Maybe that's not what you needed to do. I can show you how to take a life slowly. Taste it."

Valerie shook her head, stepping away. Her legs felt stiff, but she could still move.

The Deacon shook his head, blinking at her with his dead white eyes. He unbuttoned the sleeves of his shirt and rolled them up when he was done, casting glances at Valerie. Serendipity retreated, making herself small, pressing against the wall.

Valerie stared at her, stomach churning, mind racing. She was going mad; she was sure of it. The horrors of the ranch had caught up to her. She pinched herself, hoping to wake up from the nightmare. She wanted to find herself in bed, the sound of Nicholas sneaking out bringing her comfort. She wanted anything but this.

The Deacon walked to the mattress as he unbuttoned the front of his shirt. He leaned down, and Serendipity spread her legs, a look of pleasure on her face. At least, that's the way she remembered her. That smirk, that sly eye, that knowing face that said, "I got what you want; I will *always* get what you want." Valerie looked on in horror, in a surge of warmth. She locked eyes with her sister, and there was almost a word there, a plea for rescue. But that was wrong. Serendipity would never ask Valerie to save her. She would never stoop so low.

She heard the breaking of flesh, a sucking sound, and a sigh. Outside, the lake was quiet and there were no cars on the bridge. The town was asleep.

She wished it was that dark thing in the road in front of her now. She could take that. Not this.

When the Deacon was finished, he stood.

His mouth was covered in blood, and she fell into his eyes. White, scared at the edges, his face a shield of hard lines. He smiled and looked like a joker, a jester of the court. He looked like the nightmare thing that lived in her dreams. She tried to run, but he was fast, catching her at the elevator entrance. His hands grabbed her arms, and he held her still. Valerie thrashed, furtive *no*'s falling from her mouth.

"Sweet girl, sweet girl, don't be afraid. I want you to taste it," he said. And she imagined the words in another way. A sin in name, but nothing like this. He grabbed her jaw, making her face him. She closed her eyes, clutching them shut, afraid to look into them. And then his mouth was on hers again, pushing his wet and bloody tongue inside—so like a snake she almost gasped when she felt the forked shape. It hadn't been like that before. She opened her mouth, and when his tongue entered her again, she practically gagged on it. He yanked her head back, and she opened her eyes in reflex. When she stared into the white orbs every part of her drifted to heat. She felt warm all over. "Stop resisting," the Deacon said. "I don't enjoy doing it this way." And like a dog, she stopped thrashing. She stood perfectly still, and he let go, stepping back.

"Are you afraid of me?" he asked.

CHAPTER TWENTY-FOUR

Valerie nodded. She was at his command, but her truths were still there.

"Did you not believe Markus?"

"He was false," she said, voice monotone and flat. Her mind whirled inside, but she felt drugged.

"He was ... an unfortunate disappointment. He asked you to call him your father, but he was not that. Could never be that. He knew the call. He knew who I was, and he still wore his false titles. Do you not feel good when you're with me? Or was that a lie?" the Deacon asked.

"I feel good when I am with you," she said.

"Do you not believe I will absolve you from your sins? Why do you think you have been this good this long? Were you not waiting for me?"

"I was ... I was ... I d-dreamed," she stammered.

"Of who?"

"A man, a bath of white. The blood is the cure, the tie. A winged being. An angel, maybe."

"Not an angel. Something new. Old. Everything."

"Why did you touch her?" Valerie cried. "Everyone wants her. Why?"

"Do you want to make it end?"

"I thought I did. I thought I had ended this. She's dead."

"Would you rather be sure?"

Valerie nodded, her voice a scream inside, begging her limbs to take her back into the elevator. Press the button. To leave and never come back. Take Nicholas and leave that wretched town.

Tabula rasa. They'd picked the wrong place. *She'd* picked the wrong place.

"If you want that voice to stop, the dreams to stop, finish it. Do you want to finish it?" he asked.

Valerie swayed, and the word was on her tongue, ready to fall out. *Yes.*

The Deacon smiled and then jerked his head, looking out of the cave. His brow furrowed, and he sniffed the air. When he looked back at Valerie, his earlier patience was gone.

He shoved Valerie into the elevator, pressing a button on the outside, sending her up. He shouted to her, his white eyes staring as she watched from the door as he grew smaller.

"Come back at dawn if you're tired of being alone. I need you here with me forever." The words bit her like a snake, and the image of his red lipped smile would keep her from sleep no matter how hard she tried.

TWENTY-FIVE

My inability to take any order at the time felt like my strength. My defiance was intoxicating, and I felt euphoric in my rebellion, in my ability to firmly defy those who tried to order me around. Sorina had said to stay away, and I didn't plan to listen. Valerie had asked me to join her for dinner at the Deacon's for the holiday—finally naming her *friend* —and I'd said no, leaving out the *fuck* I'd wanted to throw in for flair. And so school let out, and I reveled in the quiet of my mind. I walked the streets, the cold not scaring me, hoping to find Sorina and her black rope, too afraid to show up at her house again demanding another game of mirrors and flesh. I was firm in my answer to the women in my life, but still treading a line of fear and want. I had yet to chase as I wanted to in my dreams. But I would soon.

It was as if the Archer house called to me that cold night at the end of Thanksgiving break when I set out alone. We'd made plans to check it out in our small groups, but the more time I spent with Billy, Jessica, Nicole, and Kyrie together, the more we bickered and laughed, and fell into an unusual sort of unlikely friendship. Amber was still gone, Samantha was still a memory, and maybe we were scared to learn if the Archer House was important or not. If we kept putting it off, we'd never know. And there was safety in that.

But my dreams were never safe and often pushed me to wake, to wander. I'd seen the house before I woke, with the red circle behind it, glowing in the night like a portal. I didn't want to step through, but my feet carried me to the entrance, my hand reached for the door just as I woke in a sweat, cold air slipping into my room from the cracked window.

I'd looked up, hoping to see Sorina. Disappointed that she wasn't there, I dressed, spurred by my dream, leashed by my defiance.

I didn't turn on my flashlight until I shut the front door of the Archer house.

Spiderwebs glittered, and an orb of light flashed back at me from a door on the opposite end. I quickly shut the flashlight off, worried someone on the other side of the house would see it.

Maybe I'd watched too many scary movies on TV through the Halloween season, read too many horror stories. After burning through the King novels I owned, I'd read a depraved novel called *The Girl Next Door* by Jack Ketchum that had almost turned me off from the written word. I'd reluctantly taken a collection of Christopher Pike novels from Nicole after confiding in her about the horrors I'd read in the Ketchum novel, leaving out the part that it all felt too close to home in some ways. The pallet cleanse had been nice, and as I read about teenagers hunting ghosts and hiding from killers, visions of the Archer house lingered in my mind, blurring with the fictional houses in the stories I consumed.

Now the house was real, surrounding me. I thought I felt it breathe. But maybe that was something else.

Someone else.

CHAPTER TWENTY-FIVE

I clicked the light on again but kept it low to the ground, illuminating my shoes.

The old floorboards creaked beneath me, and every sound felt amplified. I explored the house in quiet concentration, the sound of the house and its age lost to my wandering thoughts, though my ears and eyes were alert. I held my breath when I heard the Sheriff drive by, but he never paused, never pulled in. I didn't dare go up the stairs when I took in the state of the steps.

I went to the basement, my heart beating, my imagination whirling between fiction and my dreams.

In the dark, with you, I am unafraid.

But Sorina wasn't there to shield me from dark things in the night. Real or not. When no winged beast emerged from the dark of the basement, and my investigation showed me nothing more than an old house littered with beer bottles, condoms, and cigarette butts, I felt more disappointment than relief.

Defeated, I left the Archer house, and cut across the road after watching the Sheriff's taillights fade into the dark as he drove toward the grocery store.

I stared at the sky as I slipped onto Kyrie's street before cutting across the town's main cemetery, under the protection of the trees. They felt watchful as usual, as if they had eyes.

When I emerged from the cemetery, I ran across the Raven's Nest parking lot and past Casey's gas station, hiding behind the car wash as I listened for tires. The Sheriff rarely patrolled at night, and I wondered if the holiday break had him restless. Or if those in charge of the town knew more about the missing girls than they let on. When I thought it was safe, I ran out of town along the bridge where I could finally see Moonies. It was quiet, past closing time, but the light was on in Diana's place.

I turned left at the road, heading to the small island Sorina told me to stay away from.

I remembered the man, the blood, the slope of his back, the ridges of his face.

It was inhuman, something from nightmares. But not from the nightmares of a young boy watching too many scary movies or reading horrifying books. It was from my nightmares. Nightmares that began before my life in Hart Hollow—where the most worrying things I had to endure were fiction and the lingering memories of my past in my mind like a virus.

My heart beat in my chest as I walked across the dead grass. I expected Sorina to grab my arm at any minute. To reprimand me. But I didn't care.

No one was on the island, and the moon was gone, but I could still see well in the chilly night.

My Converse clapped on the wooden boards as I walked across the bridge, over the water. When I made it to the island, I was struck by the ordinariness of it.

It was simply dirt. When I looked down, I saw bird droppings, maybe goose or duck. I walked to the center, taking a seat in the middle. The surrounding water was placid. I waited for a car to drive by the bridge or the dirt road, but the town was asleep, dead to the nocturnal world save for the wandering Sheriff.

The sudden thought that the beast in front of the Deacon's house might come out struck me, and I shivered.

I almost wanted it to. Because it didn't scare me the way it should have.

I'd wanted to help the animal that night.

And the way the Deacon had spoken, the tenor of his voice, told me he wanted to do the opposite.

CHAPTER TWENTY-FIVE

Leaning back, I rested on the ground, hoping I wasn't laying on some bird shit as I cradled my head and closed my eyes. As my ears adjusted to the quiet, without my sight competing to control my senses, I heard more. No frogs chirping as they had in late summer nights after I arrived, but still small beasts moving. Most animals were asleep, but some were wakeful like me. My nocturnal friends.

It soothed me, and I cursed Sorina in my head. I'd almost convinced myself that I'd made it all up, that I never saw the man with the blood. It was another nightmare. But Sorina had seen him too, warned me away.

And then I heard something in the woods. The world around me hadn't been silent, but something about the sound made me shoot up, and I clicked the flashlight on, shining it across the water. A flash of white disappeared into the trees, long flesh, the shape hard to recognize. It would become some nightmarish thing if I let my imagination paint it, so I closed my eyes and tried to compartmentalize my memories, my dreams, and the things I made up in my head.

In the dark, with you, I am unafraid.

I was alone with a mixture of fear and some instinct to run into the woods, give chase to something just to see if it would run.

And then I heard a girl scream.

I scrambled to my feet, running to the edge of the island, my flashlight waving wildly in the dark.

The scream came again, piercing the night, then abruptly stopped.

I imagined a hand clamped over a mouth as I tried to see across the water. Instead, I saw only trees, a pair of small green eyes— likely a raccoon or something.

Not Sorina, not anything to fear. No leader with a rope to bind me.

And then a hand clamped over my mouth, and my mind reeled at the blurring of memory and imagined things.

I whipped around, but the grip was tight. And though she let me turn, she didn't let go.

I peered into Diana's eyes, and she placed her finger to her lips, urging me to be quiet.

I nodded my head, and she let go.

"I heard—"

"Shut the fuck up, Nicholas," she whispered, grabbing my hand with one hand and my flashlight with the other. She clicked it off and drug me across the island, impossibly strong.

"Wait, we're going the wrong way—" I protested.

She whirled around, eyes wild. "If you don't shut up now, I'm going to hit you with this fucking flashlight and carry you off this island," she seethed.

I narrowed my eyes. "Well, if you would listen to—"

And then Diana made good on her promise.

○○

I woke on Diana's couch in her living room as a scream pierced the night.

I turned toward the sound and saw Diana at her window, peering out into the dark. It had begun to rain, and when she turned to me, her face was melancholy and disappointed.

CHAPTER TWENTY-FIVE

I swung my legs onto the floor, rubbing the knot on my head. "What the fuck did you do to me?" I asked, my voice ragged.

"Saved your life, damned another," she replied, graven.

She walked away from the window into her kitchen. A dim light above her stove was the only light in her place. "Want something to drink?" she asked, as if we hadn't just heard a scream, a cry for help, or worse.

I walked into the kitchen area. "No, I don't want a drink. I want you to answer my question and not in the way Sorina would answer," I said through clenched teeth.

Diana ignored me, reaching for a kettle, filling it with water. "Don't ask questions you don't want an answer to, young wolf."

"What?" I asked, annoyed.

"Why do you use the name Hemming? It is not your birth name. And it's not what you are. Not really ..."

I bristled at her knowledge of my life, crossing my arms. "How do you know it's not my name?"

"Your *aunt*"—the word sounded like poison on her tongue—"may have covered your tracks for people who don't know where to look or know *to* look, but I know more about you than you think."

"Aiight." I chuckled, mocking her. "So we're going in the direction of let's talk like Sorina. Cool. Why don't you call her up and have her come over so you both can piss me the fuck off," I said, walking toward the door.

Diana was in front of me in a flash, blocking my path. "It's not safe out there. You heard it."

"Yeah, and someone may need help."

"And you're the one to help her?" She cocked an eyebrow, grabbed my arm, then turned me toward the kitchen. I moved to brush her off, pissed that she'd touched me, but I couldn't. She was stronger than I expected.

"Let go of me," I said, voice laced with anger. I liked Diana when I met her, but that didn't give her the right to touch me. "I don't like people fucking touching me."

She let go, eyes softening. "I'm sorry. I just, you can't go out there. If you got hurt, I would never forgive myself. And Sorina would never forgive me."

"Sorina doesn't give a shit about me," I said, shocking myself. We played games; she let me touch her and taste her. But she frightened me, haunted me. She was the girl of my dreams, but my dreams were nightmares.

Diana smiled, sorrow at the edges of her eyes. "That's not true. You mean more to her than she wants."

"What are you two hiding?" I asked, walking back into the kitchen.

Diana joined me, putting the kettle on. She spoke as she worked, pulling loose tea leaves from a jar and placing them in a metal ball. "I know you and your little friends have banded together to uncover the mystery of the runaway girls. But you're messing with things you cannot fathom, a force you cannot defeat. Not yet, anyway. If the prophecies are true, that is."

"Prophecies?" I closed my eyes, seeing red from her words. "If you know as much about me as you say, then you know where I came from. I'm not going back to that life. Prophecies and omens and the wrath of God. I left that life behind. I'm not going to church with Valerie, and I'm not listening to made-up tales from you. There is no God. There is no Devil. Omens aren't real.

They're made-up stories we tell ourselves to explain why people do bad shit. It's what he did."

"Markus was an evil man. An arrogant monster who paid the price. He was sick. "

I shivered at his name, confirming that Diana knew about my past. "He was."

"He was a pretender. He has nothing on the man …" She let the word linger for a beat. "He has nothing on the man doing this," she finally finished.

"Everyone has written this Amber Hughes girl off as a runaway," I said, running my hands through my hair, tugging in frustration. "If we don't look for her, who will?"

"No one will look for her soon. In the morning, there will be a body. I don't know where it'll be, but someone will find it. And someone will take the blame."

"A body? Why the hell aren't we out there?" I waved my arm at her front door. "Why aren't we stopping her from becoming nothing more than a fucking body?" I asked.

"I'm not this town, Nicholas. I'm in it, but I'm not one of them."

"Then what the fuck are you?" I asked.

"Something like you." She smiled. The tea kettle cried out, and she pulled it from the stove. I watched her pull two mugs from the cabinet. She set the metal balls inside each mug, then poured the water in. Finally, she brought a mug to me, setting it on the counter. "Let it sit for a moment. It's hot."

I nodded, watching the steam. "What are *we*, then?" I asked.

Diana gripped the mug, ignoring her own warning about the temperature. Her hands didn't seem to burn. "Beings in sheep's clothing," she whispered. "Me as I see fit. You—" Her eyes darted to the door, and mine followed.

I'd heard it too, and the hairs on my neck stood up. "Is someone here?" I asked.

Diana nodded but didn't go to the door.

Her lips turned down, a frown all I could read. I shook my head, reaching for the mug. I took a sip of the hot tea, closing my eyes as it went down my throat. It calmed me immediately, and I wondered what was in it. It might have been drugged, and I took it recklessly.

These women scared me, and I wanted the company of my friends. I wanted to plan with them and figure it all out. To be coddled. I just wanted to spend time with them, fight and laugh and pretend the reason we were all together wasn't because girls were missing and violent ends weren't what we feared.

I set the mug down, swaying a little.

"I'm going to drive you home, Nicholas," Diana said, her voice far away.

I could only nod.

No one knocked on the door.

※

Diana parked at the entrance of the trailer park so Valerie wouldn't wake. After killing the lights, she got out of her car and walked to the passenger side. She opened the door and offered me a hand, like a snake coiled. I felt warm from the tea, my rage simmering, caged by whatever was in it.

CHAPTER TWENTY-FIVE

"What did you give me?" I asked as I took her hand, stepping into the icy rain as the sky woke. I flinched at the downpour, wondering how long I had been knocked out on her couch, but Diana seemed unfazed.

"It's just an herbal tea. You're just very ... It's easy for you to feel it."

"Why? Because I'm whatever the fuck you are?" I snapped, walking toward my trailer on legs that felt liquid.

"Kind of," Diana replied, moving me along.

"Mhhmmm, okay," I mumbled, ready for bed even though the sun would come up soon. If it meant a dreamless sleep, I'd fucking get over it and be late to school. Maybe I'd start asking Diana for tea the way I asked Sorina for a light. I was turning into the deviant Kyrie feared I'd be.

We walked around the back of the trailer to the picnic table. The sun wasn't in the sky but a warm glow crested the surface, illuminating a white figure by the tree line. Sorina stood there, drenched from the rain, her red hair sticking to her, but I still saw the deep color in other places, similar to the color of her hair when the sun shone on it.

She was covered in blood.

Diana's eyes flicked to the tree line, and she cursed.

I pulled away from her, stumbling to Sorina, my anger at everyone flying away as another emotion took over. Worry.

Diana followed. "Nicholas, she's fine. We need to get you to bed."

I ignored her, and Sorina flinched when I reached her. Her eyes were completely black. "What the fuck," I whispered. Then, "Are you okay? What's wrong with your eyes? Is this whatever the fuck you gave me, Diana?" I asked, reaching for my head, closing my eyes briefly before looking back at Sorina. She looked the same. Like a wraith.

"What did you give him?" Sorina asked—black eyes unblinking.

Diana was next to us, arms crossed. "Just some fucking tea, but he's a goddamn sponge."

"What the fuck is going on?" I asked, ignoring Diana. "Are you okay?"

"It's not her blood, Nicholas!" Diana yelled, the rain drowning out the quiet of the night that always felt like a warm blanket when I roamed the streets.

"Then whose blood is it?" I asked, ready to run inside to call the Sheriff. Or Billy. Anyone.

"It doesn't matter," Diana repeated.

I reached forward, ignoring Diana. I explored Sorina's body, my hands becoming bloody. When I found no wounds, I dropped the hands I'd been holding like poison. "What the fuck did you do?"

Sorina looked at me, blinked, and the black of her eyes went away; all I saw was the blue and something in the corner of her eyes. More blood, but this seemed to leak from her like tears. "I tried ... I tried to fix it. It didn't work. It never works. I can never save them. I couldn't save her," she mumbled, shivering in the rain.

"Sorina, go home. Clean up. I'll get him to bed," Diana commanded, and my red-haired girl turned to Diana, eyes sharp. She looked like she was ready to say something, a command, but she opened her mouth, then closed it.

Diana nodded, a wordless exchange taking place between them.

I was ready to fight, prepared to yell; I'd wake up the entire trailer park if they would just fucking listen to me. But Sorina looked at

CHAPTER TWENTY-FIVE   265

me, and I saw in her eyes what I saw when we played our games, something tender, something longing. "I'll talk to you tomorrow, Nicholas. If you want to ..." she trailed off, turning to the woods.

I felt it then, my anger bubbling to the surface, the lingering effects of my past bundled together like raw nerves. "Fuck you both," I said, walking away.

I heard Diana call out to me, but I kept walking. Sorina didn't say my name, didn't fight.

I ran to the bench under my window, opened it, then crawled inside. When I closed it and fell to my bed, I shut my eyes, listening.

The trailer wasn't quiet. I could hear movement, and it spurred me to action. I stripped my wet clothing, throwing it in a pile on my closet floor that was my hamper. I grabbed my covers, threw them back, jumping into bed. Just as I covered myself, I heard my bedroom door open. My eyes were closed when the light from the hall spilled in.

I was turned away, and the silhouette on my wall was Valerie's form.

I wondered if the sounds outside had woken her, or if she had been awake getting ready for work.

If she saw Diana leading me down the driveway to the back of the trailer, I knew she wouldn't say anything. She was good at biting her tongue. But if she saw me with two women in the woods, one covered in blood, that might be another story. I steadied my breathing, pretending I was somewhere peaceful. All I could hear was my heart breaking.

After a moment, Valerie closed the door, and I opened my eyes.

I didn't hear her go down her hall, back to bed.

I heard her walk to the front door, leaving.

When her engine turned over, I jumped out of bed, sneaking out of my room. I moved the curtains only slightly as I looked out.

She was sitting in her car—not in the uniform she wore when she worked at the café—her hands on the wheel and she was talking to herself.

I couldn't be sure. My mind was fuzzy from the tea, from the events of the night.

After a moment, she put the car into reverse and left.

It had never occurred to me I might not be the only one sneaking away.

TWENTY-SIX

Valerie was in bed when she heard the noise. She could not sleep, could not move. The drugged feeling that had left her limbs feeling like cement still lingered. She couldn't see his eyes, but the feeling remained. She felt dirty, wrong, and beckoned.

She was under her covers, fully clothed, staring at the ceiling. She had been there since she arrive back home. She wanted to sob in the dark, in the quiet. Nicholas had been gone when she pulled up, blood on her chin, the Deacon's spit on her lip.

She'd been grateful for that. Grateful and incredibly sad. Some part of her wanted him to be there so she could beg him to pack a bag. So they could load up her car and leave Hart Hollow. The image of the Deacon's red smile blinked in her head with the rest of the images. The winged beast. The fire on the ranch. The red-haired girl sheathing Nicholas.

At the sound of the second noise Valerie shot up in the dark, her nightmares melding with reality. She'd seen the red-haired girl in her dreams before, her naked body wrapped around Nicholas, holding him close. She blinked her eyes, rubbing them, then holding entirely still, she listened. She heard rustling, and without a second thought, she threw her flannel comforter off her legs, leaving her bedroom. She walked through the kitchen, past the sparse living room, to the hallway. She slowly opened Nicholas's room, finding him asleep under the covers. She watched his breathing for a moment, then closed the door.

She thought she was going mad, and hastened down the hall, tears welling in her eyes. She thought she'd seen her sister tonight. Her sister, whom she had killed. Alive and well, below the house on the hill. The Deacon had touched her, teased Valerie. She hated him, his vile lies, and how he had sounded just like Markus. Fuck him, she thought. She wanted to expose him, to let the town know a pretender sat on the hill, watching over them. She'd made it all up, what she saw, what she felt. It was a Halloween trick, though the month had passed.

She dressed quickly and quietly, the words in her dreamland repeating in her head. The words the woman had said that last night at the ranch.

Omens and witchcraft.

The woman had looked wild—blonde hair and blood everywhere. And in some deep part of herself, Valerie felt reverence for the woman. So young. So full of power and purpose. She had set forth the events of the night—the death of the family—Markus, and his children. His inbred daughters. His vile sons. She'd lived with them, mingled with monsters. And what did that make her? She wondered. What kind of monster would leave that girl—whoever she was—alone in that cave with the Deacon?

She threw on her coat, rushing out of the front door. She would confront the Deacon. Demand he take her down to the cave again. She wanted to see in the light of the early morning what he had shown her there.

CHAPTER TWENTY-SIX

When she sat behind the wheel of her car, she closed her eyes, repeating the words. They sounded like something Nicholas would read in his horror books. Tales of fangs, and small towns, all the morbidity of a novelist bringing forth images of pain. She wondered if Nicholas would become a writer one day. Let the world see his talent. She'd only seen scraps, but she knew he had it. What was the point of trauma if you couldn't flay it alive for the page?

Valerie did not have that talent. And she envied him the pen, however small.

She thought she saw movement in the trailer, and she stopped mumbling and watched the window. Then, after a moment, she cursed, put the car into reverse, and drove out of the trailer park down the street. Slowly she wove through town, to the outer limits, to Steele Bluff road. The trees looked menacing as her headlights illumined their dark, spindly branches and fallen leaves. They were sleeping, wasting away until the spring. The waking sun shone through the dark branches, reaching for her.

She wanted to see spring there, a fresh rebirth. But she feared she could not do that. The Deacon had ruined the romantic image she had created for him in her mind.

Godly man.

Ghastly man.

Ghoul.

They never failed to let her down, just as her own hands and dark thoughts often did.

She parked next to the lookout, killing the lights.

She sat there for ten minutes, hands on the wheel, then her lap, and finally, covering her face. Tears came in waves until finally she composed herself and reached for the door handle. She gasped when she looked at the long driveway that led to the Deacon's home.

He was waiting on his front steps, watching her.

Naked, glasses off, white eyes hypnotizing her.

She shut the car door and walked to him.

TWENTY-SEVEN

There was no grace period, no reprieve from the worry.

When I walked into school after sleeping in late the next morning, it was clear nothing would ever be the same.

I pulled my backpack higher on my shoulder as my eyes canvassed the scene. Students were sitting on the hallway floor, blocking the lockers and some entrances to classrooms. I could hear crying, soft words, and an argument down the hall as I walked toward my locker in a trance. Every person I made eye contact with had red eyes and tears streaking down their face, so I walked faster, rounded the corner. When I looked at my locker, I saw Kyrie holding Nicole. Jessica stood a few feet behind them, a furious look on her face, but eyes still red.

I rushed forward, reaching for Kyrie. Her eyes opened wide when she saw me. "Nicholas where have you been all morning?" she cried, moving away from Nicole, wrapping her arms around me. I stiffened in her embrace but tried to endure it.

"What happened?" I asked, but maybe I already knew.

"They found part of her," she cried out.

Jessica stepped closer, jerking her chin at me. I pulled away from Kyrie, and she grabbed Nicole again as I moved to the side, following Jessica to my locker. She was blunt. "They found Amber's head."

My heart stopped. "Her ... her head? Just—"

"Just her head. With some necklace in her mouth," she whispered.

"Where?"

"Ten miles out of town, toward the Grave."

"The what? Who's grave?" I ran my hand through my hair, closing me eyes. Images from my dreams flared through my head. "Who's grave?"

Jessica pinched the bridge of her nose. "Sorry, I forgot you're not from here. Gravespring. You know, the Grave kids?"

I knew, and the nickname for the bordering town should have been apparent to me, but I heard *grave* ... and well ...

Jessica turned her back away from her sister and Kyrie. "They're a fucking mess. We gotta get outta here."

I nodded, eyes taking in the morbid stillness of our world. The bell rang for first period, and no one moved. Instead, teachers walked around the halls, comforting students and leading some to the guidance office. There would be no class that day, and no work would've been done if there was. The town had lost a young girl.

"They can't call her a runaway anymore, huh?" I asked, looking at Jessica.

She nodded her head. "Billy ... he's not okay. He didn't go to work but wouldn't let us stay with him at home either. Said we needed to be with you guys," she said, referencing Kyrie and me.

CHAPTER TWENTY-SEVEN

"Fuck," I said, running my hands through my hair. "Okay, let's get out of here."

Relief flooded Jessica's eyes. "I was thinking the same thing, but maybe we should stay? Listen in? I don't know. Fuck."

"Listen in on what?"

Jessica shook her head. "I don't fucking know. What? We aren't going to try to figure out what's happening because she's dead? We've been playing at Sherlock and Watson, but we haven't actually *done* anything, have we?" She looked over her shoulder at Kyrie. "She's fucking scared. Thinks she's next. She kept saying that until Nicole got here. She's going to lose it. We can't leave her alone. And her parents? If she thought they were overbearing before …"

"Yeah," I said, not sure which way to turn, and after a beat the doors at the end of the hall burst open, and as if we conjured them—Kyrie's parents rushed through the entrance. Kyrie looked up at the commotion and pulled away from Nicole, running down the hall.

I knew their relationship wasn't the best, but at that moment, it was something I envied. Valerie wouldn't be barging into the school to see if I was okay when she heard the news, if anything she would be packing a bag, ready to tell me we were leaving Hart Hollow when I got home.

Kyrie's parents hugged her, and her father broke away, walking to Principal Garrison, who stood against the wall, watching his students. They spoke briefly before nodding in agreement. Kyrie's father walked to his wife and daughter, leading them out of the school. Kyrie looked back at us, eyes red, pleading for something, but I couldn't be sure what. She always spoke what she felt, what she wanted. I'd never had to read her face alone.

Nicole joined us, wiping her eyes. "Who ... who could have done that? Who could have done that to a girl? Someone like us?"

Jessica grabbed her twin, pulling her close. It was the first time they seemed like sisters, or remotely alike.

I balled my fists at my side, aching for someone to tell me how to act, something to hit, or rip apart.

I'd seen death before, all in one night, a slaughter. But this was something different. This would draw attention to the small town of Hart Hollow.

Fuck. Would Valerie want to leave? To move? The fear from moments before crept in again, making me shake. We were supposed to disappear, fade into the middle of America.

I thought of Sorina and the blood. Her mangled words. If you decapitated someone, how much blood would cover you? I pushed the thought away, but it lingered. I didn't know her. I didn't know what she was capable of, but how she moved reminded me of a serpent. It scared me and aroused me. I hated who I was, the strange way my mind worked.

I grabbed my backpack, walking away from Nicole and Jessica. I heard Jessica call after me, but I kept going until I hit the double doors, opening them to the bright light of the morning.

The grass was still damp from the rain the night before, and the sun was out. It looked like a normal day, like any other. Except it wasn't. A girl was dead. A girl I never knew but felt the loss of in the vibrations of the surrounding people.

I wanted to scream and howl into the sky until the night fell, the image of Amber Hughes face on the supermarket bulletin board haunting me.

I wanted to know where the fuck Valerie went that morning.

CHAPTER TWENTY-SEVEN

I wanted a fresh start, a new life away from the horrors of the ranch, but my life hadn't changed in one way. I was still terrified of the women in my life.

I don't know what I'd expected to find when I arrived at our trailer.

Valerie looking for me, concerned, like a mother figure should be?

Billy on my porch, devastated, sure this meant the same fate fell upon Sam?

Or Sorina, not covered in blood, but with an open mouth and honesty ready for me. But all of those scenarios were foolish, especially any that involved Sorina in the morning light. She was never seen that early in the morning. I wondered if she would come to afternoon classes and mourn like the rest of the students. But she couldn't cry, could she? Would the tears be red? Blood? I grappled with myth, legend, and the omens the town seemed to be ruled by.

I didn't know where to go. I thought about going to Diana's, but I didn't want to hear the same old shit.

I also wanted to go to Kyrie's, to calm her down, to comfort her. The warm blanket of her parent's worry had likely faded, and she was probably scared. And I wondered if her parents would even let me see her.

It was my fault. My fault for not listening, for not staying away from Casador Lake. Maybe the person, or that thing, would have let Amber go.

I walked to my bedroom in a daze, laid down on the bed, then closed my eyes. Was my nightmare real? Did I imagine that thing by the water? I thought my past was catching up to me, haunting me in waking hours, taking from the ones I cared for. But Hart Hollow had been hiding from these demons long before I came around. I just didn't know it yet.

Eventually, I left my trailer and walked to Sorina's house through the woods. I didn't care what she did in the morning, why she wasn't seen. I was going to see her. I was going to make her tell me the truth.

I approached her house slowly, looking for anyone around, looking for her. But there was nothing. When I knocked on the door, the echo rang back to me. I was met with nothing but silence as I peered in the ornate windows on either side of the beautiful door before I tried the handle. Locked.

Determined, I walked around back to the door that led to the kitchen. Locked as well.

There was a low window along the back of the house. I walked to it, saying a silent prayer to anyone but God, and pulled myself up. It unlatched, and I opened it wide, sneaking in.

The house was cool, shrouded in darkness.

I hadn't noticed the curtains when I was there before. Every window was covered in dark fabric, drowning out the light.

I closed my eyes, then opened them again, adjusting to the darkness. Everything became clear, and I sniffed the air, catching her scent. Quietly I crept down the hall to the staircase, placing my palm on the railing and taking the first step.

The floorboard creaked, cursing me, and I closed my eyes, saying my own curse in my head.

Slowly, I ascended toward the second floor, where I knew her bedroom was.

CHAPTER TWENTY-SEVEN

I made it to the second floor and strolled down the hall to Sorina's room. The door was shut, and I opened it, peering in the dark.

The covers were drawn up on the bed, and a tiny figure was beneath the fabric.

I walked to her, and it struck me how tiny she seemed when I sat at her side.

She didn't open her eye when she spoke. "You're not as quiet as you think, Nicholas," she said, turning over.

The first thing I noticed, beyond her nakedness, was the wound on her neck. I hadn't seen it the night before. There had been so much blood on her. They had lied when they said it wasn't her own. Some of it had to have been from this wound. It was red and raw, not bleeding, but inflamed.

No large wound could have healed that much in such a short time, but she was obviously hurt.

She winced when she sat up, not reaching for the covers, not covering herself.

"What happened to you?" I asked, voice rough.

"I tried to save her, Nicholas. I did," she said.

I made my voice steel, though I wanted to pull her to me, close to my chest, and protect her. "From who? Or what? Tell me what the fuck is happening so I can help."

"There's nothing you can do. She'd dead."

"And what about the next girl?" I asked. "What about Kyrie?"

"Enjoy what time you have with her. She'll graduate next year. He doesn't want her. She can go; she can escape it."

"Escape what?"

"He's full," she said, almost dreamlike. It was as if I wasn't there, as if she were far away, somewhere else, telling a story.

I touched her then. My large hands gripping her small shoulders. "Sorina, what the fuck is going on?"

She reached up, gripping my wrists. "There is a beast in this town, Nicholas. It feeds on the town, on the daughters of men of God. Stay away from God, and you'll be safe. Stay away from the girls whose fathers spread the *Word*, and you won't get hurt. Stay away from me—"

"And what?" I asked, pulling her closer.

"He won't hurt you. You won't hurt me." The last sentence was a whisper.

"Who is doing this?" My hand trailed down her shoulders, catching on her elbows.

"What would you do if you knew?" she asked.

"Turn them in."

She laughed then, small and hollow. She pulled away, then pushed the covers off of her legs, reaching for her nightgown on the edge of the bed before slipping it over her shoulders.

I stood, stepping closer to her, and when she turned to me, she wrapped her arms around me, and the tenderness was so unlike her, like the ways I never wanted to be touched. But with her, with Sorina, I welcomed it. I wrapped my arms around her petite frame, and she tucked her head under my chin, only reachable because I was leaning down, forever toward her like she was the sun.

"I want you to have a normal life. Go to the winter formal. Fall in love. Get married. Have kids. Live in the charade created for you for as long as you can."

"What the fuck are you talking about?" I asked, pulling away.

Sorina was crying, and her tears were red. She shook her head, running her hand up my chest. "You're getting bigger," she remarked.

"I guess," I said. But it was true. Ever since we'd settled in Hart Hollow, I felt my skin stretched thin. When I slept, though rare, I ached in the mornings. Growth spurts.

"You won't be able to help yourself, not if he lets you out."

I let go then, dropping Sorina's hand. "You're going to stop that right now, and you're going to tell me something, fucking *anything* real. Or I'm going to tell someone what I saw. That I saw you covered in blood last night."

Sorina's jaw tensed. "I didn't kill her, Nicholas. You know that. You know I tried to save her."

I groaned, and it sounded like a growl. "I don't know shit. All I know is this shit is pissing me off. Tell me something now, or I'm gone."

"What if I want you gone?"

"Do you?"

Sorina didn't speak; she didn't tell me the truth. Instead, she walked to me, and I stood still. She placed her hands on my chest and moved them up to my neck. Her skin glowed in the darkness of her room, and her pale face beckoned me. I wanted to kiss her, strangle her, tie her up again. But, when I looked into her eyes, they were black. And she opened her mouth, exposing the teeth. The incisors that had always seemed a little longer were longer now than the rest of her teeth.

One hand traveled higher, gripping my throat. I reached for her hand. Trying to pull it away, and it wouldn't budge.

"What are you doing?" I gasped.

"Giving you what you want," she replied as she backed me out of the room to the staircase, and I struggled in earnest, grabbing her arm, yanking at it; it was useless, I couldn't get her off of me, and she was backing me to the steps. I panicked. "Sorina," I begged—her voice a prayer and a plea, the only pleasure I'd ever known.

She smiled, incisors gleaming white. Then, when my feet hit the top of the staircase, I thrashed. She pushed me one last step, and I didn't fall; I didn't tumble down. Because she still had my throat in her hands, and I was in the air, dangling from her small, outstretched arm.

It was impossible. No girl that small should have been able to hold someone like that. I was not yet my full height or strength, but it shouldn't have been possible.

I struggled, gasping for air, and she stepped back, letting my feet hit the hardwood, releasing my neck.

I grabbed my neck, dropping to my knees, gasping. "What the fuck?"

"Am I? I think you know," she said, backing away.

I straightened to my knees, one hand on my neck, one hand gripping the banister. "No," I said, the reality washing over me, overtaking me. I'd left that life behind. It was fairytales and made-up stories to manipulate. It wasn't real.

"Markus worshipped the son of a demon. And that son is here, Nicholas. The Devil has a need, has a hunger."

"No."

"I do too. And think you should leave," she said, walking back into her bedroom, shrouded in darkness.

CHAPTER TWENTY-SEVEN

I wanted to follow her, to get more answers, but the flash of her teeth haunted me, aroused me, and made me sick.

I ran down the staircase, out the back door, and into the light.

I ran down the street.

Past the trailer park.

Only slowing to a jog when Kyrie's house was in view. Her parent's vehicles were in the driveway, and I had a hunch I wouldn't be a welcome guest. I'd moved to town right after Amber went missing. And I'd seen the way Kyrie's father looked at me. Like he thought I wanted to steal his daughter away.

I walked into the yard, crouched low, looking like a common thief.

I knew you could get to Kyrie's window by climbing the tree in front of her house, but what if they were in her room? I took a chance, grabbing the lowest branch and hoisting myself up. I climbed, heart still racing from what happened with Sorina, fear gliding down my spine like a drop of blood.

I pulled a penny from my pocket when I had Kyrie's window in sight, tossing it at it, saying a silent plea that she was in here.

After a moment, her curtain moved, and I saw her stricken face. Then, with wide eyes, she opened the window. "Nicholas, what are you doing?" she hissed, looking back into her room.

"Are you alone?" I asked.

"Right this second, yeah," she whispered. "But they could come back up at any moment. They're freaked out."

"So are you," I said, looking her in the eye.

She nodded, and I worried she would cry right then. She didn't. That would come later, when I was in the room.

After one more hurried glance into her room, she opened the window wide, reaching for me.

I pulled myself in, sliding to Kyrie's floor. She clamped a hand over my mouth, moving to my ear. "I think my dad is leaving soon. Come here." She let go of my mouth, and I closed my eyes.

The memories came flooding back, hands over my mouth, hands on my shoulder pushing me down, hands everywhere. I felt those moments, at the fringes of my mind, when anyone touched me. Anyone but Sorina. When I didn't move from the floor, Kyrie turned back to me. "Are you okay?"

"Please don't ever put your hand on my mouth like that again," I said, robotic, staring at the ceiling. I'd kept my voice low, but Kyrie still looked at her closed bedroom door.

When she looked at me again, she nodded. "Okay. I'm sorry."

After a moment, I got up. Kyrie motioned for me to move toward her closet. I crawled along her hardwood, turning around once I was shrouded by her clothing.

"Sit in here. If they come up, I'll close the closet door."

"Okay," I agreed, leaning into the dark space. It almost felt comforting. I didn't have a big closet in my room, not one that you could sit in like this. I ducked under a section of shirts, batting away a dress that hit me in the face. I crossed my legs, then ran both hands through my hair.

"We're going to keep trying to figure this out, aren't we?" she asked, sitting on the floor, moving close to me. I backed into her closet a fraction more. "Seriously, this time?"

"Yeah, we'll ... we'll figure this out."

CHAPTER TWENTY-SEVEN

Kyrie steepled her fingers, bringing them to her forehead. "I don't want to be next. I don't want to be ... taken ... I'm scared."

"We won't let anything happen to you," I said, making a promise I didn't know if I could keep. Not if the horror was true.

Markus had been a madman, a monster, and his flock was broken like he had been. But he was dead. He couldn't hurt anyone anymore. But what of his God? The son of a demon?

I opened my mouth to speak, to tell Kyrie what I'd seen at Sorina's, what she'd done, but the words died in my throat when we heard footsteps coming upstairs. Kyrie looked at me with wide eyes, and I leaned back into the closet, closing my eyes when she shut the door, shrouding me in darkness.

I heard a door open and a man's voice. "Honey, how are you?" Kyrie's father asked, his deep baritone concerned.

"I'm okay," Kyrie's voice came from the other side of the room, near her bed.

Another set of footsteps entered the room. "Your father and I both have appointments in Springfield today. Do you want to go to your aunt Viviane's house while we're gone? We don't want to leave you alone. Or you can come with us, whatever you need sweetie."

After a moment's hesitation, Kyrie said, "It's okay. I'll be fine." She sounded convincing, and I almost believed her.

"I just don't know how comfortable I feel about leaving you here by yourself with everything that's happened today," her father said.

"I promise I'll be fine, Daddy. I just ... I want to take a nap."

"You could always come with us, darling," Kyrie's mother repeated. "We can go by the mall after. Get that ice cream you like at the food court."

"I'm not hungry. Thanks, Mom. I think I just want to sleep."

The conversation continued for a bit longer, and Kyrie finally convinced her parents she would be okay alone. She promised not to leave or open the door.

The whole time I sat still, quiet, wondering where Valerie was and if anyone would ever worry and protect me the way Kyrie's parents worried for her.

Likely not.

I stayed still like that, writing melancholy poems in my head about my life as her parents walked down the stairs, as Kyrie sent them off, as she locked the doors, finally returning to her bedroom. She left the bedroom door open and walked to the closet door, letting me into the light.

"They're gone," she said.

I sat in the back of her closet, staring at her ceiling, noticing plastic stars pressed to the top. "Why didn't you go with them? Any place has to be safer than here."

"Than Hart Hollow? Or with you?" She laughed, knowing her father would hate this.

I let the silence wash over us, and eventually, Kyrie moved close. "What's wrong?"

I looked at her.

"I mean, besides a girl being dead." She smiled, a sad thing.

"I need to tell you about where I came from."

"The ranch?"

"Yes," I said. After clearing my throat, I started. "I don't know who my father is. I never have. For years I thought I did. But the man my mother was with, he wasn't my real father. I didn't

CHAPTER TWENTY-SEVEN

live on a cattle ranch in California. It used to be a ranch, though it'd been years. I don't know how Markus got it. He didn't even have a job." I cleared my throat, leaning against the wall. "Markus was the leader. There were thirty of us living on the property. It was all self-contained, self-sufficient. We had gardens and our own little houses. A cafeteria where we all ate together. And there was a church. Where we prayed and congregated."

Kyrie was listening intently, no horror on her face. Not yet. If I stopped there, it would be a lovely tale. A quiet life on a ranch with a community of people surrounding us. It could have been nice, could have been a haven.

"Markus believed Jesus Christ was a vampire," I said.

Kyrie's face jolted as if she'd been slapped.

I continued. "He believed he was a chosen one. That Jesus had chosen him to spread his message, his pure love, his pure ... seed." I swallowed. "There weren't many men on the ranch. Just his sons. His son, Leo, was with my mother. His other son, Adrian, was with my aunt Valerie for a while. But ... the couples ... it was all a lie."

"What do you mean?"

I closed my eyes. "They were all fucking each other. He was spreading his seed, securing his line. And so were his sons. Any sons had to come from his line. Sometimes, though, they brought in new women. When my mother was fishing for new prospects, I guess she had a one-night stand with my real father? I don't know. I don't look like Leo, and I know Markus watched me closely, didn't think I was a part of his family tree. He was right. Because of that, I was their plaything."

"What do you mean?"

I wanted to break open, to cry, but I swallowed, pushing down the knot in my throat, the aching in my body. "The women. He let the women have me when they wanted me."

Kyrie brought her hand to her mouth, stifling a gasp, eyes wide. "They … what did …" she whispered.

I couldn't say it. The shame mingled with what I knew I should say. I should have said I liked it and enjoyed them using me. But I couldn't. I didn't. My body betrayed me when they pulled me into darkened rooms, when they touched me, brought me to the brink, let me spill over into their hands, on their flesh, and sometimes, inside of them—though it was forbidden.

I saw them at night, hungry mouths, open palms, the dark abyss of my captors.

All to keep them happy, to keep them there. Because they did not always welcome the flesh of Markus—his seed. Not all of them. Maybe deep down, they saw it for what it was. Incestuous, a violation. So they violated me. Thought it was okay because we did not share blood.

"Do you believe in vampires?" I asked, half a sad laugh on my tongue.

Kyrie shook her head furiously. "No."

"Neither did I." I said, staring at the window, wanting to leave, to end this sad confession.

"And now?" Kyrie asked. "What's going on, Nicholas?"

I wiped at my eyes. "What if he was right? What if Markus was right? What if the myths are real?"

"They're not. It's just … stories."

"So is the Bible," I spat, regretting it the instant it came from my mouth.

CHAPTER TWENTY-SEVEN

Kyrie looked wounded. "Stories ... we need them."

"To lull us to sleep? To tell us about the past? Secure our future?"

"Nicholas, you're scaring me. Tell me what happened. We were just at school an hour ago ..."

"I think a vampire is doing this." I hated the words and how I sounded like a madman blaming bad things on the bogeyman. When I looked at Kyrie, I saw a look I didn't want to see. Concern. Worry. Not for a vampire coming into her room and grabbing her next but worry for me. Fear for my fucked up head.

"Nicholas ..." she started.

I cut her off. "I know. I know how it sounds."

"It sounds like you're trying to scare me. You don't have to. I'm already scared."

"I'm not trying to scare you. I'm trying to ..." I tried.

"I want to find out who did this, who's *doing* this ... but we can't do that if we're chasing made-up monsters." Kyrie sighed.

I wanted to tell her what Sorina did, about the blood, about her teeth. I wondered if I was losing it and if the years on the ranch were finally catching up. Was I becoming like Markus? "Sometimes the monsters are real," I said. It'd always been men, women, the humans of this world. I didn't believe in fairytales and the omens humans made up to justify their cruelty. But now I didn't know what I believed.

Kyrie softened, indulged me. "Then ... who is the vampire in his town? Are you still reading that book?"

I remembered her seeing the worn copy of *Salem's Lot* in my locker.

I nodded. "Yeah, but I'm not—"

Kyrie stood, walking to her bed. There was one book on her nightstand. One. The Bible. She placed her hand on it, and I looked away.

That was not the answer. Not really.

I held Sorina's secret—her sharp teeth and black eyes—in my chest like a promise, a part of me I couldn't let go of.

If I said what she was, what I'd seen, I'd be putting a bullseye on her. But I didn't think she was the one doing this. She spoke of *him*, of someone else.

The Deacon lives on the hill, above the lake, above the island.

He scared me.

And he had Valerie hanging on his every word. I remembered the look on her face when she sat in her car talking to herself.

I'd been mad she wasn't worried about me.

But maybe I was the one who should worry for her.

After driving by the café to see if Valerie was there and safe, Kyrie and I drove up the drive to the school, parking in the student lot. When we walked in, the hallways were no longer lined with students. Instead, it was eerily quiet until we made it to the gym.

We walked in, halting at the top of the stairs that led to the bleachers to search for our friends. I found Nicole and Jessica in the crowd, and we headed to them, taking the two seats they had saved for us. "What going on?" I asked Jessica, who was closest to the seat I took.

"I don't know," she said, annoyed. "Where the hell did you go?"

"Kyrie's house," I said, and Jessica narrowed her eyes.

Nicole leaned over Kyrie, who was next to me. "Principal Garrison said he had an announcement. And the Mayor is going to be here."

I shivered, but I didn't have long to dwell on the thought because Principal Garrison walked onto the basketball court, followed by Mayor Wynn. The whispers of our classmates dulled as the Mayor stepped up to the mic.

Beside me, Kyrie reached for my hand, and I tried to bear it.

I saw Jessica glance at us before looking ahead.

"Students of Hart Hollow High. It is with deep regret that I meet with you today. I know it's been a difficult day. Unfortunately, one of your fellow students is gone." He cleared his throat, reaching for his tie. "Amber Hughes was taken too soon, and the investigation into her murder will be the sole focus of the Hart Hollow Sheriff's department. I know there has been speculation about other disappearances in the past, and I want to state that at this time, we see no relation between the murder of Miss Hughes and any other missing persons."

Beside me, Jessica swore. "If Billy were here ..."

Kyrie leaned forward, shushing Jessica.

I tried to ignore them.

"For the time being, we will instate a city-wide curfew on any underage individuals. No one is out past nine o'clock in the evening without parental supervision. No sleepovers. No parties. No cruising. The Raven's Nest will close at eight o'clock sharp every night so everyone can get home safely."

A collective groan resounded through the auditorium, mostly from guys. They weren't worried. It wasn't as if they were in danger—as Nicole had pointed out.

The Mayor raised his palms. "I know, I know. Of course, you all want to go out and have fun. But still, I urge you to remember it's not safe right now, and having Hart Hollow be a safe town for your parents to raise their families and for you to raise families in the future is our top priority."

"What about the winter formal?" I heard someone ask from the back of the bleachers.

Principal Garrison cleared his throat, and the Mayor nodded at him.

"The winter formal in December will be the one exception to the curfew. The tragedy of Amber Hughes is in all of our hearts, and we will take every precaution. We are going to have a safe and orderly dance. The PTA is organizing more parents to be on standby to ensure everyone is watched and cared for. So, let your parents know. Urge them to sign up."

"What a buzzkill," someone said behind me, and there was laughter.

I clenched my fist and pulled my hand from Kyrie's.

I'd wanted to ask Sorina to be my date for the winter formal, held the question on the tip of my tongue in the pool, in her room, late nights spent by her, wondering what was going through her head.

Now, I didn't know. The image of her sharp teeth flashed in my mind, and I closed my eyes, lost in it. I adjusted in my seat.

I still wanted to see her, talk to her, listen, and be afraid.

My *normal* life was unraveling; it couldn't last. Nothing lasts.

Fuck Tabula Rasa.

"For now, we are going to go home early. Buses will take you home if you feel safe. If not, you can call your parents to pick you up or go home at your normal time. If you're leaving later, you can stay here in the gym. No leaving to your locker without checking out with a teacher at the door."

"It's like a prison," Jessica whispered.

Kyrie looked at her. "They're being safe."

"Amber wasn't taken from school. She was last seen in the fucking woods. Just like Sam."

"I guess I won't go into the woods then," Kyrie remarked.

I saw her wring her hands together, and I knew she was scared. I wished I could stay with her at night, hide in her closet or something. I wanted to protect my friend. But did I need to protect her from Sorina?

The Mayor and Principal Garrison prattled on about the new rules for a while, and I leaned back into my seat, closing my eyes, trying to formulate a plan.

I looked over at Nicole, and she was watching me, eyes red. I grabbed her hand, pulling her from her seat. "We'll be back," I said over my shoulder. Jessica and Kyrie shared matching looks of suspicion.

We checked out with the teacher at the entrance, lying about needing to go to our lockers. I held onto Nicole's hand in pretense to convince the teacher she was my girlfriend, but I wasn't sure whether the lie landed. I didn't care.

When we made it to the hallway, Nicole pulled her hand from mine. "What's going on?"

I walked down the hall to my locker wordlessly.

"*Nick*, what the hell?" she called after me, hurrying up.

When I made it to my locker, I grabbed the lock, twisting it, putting in the combination. "I want you to tell me more about your friendship with Amber."

"What do you mean? She was my partner in science. That's it," she said, the lie making her choke up.

I opened my locker, reaching for the little notebook I kept in my pocket when I went to class. "Stop lying to me," I said, staring Nicole in the eyes.

She crossed her arms, eyes glassy. "I'm not."

"Yeah, you are," I said. "I've felt it ever since you first said her name. Something was going on."

Nicole rolled her eyes. "What do you mean, something was *going on?*"

"I don't fucking know, Nicole. But you gotta stop keeping us in the dark about whatever the hell it is."

Nicole stomped away, and I chased after her, glancing around the hallway. She ducked into the girl's restroom, and I swore before following her in.

She whirled around. "You can't be in here, Nick."

"Quit calling me Nick," I replied, crouching down to look beneath the stall doors. There was no one in there.

"Fuck off," she said, reaching for a stall door. I blocked it.

"And that's how I can tell you're lying."

"How?" she asked, her voice sounding off.

"You sound like Jessica right now. You don't swear, you don't call me Nick. You're pissed."

"I'm scared," she admitted as she reached for a chain around her neck.

CHAPTER TWENTY-SEVEN

"No, Kyrie's scared. This is something else. Tell me what's going on, or I'll ask Jessica."

Nicole laughed. "Jessica doesn't know shit about me."

"Yeah, but she'll never leave you alone if she thinks there's something to figure out. Billy won't either."

"Billy wasn't fucking Amber. He only cares about Sam."

"So who was fucking Amber, then?" I yell.

Nicole shoved me, tears falling. "I was. Are you fucking happy? They said she had a necklace in her mouth," her words broke at the end, and I stepped back, hands falling to my side.

Nicole reached into her shirt and pulled out a necklace, tears running down her face. We stared at each other before she tucked it back inside her T-shirt.

Whatever I thought Nicole was hiding, it wasn't that. And I hated myself for pushing her, for pulling it out. This time, I didn't block her when she grabbed the stall door, opening it wide.

Suddenly the tension made sense, the way she had been looking at Kyrie, the way she had mourned the disappearance of Amber. Someone she cared for, maybe even loved.

I walked to the stall door, placing my hand on it. "Fuck, Nicole. I'm sorry. I didn't know. I didn't know that what—"

"Just please go away, Nicholas. Please. I've been handling it this way. Alone. If you tell them ..."

I pressed my forehead to the stall door. "I won't. We'll find a way to ... don't worry. I won't say anything." It wasn't my secret to tell, and anything she knew, I'd tell them I got the information somewhere else. I'd lie. I'd figure out a way to lie for her.

I'd lie for Nicole, and I'd try to save Kyrie from her fears—I'd keep them there with me, as long as I could.

TWENTY-EIGHT

She'd been a healthy meal. Drawn out, as always, until her parents' grief had been so exquisite the Deacon knew it was time to end the suffering.

He'd wanted Valerie to do it—to take the life, he thought the magic of making Amber's face look like Valerie's foster sister would do it. But Valerie had been too long in the fire. The ranch had been a holding cell, a place for Nicholas to build his mocking, impenetrable rage and a home for Valerie to remain untouched. He'd planted fear into their minds. The men at the ranch knew never to touch Valerie. She thought it was her deformity. But it was the Deacon's will.

She was the red virgin, a missing piece in his ascension. The reds were few, and they were always unique to him. It was why Sorina was so special to him—why he let her out, let her pretend she was fighting him, carrying out her ill-fated plans. *You should let your children play.*

And the townspeople were precisely that. His children. His little lambs.

CHAPTER TWENTY-EIGHT

It was a disappointment, the way Valerie had run out. But then she came back—they almost always came back.

And he'd ushered her into his home with open arms. The seed had been planted, and he saw the fire in her eyes dim. Now he just needed her to bring the boy with her. Bring him into the home, into the family. He didn't want to drag him kicking and screaming. There was no fun in that. He wanted the chase to be real to the boy. He wanted him to nip at Sorina's feet with delight. Right now he was only playing. And children shouldn't play with their food.

He hadn't wanted to tear Amber's limbs from her body that night as she screamed in the dark. But Sorina had pushed him. He'd grown bored with her circling, her playtime in the water, her stalking of the cave entrance.

She could not get in.

The way was barred, but she liked to taunt him. And she liked to offer the girl promises she couldn't keep. So he'd stared into Sorina's eyes as he ripped the girl's flesh apart. Tore and drank and smiled as Sorina thrashed at the entrance, forever barred until she could be good.

And she was never good. Not the way Valerie would be.

The funeral for Amber Hughes took place on a Sunday at the Holman Howe Funeral Home. The only funeral home in Hart Hollow. And her body was laid to rest, not at the cemetery near the woods by her father's church, but in town at the Steele Memorial Cemetery.

Amber's mother and father had fit in nicely in his small congregation.

The weight of leading his flock at the Hart Hollow Free Will Baptist Church was lifted from the pastor, and the grief had lessened. That's how the Deacon knew it was time. Time to end their daughter's life and renew the grey feeling of hollowness in their eyes.

They'd wept in the Deacon's small, round church. They'd cried on his lawn. And he took them in. Fed them with Valerie by his side.

And when he ushered the pastor into the confessional, every ill thought he'd planted into the man spilled forth. The way he'd touched his daughter. The way he'd sinned. The way he'd strayed from the path. *This was my punishment,* he'd said. And the Deacon offered him forgiveness. Afterward, he held the hands of the Hughes and planted new seeds. They would pack up. They would move away and start over. He didn't need their hollow shells. He didn't need their gaunt faces in his church. He needed fresh meat. He needed a new family to take the mantel of the Hart Hollow Free Will Baptist Church. He needed new guards at each point of the cross.

TWENTY-NINE

Life had a way of going on despite tragedy. It was something I knew innately, a reality I cursed when my body and mind were used on the ranch. Each morning after, the sun would shine. There would be birds singing, and there would be smiles—even from the most desolate souls.

That's how life went on in Hart Hollow. There was a funeral for Amber Hughes. I did not attend, though my friends did.

It felt wrong to show up, to mourn a girl who was nothing more than a face on a grocery store flyer.

I mourned future ills, my dreams and manifestations.

I mourned Sorina, who did not come back to school.

I mourned Nicole, who mourned in silence.

And I mourned Valerie, who rarely came home, leaving our shallow dance at family in the past.

Amber was not laid to rest in the cemetery near her father's church.

We'd heard the rumors and discussed it in passing.

Pastor Hughes's church, just out of town, had become a solemn place. People were leaving. Pastor Hughes had taken to sobbing at the podium. Ranting about the sins of our children, the way they were being led astray. He preached hope, and his hope had soured to sorrow.

Then he stopped showing up. The doors stayed locked, and he found a new place to talk to God.

Pastor Hughes and his wife gave up leadership in favor of being the sheep. They joined the Deacon on the hill. They rarely came into town. They rarely spoke to others who were not part of the Deacon's church.

And then one day, they were gone. No one saw them leave town, but they followed the same path as Sam's parents did. Out of town, far away from the sorrow of their gone daughter. We connected the dots, but to the people of Hart Hollow these two families were not the same. Sam had been runaway. Amber had been a victim.

The rumors persisted, small town gossip and bile.

But in our world, some things calmed. The dreams no longer came to Kyrie. She did not hear something on her roof, did not feel the eyes anymore. She looked rested, a worry dropped from her skin, leaving her lighter. She mourned her classmate, but she did not mourn herself anymore.

I tried to convince myself that my dreams meant nothing, and I didn't share them with my friend. I didn't care that on the nights Valerie did not come home, I thought I heard the animal from the hill in the dark outside my trailer, sniffing, crying out, growling.

It was the first time I was afraid of the darkness outside, and in turn, I found a strange comfort in the darkness of my bedroom.

The trailer felt different when I was alone.

CHAPTER TWENTY-NINE

And I was ashamed to admit it was a different I wanted.

I didn't want to think about what it said about me that I wasn't upset Valerie had left me behind like a forgotten toy.

At school, the basketball team won games and traveled. The choir sang. The drama club whispered in huddled groups. The lost smiles returned to students' faces. Life had a way of going on despite tragedy, and the winter formal loomed in our minds like a beacon to better days.

We also got a new transfer student from Florida. Her name was Lauren, and she had blonde hair, dark brown eyes, and was almost as tall as me.

The jocks eyed her for different reasons, and Kyrie chatted with her during a few lunch periods, leaving me with the twins.

On Lauren's first day Kyrie ate lunch with her, and she came back to our table beaming before the bell rang, telling us Lauren's father had been a pastor in Orlando.

I stared at Kyrie when she told us this news, and when I glanced back and forth between Nicole and Jessica, their faces matched my own.

"What?" Kyrie asked

Jessica leaned in as Kyrie sat down. "Tell that girl to get the fuck out of town right now."

Kyrie closed her eyes, and I wondered if the town curfew had also dulled her sense of reality. Things had been quiet. We'd met after school at the Nest from time to time, discussing timelines, missing girls from the past, and the Archer house.

The five of us thought of nothing dark, just enjoying each other's company. Pretending funerals had not recently passed, bodies had not been cut in the night, and I was not an orphan.

Each night we hung out together we had all gone home early, beating the curfew.

I'd joined Billy in the cemetery on the nights he brought up Sam, hoping my presence was a salve in some way. We smoked and played cards on the picnic table beneath my window. Some nights I went over to the trailer and hung out with Jessica and Nicole as well.

I'd worried it would put a wedge between Kyrie and me, and I could see the wedge inching in each day. We had inside jokes, and Kyrie rolled her eyes at them. I'd asked if I could come to Kyrie's house for dinner on the days I worried the dynamic in the group was blurry. And the answer was always the same. My first friend in Hart Hollow said she would love me to come over, but her father wouldn't allow it.

When I looked at my friend now, I saw what she was feeling. I saw the wedge between us when she looked at us.

I was on their side.

And Lauren and Kyrie had something in common. Something Kyrie and I would never have.

Because in my heart I did not believe in miracles. I did not believe in the forgiveness of sins and the love of a father. I believed in the wrath of the wicked. I believed not in fairytales, but in horror stories.

Life had a way of going on despite tragedy. But my life was stuttering and starting, unable to go on after what I'd seen in Sorina's house.

Life had a way of sinking when reality was worse than your darkest nightmare.

She was not human.

The girl next door was not human, and I was in love with her.

I was in love with the blood that soaked her in dreams, with the way she made me hurt in the softest places. I was in love with an unearthly thing, and I felt my wrongness seep out when I was among my friends.

When Kyrie looked at me, I reached into my sleeve, running my finger over the friendship bracelet she had given me. I'd asked her if she would make one for the Clement siblings. And she dodged the question every time.

"I don't want to feel like this," she said, leaning in. "I want to go back to normal."

I thought of my first day, just a few short months ago. I'd wanted a fresh start, and I got fresh horrors—my first fall into desire. And I got these people. These friends.

"Did you tell her she was the fresh meat? Did you tell her what would happen?" I almost smiled but held it back.

Jessica rolled her eyes at Kyrie. "You gonna be lookout when they TP her house?"

Kyrie mocked a shocked face, and Nicole smiled. For a fleeting moment, we slipped into normal. The voices around us were lulling and comforting. The smell of the food and the laughter, it almost made me believe I'd never seen Sorina's fangs. Never seen the black of her eyes.

Never wanted to walk arm and arm with her into the gym.

I looked across the lunchroom to Lauren. She was leaning against the wall, rifling through her book bag. When she looked up, her eyes went to Kyrie. Kyrie who made every new student feel at home. Kyrie who was funny and kind and judgmental and real. The new girl's eyes landed on me, and I smiled at her, then looked at my friends.

I looked at Kyrie then, and before I could stop myself, I reached across the table to place my hand on hers. "You should be her friend. Everyone needs friends," I said, and Jessica did not scoff this time.

The lunch bell rang, and we stood, walking back to our lockers.

Kyrie hung back and walked with me. "Maybe you should ask Lauren to be your date for the formal," she said, looking up at me.

"Absolutely not," I replied.

"Why? Who else would you take?"

Sorina's name hung in the air like an omen, but I didn't say it. It was a game I played. I wanted to see if she lingered in their minds, or if she drifted away. She often vanished and was only real to my friends when I brought her up. I wondered if it was some sort of magic, something dark. How else could someone—a being such as her—survive in this world if people didn't forget her?

I shrugged away my thoughts, vowed to work them into a story, and looked at Kyrie. "Let's all go as friends." I was reluctant to add another to the group, but what we all were to each other was changing. I had the key to something, and I was reluctant to let it free. They would think I was insane. They would think I needed help. They would leave me behind, just as Valerie had.

"Okay. I'll talk to her." Kyrie smiled. "Lets all meet at the trailer park."

It did something to my heart to see her smile like that. I wanted that for my friends. Normalcy of some sort. So I told myself I would keep my secret, even if it ate me alive. And I would go talk to the one person I knew would not think I was going insane.

CHAPTER TWENTY-NINE

After school, I took a walk across town in the daylight.

I needed wheels. That much was apparent, but it hadn't been a priority when we arrived, and I'd wanted an excuse to explore the town.

But now, with Valerie rarely home, I knew it was time to broach the subject. I knew we had money stored, and I was half tempted to help myself to it. But I also knew I needed a job if I was going to sever the cord entirely between myself and Valerie. Relying on her for the past two years had been like breathing. We relied on each other in silence, in ease. But now it felt like a crutch. Or a cage.

And I didn't like the idea of being caged.

When Moonies was in sight, I sped up, crossing the bridge over Casador Lake at a brisk run. I hesitated when I made it across the highway to the gas station that sat between Moonies and Diana's place.

I could hear music from the derelict bar, and smoke came from the chimney of Diana's house.

I walked to her front door, clearing my throat as I knocked.

She didn't answer the door, but a loud whistle sounded behind me. I turned to see Diana at the entrance of Moonies, waving me over.

I jogged past the gas station pumps to her, slowing when I saw her raised eyebrow.

"What are you doing, kid?" she asked gruffly.

I glanced at her throat, noticing what shouldn't have been there—what I hadn't noticed before. I looked her in the eye. "Can we talk?" I asked, running a hand through my hair.

Diana glanced back into the bar and nodded to someone before shutting the door, drowning out the jukebox.

We walked across the pavement in silence, the late fall wind stinging.

When we made it to her place, she opened the door. It hadn't been locked.

I walked into her living room, the familiar smell of tea and weed hitting me. It smelled comforting.

Diana walked into her kitchen and put the kettle on.

"No tea for me," I said, staring at her.

She laughed. "So, for what do I owe the honor of this daytime visit, Hemming?" she asked, grabbing a porcelain mug from the cabinet.

I walked into the kitchen. "I'd like to have a no-bullshit conversation about that night."

The most honest conversation I'd had was with the paper in my pocket. Only there could I admit what I believed in. I told myself when we left, I wouldn't believe in anything anymore. Not God. Not angels. Not the Devil. I could feel them all around me now. And not in a good way.

"Okay," Diana said, crossing her heart. She smiled after that, and it was the look of someone with a secret they promised never to reveal. The face of someone about to reveal that secret.

Diana offered me water, and I filled it myself from the tap, unsure if I could trust her.

We walked into the living room and sat on the couch.

CHAPTER TWENTY-NINE

After taking a sip of my water, I jumped in.

"Sorina's a vampire?" I said, not sure if it was a question or not.

Diana took it as one.

"She wouldn't call herself that."

"What would she call herself?" I asked, annoyed at the toying already.

But when Diana spoke again, she gave me what I wanted. Finally. "There are many names for it, and where one is born, where they live and mingle with humans, they often adopt that term. Sorina is a living thing. Her heart beats, she cries, she eats, sleeps, breathes. She would call herself a Moroi. As her people did before she knew what she was."

"Before she was turned?" My mind flipped through stories, through lore, searching for anything that felt real.

"No one *made* her. She was born that way. No one bit her." She laughed.

"So ..."

"I know you have a mess of facts from movies and comics and TV shows going on in there," she said, calling me out. "She can't turn into a bat, and she won't turn to ash in the sun. But she won't be watching it rise with you."

I stopped her. "I'm just trying to figure out if any of this shit Markus said on the ranch was real." I never believed him, but as a kid, I found some of his stories fascinating. He called it the gospel, and I listened like someone was telling me a fairytale. I studied his scripture and turned it into the stories I fed to the fire.

Diana scoffed. "His head was full of scrambled eggs, and we both know that."

"Yeah," I spat. "He was a rapist and a murderer. A monster. And he's dead now, but he believed in that sort of thing. Maybe that's why he's dead. And now I'm on the same fucking track."

"That's not why he's dead. Believing in us doesn't make you stupid."

"In us?" I asked, my stomach dropping.

Diana smiled, and I noted her teeth. They looked ordinary. "Oh, I'm no ... vampire ... as you say. I'm something else. Something you'll understand one day."

When I dreamed, it was of people, creatures, and the Devil in the night sky. All in the dark. The places blurred—the ranch, places I'd never seen.

And after arrived in the Ozarks I dreamed of different places.

The pond by the school.

The pool out on Highway 38.

And the Archer house.

I dreamt of a glowing red circle. Sometimes in my dream I stepped through. And I would often wake then, never knowing what was on another side.

When I had visited the pond, the pool, and the Archer house, I'd never seen a red circle glowing in front of me.

But I'd heard a strange hum. I'd felt an unmistakable dread, as if there were a key I'd left behind to open the doors. When I visited the Archer house alone, I thought I imagined the glow inside. Red inside the house, seeping out of the windows. But there was never anything inside. Sorina looked afraid when I told her what I saw. She told me it was nothing but a dream. But I knew that was a lie. I'd heard her pulse. But convinced myself I'd imagined it. Diana said she was alive, a living thing.

CHAPTER TWENTY-NINE

And I'd felt, touched, and sucked at that pulse as I took her throat in.

I hadn't known what she was, but now I had a word for it. The word she chose.

Moroi.

Horror stories soared in my head. Reality and fiction blurred at the edges. What was a myth and what was magic remained to be seen.

I was tired of some mysteries.

I looked into Diana's eyes, pleading with her to tell me something real. I remembered Sorina's words.

He's full. There's a beast in this town.

"What is the Deacon?" I asked, leaning forward.

Diana opened her mouth, a look of resignation on her face, but our conversation was cut short when someone knocked on the door.

Standing on the other side was Sheriff Childress.

⊙

Sheriff Childress stood all of five foot nine and had an unfortunate mustache. I'd never spoken to the man, but I'd been playing a game of cat and mouse with him for weeks, though he was none the wiser.

I stepped out of Diana's house as the Sheriff stepped back. "Sheriff Childress," I said in way of greeting, my mocking getting the best of me.

The lawman stared past my shoulder into the house.

"Miss Rollin, I'm going to assume you know this boy who was just *in* your home."

Diana walked past me, her height startling when she looked at the man before her. "Yes. Nicholas was just leaving. I was going to drive him home."

"Is there a reason *you*, a bar owner, have a minor in your house?"

I looked at Diana. There was no reason for me to be in this woman's home that didn't sound completely ridiculous. *Oh, sorry, sir, we were discussing vampires.*

I smirked, and the Sheriff looked at me.

"After school tutoring," Diana mocked, crossing her arms.

The Sheriff glared at her, then looked at me. "You, I need you to come with me. There've been reports of vandalism at a house in city limits. An anonymous tip said they saw you leaving the premises."

"What premises?" I demanded, walking past Diana.

"You tell me, son. Have you been breaking into more than one house in town? I know you're new here, but vandalism and breaking and entering don't fly in Hart Hollow. We're a quiet town, and I'd like to keep it that way. Now come along so I can take you to your guardian."

I heard Diana make a noise behind me, and I turned to her. "It's fine. I'll talk to you later," I said, walking to the police cruiser.

The ride into town was short and rife with tension. Behind the partition, I watched the Sheriff's jaw twitch, and I couldn't figure out why he would be that pissed at a teenage boy possibly breaking into a house.

As we pulled up to the stop sign, we turned right toward the café instead of turning left to take us past the school and to my trailer.

CHAPTER TWENTY-NINE

When we pulled in, the eyes of every person on the street and in the parking lot turned toward the car. I looked like a deviant, and my anger didn't quell when the Sheriff came to my door to let me out of the vehicle.

Without a word, he escorted me to the back of the café, where Valerie was leaning against the side of the building. When I turned to my right, I saw two workers at the feed store eyeing me from the open dock doors.

"Miss Valerie, I was able to find your nephew. But, unfortunately, he was in the house of an adult woman. A woman who owns the bar here in town."

Valerie pushed off the wall, and every tense moment we'd danced through since she decided to return to God flashed in my mind.

"Nicholas, please get in my car," she said.

I saw her car parked a few feet away, but I didn't move. "Can someone explain to me what's going on here?" I asked.

The Sheriff looked at Valerie, and she nodded. "There have been anonymous tips about suspicious activity at the Archer house. Do you know it?" he asked.

I nodded. "Everyone does. They call it a haunted house at school."

The Sheriff smiled. "I know that's not what your peers call it. You call it a party house. It's been a problem for years. But I'm putting my foot down on it now with everything that ..." he trailed off. "Anyway, I know there is a very important formal tonight, and often, your peers like to have themselves a good ol' time at that house after the dance. It's close to school. No one can watch you. I get it, I was once young too. But I've had enough. This has been a peaceful town for many years, and it will return to that."

Valerie stepped forward and spoke in a voice I had never heard before. "I can assure you, Sheriff Childress, Nicholas will not be going into that house again. He's also not going to the formal tonight."

At this, I lost my thinly veiled composure. I looked at Valerie, hard. "Tell me why I should take an order from you?" I asked.

The Sheriff shook his head. "Son, you should—"

I ignored him. "Tell me here and now why I should take an order from you?" I asked, my fists clenched.

Valerie stared at me, and her lips trembled. I remembered that moment in the trailer when it shook with my anger. I remembered her murmuring mouth when I saw her talking to herself in her car. She was losing it, losing herself to something. And I hated that I knew how that felt.

The Deacon had her on a leash and hadn't Sorina had me on one? I hated them both in that moment.

"I'm going home now. You don't need to drive me. Don't worry about driving me ever again," I said, walking away.

I heard the Sheriff call after me, then Valerie's assurance that it was okay. He hadn't brought me in to question me or formally arrested me, and I wasn't scared of the Sheriff. I wasn't scared of Valerie.

And I wasn't scared of walking into the Archer house again.

But, someone wanted me out.

And that was the reason I would visit it again that night.

THIRTY

I wasn't a runner, but after I left the café parking lot, I sprinted back to our trailer. *My trailer*, I thought sullenly. Once home I changed into the black jeans and suit jacket I'd laid out that morning. I had a white button up to wear underneath that I'd found at the thrift store downtown. I didn't have a date, but I pinned a red rose to my lapel. The same color as Sorina's hair. I'd taken it from the bush outside her front door a few nights ago, hoping she would come out.

Once my shaggy hair was combed, I ran into Valerie's room, opening her curtains so I could see outside incase her car approached. It didn't take me long to find the safe in the back of her closet. A ratty old blanket she brought from the ranch covered it. I tried Valerie's birthday for the combination first. It didn't unlock. But when I used my birthday, the lock clicked, and I felt no triumph at my win. My birthday. My one tie to my past, fading away.

Pushing away any warm thoughts I had of my time with Valerie on the road, I grabbed a stack of bills, counting. I didn't plan to take all the money. I didn't even want half. Because Valerie had worked more than I did due to school. But I would take what I thought was enough to buy my freedom.

After setting the stack aside, I moved to another one, and my hands stilled. It was covered in blood. I brought it to my nose, smelling it, wondering why I was fucking smelling it.

When I closed my eyes, I saw the ranch, I heard the screams, and I saw the blood. I knew instantly where the money had come from. Blood money.

And hadn't I bled for it, too? I screamed in the closet, the echo shaking the trailer. Then I put my first through the back of her closet. I lived in the past the way I breathed, and I was going to be suffocated by my memories.

I closed my eyes for a moment, slowing my breathing, calming myself down.

At the ranch I'd been a spectator, a plaything. I'd been someone who had things done to them. I was passive and weak.

I would not be that anymore. I was taking control. Starting now.

After I put everything in her room back in order, I grabbed a handful of sandwich bags from the kitchen. I shoved the blood money inside and headed out the back door, across the yard, and through the cemetery. I didn't feel safe putting the money anywhere in the trailer, so I went to the safest place I knew. The scariest place I knew. I pulled my notebook from my pocket, then a pen.

I wrote a note to Sorina, then shoved it into the bag with the money before pushing the bills through the mail slot on her front door. I waited a moment for her to come, but she never did, so I left after casting a fleeting glance at the window to her bedroom.

Once back in the trailer park, I ran to the Clement trailer.

CHAPTER THIRTY

When Billy answered the door, he grinned. "Nice shirt, Hemming. Is that vintage? What are you doing here?" he asked.

I walked in, looking down the hallway where I saw the open doors to the twin's separate bedrooms. Jessica stepped out, calling over her shoulder. "The curls look good, don't touch them." The smile she had on her face warmed me. I wanted us to all get along tonight—to have fun tonight. I wanted a sense to normalcy before I plunged into danger again.

When Jessica looked at me before heading into her room, her eyes went wide. I blushed before I could register the feeling she pulled from me. "Fucking hell, Hemming. Look at you," she whispered.

I'd bought the clothes for the formal during Thanksgiving break. I was growing out of clothes all the time, and my height had reached six foot two. I thought I'd looked decent when I left the trailer, but she made me feel weird.

Billy grabbed my arm, pulling me away from his sister. "Finish getting ready Jess, you can eye fuck him at the dance later where I don't have to see it." He groaned.

I walked into Billy's room, following the sound of loud music, which he turned down. When he turned to me, I reached into my coat pocket and pulled out a wad of cash. None of it had blood stains. "Is your uncle's truck still for sale?" I asked.

Billy grinned wide. "Fuck yes, Hemming. I've been saying you need wheels. Those wheels are so you. You're going to eat them alive up there."

Jessica walked into the room as he clapped me on the back. She looked no more ready to go than she had moments earlier. "What the fuck are you going on about?" she asked.

"Hemming is buying the Silverado."

"Yes! That means we don't have to babysit you anymore!" She punched me in the arm, and I wondered where Nicole was. She was the sibling least likely to assault me.

"Yeah." I laughed as Billy rummaged through his desk.

In my peripheral, I saw Jessica eyeing me up and down as the prospect of having the truck made me suddenly even more irresistible to her. I pushed away memories of the first day of school, of her spreading her legs, and the way she'd looked at me just moments ago.

Following a few curses and slammed drawers, Billy turned around triumphantly. After we'd exchanged cash for the title and key, I felt a weight lift from me. Valerie would be pissed I took the money without discussing it with her. But I was pissed she'd never brought up the amount she had stashed away to me. I knew she was saving. I knew that's what we were both doing.

But she never mentioned the money she took from the ranch. She never mentioned a plan for it. I suspected college after I graduated, or a house for her. The woman I fled with was practically a stranger, but familiar to me. And maybe that's where the guilt lay. I didn't believe she kept it from me for a nefarious reason. But perhaps that was my naivety living on.

I wondered if she'd seen who spilled the blood, if she'd taken part in it.

She'd been practically mute for weeks after we left the ranch, but I chalked it up to everything we'd been through. And I'd like the silence, the quiet of our existence. It was as comforting as the sounds surrounding me now.

After Jessica left Billy's room to finish getting ready, I shut the bedroom door. Billy raised his eyebrow, and I walked to his desk.

CHAPTER THIRTY

I held the title of the truck in my hand like a lifeline. And it would be. "I need you to be cool about some shit here for a minute," I said.

Billy looked at his door and cocked his head. "Is this about Jessica? She's just fucking with you, and I'm not sure how I'd feel about you—"

"No. No." I said. "It's about the … it's about a lot of things."

Billy leaned forward. "Okay. What is it?"

I let out a breath. "It's about Amber. And Kyrie. Sorina. And … Sam."

Billy's jaw twitched.

"I was at Sorina's house the other night—"

"Who?" he asked.

I squinted my eyes. "Sorina. The girl next door to me."

Billy stared.

"The house through the trees?"

He blinked, then his mind seemed to clear. "The red-haired girl you fucked."

"I …" This was not going how I wanted things to go. I cleared my throat. "Anyway. The night after Amber's body was found, I went to her house after I left the school." Every ounce of fight left me then.

I knew the words. I'd said them a thousand times. But with my friend staring at me, I couldn't find the will to tell him. He would think I was insane. He would think I needed help.

I looked into Billy's eyes as Nirvana played, heard the twins getting ready, and clutched the title to the truck in my hands.

Everything felt like it was falling apart, but then I remembered the first time I saw Billy smoking in the cemetery. I remember his words. *The Vampire King resides high on the hill.* Billy *knew*. Billy knew something about Hart Hollow was wrong, and maybe it's why he hadn't left. Maybe it's why he was here, staying for his sisters. Perhaps he couldn't leave them behind. Not the way Valerie was leaving me.

"You remember what you said to me the first time you saw me?"

Billy shook his head.

"You said the Vampire King resides high on the hill. You said that's who took Sam. And I thought *this guy is nuts*. This guy is playing a joke on me. Because how could he be using the same words that had become synonymous with Jesus all my life? You said the vampire on the hill, and I laughed it off. I tried to pretend I didn't think it was crazy. But Sorina ... vampires or whatever the fuck they want to call themselves, they're real. And she tried to stop the thing that killed Amber. But she couldn't. She said he's *full*, and eventually he won't be anymore ... and he'll take another girl. And my best friend could be one of those girls. That thing ... that thing took Sam. And it will keep taking girls from this town if we don't stop it somehow. You said Hart Hollow is a forgotten town, but this is our home. It's my home now," I said, surprising myself. This dark town, with all of its secrets, had seeped into me, and maybe the horror of it all is what I found comfort in. However fucked up that was.

Billy stood, placing his hands on his hips. I didn't know what to make of his dark eyes. "I was joking when I said that. It's a story passed on from generation to generation in this town. My dad used to say that shit when he was drunk with his buddies. He *used* to have buddies back when he pretended to live here. And when he found out I was hooking up with Sam after she left, he said it was her punishment for fucking around with someone younger than her. The vampire king on the hill is the bogeyman,

Nicholas. It's what you say to scare kids and why they're punished. I kept going to the Archer house because Sam and I went there together a couple of times. Even though it felt wrong, I felt like she was still around when I went in there. I said it was just a place to get high, but that's not why I went there. I went there to remember her."

"It's more than just a memory house," I said. "I think it's the key to something." Billy stared at me and I held his gaze when I spoke again. "Sorina is not human. She showed me. She couldn't stop it. And if something happens tonight, even if it means I fail like she did, I'm going to do whatever I can to save the people I care for. And I'd like you by my side if it comes down to that."

Billy's jaw twitched, and I saw he didn't want to believe me or join me, but some part of him did. "It won't bring Sam back," he said, his voice gruff.

I heard a car approaching, and I knew we needed to leave soon. The fate of the night would soon be set in motion, for better or worse.

We both looked out of the window to the familiar headlights of Kyrie's car. "But what if we can save *her*?" I asked.

When my friend looked back at me, he nodded.

THIRTY-ONE

We drove to the school in two vehicles. I helped Kyrie into my new truck, while Jessica and Nicole drove themselves. The girls didn't know, but I planned to sneak Billy in later in the night. If only to help me if things went south before I slipped away from the dance. I couldn't forget that the Deacon had told Mrs. Vaughn he would be at the winter formal to chaperone.

When we walked up to the entrance of the school, I waved the girls on, hanging back. Kyrie lingered in her blue dress, but I told her I'd join them in a minute, and as she'd reluctantly went inside, I saw a strange look on her face. She'd wanted everything to be normal for a while, but she was always searching for a crack in the facade I was crafting for her.

When I was alone, I stared up at the moon, then closed my eyes. I didn't know what I was listening for, and maybe I was merely hanging onto the moment. The pure moment of being a teenage boy with a new truck and a group of friends who were more family to him than any of his family had ever been. Tabula Rasa. I'd made that for myself in some ways, failed in others. *If our hearts had been made of steel, would we be unscathed right now?*

CHAPTER THIRTY-ONE

My memory drew my eyes across the highway, to where I knew my trailer was and where Sorina's house stood like a sentinel. I wanted her there with me, on my arm, walking into the gym. Her hair the color of the rose pinned to my coat. I wanted to watch their eyes when they saw her again.

The teachers never said her name or asked where she was. When she skipped school, it was as if she never existed; no students mentioned her. She was a ghost, and only my friends seemed to know who she was when I forced them to remember her.

I didn't know what the night would bring, and I wasn't sure if I wanted them to remember her anymore.

Before I could stare at the long drive that led to the school for any longer, I heard my name called from the entrance of the school, followed by the muffled sound of music. I turned to see Jessica standing at the entrance, her brow pinched. When I reached her, I noticed her nipples were hard from the cold. She didn't move to cover herself, and I didn't blush. When she held out her arm, I reluctantly let her loop her arm with mine, if only because I knew her flesh wouldn't touch mine.

"Kyrie is being insufferable about what's taking you so long," she said.

I didn't reply as we walked into the gym, heading to the rest of our crew. When I pulled away from Jessica, Kyrie looped her arm into mine, and Jessica and Nicole reached for each other, holding hands, finally looking like sisters. The ominous feeling we'd all felt was at a breaking point, and the way Jessica kept glancing at me was unnerving.

Around us, our classmates mingled, laughed, and danced.

We walked to the punch bowl together, and Jessica bent down to fiddle with the strap of her high-heeled shoe, and when she stood

I saw she had pulled a flask from under her dress. I shook my head.

"What? You've been around the preacher's daughter too much." She scoffed as she spiked the punch.

Kyrie grabbed a plastic cup, then looked Jessica in the eye as she poured herself the now spiked liquid.

"We've corrupted you." She smirked in admiration.

Kyrie took a big gulp. "Well, if I'm going to die tonight, I might as well feel good," she said, turning to me.

"If you're going to what?" I asked as I waved the drink away, confused. I wanted to have all of my senses and be ready for anything, and Kyrie's words had my heart racing.

Kyrie shrugged her shoulders before setting the empty cup down. "It was just a joke. Wanna dance?" she asked.

I nodded, though it was the last thing I wanted to do. But I could spin her around as I took stock of our surroundings.

Across the room, I saw Valerie, and she waved, as if the scene outside the café just hours earlier had never happened. Her eyes seemed vacant as she looked away.

Beside her stood the Deacon, his long hair in a ponytail, his face tilted toward Valerie's. He spoke into her ear, and she looked at me again, lost in whatever he said.

I placed my hands on Kyrie's waist as we swayed.

"I'm glad we came," she said, playing with the collar of my shirt.

"Me too. I only have a year and a half left of high school. I want every experience I can get," I said. It was true. I wanted to experience everything I could. I craved it. And whenever it felt like life was spiraling into the horror of the past, I clutched to ordinary thrills even tighter.

CHAPTER THIRTY-ONE

The title to my new truck in my coat pocket.

My friends around me.

The promise of the night.

It all felt like it could float away, be burned from my hands.

Nothing about the night felt normal, if I let myself be honest with myself. I felt as though I were on the edge a cliff, ready to tip over the edge. And if I was falling, I wanted one person with me. I didn't want to be swaying with Kyrie. I wanted to be close to Sorina, to have her whisper her vague stories into my ear, pull me close.

I wanted to undress her, pretend I was in a dream, and that she would never let me wake up.

I looked down into Kyrie's eyes, and she smiled. "Who are you looking for?"

I smiled, grateful my friend knew me, even if she didn't know who I was searching for. "Sorina. I doubt it she'll show up, though. I think she may have left town."

Kyrie surprised me when she answered. "I'm sure you would have seen moving trucks at her house if she left."

I blinked, and a question hung between us. *You didn't forget her?* I pushed it away. "I think if she wanted to leave, no one would know. No one could stop her."

Kyrie nodded, looking down. "You're in love with the girl next door. That's a normal thing. An ordinary thing. It's what you want, right? What we both wanted for just one night."

I shook my head and closed my eyes. *Not if she isn't a girl, if she isn't ... normal.* "Not if she doesn't love me too," I said.

Kyrie didn't argue, couldn't. Then she looked over at the bleachers, her eyes on Nicole. She pulled one arm from my neck, and I saw the friendship bracelet there. I'd wanted her to make one for the rest of the group, and she hadn't yet. But I saw her ease with the Clements grow. I saw the way she was opening up.

I wished Kyrie and Nicole could see what I saw when they looked at each other. I wished they would go to each other. But I didn't understand it, didn't see the big picture for them. Though I tried.

"You should ask her to dance," I offered.

Kyrie's eyes flew to me, and her face turned red. She glanced around the room, and I saw where they fell. Her parents were in the corner, talking to another group of parents. I had no idea they'd signed up to be chaperones.

Kyrie looked up at me, a sad smile on her face. "I can't. And you know that."

"Why?"

She kept dancing. "I just can't, Nicholas. I can't. I don't even want to be here."

She dropped her hands, fiddling with the bracelet now.

I grabbed her hands, willingly touching her. She looked into my eyes. "What's going on with you tonight? You don't want to be here? It's all you've talked about for weeks."

Kyrie stalked away, and I followed. She walked past Nicole and Jessica to an empty spot on the bleachers. I sat with her, glancing around the room to see if anyone was watching us.

When I was close enough that no one could hear us, Kyrie turned to me. "It's all I've been talking about because I don't want to think about everything else. I don't want to think about what's going to happen to me."

"You said the dreams stopped, Kyrie," I said. "Has something happened?" *He doesn't want her.* I'd found solace in Sorina's words,

CHAPTER THIRTY-ONE

a strange comfort. I thought Kyrie would be safe, and her assertions that she wasn't having dreams anymore had strengthened that comfort. It never occurred to me they might lie to me.

Kyrie ignored my question. "The worst part about wondering if I would be taken, and if my parents would think I ran away, is that ... I've wanted to. I've wanted to for years. I've written these notes, only to throw them away. I want to be a runaway sometimes. Start over, new town, new name. Somewhere where it wouldn't be so hard to love ... just to love. They think I don't know what Jesus would think of my yearning. But I do. He would love me anyway. Because that's what he is. But them?" She looked at her parents again. "They wouldn't. They would think I was a failure. They would disown me. I would tarnish their beautiful image. I would lose my parents."

"Is that worse than losing yourself?" I asked.

Kyrie looked into my eyes. "I don't know. But—" She pulled her hand from my chest and placed her palms in her lap. I reached for her wrist and grabbed the friendship bracelet. I'd lost mine, though I couldn't figure out where.

Kyrie looked at me again with a smile on her face that was almost sad. "When I'm with you and Nicole, and Billy, and even Jessica ... I feel like I can be myself. Not the self everyone here knows, but the real me. I was so judgmental in the beginning, and I regret it. I've known them my whole life, and it took you bringing us together for me to really see them. It's important to be around people who see you."

I nodded, running a hand through my hair.

Kyrie leaned in, bumping my shoulder. "She sees you," she whispered.

I turned to my friend, and her eyes were trained past me.

My heart stilled when I saw Sorina walk into the gym.

Her long red hair was up, and her eyes were rimmed in black, shimmering eyeshadow that made her blue eyes shine. Her pale skin was luminous, and I almost ran to her. My body reacting to her, desperate for her.

Kyrie squeezed my arm. "Go talk to her," she said.

Before I could respond, Kyrie was gone. And I didn't have to decide. Sorina walked to me, her body liquid, her white dress trailing behind her.

When she reached me, I stood, holding out my hand. She took it and I spun her, resting my hand on her hip, the other in her hand.

We didn't speak for a moment, and I saw the Deacon watching us before I could open my mouth.

I moved so he couldn't read my lips, but I doubted that mattered.

"Where have you been?" I asked.

"Hiding," Sorina said, looking up at me. She looked small, almost grey up close. I wondered what her attempt to save Amber had cost her. "I found the envelope you left at my house."

"Who have you been hiding from?" I asked, ignoring her mention of the money.

"From you."

I gripped her waist, dropping my mouth to her ear. "Why?"

Sorina brought our clasped hands between us, holding mine tight. "I won't give you poetry, nor bedtime stories. No letters to long-dead loved ones. I'll give you the truth, but nothing will be the same when I do. The night will break open. And someone will get hurt."

"I don't mind being hurt," I said. I thought she meant my heart, something mendable, something inside I could pretend wasn't broken. But that wasn't what she meant.

Still, she spoke. "I know Diana talked to you about me."

"She said some crazy things." I cleared my throat, remembering her teeth, the way her hand felt around my throat. "But maybe the craziest part is I know it's true, everything she said."

Sorina smiled, looking away.

"What would happen if you bit me?" I asked.

"I would like it," she said, looking back into my eyes.

"No, I mean, would I become one?"

"No. You could never become one of us," she whispered. "And besides, it takes an exchange of blood. And that's rare because we give away our memories."

"What do you mean?" I asked.

"If I made someone like me and let them taste me, they would know every moment of my life. Every memory, every horror. We would be one. That is why it is so rare, why we never do it."

"So you, you've never done it?" I asked.

"No. And I have no intention to."

"You want to be alone forever?"

"If the alternative is to give away my memories, yes. Loneliness isn't what humans make it."

"I enjoy being alone. After the ranch ... I like the quiet. When Valerie is gone," I admitted.

"She was making you sick, you'll feel better when she's gone for good."

"What do you mean?" I dared a look toward the Deacon and Valerie, but I did not see them. I didn't know if I should feel comforted by that or concerned. I turned my head, looking for my friends. I saw Jessica talking to a guy by the punch bowl, and Nicole talking to a girl from my science class.

I didn't see Kyrie.

"Do you eat people?" I asked, thinking of Amber. Of how they only found parts of her.

"Some do," Sorina said.

"But ... do you?" I asked, looking down at her.

"No."

"Could you make me forget anything I want to forget?" I wondered who I would be if I slept through the night. If I cared about normal things. If I never remembered the hands that touched me. Tabula Rasa and a life started over. I wanted to know what I was, where the rage inside of me came from, and what I was capable of.

Sorina's hand grazed my neck. "I could make some people forget."

"Will you?"

"No."

"Why not?"

"I know what plagues you. If I could make the memories disappear, they would still live in your body. And you wouldn't know why you hurt, why you ached. Because the things that trigger your pain would still trigger your pain, except you wouldn't know why. And that would tear your mind apart. There is great risk when doing it, it leaves scars that will never heal."

"I already have those." We danced for a moment, my hand fisting in her white dress, her red hair grazing her collarbone. "What would happen if someone became like you? Would they forget? Could they forget everything bad from their life?"

"No," Sorina said, looking down between us. "They would remember every detail of their life. With clarity. For eternity."

"Can you hypnotize yourself?"

Sorina laughed then, and it was strange, a sound I'd never heard. I wanted to bottle it, to keep it with me forever. When she looked at me, her face was one I'd never looked at before. She looked young; she looked timeless. She looked happy and full of sorrow. "Nicholas, this isn't a story. No, I can't hypnotize myself. Yes. I have a reflection. I can't be hurt by a cross or holy water. I can't fly. I have a heartbeat. Do you want to feel it?"

I looked at her pale skin, her neck.

Her tiny hand between us and her dark red nails.

"Yes," I said.

She brought my palm to her chest, pulling her dress down slightly. I closed my eyes and listened to her heart. I could feel it through my skin, hear it in my ears. Everything drowned out. It was just us in the room, and I wanted to kiss her, take her there. *If I kiss you, will I die?* I wondered, poetry spilling forth with no paper to take the ache.

Sorina's other hand slipped into my shirt just a little, her fingertips tracing my chest. "I've been alone for a very long time, Nicholas. And I've been alive for a very long time. When I was a girl, I dreamed of a man. The other half of me—darkness, something my body could envelop, like the black in the eye of a crescent moon. I've always known I was destined for someone. And I thought I found him many years ago. But I was wrong, though I'm not sorry I had my time with him. He gave me my greatest gift in this life."

"What was that?"

She looked up into my eyes, blue and pink at the edges, like she was about to cry. "A child. A beautiful baby girl. And she was mine for a while. I raised her, loved her, and taught her everything I knew—how to be strong, how to be careful, and how to protect herself. But, it wasn't enough. And she's gone now."

I pulled Sorina closer, my mouth at her temple. "I'm ... fuck. I'm so sorry."

She was still in my arms, hard. "I don't have time to love someone, Nicholas. I don't have time to nurture, be soft, or be open. Because I have a job to do."

I pulled away, looking down at her. "What do you mean?"

"I know who took my daughter. And I won't rest until I've drained him, taken from him all he loves and holds dear. And if I love something again—love *someone* again; their fate is to be hurt by him. I don't want that for you. I can't love until he is gone."

"Where is he?" I asked, though I knew. I knew with every part of me.

Sorina smiled, eyes alight with something fearful. "He's in this very room."

THIRTY-TWO

School dances were ruined for me.

As I looked around the gym for the Deacon and my friends, Sorina slipped away, her white dress pooling around her. Before I could chase after her, I finally caught sight of someone. Jessica stood near an exit, waving me over. I snuck through dancing bodies and students mingling toward her. Everyone was a blur, but the sight of Eric Childress dancing with the new girl, Lauren, caught my eye, but before I could think much about it, I was at Jessica's side. Just as she began to speak, the music stopped, and Principal Garrison's voice came over the intercom. "Are we ready to crown the Hart Hollow Winter Snow Queen?" he asked. Cheers and hollering rang out as Jessica grabbed my arm.

"So when's it going down?" she asked.

I looked down at her hand on my arm, and she let go, rolling her eyes. "When's what going down?" I asked.

She crossed her arms. "I heard you talking to Billy. I know you're sneaking him in."

"Jesus Christ." I groaned.

"Is a vampire," she added as she narrowed her eyes.

We stared at each other as names were announced and our classmates carried on.

Finally, I spoke. "Did you hear everything I said then?"

Jessica nodded, and I stared into her eyes, daring her to tell me I was crazy.

She didn't. "You can be incredibly dense sometimes, Nick."

I corrected her, and she held up her hand. "Save it. Yes, I heard it all. And Billy's right. Our dad used to peddle that vampire shit and MoMo and every scary story parents tell their kids when they're young and dumb. But we aren't little anymore and we have minds of our own."

"And what does your mind think?" I asked.

"I think you've been too lovesick to notice your best friend is lying to you," she said.

"What do you mean?" I asked.

"Kyrie's still having dreams."

My heart stopped. "What? Did she tell you that?"

"Like she would tell me shit." Jessica scoffed.

I ran a hand through my hair, looking around the gym. "Then—"

"She told Nicole, and I heard them."

"Who *don't* you eavesdrop on?" I asked.

Jessica looked wounded, and I grimaced. "Maybe if you guys would tell me what's going on, I wouldn't have to. You and Kyrie are best friends, and you and Nicole have your study shit. You smoke with Billy. Even Kyrie and Nicole have a little friendship. So where does that leave me?"

I hated myself then—for my walls and my selfishness. I'd spent my whole life feeling like outsider, and I hated that I made Jessica feel that way.

"I'm sorry," I said. "You're my friend, you—" I didn't know how to say it. I never knew how to say it.

Jessica watched me struggle, her arms crossed. And then, finally, she let out a breath. "I get it," she said. "I'll lay off. But Nicholas, you make it so fucking hard, sometimes," she whispered. Her eyes roamed over me—my height, my arms, my eyes—and for a second, it didn't make my skin crawl. It made me feel good about myself.

"Okay," I said.

And Jessica nodded. "Okay." We let the unspoken thing fade away.

When Principal Garrison started announcing the Snow Queen candidates, Jessica leaned in.

"So where are we letting my dipshit brother in?" she asked.

I motioned toward the stage. "There's a door at the back of the stage that leads to the back parking lot where the buses drop off for band. He said he'd be back there waiting."

"And you both think he won't get kicked out in five minutes?" She raised an eyebrow.

"He's going to lie low. We need every set of eyes we can get."

"On who? The Deacon? Is he your Dracula?"

I glared at her before stalking across the gym, my eyes searching for the Deacon. *He's in this very room.*

After finding Nicole, Jessica and I grabbed her arms and pulled her from the crowd. The three of us snuck away behind the curtain at the edge of the stage as the Snow Queen was announced. The cheers and commotion made it easy to sneak away, and as we walked across the stage, Nicole scurried in her heels to keep up with me.

"What's going on?" she asked.

Jessica leaned into her twin and grinned. "We're sneaking Billy in so we can stake a vampire."

I rolled my eyes as we moved into the back room behind the stage. "Have you seen Kyrie?" I asked.

"She was with me, but then she said she wanted more punch and then all the announcements started," Nicole said as I opened the door to the back lot of the school.

We were greeted by a puff of smoke, and Billy's grin was devilish. I couldn't tell if it was real or if the haunted look he'd had in his room was merely masked for the benefit of his sisters.

"Normal punch or more spiked punch?" Jessica asked as her brother walked into the school. "She shouldn't be drinking. She'd be a fucking lightweight."

"Who's drinking?" Billy asked.

"Well, she's been having more dreams, and she's been freaked out but faking it for *you*," Nicole said, pointing at me.

We rushed across the stage, slipping out onto the dance floor as music started for the newly crowned Snow Queen to dance to.

"Where's the Deacon?" I asked, looking for Valerie. I saw her by a teacher, talking and mingling. I couldn't linger on how odd that looked.

CHAPTER THIRTY-TWO

"Where's your fucking girlfriend, Nick?" Jessica barked, walking over to the punch bowl. We followed and I leaned in close to her.

"I don't know. We were dancing and she …" *She said she had a job to do.*

"So two supposed vampires are missing, and so is our friend." Jessica laughed, throwing her hands up, and for the briefest of seconds I found happiness in her calling Kyrie her friend.

"This is supposed to be a lockdown. No one in or *out*," Nicole said, before whispering, "A vampire? What?"

"Yeah, like the shining professionals of Hart Hollow High are competent enough to pull that off. Look at me." Billy laughed.

He was proof that someone could sneak in. Proof that someone could sneak out.

"Fuck," I whispered, looking around. "Could she be in the school? Are her parents still here?"

We moved around the gym until we could see the Davis's by the food table.

"What about her car? Should we check for it? What the fuck is going on?" Nicole asked.

"She wouldn't just leave a school dance without saying goodnight. Something's up, and we all know we need to go in that goddamn house." Jessica glared at me and Billy. He narrowed his eyes at her and then shook his head. He was probably used to her eavesdropping over the years.

"Let's check the classrooms and the restrooms, then we'll go," I said. The entrance to the hallway closest to the student lockers was manned by Mrs. Vaughn. Jessica saw me eyeing her.

"Go distract her. You know she wants to fuck you," she said.

My stomach turned because I knew she was right. I hated her class because she reminded me of the woman at the ranch. Her hands didn't touch me, but her eyes were hungry.

Billy clapped me on the back. "Lucky dog," he said.

I wanted to shove him, to tell him why I hated it, but he didn't know. Couldn't know what I'd been through. Fucking an older woman like that was a badge of honor for some young men, but not me.

"Okay, I'll get her away from the door, but what about me?" I asked.

Billy stepped forward. "When you lure her away from the door, the twins will go through while I cause a distraction, then you can go."

"What about you?" I asked.

Billy grinned. "Well, I'm not supposed to be here. So what do you think they're going to do with me?"

We all smiled.

"Once I'm out, I'll circle back to the student parking. Let me in and I'll help knock out all the classrooms. If we don't find her, then..." He hesitated, the music around us upbeat and loud as we planned our dark night. "Then on to the Archer house."

"You think something is going on here?" Nicole asked, far more innocent than her eavesdropping twin.

"You never know," Billy replied, walking toward the punch bowl.

Jessica and Nicole smiled at me encouragingly, and we walked toward the door before breaking off as we neared Mrs. Vaughn.

I cleared my throat, adjusted my shirt collar, then rolled up the sleeves of my white button-down, exposing my forearms.

CHAPTER THIRTY-TWO

Mrs. Vaughn smiled wide when I approached. "Mr. Hemming, so nice to see you all dressed up. Are you enjoying yourself?" Her eyes were greedy as she took me in, looking up at me when she was done. I smiled my fakest smile and hoped it landed. It did, and I tried to keep my rolling stomach in check. "I sure am. You look nice tonight," I replied.

In the low light in the gym, I saw her blush slightly. "Thank you. Mr. Vaughn hates this dress." She smirked, tugging her neckline down slightly as she moved closer.

"That's a shame," I smiled, backing away from the door slightly.

Mrs. Vaughn moved forward as I'd hoped, away from the door. "Do you have a date tonight?" she asked.

Behind her, I saw Nicole and Jessica slink along the wall, Jess whispering in Nicole's ear as they moved. Nicole's eyes were wide as she likely took in the knowledge that we were hunting a vampire like a bunch of idiots.

I shook my head, then took another step back, pretending to stumble over my Converse. Mrs. Vaughn narrowed her eyes. "Are you okay, Nicholas?"

I reached into my pocket and pulled out my new truck keys. "Yeah, uh …" I hiccuped. "I think maybe I need to go home. Or lie down. I don't know. That punch tasted weird."

I saw Jessica and Nicole slip through the door as Mrs. Vaughn reached for my arm. I slipped, then let the keys fall to the floor just as I heard a loud crash behind me. When I turned around, I saw Billy faking a spill, bowling over a stack of plastic cups. Mrs. Vaughn rushed past me, and I snatched my keys up, walking backward toward the door as teachers started converging on Billy. Across the gym I saw Principal Garrison excuse himself from a conversation to march toward Billy.

I turned and ran toward the door, slipping through. Nicole hugged me when I made it to the other side.

"Your brother should be getting kicked out any second now." I laughed. Together we ran down the hall that led to one of the front entrances of the school that was locked from the outside. We squatted down, pressing our noses close to the glass. After a few minutes, we heard raised voices outside, and eventually we saw Billy walking away from the main entrance, waving his arms back and forth as the Principal advanced on him. Eventually Principal Garrison waved his arm, and I heard a threat of the Sheriff being called. Billy yelled he was going home and started toward the drive that led down the hill, toward the trailer pack.

We ran back down the hall, making a right, taking us farther from the gym toward the entrance that led to the student parking lot. I made it there first, but when I glanced back, Jessica had caught up with me, and I noticed her shoes were in her hands. I opened the door to the student parking lot, and we saw Billy running along the pavement from one of the side streets in front of the school. He sprinted across the pavement where I saw his Camaro parked, then up the walk to us. "Such brilliant educators. I miss this place." He laughed.

As he ran up the steps, he pointed to the parking in front of the main entrance. "Kyrie's car is still there. I saw it," he said as he rushed inside.

I crossed my arms as we all moved into a circle. "Okay, fuck. Then she should be in here somewhere or …" I ran my hand through my hair. "Let's check out the school, and if we find nothing, we head to the Archer house."

We all nodded, heading in separate directions, and I cursed my plan. I knew what we were up against, and I knew it was something I needed to face alone. My friends had long lives ahead of

CHAPTER THIRTY-TWO

them, futures I wanted them to see. The word was a fantasy to them, a horror story, all make believe. Vampire. Moroi. Demon.

He's full.

I'd begged for death countless times on the ranch. I'd give up my waking nightmares and my sleepless nights for Kyrie. But I couldn't ask my friends to do the same.

I checked empty classrooms with my friends, giving thumbs ups each time I caught one of their eyes in the hallway as we moved further away from the gym, and closer to the end of the school, closer to the Archer house.

As I walked down the hallway toward the classroom at the edge of the school, I heard someone say my name in the dark of an open door, and the pitch black entrance of the AG room made me shiver, but I walked in behind an ivory train of fabric like a fool— a lamb heading to slaughter—as I shut the door behind me.

When I stepped in front of the window on the far wall, next to Sorina as she stared into the night, she reached for my hand. "You cannot go there."

I laced my fingers with hers, and turned toward her, tipping her chin up. "Where?" I asked.

Her eyes were incredibly blue in the dim light of the classroom. Her touch calmed me, soothed, and set me on fire. I pulled her closer, pressing my forehead to hers. "The Archer house," she whispered. "He's waiting for you there. He thinks you can open the door."

"Who is?" I asked.

"The Deacon," she replied.

"Why's he waiting for *me*?" I asked, running my hand up Sorina's arm. It had always been about the girls. The girls on the ranch. The missing girls here. What did I have to do with any of it?

"He has Kyrie with him. He has Valerie with him."

I dropped her hand as I walked toward the door, and in a flash, Sorina blocked my way, her eyes black. "You cannot go there," she repeated, and her voice sounded ancient, hard.

"I have to. *We* have to. And you know that shit doesn't work on me anymore." On the first day of school her magic had worked. I remembered the way I'd smeared the applesauce on Kyrie's nose, remember her laugh. I'd do anything to make my friend laugh again.

"Who is this *we*? You and your mortal friends?" she hissed. "Or us?"

I shook my head, trying to move around her. Sorina spread her arms wide, covering the door. It would have been comical, her five foot nothing and scarcely a hundred pounds attempting to block my way. But I knew what she was, that she could stop me if she wanted to.

"I have to," I said. "But no, not with my friends. I don't want them with me."

"What if you die?" she asked as she stepped forward, reaching for me.

I backed away, out of her grasp. "I've wanted to die my whole fucking life," I admitted.

The black of Sorina's eyes vanished in a blink, and I saw blue, the red of a tear forming. "You would go into a trap, knowing you'll lose? That you are the prey?"

"Aren't *they* the prey? Quit playing games, and tell me what *I* have to do with this," I demanded.

Sorina shook her head. "They're bait."

CHAPTER THIRTY-TWO

"Why does he want me, Sorina? Why?" My voice was deep, and the room shuttered and shook.

Sorina looked around, a look of fear and bewilderment on her face. When she looked at me she looked both frightened and awestruck. "I'll tell you the prophecy if you sit down with me," she said, moving from the door.

"No. You're trying to stall me," I replied as I opened the door. I didn't look back as I raced down the hall. I saw Jessica come out of the girls' restroom, Nicole and Billy in front of a row of lockers.

I didn't hear Sorina follow.

I thought of what she was, what the Deacon could be.

I couldn't let them go with me. I couldn't let them step into that house. I needed to lie to my friends.

I caught up to them, calling out.

Billy turned, then his sisters did. They stopped.

"So, what's his plan?" Billy asked. "Archer house? Do you think Kyrie's there?"

I shook my head, pretending to pant from the run, from my exciting news. "No, no. I just talked to Sorina. She says she knows where Kyrie is. She's out of town. The Little Creek Baptist Church. Something about the woods there."

I saw the shock on Billy's face, and I regretted my lie immediately. "Sam's father's old church? Why would she be there?"

"I don't know," I said. "She said something about there being a significance to it, to the woods there. She's going to fill me in on the way, but we need to get there now."

Billy looked at me like he didn't quite believe me, but Nicole and Jessica nodded, accepting my lie.

"Okay," Billy said, his voice harder than normal.

"You guys head that way. We'll meet you there," I said.

Again, Billy watched me, but his sisters walked to the door, and after a moment, we ran to catch up with them in the parking lot.

I was buying time. And I had little of it. It would take them ten minutes to get to the church and ten minutes to get back when they realized I wasn't coming, and I had to hope the time they spent waiting was enough to end whatever would take place at the Archer house. I needed to get Kyrie and Valerie away from the Deacon. Though I didn't know how.

"Where is your girl parked?" Billy asked.

I surveyed the parking lot. On the far side of the school where the teachers parked, I saw Sorina's Firebird.

I pointed to it, and Billy nodded, then looked at me. "Okay. We'll meet you there. But if you're late, we're going to her house. I don't trust her, and neither should you."

"I know. But I can't risk Kyrie being there and not going," I said.

That worked. Billy clapped me on the back, then turned around, following his sisters to his Camaro.

I jogged across the parking lot toward Sorina's car as they started the engine, and when Billy and his sisters were gone, I turned back around, running down the parking lot to the road that led to the Archer house. It wasn't far. And when I turned onto the main road, I saw Sorina standing on the sidewalk, gazing up at the moon. When I reached her, I saw the red stains on her cheek.

She'd been crying.

I'd meant to walk past her, be defiant, and make a point. But her tears struck me, cementing me.

CHAPTER THIRTY-TWO

I towered over her and pressed my fingertips to her cheek, wiping the blood away.

The next moment would stay with me when she was gone, when I knew she was lost to me.

She grabbed my hand and turned it. I stared at the red on my finger in the moonlight. With her other hand, she reached for my jaw and ran her thumb over it, up to my lips. She pulled down on my bottom lip, opening my mouth, and with her other hand, she brought my bloody finger up.

I didn't protest. I didn't ask her what the fuck she was doing. I just stuck my finger in my mouth, my tongue swirling around, tasting her salty, bloody tears.

She let go, dropping her hands, a small smile on her mouth.

I pulled my finger from my mouth and stepped back. "What are you trying to tell me? I'm not a—"

"No, no. You're not what I am. I just wanted you to ..." she trailed off.

And when I closed my eyes, I saw an image of a man in the road —stark naked, outstretched hand. He was beckoning me. Except, it wasn't me. Red hair blew in the wind, and I realized this was a memory. Sorina's memory. The man was blurry in the memory, but his hair was long.

I shook my head and blinked. "What the fuck was—"

"The blood is the tie, a red thread."

"What was that?" I demanded.

"A memory. One of mine. What did you see?"

"A man in the road. Naked. Long hair."

"And who might that man be?"

I turned to the right, the Archer house one block over. "The ... the Deacon," I said.

"He was waiting. He was waiting for me that night. In the heavy weather, I walked to him willingly, into the woods, into his arms. I didn't know what he was, and if I had, maybe I could have saved myself. But I didn't know. *You* know. I'm giving you the warning I never received. Please, Nicholas, please heed it," Sorina whispered before she dropped to her knees and gripped my hands. When her eyes met mine, they were begging. She was ice, stone, cold, and at that moment, a prayer. I never wanted to bring a girl to her knees.

I wanted to wake from this nightmare.

"I could never live with myself if I didn't save them. What happened to the girl who said she wasn't scared of anything? The girl who sang to me?" I asked, tipping Sorina's chin up. She closed her eyes, and another red tear fell.

I dropped to my knees without a thought, ran my tongue up her cheek, lapping at the blood like a dog, and she gasped, then grabbed me, pulling me closer.

I wanted to fuck her on the sidewalk, wake up sleeping townspeople.

I wanted the Deacon to hear.

But I didn't act on the desires of my heart or my body.

I let go, pulled away, and walked toward the Archer house.

THIRTY-THREE

When I stepped into the Archer house, it felt like the old building sighed with relief. As if it had been harboring a deep secret and knew my arrival would mean it could whisper it into my ear.

I'd come in through the kitchen, and a flash of white moved by the doorway that led to the foyer.

I closed my eyes. Maybe a foolish thing, but I knew what I was facing.

Or, I thought I knew.

I heard a soft cry, and I ran into the foyer, where the room opened up to the staircase and the living room on the far side of the house. There were candles lit everywhere, and in the center was a chair. Valerie was sitting there, and below her, on the floor, with her neck exposed, was Kyrie. Her eyes were wide, and a piece of cloth was tied around her face, stuck in her mouth. Her blue dress was dirty and when she saw me, she cried out, and Valerie's face jerked.

It's then I saw Valerie's eyes—black, no pupil, no iris. Nothing but black. There was blood at her temple, as if she had been hit. It dripped down her face, stopped at her jaw. A few drops were on her dress.

She had a blade in her hand, and it was at Kyrie's neck.

"What the fuck are you doing?" I asked, palms up in surrender.

"She can't hear you," a voice said behind me. I whirled around and watched as the Deacon walked down the stairs that led to the second story. His long hair was pulled back, his white button up undone, untucked from his grey pants. He was shoeless, and I glanced at his feet as he took each step toward us. The staircase was littered with dirt, debris, and broken glass. And he looked as though he were walking on water.

When he made it to the landing, he strode past me to Valerie and Kyrie, and I flinched, wanting to run forward, afraid for Kyrie.

"What do you mean, she can't hear me?" I asked.

"Well, maybe that's not completely true," the Deacon said. "Her ears hear you. But her mind, who you know her to be, it's in a box, shut soundly and locked with a key. She cannot understand you."

I looked at Valerie. No mind, no will. Just a dagger in hand, her master close by. "What, like a zombie?" I asked.

The Deacon strolled behind Valerie and Kyrie, placing a hand on their shoulders. He leaned into Valerie and nuzzled her. "No. Zombies don't exist. What purpose would they have? Mindless, flesh-eating beings. I do love their stories. They tell the best stories."

"They who?" I asked.

The Deacon smiled wide, and I realized how silly he looked in the dead of night with his glasses on. As if he read my mind, he

CHAPTER THIRTY-THREE

reached up, pulling them from his face. His eyes were closed for a second, but when he opened them, I saw they were white. But were they unseeing?

I saw scars, too, across his eyelids. As if he's tried to cut them out. His grin was pointy, menacing. "Humans, of course," he said.

"And what are you?" I asked, trying to keep him talking.

I wanted Sorina there—to have her by my side to fight whatever this was. But she'd told me not to go in, and I wondered if I was on my own.

The Deacon chuckled, taking his hand off Valerie. "But hasn't she told you? Hasn't the little traitor warned you about the bogeyman? Well, her bogeyman anyway. She likes to tell stories, too, you see. And I've watched you. Your coupling. Your feeble attempts to satisfy her hunger. You cannot quench it, boy, that thirst. You'll never give her what she needs."

"And what is it she needs?" I asked, seeing a flash of red in the window behind him.

"Revenge for her supposed slights." The Deacon laughed. "I'm sure she told you all about our history." I shook my head involuntarily, and the Deacon caught it. "Oh, so she hasn't been so forthcoming. You've fallen far, and she is still on the first step. Reach up all you want. She'll never fall down that dark hole for you."

"How do you know Sorina?" I asked, glancing down at Kyrie. Her tears stained her cheek and wet the cloth in her mouth.

The Deacon stepped to the other side of Valerie, swiping her hair from her shoulder. He knelt down, bringing his mouth to her neck. She moved ever so lightly, inviting him in.

And when he opened his mouth, I saw the long, sharp, needle-like points at the tip of his incisors. He grazed them over her neck, and she sighed, black eyes blinking. His own were closed, but I didn't dare believe he couldn't see everything in the room.

"I know Sorina in ways you'll never know her."

I changed tactics, waiting for Sorina to make her move.

"Why are they here? Why is Valerie here if this is about me, you, and Sorina?" I asked. "Why have you been spending so much time with her? And why Kyrie?"

"Because you love them. In your own way. Kyrie was never next, but the way you took to her ... I couldn't help it. That was a sweet bonus. It'll be your punishment for misbehaving. And Valerie?" The Deacon laughed. "Valerie's mine. She's always been mine. She's just finally come home."

"Then what happens next? Who makes it out of here alive? What the fuck do you want from me?" I asked, stepping closer.

"I want you to choose," he said.

"Between who?" I asked.

The Deacon smiled. "The women you love, of course. What a gift, right?"

"What is?"

"To love these women, when you thought it not possible. After everything they've taken from you. I know what happened in California. What a beautiful teaching, just as I'd hoped," he said, smirking.

"A teaching?" I asked, the wind knocked out of me.

"Yes, the flesh has a long memory."

"I didn't want it," I gritted the words out. One word lodged in my throat.

Rape.

CHAPTER THIRTY-THREE

The Deacon laughed. "You're so like her."

"Who?"

"That's the question. Who will you choose, boy? Who?" He stepped to the side, and my eyes landed on Valerie and Kyrie again. My heart hammered in my chest. I foolishly wished my friends were there as I stepped forward. Before I could take another step the Deacon made a noise, alerting me I could go no further.

"Just let them go, please," I begged.

"Make a choice, and I will grant freedom."

"To them both?"

"To the one you love most."

"No!" I yelled. The house shook with my scream, and my shadow on the wall grew taller for a fraction of a second. I would have thought I was hallucinating, but I saw the Deacon flinch.

When he spoke again, his toying tone was gone. "Choose, or I will take them all. Every person you love," he hissed.

I looked at Kyrie and Valerie again. I knew who I would choose. I would choose Kyrie. Kyrie with so much life to live. Kyrie, who was innocent. Kyrie, who could see. Maybe Valerie wouldn't know what was happening. Maybe it would be fast. Or maybe he couldn't hurt her. Maybe he'd become attached to her. *She's always been mine.* I didn't believe belonging to someone made you safe but had to hope there would be a second chance to set her free.

"Kyrie. Let Kyrie go," I whispered, clenching my teeth and closing my eyes.

The Deacon laughed, snapping his fingers. Valerie's hand dropped the blade, and she leaned back, letting go of Kyrie. Kyrie fell forward, reaching for the cloth at her face, pulling it away. She coughed and heaved on her hands and knees on the dirty floor.

"Go to him," the Deacon commanded. And Kyrie scrambled up, running to me. My eyes were fixed on Valerie, even as Kyrie hugged me tight. She looked like a dog, frozen in place. The puppeteer was no longer moving her limbs, but the strings were still in his grasp.

"What are you going to do to her?" I asked as I clutched Kyrie to me.

The Deacon did not speak as he removed his crisp white button up. I watched his muscles move as he folded it neatly in his hands before turning to Valerie. He placed it in her lap, and she pressed her palms to the fabric, content.

As Kyrie turned in my arms, the Deacon wiped the hair from Valerie's face and leaned down, opening his mouth. When his tongue came out, it was long, forked, and I stepped back. In my arms, Kyrie did not recoil in surprise, as any normal or coherent person would, and I wondered if she was in shock.

The Deacon licked the blood from Valerie's temple, and I wanted to kill him for doing what I had just done to Sorina.

When he was done, he placed a tender kiss on her temple, then stepped away. "I'm not doing anything to her."

"But you said—"

"I said you had to choose the one you love the most. You've chosen. He didn't choose you," he said, his head turning to the side slightly. The last sentence not directed at me.

I stepped to the side, pulling Kyrie with me, and glanced in the direction the Deacon was speaking. From the dark of the kitchen behind us, Sorina stepped out.

CHAPTER THIRTY-THREE

The Deacon smiled wide, his sharp teeth making me stare at him again. "Did you hear that, Sorina? He didn't choose you," he said, his lips peeled back, sharp teeth menacing.

Sorina walked past us, into the room, a dagger in her hand and tears of red down her face. I could barely breathe, fearful for everyone but myself, half ready for death.

The Deacon turned Valerie around, hand on her shoulders. Her black eyes darted wildly for a movement until the Deacon pulled her forward, opening his mouth.

I heard a noise come from Sorina, but I didn't know what it meant.

The Deacon's long tongue slid into Valerie's mouth, and she closed her eyes and moaned into him. When he pulled away, he looked at her with his white eyes, and she seemed dazed again, blinking. He let her go, and she stumbled a little.

"Go home, my love. I'll be there soon. You don't feel well," he said. "You had fun at the dance, but needed to get home to rest. You bid your nephew goodnight before your departure. When you hit our bed, you will fall into a deep sleep."

Valerie nodded, walking past Sorina, toward Kyrie and me.

"Valerie, Valerie, wake up," I yelled as she passed me, reaching for her hand as Kyrie flinched at the woman who'd held a dagger at her throat. I let Valerie pass, whispering that it would be okay into Kyrie's hair.

"Don't worry," the Deacon smiled as Valerie left. "She will get home safe. She will sleep well. She will remember none of this in the morning."

"What the fuck are you?" I yelled, watching Sorina, who didn't move—eyes trained on the Deacon.

"I think you know what I am. I think our dear girl here warned you. Don't be a dumb dog. Open your ears." The Deacon smirked.

"You're a vampire, then?" I asked. I knew it. I'd felt it. I'd smelled it.

But I wanted him to say it.

The Deacon laughed, throat vibrating. His shadow seemed to move. To shake with his laugh. "Ah, that word. I admit it sounds nice, such lovely letters, lovelier fairytales. Or what do you call them? Horror stories."

"Just say it," I gritted out.

"That word means nothing to me," the Deacon stated. "That little brain of yours cannot fathom what I am. You want to know what I am? I'm *the* Father. Address me as such."

"I thought you were a Deacon," I mocked.

He smirked again, shaking his head. "Family is everything, boy. Family is blood, life, community. You don't appreciate the women in your life, boy. Valerie feeds you, clothes you, *saved* you. And what did you do? Ignored her as soon as you got to this little town. Running around in the night like a dog with a bone. She saved you. Just like I told her to."

"She saved me from a man who thought Jesus Christ was a vampire. A blind lunatic who controlled people, used fear and the wrath of *the Father in the sky*."

"People need a savior. A veil. They can sleep at night knowing all the bad things they've done will be forgiven if they just ask. They just have to ask me. *You* just have to ask me. Ask me for forgiveness," he commanded.

"I don't follow him. Nor do I believe in *him*," I sneered. Kyrie turned in my arms, looking into my eyes. As if the most horrifying thing in the room was me not believing in God. Not the man across the room. But maybe she thought this was the end, and she wanted my soul right.

"Ah, but what of heaven and hell?" the Deacon asked.

"More made-up shit to keep people in line, to play games, like you said," I replied.

"But who doesn't love a good game?" The Deacon smiled. Then he whistled, and Kyrie jerked her head, looking into his white eyes. "Go home, little girl. You don't feel well. You had fun at the dance, you danced with your friends. You bid them goodnight before your departure. When you hit your bed, you will fall into a deep sleep."

Kyrie jerked from my arms, and I reached for her, trying to make her stay, but she was strong, slipping out of my arms.

The Deacon looked at me, smiling wide, his voice deep when he spoke. "Go home—"

I laughed, staring at him, and I saw his eyebrow raise and his nostrils flare, his white eyes narrowed.

When he spoke, his voice was toying. "Dear Valerie wasn't wrong. You've taken to that skin a little too well. Rebellious. Raging with hormones. Petulant. A little lost, like most teenage boys. But you're not that, and you need to remember what you are."

"What am I?" I asked between clenched teeth.

"Your existence is steeped in the legends of humans, boy. But in reality, I let you have it. I let you exist, Skoll," the Deacon said, smiling.

"My name is Nicholas," I seethed.

"Ah yes, the name the humans gave you. Cling to it. But it's not who you are. You and your brother are meant to take care of the thorns in my side."

I stepped back; the wind knocked out of me. "I don't have a brother. I don't have any siblings."

"Boy, why do you cling to what you think you know? The lies you've been fed? And from those who *slighted* you. You know your father was not your father. But your mother was also not your mother. You were gifted to them, meant to be in safe keeping on the ranch until I saw fit to set you free."

I growled, something guttural rising to the surface. "I was there because of you?" I asked. "They, they—"

"You can't be broken, not by them. Not by anyone but me. Your time there has prepared you for this. They sharpened your claws. The flesh has a long memory."

"Fuck you," I snapped.

"You'll see, once you wake up from the fog she's put you in." The Deacon chuckled, looking at Sorina. "I allowed you the gift of sleep for centuries. This town you love to wander? You wander it because you've spent years sleeping, and now your body rejects it. You're never tired, are you?"

"I have nightmare because of what you let them do to me," I said.

The Deacon waved off my answer. "And nothing nourishes you, does it, boy?" He motioned to my slim form. "You have an insatiable hunger, don't you? Nothing tastes as sweet as … well, as sweet as she would." He motioned to Sorina. "Your destiny is to devour the sun."

"What the fuck does that even mean?" I asked.

"You think you love her but you were born to end her shining. Yet she hasn't shined in years. So ungrateful. I should have punished her for meddling and biting at my ankles years ago. But I haven't because, just like you, she serves a purpose."

"And what's that?" I asked.

"Sorina, care to enlighten the boy?" the Deacon asked.

Sorina looked into my eyes, blue to blue, a pleading look on her face. "You're supposed to ... you're supposed to kill me. That's your destiny, Nicholas."

I shook my head, willing her words away. When I spoke, I stared at the Deacon. "Why?"

"To bring about the long night. In the winter, we will forge a fresh path in a new world. We are the strongest, hiding away in the dark, pretenders during the day—to fit in among them. But why? Why do they get to rule this place?"

"So you want to rule the world. How original," I mocked.

The Deacon smiled, and for the first time I saw an imperfection in his two front teeth, turning inward slightly. "When the humans are at our feet, I will be their king, their father. I am the first of my kind. You are the second."

"Second of what?" I was begging for answers, and though I didn't trust him, I believed he would tell me why I'd felt wrong in my skin my entire life.

"Your father would be heartbroken to see what I've turned you into—resembling them, walking among them instead of making them a meal. You're a wolf—castrated, so to speak—because it was my will. But I will give you everything back if you do as you're told, like an obedient dog."

"Give what back?"

"Your black, your red eyes. You're not meant to look this way. Don't get caught up in the human stories of werewolves and

Lycan that are swirling in that little brain of yours. You are neither. You are the wolf they came from. Not human. You were never supposed to be human." He laughed. "But I couldn't keep a black beast such as you locked up where you could be found, now could I?"

"What about ... the other?" I asked.

"Your darling brother? I let him out to play, too, sometimes. But he's not as easily manageable. Not like you. He's hungry, and he's almost sniffed her out countless times. It was not time yet, and I grew tired of his yapping. He couldn't be an obedient dog like you. "

I smirked, livid and cracking, making the Deacon smile wider. "Do you know what your name means? *He who mocks.*"

I smiled, a retort on my tongue, but the Deacon pressed on.

"Well, your brother is he who hates, and his hatred is a beautiful thing to behold. You resent this lot you've been given, and he thrills in it. He's ready to eat your darling Sorina's daughter right up. But not eat her the way you've..." He raised an eyebrow.

I stepped forward, and Sorina was in front of me, pressing on my chest. "Nicholas—"

The Deacon scoffed at my name on her lips. "Why do you cling to these human names and titles? I taught you better than that. I never taught you to be so arrogant, though."

"I'm nothing like you," Sorina seethed as she turned to the Deacon.

"But aren't you? Wanting what you cannot have? Again? You're so blind. Did you get that from me, too?"

"But you see all, don't you?" she snarled.

CHAPTER THIRTY-THREE

"I know this boy will break your heart, just as his brother is meant to break your daughter's heart. But I'm protecting her from that."

Sorina lunged for the Deacon before I could grab her, and in a blink, she was in the air, dangling from his outstretched hand.

"I see everything, Sorina. I see everything you want to do before you do it. Every desire you have. Your craving for this boy. You're so flushed, wanting for him. You'd make a lovely display encased like that. Maybe I'll finally let you rest next to your darling daughter."

Sorina struggled, scratching at the Deacon's arm, legs kicking. "Please, please take me to her," she begged.

"Are you tired?" the Deacon asked, his voice almost soft.

She cried out, still fighting, slower. "Yes."

"Then I'll let you sleep," he whispered.

I felt a humming then—not unlike what I felt when I first laid eyes on the Archer house—but stronger, a crackling in my bones. It doubled me over, and when I spoke again, I did not recognize my voice. "Let her go," I demanded, and they both looked at me, sharp turns of their neck.

The Deacon smiled. "Ah, there he is." He turned, shielding himself with Sorina, forcing her to stare at me.

Pain radiated through me.

Overtook me.

I doubled over, clenching my eyes, and when I looked up, everything was crystal clear. The Deacon looked satisfied, and Sorina looked scared.

He leaned in close to Sorina's ear. "How does he look?" he asked, squeezing her neck.

I didn't know what he meant; I couldn't see myself, couldn't see my eyes. Bloodshot, bulging. I'd see them in a memory that was not my own.

"Has he tasted you?" the Deacon asked. "You let him. You were always so foolish. Arrogant. You're meddling with things you shouldn't, tempting fate. I should leave you here with him. Let him feast on you. Do you want that?"

"Yes," Sorina breathed, staring into my eyes.

I felt myself growing, breaking open—as if every morning I woke feeling stretched, compounded to this, magnifying my pain and ache. And when I stood, the ground seemed farther away. I held my hand up to my face, stumbling back at the sight of my long fingers, the growing fingernails. They looked like claws.

"Should I let his brother have your daughter?" the Deacon asked.

Sorina's face fell, and she closed her eyes. When she opened them, a red tear fell.

The Deacon leaned close, his long tongue lapping up the tear. "And what about *our* daughter?"

My reaction was instinctual, enraged. I growled. *Our daughter? What the fuck.*

The Deacon laughed. "So you did not tell him, then? He doesn't know. Maybe I really should leave you to him, let him punish you. They can be quite territorial, his kind. Maybe I should let him think you're his."

I stepped forward, and the Deacon stepped back. "Ah ah ah, not so fast."

Everything in my body begged me to leap on him, rip him apart. I looked down at my hand again and brought the other forth. My fingers were black, the darkness extended to my wrists, and my shirt bulged around my arms, threatening to tear.

CHAPTER THIRTY-THREE

I looked up, ready to jump and tear the Deacon apart. But I stopped short.

Before me, he twitched and shuddered. Sorina's legs grazed the floor as he stooped. Behind him, two giant wings spread out from his back, white as the moon, black claws at the tips. They stretched wide, scratched the walls, and pushed into the ceiling. The Archer house moaned with the invasion, with the darkness.

The Deacon stood tall, stretched a grin. When he looked at me, he laughed and all of his teeth were jagged, and his forked tongue ran over them. "Ah, this is much better."

I stepped back, stumbling over my limbs, larger and foreign to me. I cursed my vision as I stared at the beast before me. He was the nightmare of my dreams. The winged creature looming over the town, devouring everything and blotting out the sun, consuming the moon.

When I imagined the horrors of the night, vampires of old, this was the image that haunted me.

And it was real.

He was real.

"Did she tell you everything as she lured you to her bed, Skoll? Everything our kind does? That pretty human word is nothing. Cannot live up to your dreams. Did she comfort you by telling you I am the villain? She weaves a pretty story. But you don't want pretty stories. You want this—reality unveiled."

"What the fuck are you?" I asked, my voice deep and guttural. There was more to him, more to his vile existence, and I wanted to keep him talking.

The Deacon leaned close to Sorina's ear. "Tell him what I am, my darling daughter."

I stumble back; my shock was violent, unearthly.

Daughter.

"You ... you ..." I stumbled over the word, the one I buried, the brand on my flesh. I thought of the naked man on the road, beckoning Sorina in her memory. *He was waiting for me.* I stood to my full height, grazing the ceiling of the Archer house, growling. "You raped your own daughter?"

"Oh, is that what she said? They always do love to sell a good tale, my daughters."

Sorina sobbed and thrashed again.

The Deacon reached for her leg and spread it, exposing the white of Sorina's skin. With one long fingernail, he broke her skin, spilling the blood on the floor. "She's not yours anymore, Skoll. You want her? You'll have to lick her from this floor." The Deacon sneered.

And then he pushed off the ground, bursting through the ceiling, taking Sorina with him. I ran to them, too late, my eyes peering at the sky. They rose high, and I could see the blue of Sorina's eyes looking down at me.

Then he spread his wings, taking off into the sky.

I thought I heard her cry—my name on her lips—but in a blink, they were gone.

THIRTY-FOUR

The rain was beating on the surface of the roof when I woke in a basement, chained to a wall.

I strained against the metal, body aching, eyes searching for something to anchor me.

Diana sat on a chair twelve feet in front of me, arms crossed, eyes dark and haggard.

"Where am I?" I asked, and my voice sounded like it always did. Gone was the guttural growl, the inhumanness of before.

"You're in my basement, below my place," she said.

"I didn't know you had a basement," I remarked.

"I like it that way," Diana said, standing. "How do you feel?"

"Like someone broke every bone in my body." I strained against the chains, anger swelling inside of me, masking the panic.

Diana smiled, shaking her head. "Yeah. That sounds about right."

"Where is she?" I asked, no longer caring about my own broken body.

Diana's face fell as she walked to me. She unlatched the chain on my left wrist, then the right, before answering. "He has her. She's gone."

"What do you mean?" I asked, as I rubbed the aching wrist of my right hand with my left. I took a step forward and Diana stepped back, almost wary.

"I mean, if the Deacon has her, there is nothing we can do. She's in the deep sleep," she answered, clearing her throat.

I looked down then, noticing I wasn't wearing my clothes from the formal. Instead, I had on a pair of dark jeans and a shirt that said *Moonies*. "What the—"

"Yeah, you shredded your clothes when you changed." Diana laughed, though there was no humor there.

I shuddered at the thought of someone seeing me bare, and I crouched down, head spinning as I clutched my shaggy hair. "Changed into what?" I asked, voice breaking, memories blurring in my head.

"Into what you are, what you've always been."

"He called me Skoll," I said as I rose to my full height, staring at the ceiling.

"Do you know the story of Skoll and Hati?" Diana asked.

"No."

"Fenrir?" she tried again.

I nodded. "The giant wolf?"

Diana walked to the staircase, leaning on the railing. "Yes. Skoll and Hati are Fenrir's sons. They're meant to chase the sun and the moon until the end of days; that's an old myth taught in books. You'll probably learn about it at your little school. But you won't learn about the omens that rule this fucking town. Not in books."

"What omens?" I asked, stepping toward her.

Diana's deep voice sounded hard when she recited the words that bound me to Sorina.

> *From their blood, a prophecy will be woken*
> *No cycle broken,*
> *Twin Princes of black beast;*
>
> *Treachery, the wolf*
> *Who chases the bright bride of the sky*
>
> *The other He Who Hates*
> *Who follows the lunar daughter*
> *Into the desolate forest*

We stood there for a moment, dark words between us, my mind spinning. "None of this makes fucking sense." I went for the stairs, ready to leave the basement, but Diana stepped in my way.

"Do you want to hear this or not?" she asked, her hand on my chest, pushing me back. "I won't give you riddles like Sorina. That's not what this is. She was trying to protect you. I'm going to arm you."

I stepped away from her touch and crossed my arms. "Okay. Tell me why the Deacon said they had a daughter. And why he called Sorina daughter."

Diana's face fell, and she shook her head. "Because he is her father, and they have a daughter."

"That's—" My heart ached, and my eyes stung.

"Incest. Yes."

"She—" I started, and Diana shot a look at me.

"She didn't know. They never fucking know when he tricks them. He makes them for this. There are to be no males like them."

"No male vampires?" I asked.

Diana shook her head. "He won't allow male offspring. Only girls may live—to keep the bloodline pure, his bloodline. He creates new daughters with his daughters. He comes to them when they're grown. When they don't know what they are. He seeps into their dreams and bends their minds. It's a game. He finds them alone, rapes them, and plants his seed. And if they have a male son? He eats them."

"What the fuck—" I said as I stepped back farther into the basement, deeper into the nightmare.

"He is the first of his kind. The first *vampire*. He isn't alive. But she is. Or, she was," Diana said.

"What do you mean?" I asked.

"There are *living* vampires and *dead* vampires. You felt her pulse, right? Heard her heartbeat?"

I closed my eyes, imagining my ear to Sorina's chest, the frantic beat of her heart. "Yes."

"His daughters are alive. They feel, they have a beating heart, a pulse. But if they transform, they can be like him. In Sorina's home in Romania, they call them Moroi and Strigoi. The living vampires and the dead vampires. But they are forbidden to make the change. He fears them."

"How do they make the change?" I asked, though somewhere inside I thought I knew.

CHAPTER THIRTY-FOUR

"Suicide. She has to want to overtake him—want to still her heart. But her daughter is all that has kept her from it. From chasing. She thinks she'll be like him if she does."

"Where is her daughter?"

"He has Salina," Diana said, raking a hand though her black hair. "She's a half-breed, part of the prophecy that will undo him."

"What is she?" I asked, remembering the headstone in the cemetery the first time I saw Sorina in the flesh. *Salina.*

"Half her, half wolf," Diana said.

I buried my head in my hands, my mind spinning. "This is too much. Fuck!" I yelled, and the house shook.

Diana stepped back, one foot on the stairs, her eyes on me. "I know," she said tentatively. "But you need to know what he is, what she is, what *you* are. The Deacon was the first vampire, and the first of our kind came later. Moments before you."

"What is our kind?" I knew what it was; but I needed her to say it.

"We are from the wolves. You are *the* wolf."

I looked into Diana's eyes, waiting for more. It never came. "The Deacon said something about stories of werewolves and Lycan, not to get caught up in them."

"Those are human stories meant to make sense of the things that lurk in the night. Our kind came after the vampires. You and your brother are the sons of Fenrir and the demon that made the Deacon."

"Who is the demon?" I asked, unsure if my mind could take much more.

"Incubus, succubus. Whatever it wishes to be. It takes, just as he does. *Lilit* as the father of vampires. *Lilith* as the mother of wolves."

My mind stuttered and started on the words. Father. Mother. I didn't have to wonder why a father would rape his daughter. Family was a meaningless word. "He cut her. Right in front of me. Spilled her blood on the floor," I whispered.

"Where?" Diana asked.

"Inside the Archer house."

"We need to go there," she said, running up the stairs.

⊚

When we walked into the Archer house in the dark of the early morning, the creaking floors sounded loud in my ears. Diana was ahead of me, standing next to the blood on the floor, staring up at the ceiling where the hole was. The moon was obscured by the clouds, and I wished for nothing more than the sun. Not the sun in the sky, but the girl who had been taken into the night.

Diana turned to me, and for the first time, I saw her cry, though it wouldn't be the last time. "Everything you want to know is in the blood," she said, reaching her hand out to me.

I walked to her but did not take her hand as I looked down at the blood on the floor—half congealed, some still wet. "What do I need to do?" I asked, though I knew. My body stiffened with the thought, but I held the shame at bay.

"You need to drink it," she stated.

I shook my head as looked down at the dirty floor and the red blood. It called to me, and I was ashamed of that, aroused by it, haunted by the color in daylight and the dark of night.

"Their kind does not let anyone drink from them. Not unless they want to give their memories away. When you drink another's blood, you take in a piece of them. You see their memories; they become your own. It exacts a toll. That many memories, over time can drive you mad. Unless you are undead, like him," Diana said.

"Do they survive? Those who do it?" I asked.

"They don't survive long. His daughters grow mad when they take the blood of others, and they're forbidden to change into Strigoi. If they do, he kills them. That's why he's always making others, making new daughters. He tests them, and they fail, over and over again. I don't know what the fuck he's looking for," Diana admitted, voice cracking.

"She let me drink her tears, her blood," I admitted. "I saw a memory."

Diana cursed. "You're meant to be her undoing. Sorina means the sun. You're meant to devour her, to take care of the problem he cannot correct himself. He made her what she is—a lethal killer, but her hatred for him weakens her. It's all she sees. She wants to kill him but cannot, because only he knows the fate of her daughter. Knows where she sleeps."

"Salina. Salina, her daughter," I said, my voice dreamy and faraway as I stared at her red blood on the dirty floor.

"Salina means the moon. Your brother, Hati, is her undoing."

"Who is Salina's father? Who did she love?" I asked as I tore my eyes from the red and stared at Diana.

Diana smiled a sad smile. "It wasn't love; it was defiance. He forbids his daughters to breed with our kind. Because a daughter of such a union will be his undoing, the daughter will complete the circle before he can shroud the world in darkness. He wants to bring eternal night to this world."

I shook my head as everything Diana said swarmed around inside of it. "Fuck this shit. Fuck this town. Fuck this house and this goddamn *world* and all this—"

"Do you believe me?" Diana asked, voice hard.

I looked down at my hands, blood under my fingernails from when I changed. "How can I not?"

Diana looked down at the blood again. "Nicholas, drink it. You have to."

I dropped to my knees in the dirt and leaned down, and Diana stepped away as if to give me privacy as I brought my nose to the blood.

I should have been disgusted, but I closed my eyes and saw myself in a dream—a black wolf lapping at a creek, running red with blood.

I got closer, opened my mouth, and stuck my tongue out as the blood of my mind was left behind.

White light flashed behind my eyes, and I groaned as I heard the faint sound of Diana's retreating footsteps, and I grew hungry, taking the dirt and blood into my mouth.

My body broke again, bent, and I grew large, ravenous. I licked it all up as my body grew and changed, and when I was done, I howled into the dark, into the gaping hole in the ceiling.

When the sound left my aching throat, I fell over, convulsing, eyes closed.

I saw Sorina, a young girl, walking into the woods. Before her stood a man, his hand outstretched.

In a flash, the image changed, and she was bent over a tree trunk as he raped her.

Her eyes were closed.

CHAPTER THIRTY-FOUR

Her tears were streaming.

Flash.

Her mother was angry, begging her to tell her who did it, who she was with.

Flash.

Sorina on the streets, belly large, homeless, a runaway.

Flash.

A baby boy in her arms, ripped away, a blind man flying into the night with her child.

Flash.

Sorina was older; another woman held her and rocked her. It was Diana. The rain pelted them.

Flash.

Sorina with a man, dark hair, their hungry bodies clinging together.

Flash.

His lifeless animal body, the Deacon standing over it. Sorina in a pool of blood, her lover dead, her daughter gone.

I saw myself then, young, in California at the ranch, and Sorina in the woods, watching me, sneaking into my room.

She'd known me before I knew her.

I saw her sneak into my bedroom at the trailer. Climb under my covers, our bodies wrapped around each other.

I felt her heart swell with it, with her longing for me.

Love. Love for me. Jealousy mixed with desire as she saw me with the girls.

I saw us in the pool, my tongue on her skin, her hand wrapped around me. The beating of her heart when I looked into her eyes.

Love. Love. Love.

Fear and love wrapped together, love devouring fear, fear consuming hurt.

I saw her in bed, naked, a snake wrapped around her throat, eating its tail, pulling tight around her.

I saw her in the woods, outside the Deacon's house—the Deacon in the pale moonlight, wings outstretched.

And then I saw another red-haired woman.

Valerie against a tree, naked, tied tight against the bark.

The Deacon feeding on her, taking her blood, knowing everything about me, everything Valerie has seen, everything she has felt.

He had her memories.

I saw the girls then, the missing. The Deacon drinking from them in a cave. Their hands searching, pleasuring themselves as he fed. Weeping in the dark all alone, waiting for death the way I always have.

I saw his white eyes turn away, searching for a sound and Sorina escaping into the night.

I saw it all, the horrors of her life, the beating of her heart when I was with her.

Solace in a nightmare.

My sun.

I was meant to devour her and as her blood burned in my body, as I writhed on the floor, her blood and memories surged through me. Waking me. Burying me.

CHAPTER THIRTY-FOUR

I needed to find my home again.

When I walked into Sorina's room, the sun was cresting the horizon, but the dark curtains kept all the light out. I touched them as I walked around, my human fingers tracing the edges of her things.

I could smell her everywhere, and I missed her with parts of me I didn't know existed. We had few words between us, more touch, more reassurance that I was not broken inside.

I didn't know what I was—a beast dressed in magic? A mirage? I shouldn't look the way I did. I shouldn't have been able to fit my body into hers, a phantom with her on that bed in the trailer. But I did. And I was scared.

I walked to her nightstand and saw the worn paper and a pen where I'd seen it before. I shouldn't have opened it. I shouldn't have invaded Sorina's privacy that way, but I couldn't stop myself.

I wanted to see every dark thought in her head, devour the pieces she kept locked away.

I wanted to know what she thought of me when she spoke to the pages. *If* she spoke of me. I was more teenage boy than beast when I opened the pages. And I blinked when I saw it was not a journal, but letters to someone.

My eyes roamed over the first words on the page.

My Moon

I skimmed her slanted handwriting, the sharp ink piercing the pages. They were letters to her sleeping daughter.

Salina.

A beautiful name like her mother's. I skimmed through the words, suddenly feeling foolish and wrong. The end of each page ended with *Your Sun*, and I ached with the letters.

She said she had raised her daughter for a while, and I wondered if when she slept, that was what she was doing—shining on her daughter.

I fucking hoped it was not a forever sleep.

I flipped more pages, perhaps looking for my name, maybe just wanting to fucking feel her again. And I stopped flipping when I saw an entry not addressed to her *Moon*. Instead, it was simply addressed with one word—*Daughter*.

The letter was one sentence, one jagged edge of words scribbled. The pages were crumpled a bit, as if she almost ripped it out and thought better of it.

I wish you were never born.
Your Red Sister.

Daughter and sister, sister and mother, the same in their morbid bloodline. Daughters who went mad, who were driven to insanity by their father—*the* Father.

Daddy dearest longed for the long night. *In the winter, we will forge a fresh path in a new world.*

Fuck him, I thought, and my face morphed into a mocking grin.

He was the oldest being on this earth, but Hati and I were not far behind.

CHAPTER THIRTY-FOUR

I let the notebook fall closed as I turned toward the bed. I pulled back the covers and slipped under. The scent of Sorina enveloped me, and it was almost like she was there with me—covering me in her dark embrace, whispering her omens and her riddles. I'd give anything to hear her voice fall away in my dreams, hush close in my waking hours.

What a gift to love these women, the Deacon had said.

He was right about that, at least.

Though it hurt to admit, I loved Valerie in my way. And I'd save her if I could. Just as I would guard Kyrie. Shield Jessica and Nicole.

Perhaps the Deacon thought once I found out I was not human, I'd leave them behind and finally take pursuit, snuffing out Sorina's life as he couldn't.

But I was the mocking kind, the killing kind.

And I'd tear him apart before I let him snuff out the light in this world.

No one was allowed to devour the sun but me.

EPILOGUE

It was always the icy breath of the trees that made Maria feel at peace.

She came to the woods to be alone. Away from the yelling voices and the shuddering exhale of her young life.

In waking days, her family was pristine and respectable.

Godly.

And in the nights came the arguments—the icing. The silent stares and aggressive exhales meant to wound.

So she left her parents and took to the woods near her home and the family church. In the heart of the trees was an old dumping ground, and she liked to look for treasures, though any she found were useless in the eyes of others. But in her bedroom windows, catching light, were old bottles, a tarnished bracelet, and a worn-down rock.

She would worry it each night.

But in the woods, she would sing. Not the hymnals of her church, not the songs led by her mother before the congregation. But the

EPILOGUE

songs she played low in her room on the radio.

She wanted all she did not have—a life far from Hart Hollow, far from the Ozarks. Far from mother and sister.

Far from the ways her father suffocated.

She brought a book with her that chilly night that she'd checked it out from the library. She'd kept it far from her parents and siblings, often stuck between her mattress and box spring. But now Maria carried it like a lifeline, like a weapon, out into the fading evening sun.

Under the cover of the dead trees, she couldn't see the words well enough. So she pulled out a flashlight and sat on the old washing machine in the center of the dump. When she wasn't singing, she read aloud sometimes to an imaginary audience, to herself on days she was not pretending.

And she didn't see him watching. The girls never did.

He hovered closer around the opening in the trees, a slow circle.

Curious, the scent in the air intoxicated him, as it always did, even so soon after his last meal.

Maria was fifteen and seventy days. Sophomore year was fast approaching, young life ahead, vibrant red in her veins.

He smiled as the sun left them, inching away from the crime scene. He smiled as she read the words on the pages so confidently, so clearly in the woods, alone with her thoughts, his eyes watching, roving over her slim leg in her winter stocking, over her dainty hands.

There wasn't much meat on her bones, and for that, he was sorry.

But the devastation.

That is where the actual marrow was.

Maria's parents were godly and named right. Ancestors bred and chained to the town for decades, difficult to drive out.

He needed new guards at each point of the cross. And they would serve well when they had nothing left to live for.

The Deacon flew up high, white wings reflecting the fading light, fangs elongated, sharp and eager.

He smiled as he dove, thrilled with the way a hunt could feel when all the games were forgotten.

His whisper was felt on the cold winter breeze, carried away into the nothing.

"God is out here."

The story continues in The Ghost in the Grave, book two in the Ozark Omens Series.

Pre order here.

ACKNOWLEDGMENTS

This novel would not be possible without the support of many people.

Christopher Pike—the creator of Sita, my favorite vampire.

The team at Peachy Keen Author Services for sharing my story.

My agent, Savannah, for championing my work.

My editor, Tori, for working tirelessly to appease the grammar police while also retaining my poetic voice, helping this story find a healthy balance between dream and reality.

Misty, Talon, and Maria, thank you for hanging on for years, waiting for this tale—I hope it met your expectations and that you will follow Nicholas and Sorina into the next chapter.

Ashleigh and Anna Lisa, the first to meet this story—thank you for your invaluable input.

Trish Anderson, Daniele Derenzi, Cristina Bon, and Felicia Tincher for your behind-the-scenes support.

K Leigh for always being so passionate about my books.

Kat and Cynthia for cheering me on as I descended into madness.

My mother who was our protector as we braved our new world in Misery. I mean, *Missouri*.

My husband for holding down the fort while I became a feral thing.

J.R. Rogue is the author of three Goodreads Choice Awards Nominate poetry collections. She first put pen to paper at the age of fifteen after developing an unrequited high school crush & has never stopped writing about heartache, sorrow, and hope. Rogue has published multiple volumes of poetry & novels. In addition, she is a Certified Yoga Teacher with additional certification in Yoga Nidra & Trauma-Informed Yoga.
She lives in a small town in the midwest with her family, where she enjoys a quiet life reading & telling stories.

Join her mailing list to keep up with everything she's working on.

www.jrrogue.com
contact@jrrogue.com

facebook.com/jrrogueauthor
twitter.com/jenr501
instagram.com/j.r.rogue
amazon.com/J.-R.-Rogue
bookbub.com/authors/j-r-rogue
pinterest.com/rogueauthor
snapchat.com/add/jenr501

ALSO BY J. R. ROGUE

NOVELS

MUSE & MUSIC SERIES
Breaking Mercy
Burning Muses
Background Music
Blind Melody

SOMETHING LIKE LOVE SERIES
I Like You, I Love Her
I Love You, I Need Him
I Like You, I Hate Her

RED NOTE SERIES
The Rebound
The Regret

STANDALONE NOVELS
Kiss Me Like You Mean It

POETRY

GOODREADS CHOICE AWARDS NOMINEES
The Exquisite Pain of the Unrequited
Exits, Desires, & Slow Fires
I'm Not Your Paper Princess

Tell Me Where it Hurts

Dark Mermaid Song

Songs for the Stars

After The Blackout

I'll Be Your Manic Anxiety Queen

Daddy Issues

Made in the USA
Monee, IL
10 February 2025